RED
DIRT

ANNA JARZAB

RED
DIRT

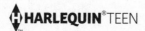

Recycling programs
for this product may
not exist in your area.

ISBN-13: 978-0-373-21251-4

Red Dirt

Printed in U.S.A.

For Dianna

WHEN THERE WERE GIANTS

I'm gonna tell you a story. You wanna hear a story, don't you, Decca? Well, I thought of a good one. And, best of all, it's true.

Long time ago, before there were humans in America, Oklahoma was the land of giants. Yes, before you were born. Before I was born, too, and Denver and Daddy—before everyone you can think of was born. Stop naming people and listen. There were thousands of giants in this country, and they were huge, just really effing big. Stop it. It's my story, I can say "effing" if I want. Don't interrupt.

Where was I? Oh yeah, the giants—they were huge suckers, bigger than houses. So big they used pine trees as toothpicks, just plucked them right out of the ground like dandelions and stuck them between their molars to knock the food out. So big, when their footprints filled up with rainwater, they turned into lakes. No, not our lake, but I got it on good authority that

Bittersweet used to be a giant's bathtub. How can I tell this story if you keep on interrupting?

Giants were nomads—you know what that means? Means they didn't have homes, just wandered 'round making temporary camps, like how Cousin Billy Little sometimes sleeps in his car when Aunt Bella throws him out of the house. Except giants didn't have cars, or trailers, or any of that. They slept under the stars. When it got cold, the giants would pile dirt on top of themselves like a blanket. That's how we got mountains, you know. The bigger the giant, the bigger the mountain.

But they didn't sleep that much. Giants were always hungry, and they were always restless, so they'd ramble through the hills and hollers looking for food, with footfalls so heavy they shook the earth.

Thing is, giants are solitary—means they prefer being alone. Problem with creatures that prefer being alone is sometimes there ain't enough room, like in our house, you know. When we get in each other's way we get cross and stomp our feet, but when *giants* ran into each other, things got violent. So it was important they always had plenty of space to themselves, and when they did, they lived in peace—not just with each other, but with every other living creature.

For a long time, that was okay, 'cause Oklahoma's a big place. Then men came over, from across a wide, blue sea, and things got bad.

How bad? Well, giants didn't have weapons, you see. They didn't know how to invent things. All they had in a battle were their fists. Humans, though—we're smart and we know how to dream stuff up that never existed before and then make it. Like guns. And bombs. All sorts of ways to take what we want from whoever had it first. The humans wanted room, too, to build their towns and raise their families and grow food, so they started to drive the giants off, pushing them closer together.

This caused war among the giants, 'cause they had to share space like never before. They slaughtered each other, ripping each other's throats open with their teeth and beating each other's heads in with rocks. By the time the last giant was gone, the rivers were running crimson and the lakes were a muddy scarlet color. And the dirt—you seen the dirt. Red as a cardinal's breast, and now you know why. Soaked with the blood of giants.

Yes, you're right, that story turned out to be sad and scary. I'm sorry. But you gotta be brave. There's lots of sad and scary stories in the world, and most of them are true, in one way or another.

Was that story true? The one about the giants?

How about you tell me?

CHAPTER ONE

Decca slams her little fists into the small of my back.

"Wake up!" she says. "Wake up, wake up, wake *up*, Sammy!"

I squint at her through bleary eyes and paw the sheets, searching for my phone. Not sure what I did with it. Tail end of last night is kind of a blur.

"What time is it?"

The sun's crooked fingers reach through the aluminum blinds, splaying across the threadbare carpet and piles of dirty clothes. My head pounds.

Decca looks up, craning her neck like the answer's on the ceiling. "Don't know. Get up!"

I rub my face and my fingers come away black with smears of mascara. I still got on my graduation dress, all wrinkled and bunched 'round my hips.

Sweat beads on my hairline. The air's hot, so heavy it's like I'm breathing through a damp rag. Summer don't come soft in Oklahoma. It barges through the front door like a long-lost relation and settles in for six months with its feet propped on the coffee table.

My eyes drift 'round the tiny, messy room, snagging on the red cap and matching polyester gown in the corner. I graduated yesterday, by the skin of my teeth, then drank to forget I got no plans for what's next. Now I'm sober, I feel it, the difference in me. Reality gut-punches me hard. It's like driving down a dark highway and realizing you done run out of road.

I groan. My stomach feels like a spitball, all wadded up and gummy, and I'm feeling shaky. All I want is to go back to sleep, but Decca ain't gonna let me. She's hungry.

"Make your bed," I say.

I head for the bathroom, where I chase two aspirin with water from the tap and take a look at myself in the mirror. It ain't good. There's a hickey just above the curve of my shoulder, but I can't say for certain who gave it to me. Tall, with dark wavy hair. Tan. Not from around here. That's all I can remember.

I make a face at my reflection.

The door opens and Decca pops her head in. "Almost done?"

"Hey! I could've been naked. Or peeing. Or *worse*."

She shudders. "Gross."

"You wanna come in, you knock. You never know what somebody's doing, and there's a lot of shit you don't wanna see. Literally."

"*Shit*," she says, waiting for my reaction with eyes wide as Frisbees. Decca gets a thrill from swearing, 'cause she knows she ain't supposed to. Don't got the energy to tell her off, not this morning.

I try shutting the door, but Decca leans against it with her full weight.

"Stop that. What's Dad doing? He up yet?"

Decca shakes her head. "Sleeping."

"Go bother Denny, then."

"He ain't here." Decca points at my neck. "What's that?"

I brush my hair over the hickey. "What do you mean Denver ain't here? Where is he?"

"Fishing with Holler, I guess," she says. "His pole's gone."

"Figures. Fix yourself some cereal, then, and give me five seconds of peace."

"Cereal's gone, too." Decca frowns.

"Bet there's another box 'round here somewhere." I kick the door closed, locking it. Decca bangs on it from the other side. "Quiet, beast! I'll be out in a second."

I wash up quick. The water drools out of the showerhead and it's lukewarm, but it helps. When I get to the kitchen, Decca's standing on a chair, trying to climb on the counter. There's a box of some generic Lucky Charms rip-off sitting on top of the icebox and she's fixing to reach for it.

"What the Sam Hill are you doing?" I swoop Decca into my arms and nudge the chair back under the table with my foot. "You want something, then *ask*, you monster. One day you're gonna fall and crack your fool skull open, and you better not come crying to me. Jesus Christ."

"Auntie Pat says don't take the Lord's name in vain." Decca wags her finger at me. "Better watch out, Sammy, or you'll burn in hell."

"Oh yeah?" I growl, tickling her belly. Decca wiggles and screeches with laughter. When she's had enough, she grabs my hand and bites down hard. I yelp—that monster's got teeth.

Dad picks this exact second to walk in. He glares at me.

"Pipe down," he mutters, crossing the kitchen in three steps and seizing the coffeepot. He tips it over, shakes it a few times, shoots me a pointed look. "No coffee?"

I set Decca down in her booster chair.

"Was just about to make some." I take the pot from him and rummage through the drawers for a filter. "Bring you a cup when it's ready."

Dad grumbles about ungrateful children, but he rumples Decca's hair, then kisses me on the cheek, scratching my skin with his sandpaper stubble.

He disappears into the other room and I release the breath I'm holding. Like all men who done time, Dad can be hard to predict, though he swears those days are behind him. I mostly believe him. Only sometimes does he give us cause to remember he's got a secret spring of danger in him. But then we all do, don't we, deep down?

I pour the last of the cereal in a bowl and set it in front of Decca.

"Eat all of it, not just the sugary parts, or I ain't never buying it again."

"Even if there's a coupon?" Decca asks.

"Even if there's a coupon."

I root around for my own breakfast, but all I find are near-empty cupboards.

Decca hunches over her bowl, slurping her milk like a cat. I smooth back the cowlick that curls up near her temple. Her downy hair is damp with sweat, skin baby-soft and rosy. Sometimes I wonder if anyone ever loved a person much as I love her.

She looks up at me and says, "You need more deer corn, Sammy. Else the deer'll starve."

There's a small herd that comes almost right up to the house most nights, looking to feed off our leftovers. We throw watermelon rinds and apple cores into the woods for them, but I also keep a stock of dry corn kernels just in case. Denver says don't go 'round making pets of wild animals, but I can't stand the thought of them going without.

I check the spot under the sink where I keep the deer corn and, sure enough, bag's empty.

Decca stuffs a spoonful of cereal into her mouth. "Told you," she says, mouth full.

"I'll get more," I say. "Don't worry about it. Did I tell you one of them is pregnant?"

Decca swivels so fast her chair nearly topples over. "Really?"

"Cool, huh? Pretty soon we're gonna have a baby deer. They call them 'fawns.'"

"Can I pet it?"

"No. But you can look at it."

Decca shrugs and goes back to her breakfast, picking through the cardboard oat bits in search of soggy candy.

She's a menace, but I love having her here. We only get her once a month for an overnight, plus a few unsupervised daytime visits. Don't seem like much when you put it on paper, but Dad fought long and hard for those rights, so it's a boon in comparison to the nothing we had before.

I glance at the clock on the microwave. In no time at all, Decca will be back in Rainne's clutches, and after that, who knows? Few months ago, Decca's mama got it in her head she wants to move to eastern Arkansas with her new husband, Duke. There's a family court hearing on Wednesday, where a judge'll rule if Rainne can take Decca out of state. I got no idea which way it'll go. If we lose, they'll be gone by end of summer. Sickens me to think of it.

Rainne and Dad never should've gotten married. She was too immature to be with someone like him, who had a rap sheet, two kids and fifteen years on her when they got hitched. Didn't surprise a one of us when she left him. Lots of folks say Dad should be grateful she did him the favor.

Odd to imagine them together, now it's over, but women like Rainne always flocked to Dad. He was born wild, to hear people tell it, and prison only made him more desirable, gave him this dark, mysterious glow that draws them in like mosquitoes to a porch light. He should've known better than to get mixed up with one of them. Now we're all paying the price.

I'm in the front room sweeping empty beer bottles and two packs' worth of cigarette butts into a trash bag when there's a knock on the door so loud it makes me jump. The trailer smells like coffee and stale smoke. I press my fingers to my forehead, trying to massage the hurt out. Dad's dozed off again, sleeping like the dead a few feet away.

I set the trash aside and head for the door. Decca's frozen midchew at the kitchen table. It can only be one person at this hour.

"Hel-*lo*!" Rainne shouts, pounding so hard the storm door rattles like a cage. "Anyone in there? I don't got all day here. Sammy!"

I sigh. "Finish up real quick, Decca. Your mama's here. Leave the bowl and go get your things."

My ex-stepmother ain't a patient woman. I made Decca pack yesterday before bed, knowing Rainne don't like having to pace the porch in the thick white heat while Decca gathers her toys.

I open the door, but leave the screen locked. No way I'm letting her in. Second she lays eyes on Dad, she'll start in with digs about the drinking, or the smoking, or the mess. Next thing you know they're screaming at each other and itching to take a swing.

"Rainne," I say. "Didn't expect you till later."

"Well, I'm here now. That a hickey on your neck?"

Rainne lowers her sunglasses and squints at me. I fight the urge to cover the bruise with my hand.

"This?" I shrug. "Got it noodling down at Terrapin Creek. Had my head underwater and this whopper of a catfish just came out of nowhere and gave me a big ol' kiss."

I make a loud smacking noise and shoot her a grin. If I let her get to me this early in the morning, it'll ruin my day.

"Grow up, Sammy." Rainne muffles a yawn with the back of her hand. I drop the smile. "Where's my kid?"

"Hold your horses, she's coming," I say. "When can I see her again?"

"I don't know. Depends what happens Wednesday."

"Give me a break, Rainne. You don't gotta bring her here. I can watch her while you're at work."

"That's what day care's for," she says. "Where's Bobby Ray at, anyway? Y'all beg for these visits and then he ain't even *around*?"

"He's getting ready," I lie, hoping she don't hear him snore.

She shades her eyes and looks off toward the woods. Our land ends at the tree line. Government owns the rest.

"He's such an idiot, not selling up when he had the chance."

"What's that supposed to mean?"

"He's had offers, but you Lesters are always holding tight to things you oughta let go of."

"There something you're trying to say?"

"You oughta tell Bobby Ray to drop all this custody stuff. We're moving, and he can't stop it. He's only making things worse, getting the courts involved."

"You can't go taking a kid away from her family. This is Decca's home. She belongs here."

"She belongs where I say she belongs till she's eighteen. Just 'cause you and Bobby Ray are happier than pigs in shit, living in the same place you always lived, don't mean other people can't want more for themselves, Sammy. Just ask Denver."

"This ain't about me," I snap. "Or Denver."

"Sure as hell ain't. But if you got anything in that head of yours besides air, you'll get gone, too. Word is those people that been buying up the bluff are close to a deal with the corps. Before you know it, the whole lake's gonna be a damn resort, and what'll you do then?"

She shakes her head. "Won't be nothing left for the old families. Trust me, you don't wanna be the last one at that party."

"I ain't leaving the lake," I tell her. "Not *ever*. Can't nobody make me."

"Guess not, if Reed couldn't," Rainne says. She lifts her hair and fans the back of her neck with her fingers. "That's why he enlisted, right? Wanted out of here so bad he went to fucking Fallujah or whatever, just to get away."

Rainne couldn't find Fallujah on a map, and she don't know nothing about Reed. I been trying so hard not to think about him, and here she is, throwing him in my face, the fact that he left me. Blood rushes to my face. So much for not letting her get to me.

"That's such bulls—"

"Decca," Rainne says in warning. My sister comes running

down the hall, clutching her backpack so hard her knuckles look like little gray pebbles.

"Sorry, Mama," she pants. "Can't find Waldo."

That's a stuffed elephant Dad won for Decca at the state fair last year. Denver named him Waldo 'cause we're always looking for him.

"Too bad." Rainne hates Waldo. "Come on, let's go. We got a busy day."

"Of what?" I ask.

"Errands." She gives me a look that says *None of your goddamn business.*

"Why don't you leave her here while you take care of all that? We'll find Waldo, and you can come get her this afternoon."

Decca wraps her arms 'round my leg and presses her sweaty face into my thigh.

"Denver's out fishing," I say. "Maybe we'll join him for a bit."

Decca's face lights up. "Yeah, Mama, can I?"

"No," Rainne barks. "You been here too long as it is. Say your goodbyes and get in the car."

Rainne walks off toward Duke's truck, which is parked halfway on the gravel driveway and halfway on our patchy brown lawn. One of our pink plastic flamingos is bent under the weight of his front tire. He flicks a spent cigarette out the window and it lands on the dry grass. What a dick.

I get down on my knees in front of Decca, whose face is screwed up like she's fixing to sob her guts out. Can't have that. Duke hates it when she squalls and it makes him nasty to her.

"Don't you cry now," I say. "Lesters don't cry, and your mama won't like it."

Decca sniffles. "Mama says we're moving away. She says pretty soon I won't see you no more."

I gather her to me and squeeze tight. "Can't nobody keep us from seeing each other, you hear?"

"Promise?" Decca asks, sticking her pinky out.

I shake my head. "No promises."

If there's one thing I've learned, it's that you never promise a kid anything.

"How about hope instead?" I offer.

"Okay. Hope."

I link my pinky with Decca's and we shake on it. Then I take her in my arms again and give her the fiercest hug I've got in me.

"Hoping real hard, sweet pea," I whisper. I twist her baby-fine blond hair gently 'round my finger. She looks more like me than she's got any right to. Denver and I don't look a thing alike and we got both parents in common.

Decca's like me in a lot of ways, which is why I hold out my palm and say, "Backpack."

She glares at me. "I didn't take nothing."

"Don't make me use this hand for something else."

She makes a face, but she gives over the bag. I go through it till I find what I'm looking for.

"You know the rule," I say, grabbing her arm just hard enough so she knows I mean it. I slip my phone in my pocket. Ain't the first time she's lifted it. "No stealing. Especially from family."

"Sorry," she says, pouting.

I sigh. What kind of person will she grow up into, if there ain't someone around who knows her tricks?

Dad clears his throat. He's standing over us, hair sticking up in the back. "What's going on?"

"Mama's here," Decca tells him. "I gotta go now."

Dad lifts Decca off her feet and cuddles her to his chest. She loops her arms 'round his neck and buries her face in his shoulder.

Puts a lump in my throat to see them loving on each other like that. My childhood memories of Dad are slippery as dreams, but he's trying with Decca, and if that don't make up for how he was when I was her age, at least it reminds me of all the good he's still got in him. Makes me glad he came back to us.

"I know you don't wanna, baby girl," Dad says, smoothing a few sweat-drenched strands of hair off Decca's forehead. Ain't even eight o'clock and must be ninety degrees already. "But it's just for a little while. The judge is gonna fix it so you can visit whenever you want."

"Don't," I say. Decca will cling to that white lie till it's crushed to dust in her pudgy fist.

Dad ignores me. "You can come and stay with me and Sammy all the time. We'll go down to Tulsa to see the animals at the zoo. Maybe Denver'll come, too. Would you like that?"

Decca nods. She's always open to bribes.

"First you gotta go with your mama and be a real good girl, you hear?"

"Do you promise—if I'm a good girl—can I stay with you?"

"Decca—" I say, but Dad cuts me off.

"Yes, baby," he says. "I promise."

CHAPTER TWO

The way I'm feeling this morning, last thing I wanna do is eat, but I gotta get something in my stomach before I puke. I make a bag of popcorn and flop down on the couch, shoveling kernels in my mouth as I stare at the TV.

Reception's spotty up in these hills, and only one channel comes in clear, so I'm stuck watching the local news. Dad's got it on mute, but the anchors seem pretty het up about something, so I switch the sound on.

"—unpopular with locals, the fate of two hundred and forty acres on Gibson Bluff overlooking Lake Bittersweet has been decided. Several years ago, LakeLife LLC announced plans for Sweet Home, a luxury residential and recreational complex, which would include vacation houses, rental cabins, a state-of-the-art marina with a high-end restaurant, and other amenities. Unable to purchase all the acreage they required from private owners, yesterday LakeLife signed a contract to sublease land owned by the US Army Corps of Engineers from Bittersweet County, which leases it rent-free from the federal government. Look for more on this story as it develops—"

I turn the TV off. Goddamn Sweet Home. My attachment to this lake is as close to religion as I've ever come, and what those bloodsucking city folk are doing just to make a quick buck is blasphemy.

The lake is changing. I know that better than most anybody. This bluff used to belong to my family, acres we raised cattle on not more than two generations ago. We Lesters came down from one of the first white men to settle here, some old English bloke. My great-great-great-great-granddad owned a shop in old Gibson town, back before they dammed the river and flooded the valley to build Lake Bittersweet. Might be you can still find the store's foundation somewhere beneath one hundred sixty-five feet of cool blue, right alongside wagon wheels, farming equipment and the roads my ancestors walked.

Funny enough, the lake is what sunk us. When we lost the shop, we had to sell off our land, piece by piece, to pay debts and bills and bail. All that's left of what we had once is this little patch of red dirt, not quite two acres, not even a house on it, just a trailer and a big shed Dad built with his own two hands. Now our grazing fields are owned by other people from other places, and it don't matter how much I like our neighbors—they ain't us. We're the last Lesters on this outcropping, the rest of them scattered through the flatland towns south and west of here. Only thing left of our English ancestor is his soft, round face and big blue eyes, common to many of us.

Common is what we are: hicks, rednecks, country folk. Okies and hillbillies at the foot of the Ozarks, the lip of civilization, where mild meets wild. It's the only place I've ever lived, and I'll most like be buried here.

Maybe Rainne's right—maybe Dad should've sold up long ago. But he never would, 'cause he knows what I know: a person's nothing without a home, and this here lake is ours. Ain't nobody gonna take that from us. I'd like to see them try.

The trailer's walls are thin as dragonfly wings and I can hear the shower shut off in the bathroom, then the clatters and clunks of Dad getting ready for work. He does construction for a company that builds fast-food joints all over the state, and he likes it as much as he could ever like a nine-to-five, which ain't much. You spend all your life outside the law, it's hard to get on the straight and narrow. But his lawyer took a hard line with him: work, or risk losing Decca forever.

While Dad's occupied, I go to my room and fish around in the pockets of the jeans I wore two days ago, pull out a wad of cash and a handful of coins—tip money.

I sit on my bed and count it out. Almost a hundred, but seventy-one of it's gotta go to bills. That leaves me a little over twenty to live on.

Dad can't give me anything. When I moved in with him, helping keep the lights on and food in the cupboards was part of the deal. I shove three fives in my wallet and the rest goes under the loose carpet in the corner, where nobody can get at it. Valuable things got a way of disappearing in this house.

Now that's done, I go searching for Waldo. I gather the laundry and strip the sheets, tossing them into a pile outside the door for washing, and there he is, cowering under Decca's cot like a frightened cat.

I hold him close. He smells like baby powder and acrylic. Decca painted nails onto his hooves with my new orange polish.

"What's Waldo doing here?" Dad asks from the doorway. He fastens his watch, shoves his hands into his pockets.

He's got on an old pair of jeans and a dingy white T-shirt. None of his clothes fit right 'cause he still shops like he's the same size he was when he went to prison.

"Decca left him. Rainne's fucked tonight. She'll never get her to sleep."

"Give him here. I'll bring him over there after work."

I balk like a spooked horse. "I can do it."

"With what car?"

"I'll get Kenley to drive me."

"It'll be fine. Gotta talk to Rainne about something anyway."

"You better not. You know how mad she makes you."

"Shut up, Sammy," Dad snaps.

"If there's a fight, she'll use it against you. That time she called the cops, it hurt us in court."

"Won't be a fight." Dad gives me a cold stare and I brace myself. I seen his temper transform him. Seen him unleash it on people. That was before, but how can I say for certain he's changed? Ain't even sure I believe people really can.

I toss him Waldo. Dad plucks the stuffed animal out of the air with one hand and just like that, he's smiling. His dark moods are like summer storms: sudden and fierce and destructive, then gone in the blink of an eye.

"Can I ask you a question?"

Dad's smile disappears. "Depends."

"Rainne said something about you getting offers on our land?"

"In the past."

"What about those folks buying up the bluff? They got the corps land today. Was on the news."

Dad shrugs and walks away. I follow him into the kitchen.

"Don't trouble yourself over it," he says, pouring himself a cup of coffee. "That thing, what's it called?"

"Sweet Home."

"Won't never get built."

"I think it will."

Dad laughs. "You lived here all your life, kid. Bittersweet seem like a resort to you?"

"No," I say. "But that's what these folks do, ain't it? Come into a place with some natural beauty, push out all the old families, then bulldoze it to build a playground for rich people."

"What person with half a brain would build a bunch of mansions in arm's reach of the Tullers? Redbreast's boys would clear them out in a week."

Dad lights a cigarette and leans against the counter, sipping his coffee.

Hearing the Tuller name makes my skin cold and clammy. My belly ain't yellow, but it's just good sense to fear the Tullers. Everybody's got a story about that family, told in whispers, 90 percent of them at least half-true.

Bittersweet's had Tullers about as long as it's had Lesters, and since they first stepped foot in these hills, Tullers been criminals. They got their start as moonshiners, but they're proper gangsters now, hands in every cookie jar: drugs, guns, women. Extortion, burglary, assault, murder.

Diversification, Dad says. But it ain't no joke. He used to work for the Tullers, and when it looked like he was gonna go to prison for it, they made sure he knew: turn traitor, and pay.

Worst night of my life was the last time Dad got arrested. I was four. Police kicked down the door and stormed through the house, guns drawn, shouting for him to come out with his hands up. They found Denver and me curled up together in the bathtub, shaking.

But second worst was the night I woke up to the smell of tires burning. The Tullers set fire to our only car, and in case we didn't get the message, they left the body of our mutt, Kibble, on the doorstep, split open chin to tail.

I still remember the feel of Kibble's blood, squished between my toes. I'm the one who found him. Ain't owned a dog since.

"They seem pretty fucking serious," I say. "Ain't easy to get land out of the corps. They build that thing, it's gonna come right up to the edge of our property."

"So what? Maybe our land'll be worth more."

"Who cares what it's worth? You wouldn't sell it." I stare at him. "Right?"

Dad stares straight back at me. "Never had a reason to sell."

I relax. "Good."

"Shit, I better get," Dad says, dumping the dregs of his coffee in the sink. "You going to work?"

I shake my head. "Day off."

"Where's Denver?"

"Fishing with Holler."

"You know I ain't set eyes on that boy in three days? You ask your son to come home from college for the summer, you want he should show his face once in a while."

"He hates it here. We're lucky he came home at all."

Dad grunts and lifts the sleeve of his T-shirt to scratch at a bug bite. I catch sight of one of his tattoos, the vulture with a pistol in its beak. He got most of his ink in prison, but he's had the vulture since he was younger than I am now.

"Thought you were gonna cover that up."

His eyes narrow into dark slits. "Now, that's none of your damn business."

"You ain't running with the Tullers anymore. Looks bad to flash the vulture all over the lake."

Dad grabs my arm so hard I gasp. "Don't *you* ever talk about the Tullers. You know better than to mouth off about things you don't understand."

I nod and keep my eyes on the ground near his feet. "Sorry."

He lets go and pats my head, like I'm a dog.

"It's all right. I know you're just looking out. You're the only one in this family ever had a real heart."

"Pretty sure Denny's got one, too, buried under all that book-learning."

Dad shakes his head at me, but the storm's passed. I let myself breathe again.

My phone chimes with a text:

Need a beach day. Boat launch, one hour.

"Who's that?" Dad asks.

"Kenley. You *sure* you don't want me to bring Waldo over to Rainne's?"

I miss Decca already. Feels like someone carved my heart out of my chest like meat from a melon. Wouldn't mind seeing her again, even if it means having to see Rainne, too.

"No, and I don't wanna hear that question again," Dad says. "Everything's gonna be just fine."

I smile like I got no reason to doubt him. "Okay."

"Got any money I can borrow? Pay you back off my next check."

"You gotta talk to Jerry about a raise," I grumble. But I give him ten, all I can spare. More than.

"Thanks," he says, then scoots out the door, leaving his coffee mug in the sink for me to clean.

The walk to the boat launch is so hot it near does me in. I can feel the sun burning up my scalp as I make my way down the steep hill roads, past little houses on wide-open lots boxed in by dark woods. Most are empty, squatting in the tallgrass like tombstones. The sight of their blank-eyed windows and patchy brown lawns stings. I hurry past them.

The Sweet Home developers lit on this hill like a pack of wolves, picking the locals off one by one with the promise of fast cash for land at double its value. Pisses me off that's all it took. Shouldn't have been so easy for a bunch of outsiders to push out families that've lived here generations. There's only a few holdouts like Dad left.

Hard to imagine how it'll be, living next door to rich people. Just one more piece of my future I ain't puzzled out yet.

I pass through a small campground crammed with RVs. People wave as I walk by, and I wave back. The campground will be gone soon, razed so Sweet Home can have its fancy marina, and these folks'll have to find somewhere else to park their trailers. Some of them been coming up to the lake for years. I wonder if they know how soon this'll all be gone.

Down past the rec area is a sliver of beach. I bring Decca here sometimes, when it's so hot in the house we can't stand it. Kenley's stretched out on a towel, baking herself brown as a nut. 'Round here, we all look like someone held us by our ankles and dipped us in gold.

"Howdy," I say. My shadow stretches over her.

Kenley lifts her shades and squints up at me, grinning.

"Well, if it ain't the hottest bitch in Bittersweet County."

I flop down next to her in the sand. "Thought that was you."

"Ain't what you said last night."

The memory rolls over me like a wave. *You okay, Sammy?* Kenley asked when she caught me standing in the corner of Holler's living room, staring into the distance.

Doing just fine, I said, draining my drink and tossing the red Solo cup in a nearby trash bag.

Looks like you're concentrating real hard on something. She tapped my temple. *What's going on in that head of yours?*

I wiped my mouth with the back of my hand. *I'm gonna go make out with that pretty rich boy over there.*

I pointed to where he stood. Some popular sophomores had crashed our graduation party, and he was flirting with one of them. I didn't like that a bit. He was the best-looking boy in the room, and I'd decided he was mine for the night. He just didn't know it yet.

Oh yeah? Kenley flashed me a teasing smile. *What makes you think he's interested? Looks plenty occupied with that cheerleader already, you ask me.*

Not anymore, I said, running my fingers through my long blond hair and smoothing the front of my dress. *I'm the hottest bitch in Bittersweet County, and if she knows what's good for her, she'll run when she sees me coming.*

"You know whiskey makes me overconfident," I tell Kenley now. It's all pretty embarrassing.

"Poor Sheyla made tracks soon as she saw you, so it ain't like you were wrong."

"I don't want people to be scared of me."

"Please," Kenley says. "You like it. And that rich boy was drooling over you like you just stepped out of *Maxim*."

"What tipped *you* off he's got money?"

This is a game we play. The Sweet Home developers ain't the first people to figure wealthy people might like it up here. They're easy to spot.

Kenley and I look at each other. "The shoes," we say at the same time. Never seen a lake rat in fancy boat shoes, and *definitely* not at a party.

"He was cute," she says, pulling one of her long dark curls and watching it spring back. She dyed the ends of her hair blue, practice for beauty school in the fall. "Think you'll see him again?"

I shrug. "Don't remember his name. You?" Kenley shakes her head. "Then I guess not."

She lies back down on her towel and throws an arm over her face to shield her eyes from the sun. I pull my knees up to my chest and wrap my arms 'round my legs, trying to make myself small as possible. The cornflower-colored sky stretches out over the lake like a bedsheet.

Granny Lester, God rest her ornery soul, used to say the sky is bigger in Oklahoma than any other place, bigger and bluer and brighter. The land is thick with trees: burr oak and black walnut, red cedar and sweet gum, hiding what civilization there is beneath a knotted canopy of leaves and branches.

The lake is calm as a millpond—it actually sparkles. This is a beautiful place.

There's a vulture circling the treetops across the cove. Most folks take them as a sign of ill fortune, but Granny Lester saw it different. She said a carrion bird means something's been put into motion that can't be undone. Could be death, she said, but could be life just as easy.

A horn blares behind us. I turn to see Wayne Evans's black Chevy Tahoe pulling up to the boat launch, his wife, Karen, waving at me from the driver's seat of the twenty-five-foot Cobalt they're hauling. The Evanses are our nearest neighbors on the bluff, weekenders who've owned their house up here so long they've got honorary native status. Their black Lab, Dolly, has her head hanging out the passenger-side window of the truck.

"What're you girls doing?" Karen asks. Her best friend, Dianna, and Dianna's husband, Andy, wave at us from the back of the boat. They're out-of-towners, but I know them from other visits.

"Just hanging out. Where you headed?"

"Party Cove," Wayne says. "We got some room up front and plenty of beer in the cooler, if you wanna come along."

Kenley's already on her feet, gathering her stuff. "Sure do," she says.

I get up, brush the sand off the back of my thighs, tilt my head toward the sun. Heat glides over me, thick and slow, like honey. Sunshine's got its own smell, like cotton from the dryer.

Wayne backs the boat down the ramp. Kenley and I hop in. I can feel myself fading from hungover to happy. It's my day off, I'm wearing my electric-blue bikini, my favorite cutoff skirt, and we're about to drive straight into the beating heart of Lake Bittersweet.

Got my worries, but right now they seem very far away.

CHAPTER THREE

"You hear that news about the corps land on the bluff?" Wayne asks.

We're near the back of Party Cove, tied up to four other boats all owned by people we know, a regular redneck yacht club. The celebration is raging near the mouth of the cove, but over here it's almost peaceful.

A large bird soars by overhead and for a second I think it's that vulture again, but it's just a chicken hawk—omen of nothing, far as I know.

"Was all over the TV this morning," I tell him. "What the hell, man?"

"What the hell is right," Karen says from the captain's chair.

"Gotta hand it to them," Wayne says. "Couldn't weasel enough land out of us, so they ran straight to Uncle Sam. This is why we'll never be rich, Karen." He taps his head. "Not sneaky enough."

"They try to buy you out?" I ask.

Wayne's smile fades. "Something like that, yeah."

"What do you mean?"

"Oh, nothing, honey," Karen says. "Those developers like to give the little guys a hard time, that's all. Acted like they were doing us a huge favor, offering on our land, then got mad when we didn't fall for it. Told us we'd regret not selling up, but we straightened them out."

I frown. "Think they tried to work my dad, too?"

Wayne shrugs. "Bet they bugged everyone on the bluff as much as they did us, but nobody on our side of the woods fell for it, thank God."

"Now they got the corps land, maybe they'll leave you alone," Kenley says. She yawns and stretches her long brown legs out over the side of the boat.

"Land's like money—you can always have more," Wayne says. "But I think we're safe for now."

He shoots Karen a look. There's something they ain't telling me, but I know better than to keep harping.

"Forget all that boring stuff," Karen says. "Who wants a beer?"

Karen and Wayne don't bat an eyelash when we grab ourselves a couple of Coors and take them to the back of the boat, where we spread out on towels to sun ourselves. Most folks don't bother themselves about underage drinking 'round here. Beer's low-point in Oklahoma, anyway. It's like flavored water, not enough to get drunk on.

Kenley nudges my shoulder with her elbow. "You're quiet today."

I shrug, flipping onto my back to look up at the sky.

"Better tell me what's bothering you. Your face gets all

scrunchy when you're thinking and Lord knows all you got going for you is your beauty—can't be giving yourself wrinkles."

I laugh and sit up, light a cigarette.

"Just worried about Decca," I say. "We got that court date on Wednesday. Judge is finally gonna decide if Rainne can move to Arkansas with her."

"She wouldn't really do it. Would she?"

"She ain't going through all this legal shit just for fun."

"Can't imagine her leaving, though. Bofords stay put. Never known one to move like that."

"She ain't a Boford," I remind Kenley. "Not anymore."

"You're never more than the family you were born to, and Rainne's a Boford in her bones."

Kenley crushes her empty beer can and tosses it into a trash bag.

"No judge is gonna let her take Decca away from your dad," she says.

"Guess we'll see."

But I ain't sure Dad's got a strong enough case to stop Rainne. What'll we do if we lose? Between Dad and me, we know just about every way there is to get what we want from this place, but outside Lake Bittersweet, every damn thing seems impossible, like the world past our borders has got different rules.

"She oughta be ashamed," Kenley says. "I get wanting to leave, but taking a kid from her family? That's low, even for Rainne."

"Incoming!" Wayne whoops from the bow.

Kenley and I scramble to see who's arrived. The sleek silver cigarette boat zeroing in on our floating house party don't belong to anybody I know. The driver cuts the engine and coasts to a stop next to Wayne's Cobalt. I look over at Kenley, who shrugs.

Wayne tosses me a length of rope and a couple fenders to slip over the cleats. The new guy is backlit against the sun and I can't make out a face. All I know is he's tall and broad-shouldered, body packed tight with lean muscle. If he's good-looking, my afternoon's about to get a whole lot better.

"Throw me the rope," he says.

The sound of his voice knocks a chunk of memory loose in my brain and I freeze. A slow, knowing grin spreads across his face.

"You," he says, in a soft, barely there Texas accent.

"Yeah," I say, looking him up and down. He's wearing the most hideous pair of board shorts I've ever seen. They're obnoxiously loud, red and green and blue and orange all swirled together in a chaotic pattern that makes me seasick. Why do rich people waste their money on ugly things?

His boat ain't ugly, though. It's a brand-new, custom-built rumrunner. I know people with nice boats, and people with *really* nice boats, but I never seen one like this close up before.

Kenley laughs. "It's Mr. Boat Shoes!"

He stares at the leather sandals on his feet. "Sorry?"

"I said nice shoes," Kenley says.

"Thanks?"

"Don't make me throw you overboard," I whisper, nudging Kenley in the ribs. She pretends she don't hear me, just keeps beaming at the newcomer with a thousand-watt smile.

"So...this is a surprise," he says.

Wayne interrupts to introduce himself and Karen, their friends, distracting him. I turn to Kenley and mutter, "Tell me this ain't happening."

"It is," Kenley says. She's enjoying the shit out of this.

"Then *please* tell me you remember his name, at least."

"I told you I didn't. If I did, you think I'd be calling him 'Mr. Boat Shoes'?"

"Shit." Ain't nothing like being trapped on a boat with the stranger you hooked up with in a drunken stupor the night before, especially when *you can't remember his goddamn name.*

When he turns his attention back to Kenley and me, I gotta force myself to meet his eyes. Be one thing if he was someone I known forever. I made out with guy friends and neighbor boys plenty of times after one too many whiskey gingers, and usually we laugh about it the next time we see each other— or, better, never mention it at all.

But even though I got no clue who this guy is, I know we did more than make out. What little I got left of our sweaty tumble is all desperate moans and hot, frantic kisses, naked friction and wandering fingers that found all the right buttons, pressed them in all the right ways.

I don't blush easy, but I can feel my cheeks warming, and it ain't from the sun. Don't help he's looking at me like I'm a bucketful of ice water on a hundred-degree day. Though for a second I can't figure out if it's me he can't take his eyes off of or the Cobalt. Boys got such big boners for boats.

"So, you going to invite me over?" he asks.

"Uh, sure."

I move aside, and he steps in, using the sunshade's metal frame for balance. Should've offered him a hand, but I'm nervous to touch him. Last time I did, I couldn't stop.

"Those beers up for grabs?"

"Help yourself!" Karen shouts from the bow.

"I'll get you one," Kenley says, scurrying off.

Mr. Boat Shoes leans in to whisper: "Didn't think I'd see you again so soon. Or, like, ever."

"Then I guess today's your lucky day."

He sits down next to me, so close I can smell sunscreen on his skin and the fresh pine of his fancy rich-boy deodorant. I feel light-headed, but that could just be the hangover.

"You okay?" he asks. I shrug. "Got it. I'll just sit here quietly and try not to bother you."

"You ain't bothering me."

He shoots me a look that says *his* memory of last night's just fine. He raises his eyebrows and I raise mine back.

A teasing smile tugs at the corner of his mouth. "That why you won't talk to me?"

"She's being weird 'cause she don't remember your name."

Kenley's standing over us, holding three beers. I glare at her.

"What?" she asks, all innocent. "Now it's out in the open, he can tell us what he's called and y'all can move on to flirting like horny little monkeys, same as yesterday."

"Jesus, Kenley." He's gonna think I'm some drunk slut, hooking up with so many boys I can't keep them all straight. Before he probably just thought I was a bitch.

"That's okay," he says, taking a beer and popping the tab. I smile. "I don't know your name, either. You wouldn't tell me what it was. I'm Brayton Foster."

"Sammy Lester."

He touches the bill of his Thunder cap and drawls, "Pleased to meet you."

"Guess my work here is done," Kenley says.

She shades her eyes and gazes across the chain of boats. There's a familiar pontoon pulling up to the other end.

"Ooh, Mike's here. I'm gonna go over and say hi. See y'all...
later."

"How long you gonna be?" I ask. "Ain't you working tonight?"

"Don't you worry about me," Kenley says, giving me an un-
subtle wink. "I'll catch a ride with Mike to Gibson Bend. Gotta
be at the Deck by six. You should come by, there's a band on
at eight."

"Maybe," I say, but Kenley's already got one foot over the
gunwale. She climbs into Tommy Preston's Malibu and starts
her trek over to Mike's pontoon. Brayton and I watch her go.

"That's the first time I've ever seen boat hopping look grace-
ful," Brayton says.

"Like being at a redneck ballet."

He laughs, but then a wave of awkwardness breaks over
us, and we both clam up. Hell if I'm gonna be the one who
talks first.

Finally, he gives in and says, "About last night..."

"It really wasn't—" I start to say, but at the same time he
says, "I had a lot of fun," so I say, "Me, too," which is the truth.
I've had my share of one-night stands and random hookups
over the last six months, but those were more about numbing
things than feeling them.

I felt *a lot* with Brayton, mostly in the region south of my
belly button.

"Cool," he says. He juts his chin at Wayne and Karen. "Your
parents?"

"Neighbors. This is their boat. I'm just party crashing."

"That makes two of us."

"Speaking of, how'd you end up at Holler's last night, anyway? Don't tell me you know him."

"Who's Holler?"

"Holler Groom. The guy who owns the house we were at. He's my brother's best friend."

"I was driving by and figured I'd go in," Brayton explains. "Find out whether it was the type of thing where people see a stranger and hand him a beer."

I ask how he could've possibly been "driving by"—Holler lives off a secluded country road.

"When I'm bored," Brayton says, "I just get in my car and go. Take random turns, don't use my GPS, no real end point in mind. Sometimes I stumble across something interesting." He smiles. "Sometimes, some*one*."

No wonder I found this boy so attractive last night. Must've sensed it from the first, what he was like, that he wouldn't want or need anything from me except a little flirting, a little messing around. He wasn't shy, or sweet, or sensitive, or earnest, someone I'd have to let down gently in the morning. He was a player like me. If I wanted him, I could have him, and I wouldn't have to answer for it later.

"Some*one*, huh?" I ask.

He gives me a slow nod, then whips off his hat and shakes out his dark wavy hair. It curls 'round his ears, and at the spot where his skull and neck meet.

I wanna wrap one of those corkscrews 'round my finger and tug on it while we kiss. He's got a pull on me, this boy. Being near him makes my brain go soft like melted candy.

"Yes, ma'am," he says, still doing his cowboy act. It's charming, but then most things are charming on a cheerful, handsome boy. "She wouldn't give me the time of day, so you got me instead."

I flick ice chips at him, and he fires back. Drops of cold water sting my skin.

"So, *Brayton*," I say. He gives me a thumbs-up. "What're you doing, tying that pretty boat up to a bunch of strangers? Ain't you got people up here?"

He cocks his head. "Are we strangers?"

When I don't answer, he says, "No people, not yet. It's my first summer on Lake Bittersweet."

"Yeah?"

"My stepdad's got some business interests in the area, so he bought a place up the hill a bit, behind Gibson Bluff. He's never there," Brayton says. "Figured it'd be a crime to let an empty house go to waste, so I hauled my ass up from OKC to keep an eye on it for him."

"Big sacrifice," I say. He's a city boy. No surprise there.

"Oh yeah. *Huge*."

"Your stepdad, he in oil?" I ask. Not having any money, I'm always curious where other people get it. In Oklahoma, the answer's nearly always oil. Or land.

"He was. Chesapeake, executive vice president of whatever. I don't know him that well. He and my mom just got married last year, and he's hardly ever around. Always got somewhere more important to be, that typical rich guy thing, you know?"

"Not really."

"Well, I've had two other stepdads just like him. What about you? You from around here?"

"Born and raised," I say, lifting my beer can in salute.

"I figured. You have that lake way about you."

"What's that mean?"

"You know. Tan." He gives me a long look. "Friendly, too."

"Just doing my best to live up to the town motto."

"Which is?"

"'Sweetest dam lake west of the Mississippi.'"

"A pun *and* a homophone! How could I not want to spend the summer here?"

He takes off his sunglasses and wipes the sweat from the bridge of his nose. "It's so hot. Want to swim?"

We spend the afternoon in the water, floating on our backs or sitting on foam noodles with beers in our hands, talking about whatever silly things come to mind. I ask about Brayton's life in Oklahoma City, but he ain't got much to say on the subject, which makes me think him being here this summer is less about keeping an eye on his stepdad's place and more about getting away from home.

I'm careful about what I share, too. I tell him about the senior class prank Kenley and I masterminded, and eighty-three-year-old Salty Bo Jefferts, a self-proclaimed miracle worker and local loudmouth who sits in a rocker outside Wick's general store and peddles profanity-laced prayers for five dollars a pop. Any funny story I can come up with that ain't too personal.

"You think I'm joking," I say, when Brayton can't stop laughing about Salty Bo, "but my neighbor Miss Virginie swears he cured her gout."

"I know where I'm going tomorrow," he says. "I got deep pockets and a high tolerance for foul language—gonna get me some miracles."

"Why not tonight? Bo keeps odd hours. He'll probably still be there."

"Can't tonight. I have plans."

"Is that right?"

"You're taking me to the Deck."

I roll my eyes and he grins.

"Heard there's going to be a band," he says.

"Uh-huh. Wayne's pulling up the anchor."

"So?"

"Means it's time to go. Think we overstayed our welcome."

"No way," Karen says, pulling a long filmy tunic over her green bikini. Karen's in her fifties, but she's got the body of someone half her age. She claims it's exercise, but I suspect witchcraft.

"You're always welcome here, Samwich," she tells me. "Your friends, too."

Samwich? Brayton mouths, grinning. I flip him off.

Dolly lifts her head and barks. She was in the water most of the day, lounging on a rubber raft, but now she's curled up near my feet. Karen tosses her a piece of pepperoni and kisses her snout.

"In my next life, I want to come back as Karen's dog," Brayton says.

"Me, too," Wayne says. "Did I hear someone say y'all are headed to the Deck?"

Brayton crosses his fingers. "I'm hoping. But it's up to Sammy."

They stare me down till I give in.

"Yeah, okay," I say. "Nothing else to do 'round here anyway."

"That's the spirit," Brayton says, putting a hand on my shoulder. It's the first time he's touched me all day, and I wish he'd keep doing it, only a little bit lower.

I didn't drink enough last night to erase the memory of his skin on mine, and I want that again. He's gotta know it.

"I guess I should do something about Stella," Brayton says.

"Who?"

He points over his shoulder. The name's printed across the bow of his rumrunner.

"My boat. Well, Jack's boat. Jack's my stepdad."

I give Brayton my hand and he hauls me to my feet. "Let me guess—he named it after a pet."

"*It* is a *her*, and he named it after his mother, I think," Brayton says. "Want to meet her?"

"Your stepdad's mom?"

"My boat."

"You mean Jack's boat."

"Whatever. She likes me better."

"And just how do you know that?"

"She told me."

I laugh. It's that point in the day when, if you've done it right, you've had so much beer and heat you'll find almost anything funny. The sun's a glowing disk, about to dip behind the foothills, and the sky's the color of a beautiful wound, all fleshy pinks and oranges and purple bruises.

The dying light plays over Brayton's dark hair, picking up red strands hidden among the brown. They glow like hot wires. My own long white-blond hair hangs limp across my shoulders, still damp from our last swim.

I probably got mascara under my eyes, and I can tell from the way my skin stings that my cheeks are sunburned, but Brayton's staring at me in a hungry way that makes it hard to swallow, so I can't look that bad.

"I shouldn't," I say. "You think you can talk to boats, so like as not, you're insane."

"Think of it as an adventure."

I give him a smile I hope is mysterious.

"I'm gonna ask you a very important question. Answer right,

I'll board *Stella* with you. Answer wrong and I'll ride with Karen and Wayne to the Deck. Deal?"

"This feels like a trick. Okay, deal."

We shake on it, but when I try to take my hand back, Brayton won't let go. He runs his thumb along my knuckles. This guy.

"What's your question?"

"How fast do you drive?"

CHAPTER FOUR

"What did I tell you?" Brayton shouts. "I drive like a *motherfucker*."

Ain't nothing I like more than racing across the lake in a fast boat. Only thing that'd make this better is if it were early morning, when the water's a sheet of glass and a boat like Brayton's—long and slender, with the same engine they put in expensive sports cars—cuts it like a samurai sword.

We can't talk with all the noise, the slap of the waves against the hull, the roar of the engine, the wind screaming past our ears. And there's something about being in motion that makes me thoughtful. My mind pivots toward all the stuff I been trying like hell to forget today: Rainne taking Decca away. Dad losing custody. My blank-ass future. What all happened with Reed. And money, always money—never enough of it to go around.

Worry gnaws at me. Like he can tell, Brayton grabs my hand,

pulling me back into the moment. Tonight, he's the antidote for life's little snakebites. I give in to it, let it comfort, let it ride.

Brayton takes *Stella* up another ten miles per hour, then stands and hollers into the night. I do it, too, yelling loud as I can, but the air pummeling my face and tangling my hair throws the sound of my own voice back to me. Brayton veers toward the brightening lights of Gibson Bend Marina and *Stella* shudders to a slow crawl. Even motherfuckers gotta respect the no-wake zone.

The surface of the water is smooth near the marina, still enough to reflect the stars: a million tiny pinpricks of light smattered across the sky like freckles. Out here is true country. We don't got light pollution or smog. Brayton looks at me, then tips his head up.

"I think I'm going to like it out here," he says, smiling. It's hard not to stare at his mouth. I want him to kiss me so bad, I feel like I done lost my mind.

When we pull into the slip, I help Brayton tie *Stella* up.

"So where is this place?" He leaps onto the dock and lends me a hand.

"Half a mile up the road," I say, pointing to a dark, lumpy hill to the right. "We gotta walk."

"My least favorite kind of exercise," he says, putting his arm 'round my waist.

"What's your favorite kind?"

He smiles. "Bet you could guess if you tried."

"Classy."

"I kind of used to be a good athlete, actually," he says. "State All Star in soccer."

I gasp. "Oh my golly gee, you're *the* Brayton Foster? You didn't tell me you were a *celebrity*."

"All right, calm down. I put my pants on one leg at a time, just like everybody else."

I glance at his ridiculous swim trunks.

"Those ain't pants. They look like something a methhead clown wears to the beach."

"Hey! Don't diss the board shorts. So what's the deal with the Deck? Is it like a bar or what?"

"Bar, roadhouse, dance hall. It's all things. Not a lot of nightlife up here, we take what we get."

The Deck's already crowded when we arrive. I lead Brayton 'round the side of the squat clapboard building just off the dirt road, toward the back where the action is. We run into Kenley on her way to the Dumpster, carrying three black bags full of trash.

"Hey there," she says. "Glad y'all could make it. Band's just getting going. How you liking Bittersweet so far, Brayton?"

"It's great," he tells her. "Sweetest dam lake west of the Mississippi, as they say."

Kenley nudges me with her elbow. "He's a keeper, Sammy."

I roll my eyes. In my experience, a guy ain't a thing you can keep. They come and they go as they like, and you ain't got a say in the matter.

"Hope you brought your own booze," Kenley says. "They're strict about serving minors here. Unless you're twenty-one?"

"Nope, eighteen." Passing worry troubles the happy look on his face as he shoots a glance my way. "And you're, um…"

"Calm down, Tex, Sammy's legal," Kenley says. "Anyway, ain't it a little late to be asking?"

"Okay." I grab Brayton's arm and tug at it. "We're gonna head on back, see who's around."

"Need help with those?" Brayton asks.

Kenley lifts the trash bags. "Nah, I'm good. I do this all the time."

"Let me." He takes them from her and tosses them into the Dumpster like they don't weigh nothing. He shrugs and ducks his head, smiling. "Keepers gotta earn their keep."

"Come on, let's go," I say, feeling the sudden need to get him as far from my pretty friend as possible. When we're out of Kenley's earshot, I whisper, "She's got a boyfriend, you know."

Which is a bald-faced lie.

"Yeah?" He slides his arm 'round my shoulders. "Well, I hope he's a keeper, too."

There are two main parts to the Deck—a huge backyard full of grass and gravel where people gather in big groups clutching beers and smoking cigarettes, and then an actual deck, like the sort a house might have, wooden slats bleached gray by years of weather and a small tiki-style canopy at one end where you can order drinks and fried food.

At the other end, there's a small roped-off area for the band and a couple square feet of clear space for dancing. The place is jam-packed with people, and on the outside it seems like just another night at the Deck, but I pick up the scent soon as everything comes into view, a sharp, metallic tang, like lightning in the air: trouble.

I look around, nervous as a long-tailed cat in a roomful of rocking chairs, trying to spot the source when I see the Tullers. There's a whole group of them, five at least, standing in the shadows just outside the pools of light thrown on the lawn by spot lamps in the trees.

Most of them aren't known to me by name, but I recognize Johnny and Luger Tuller, who are eight and ten years older than me. Luger's just out of prison after a five-year stint for stalking his ex-wife and setting her house on fire. He's got the butt of a pistol poking out the waistband of his jeans like it ain't illegal for him to carry while he's on parole. Glassy-eyed Johnny's got a beer in one hand and a jackknife in the other, keeps opening and closing it with a practiced flick of the wrist.

They're watching the crowd like animals eyeing prey, with three younger Tuller cubs about my age knocking each other around in a half playful, half aggressive way at their feet. One of them lands a heel on Luger's foot and he grabs the boy by the hair, yanking him backward.

I'm too far away to hear what he says, but not so far I can't see the kid's face, and that's when I realize he ain't no Tuller at all, he's a Boford. Ash Boford, Rainne's half brother, and my…

Well, Ash ain't nothing to me but a bad memory. What the fuck is he doing with the Tullers?

"Are we going up?" Brayton asks, pointing to the deck. "I could use a drink."

"They won't serve you. Didn't you hear what Kenley said?"

He pulls a flask out of his pocket. "Brought my own. All we need is soda. You okay?"

Just then, Ash and Luger catch sight of me. Luger speaks again and some kind of emotion—fear, maybe—flickers over Ash's face. He straightens his shoulders and heads straight for me. Shit.

"I gotta go," I mutter, taking off. "Sorry."

"Wait, what?" Brayton's right on my heels. "Hold up. Sammy!"

"*Sammy!*"

Fuck. That's Ash. I could run, but he'll chase me, and I ain't got nowhere to go. I stop, turn, face him as he reaches me.

Brayton's confused, but I don't know how to explain. I don't even know what's going on, but it can't be good.

Ash gives Brayton a once-over and says, "Get lost."

"What? No way. Who are you?"

"I'm none of your fucking business," Ash snaps. Then he lowers his voice so only I can hear and says, "Got a message. From Redbreast."

I stiffen. Brayton steps up to Ash and says, "I think you better leave Sammy alone."

"'Leave Sammy alone!'" Ash repeats in a mocking voice. "Am I bothering you, baby?"

"You're sure as hell bothering me," Brayton says. "Seriously, man, go away."

"Shouldn't you be off getting a manicure or something, rich boy?"

"Yeah, I'm going to need a manicure after I beat the—"

"Stop." I wedge myself between Ash and Brayton. "You go on. I'm right behind you," I tell Brayton.

Ash dismisses him with a dickish *move along* hand wave. Brayton shakes his head. I glare at him until he backs off.

"Fine," he huffs. He points at the deck. "I'll be *right there*, okay?"

I nod.

When he's gone, Ash laughs. "Who's that limp dick?"

"He's none of your fucking business," I shoot back.

Ash holds up his hands. "Too-*shay*."

"You got thirty seconds. Twenty-nine, twenty-eight…"

"Where's your daddy, Sammy? Redbreast's been looking."

"What the hell could Redbreast Tuller want with my dad? Come to that, what are *you* doing delivering messages for him, anyhow?"

He grabs my arm so hard I can feel the bruises blooming under my skin. "Shut up and listen. You tell Bobby Ray he better not go back on their deal. Been over a week since he stopped taking Redbreast's calls and if he don't get up to Rock Creek right quick and explain himself, next time he comes across a Tuller he ain't gonna get the chance to tell his side. Got it?"

"What deal?"

"You don't gotta know. Just give him the message."

Ash's grip on me loosens and he runs his hand all soft down my arm. "Unless you wanna trade me for the information."

He grins in a way that's supposed to be sexy, and maybe to another girl it would be. Makes *me* sick to my stomach.

"Fuck you," I say, shaking him off and walking away.

"You already did that!" Ash calls, but he don't follow. Small mercy.

My heart's thudding like I ran a mile and my hand shakes as I get out my phone and dial Dad. Goes straight to voice mail.

"Dad," I say, "you gotta call me soon as you get this. Something's up with the Tullers. They're looking for you, and I don't know why but Ash is involved and…just call me."

I slip into an unlit corner to hide out a few minutes and think things through. Ash is a loser, a boy playing at being a man. What he says don't mean shit. I go running to Dad spilling warnings, he'll laugh me into next week.

When I was growing up he called me Chicken Little, said I always thought the sky was falling. Even if what Ash said is true, they picked the wrong messenger—Dad never takes me serious. I'm only a girl, after all.

A few deep breaths, then I step out of the shadows and

head off to find Brayton. He's making polite conversation with Karen and Wayne near the band. He frowns when he sees me.

"You all right?" he asks.

"Yeah," I say, smiling big.

The act's more for my neighbors than Brayton, which is good 'cause he ain't buying it. He shifts me away and asks quietly, "You sure? That guy was an asshole."

"Been that way all his life," I say.

Brayton's hand is on my elbow and I can already feel the worry bleeding out of me. The sky ain't falling.

All the same, I'd feel better if I'd talked to Dad.

"You seem freaked out," Brayton says. "You're shaking."

"I'm cold is all."

Brayton squints at me. It's in the high eighties, no wind. "Yeah? Then we should warm you up."

I smile. "What you got in mind?"

"Let's dance."

"What?"

"Don't you know how to two-step?"

He leads me to the dance floor and arranges me so I've got my left hand on his right shoulder and my right hand in his left.

"Sure I do."

"Prove it," he says. The band starts up a Toby Keith cover.

"You're good at this," I tell him as he spins me.

"I was born with great rhythm," he says, grinning. "Makes me good at a lot of things."

We keep dancing as the band keeps playing: "Down at the Twist and Shout" and "Chattahoochee" and "Small Town Saturday Night." Brayton mouths the words and it makes me laugh. I lose the step once or twice and that makes *him* laugh.

Gotta concentrate to keep from landing on his toes, which means I ain't got enough brain space to worry about Dad, but when the band announces they're taking a ten, it all rolls over me like a mudslide. The Tullers and Ash are out back, watching. Can't give them another opportunity to pounce.

"I wanna leave," I say. Brayton nods.

"I think *Stella* is ready for dry land, anyway. If I leave her in the water too long, she prunes."

"She's a boat," I point out.

"She's not just a boat," Brayton replies. "She's my only friend up here, besides you."

"Who says we're friends?"

"We almost got into a scrap together. That bonds people."

He toys with a piece of hair that's fallen into my eyes. God, I want him to kiss me. But if he thinks *that* was a scrap, he's got a lot to learn about life on Lake Bittersweet.

"There's other ways to bond. Let's go. I just gotta pee first. My eyeballs are floating."

"Okay. No rush."

Brayton pulls out his phone. He's got a string of new texts. Friendless, my ass.

Must be an angel looking out for me, 'cause there's no line at the Porta-Potty, and once I realize I gotta go, I *really* gotta go.

I do my business fast and wash up. The door sticks when I try to leave, so I give it a hard shove. It hits something soft on the other side and someone swears.

"Sorry." I peer 'round the door to see who I've hit. Ain't a person so much as a girl-shaped blur of pink, white and camo.

"What the hell is wrong with—?" She gets up in my face, then suddenly jerks back. "Sammy Lester, that you?"

"Gypsum?"

"You know it! Come on out of there."

She drags me away from the Porta-Potty into a thin stream of sulphur yellow light. I stare at her. I ain't thought about Gypsum Tuller in a long time, but she ain't changed a bit, lookswise at least: short and skinny, with a beak of a nose and that sort of milky fair skin that fries right up in the Oklahoma sun. Her hair's a red frizzball, tied back with a rubber band.

Like most things, country's a matter of degrees. People who think the Lesters are the most redneck people they ever met ain't yet been acquainted with the Tullers. They came down from some Irish by way of Appalachia, and most of them got that red hair, which if you know anything about genetics should tell you something.

"How you doing, Sammy?" Gypsum asks. She's all energy and movement, like a terrier. "Heard about that trouble between your daddy and Rainne Boford or— What's her name now?"

"Tremont."

I eye Gypsum real careful, like she's a snake and I can't tell whether she's poisonous or not. Maybe Johnny and Luger don't think Ash got through to me. Maybe she's reinforcements.

Ain't like we were ever *friends*, Gypsum and I. Can't name a single friend Gypsum ever had, come to think of it. She used to follow me and Kenley around in high school, but we never took much notice. Lots of people followed us around. We were the shit.

"That's right, she married old Duke. He's what? Like forty years older than her?"

"More like twenty."

"Man, ain't she got a type, you know?"

"How'd you hear about all that?"

"People talk. And Redbreast's got an interest in Bobby Ray. From the old days."

Gotta wonder how old those days are, what with Ash's warning.

"My dad been hanging out up at Rock Creek? You can tell me."

Gypsum looks confused, though Tullers ain't too smart— could just be her regular face.

"Nobody tells me nothing. Sorry."

I worry my lip and let out a deep breath I didn't even know I was holding in. I'm feeling jittery, with all this mention of Redbreast Tuller. Even Dad feared him.

"Makes two of us," I say.

"Gyp-*sum*!" Johnny hollers, like he's calling a pig. Spooks both of us half out of our skins.

"Night, Gypsum," I say, stepping away from her. Gypsum's hand clamps 'round my wrist.

"You let go of me right now," I say. I'm safe here, with all these people around, but that don't mean there ain't a part of me that thinks she's the bait in some trap.

When she don't release me, I dig my nails into her skin. She yelps, pulls back.

"I was just gonna say, you know, take care of yourself. Bofords are bad news, no matter who they marry."

She glances over her shoulder, at the group of Tullers in the yard, and Ash Boford on the fringes, staring at us.

"Thanks for the heads-up."

Gypsum angles her head at Brayton, who's texting away, oblivious.

"Saw you dancing earlier. He belong to you?"

"Guess he does. Tonight, anyway."

"So it's really over between you and Reed Pourret, huh?"

I glare at her.

"Take my advice," she says in a low voice. "Grab your boy, and get gone."

CHAPTER FIVE

A text from Dad comes in at 9:48 p.m.: calm down. im fine.

I sigh and let my head fall back against the seat cushion. Brayton's driving a small navy SUV that looks and smells brand-new. My sweaty thighs squeak against the leather.

"This your car, or Jack's?" I ask, not really caring about the answer. Dad's okay. Of course he is. Goddamn Ash Boford, scaring me into thinking otherwise.

"Mine," Brayton says, fiddling with the radio dial. "It was a gift. From Jack."

"An 'I'm marrying your mama, please like me' present?"

"Technically a birthday present, but yeah." He pulls away from the boat launch. "What's there to do around here besides drive?"

I should go home, but I don't wanna. Like as not, the house'll be empty anyway.

"Fuel 'N Fun?" I suggest. "Nothing else will be open this late."

"What's that?"

"Gas station. Convenience store."

"Great, I need gas. You'll have to give me directions. I don't know where anything is yet."

Brayton rests his arm on the back of my seat and his fingers wander over the crown of my head. Makes me wanna close my eyes and drift off while he drives in circles 'round the lake.

When Decca was a baby, she had real bad colic, and Dad would take her on long rides to soothe her. Sometimes, he let me come. Never slept better than those nights, with Decca's fingers wrapped 'round one of mine.

On the way, I tell Brayton about the Fuel 'N Fun slushie bar.

"There's a rule," I say. "Whatever you choose, you're stuck with it. They don't want you putting together some gross flavor and dumping it after a taste."

"Sounds serious," he says.

Brayton pumps and pays for his gas, then we head on into the store. I wave at Kevin, the night clerk, then skip over to the slushie bar like I'm Decca's age.

As I consider my options, Brayton wanders off. When he comes back, he puts his arms 'round my waist, resting his chin on my shoulder. I relax some when he touches me. I always was better at the physical stuff than the feelings stuff.

"What are you having?"

He's standing so close to me. My back presses up against his chest. His chin nuzzles my neck. The soft hair of his legs tickles the bare skin of my own. I almost forget where we are but Kevin coughs loudly and that brings me back to reality.

"I always get the same thing," I tell him. "Strawberry and

lime, with a tiny bit of soda. I call it a Strawberry Summer Sammy. I invented it when I was five."

I take a sip and close my eyes, blissed out on sugar.

Brayton tries it and makes a face.

"Delicious," he mutters, struggling to swallow. I laugh.

"More for me, then. What flavor you gonna get?"

"No slushie. They give me brain freeze."

Brayton wipes his mouth with a napkin. That mouth. I wanna kiss him right now, and Kevin can go to hell.

Brayton jerks his thumb toward the counter, where Kevin's standing guard over a few cans of energy drink. "Ready?"

He tries to pay for my slushie, but I don't let him, even though I should—it takes a two-dollar-and-fifty-cent bite out of my last five-dollar bill.

But Brayton ain't my boyfriend. I don't want him buying me things.

Outside, he points to a bench near the car. "Let's sit."

"Can't we sit in the car?" Even in the dark, it's hot as blazes, and Brayton's SUV's got AC.

"Like I'm letting you in my car with *that*," Brayton says. "I've got one rule—only clear beverages allowed. No food, no colored drink, which means no Strawberry Summer Sammy."

I take a seat on the bench. "You think you can keep that car clean forever?"

"I'm sure going to try."

He sinks down next to me and lets his leg fall against mine, all casual, like I'm dumb enough to think he didn't do it on purpose. He opens one of his energy drinks and I smile.

"Why do you do that?" he asks.

"Do what?"

"Smile when someone opens a can. I thought I was imagining things, but you do it every time."

"You really wanna know?"

"I asked, right?"

"When I was little, my dad told me to make a wish every time he opened a beer."

"Interesting parenting technique."

"Know what the first rule of wishing is?"

"Never tell anyone what you wish for. Duh."

"Right. But I was too young to know that, so when my dad asked me what I wished for, I told him. And then I'd get whatever it was I wanted—to eat ice cream for dinner, or a new doll or something. Stupid kid stuff. He always made this big show out of not wanting to give me whatever it was, but he couldn't help it, he just *had* to. 'Cause that's how powerful wishes are."

"I hope you told him every single wish."

"Nah." I chew on my straw. "By the time I figured out my wishes only came true when I told my dad what they were, he was—"

Brayton raises his eyebrows. I just shrug.

"Well, anyway. If I'd put it together sooner, I'd've gotten a lot more stuff."

"So that's why you smile? Because you're making a wish?"

"Never could kick the habit."

Brayton sits back. "I like that story."

"Then you'll really like this—couple years ago, I asked why he always made such a big deal of not being able to resist giving me what I wished for. He said he wanted me to believe in magic."

Brayton smiles. "We had like fifteen beers between us today. What did you wish for?"

"If I tell you, the wish won't come true. That's the rule."

"Maybe it will. Maybe the only way to guarantee your wishes come true is to tell someone who can make them happen." His handsome face is pale in the moonlight.

"Kiss me," I say.

So he does.

At first, it feels like the ground is moving, until I realize the thing that's moving is me. Us. Holding on to each other like we're caught in a twister, afraid to let go or we'll get carried off by the wind.

Don't know how, but one minute we were just kissing, and the next I was on my feet. He's pushing, then pulling me back toward the car till we slam up against the side of it. My skin feels tight, like it's too small, like there's something inside of me that wants out, to get closer, no such thing as too close.

He pins me to the slab of warm metal with his hips, uses one hand to lock both my wrists above my head while the other one skates down my side, then under my shirt, skimming the bare skin stretched over my spine with his hot palm. Can't move for his body, can't breathe for his mouth covering mine, the tug and release of his lips, a riptide I don't wanna escape.

It's *so good*, his weight pressing me flat, the friction, the feel of him. I arch and he pulls away, panting and hungry-eyed, looking at me like he can't believe I'm real.

To prove it, I break his grip on my wrists and grab him, one hand on his back, fist curled in the fabric of his shirt, and one on his neck, fingers tangled in his hair. He makes a sound in the back of his throat like he's hurting, like I'm torturing him, but it ain't pain, it's desire unfolding, flapping its wings like a bird desperate to get out of its cage.

I feel it, too. I know what it's like to hunger for more than I've got. And with this, like with all other things, getting it only makes me want more.

A passing car honks twice as it passes. Brayton reaches behind me and yanks the door open.

"In, in, in," he murmurs, sliding his mouth down the curve of my neck till it finds the bruise he left last night. He licks the spot, chuckles, breath sweeping my skin. His eyes meet mine.

"You've got a hickey," he says.

I shove him with my shoulder. "Whose fault is that?"

He don't answer, just grabs me with both hands and lifts me into the SUV, so fast I don't see it coming. I yelp, surprised. He climbs in after me, straddling my legs with his knees while I scuttle backward till my hands hit an armrest. He uses his foot to close the door behind him and then, silence, except for our breathing, like we're deep underwater in a soundproof bubble.

I stare at him and he stares back.

With other boys, this is always the moment where one of two things happens: they ask me if I'm *sure*, or they realize, on purpose or 'cause it's their nature, that they don't care if I am or not.

But the look on Brayton's face says he don't need to ask, 'cause he knows I want it. I gave him plenty of signs.

He crawls up my body till he can brace his hands on the window, one on each side of my head. Then he leans in and kisses me slow, taking his time. He slides his tongue against mine, gentle at first, then bossier, pulling at my mouth then pushing in, trying to get at all of me he can reach.

My body lights up like someone put a match to it.

"Clothes off," I say and he laughs. He yanks his shirt over his head, tosses it somewhere, and I peel my tank top away.

He bends to kiss a line down my chest, and I grab hold of his shoulders when his lips brush my stomach, digging my fingertips into the muscle that bunches and shifts as he moves lower, and lower, till he finally stops.

"Keep going," I groan, but he's already got my miniskirt shoved up 'round my hips and his fingers hooked through the straps of my bikini bottoms, tugging them down.

I thread my fingers through his soft, dark hair, close my eyes and tip my head back against the window with a shiver. A thousand electric worms wriggle up my legs and back. I rock forward, begging, 'cause the word *more* is stuck in my throat. His grip on my thighs is punishing, his mouth on me a lightning storm of pleasure, good, so good, so—so—*good* and—

The world buckles around me, and I'm over the edge of the cliff before I even realize I'm in danger of falling.

When I finish shaking, I pull him up and push him back so he's sitting. His breath gushes out like he's been punched in the stomach, and for some reason he grabs my free hand, slides his fingers through mine, and holds on tight, eyes pinched shut, biting his lower lip to keep quiet.

Too bad. I kinda like it when they talk during, depending on what it is they say.

I ain't done this in a while, not 'cause I don't like it, and not 'cause guys don't *try*. But when it comes to sex I always listen to my gut and ever since Reed it ain't been too keen.

But Brayton's inspired me, and he's enjoying himself, going by the sounds he's trying so hard not to make, the way he crushes my hand in his. His skin is fever hot.

"Can you hand me...?" he croaks when it's over, pointing over my shoulder at a box of Kleenex. He cleans up, then kisses me, smiling, and says, "Well, I didn't like that at *all*."

I laugh.

He pulls his shorts up while I pull my skirt down, then he wraps an arm 'round my waist, towing me back till I've got my head pillowed against his bare chest. He traces the edge of my bikini top with a lazy finger. I stroke his knee, feeling boneless and proud and satisfied.

I must fall asleep, not sure how long, but the next thing I know Brayton's waking me up.

"Hi," he whispers, biting my earlobe.

My head's all foggy. I sit up and shake it a bit so it clears. Brayton presses his palm flat against my bare stomach. I put my hand down on top of it and turn my head. He kisses me, a little clumsy and groggy, still so, so hot.

"My phone," I say. I find it on the floor by my feet.

Brayton rests his chin on my shoulder. "What time is it?"

"Holy shit."

I've got seven missed calls and a long string of text messages from Denver.

Decca's hurt, I think in a panic. But that ain't it.

Where are you?

Have you heard from Dad?

When was the last time you talked to him?

He never came home. Do you know where he is?

Why aren't you picking up the phone?

WHERE ARE YOU?

I'm about to write Denver back telling him to stop freaking, I just heard from Dad, but the clock reads 3:04 a.m.

I got that last text from Dad almost five hours ago.

"We gotta go," I tell Brayton.

He rubs his eyes while I wriggle back into my tank top and bikini bottoms. I throw his shirt at him. It smacks him in the face.

"What's going on?" Brayton asks, tugging the shirt over his head.

I climb into the front seat and he follows, dropping down behind the wheel.

"I…I think my dad is gone?"

I look at Brayton in surprise, like he's the one who said it, and hold up my phone. "These are all from my brother. He's freaking out."

"He's probably just overreacting," Brayton says.

"Denver don't overreact. Can you take me home?"

Brayton nods. "How do I get there?"

I give him directions, then call Denver back. He picks up on the first ring.

"Sammy, where the fuck are you? I thought you and Dad were both lying in a ditch somewhere. Why haven't you been answering your phone? I've been trying to call you all night. Is he with you?"

I glance at Brayton. "Dad? No. He ain't with me."

"Dammit!"

"What's going on?"

"I don't know. Maybe nothing."

Denver sounds impatient, but it's just cover for a darker feeling. Ain't like Denver to worry about something other than himself, so if he's bothered, it's a bad sign.

I wanna be home already, and at the same time, as far away from home as I can get.

Denver's breathing heavy—must be pacing, like he does, back and forth in front of the couch where Dad sleeps, shoulders slumped, head ducked 'cause the trailer's ceilings are too low. Last time I saw him so frantic, he was waiting on his high school girlfriend to call about a pregnancy test.

"He told me he was going to be home for dinner," Denver says. "He was going to grill the fish I caught with Holler, but he never showed. Didn't call, either. I keep trying to reach him, but he's not answering his phone."

"Probably left it somewhere. You call down to the Horsefeather? Bet he's there right now."

"It's after three. The Horsefeather's *closed*. Where the fuck are *you*, by the way?"

"Almost home. I'll be there soon and we'll figure this out."

I hang up before he can press me. Less he knows, the better—just how he likes it.

"What's going on?" Brayton asks. I dial Dad's cell. "You're not going to tell me?"

I put my finger to my lips. Dad's phone rings four times then sends me to voice mail. I hit redial, three more times, same thing happens. Fifth time, it don't even ring. Either it died, or he shut it off.

We're almost at my house, just a few more turns. I think about asking Brayton to drop me at the corner of my street so he won't see where I live.

"Hey," he says, tugging my elbow. "Is everything okay?"

I give him a smile. "Just fine. A little family drama, no big deal."

"You sure?"

"Yup. Right here's good."

I've got the door open before he even comes to a complete stop. Gravel crunches under my feet as I hop out at the end of our driveway.

"Bye, Brayton."

"Wait, wait, wait," Brayton says, unbuckling his seat belt in a scramble. I come 'round to his door and lean against it so he can't get out.

"That's it? *Again?* 'Thanks for the great night, see you never'?"

"I never said thanks. Either time."

He rolls his eyes. "So start there."

"Okay." I squeeze his arm. "Thanks for the ride."

Brayton grins. "Which one?"

I flip him off and walk away. I kind of wish he was coming in with me. But I want him to think I'm sexy, and mysterious, not poor and troubled, and whatever's going on with Dad won't help.

I got an itch under my right eye, a bad sign. I never was one to believe overmuch in Granny Lester's crazy Ozark superstitions, but when you're worried, all things carry a whiff of prophecy.

Brayton leans out his window. "This is just good-night, right? Not goodbye?"

I glance back at him, over my shoulder.

"Sammy, I mean it," he says. "I want to see you again."

"Yeah?" I say. He nods. "Well, you know where to find me."

"Where the hell could he be?"

Denver flops onto the couch. We just got finished canvassing the phone tree—friends, neighbors and the tangled web of Lesters, Littles, Howards and Baskins that make up our far-flung family—looking for someone who saw Dad tonight, or knows where he is.

So far, we got nothing.

I was hoping it wouldn't come to this, but I tell Denver what Ash said.

"Why were you talking to Ash Boford?" he asks. "I thought you hated him."

"He didn't give me much of a choice," I snap. "He cornered me."

"And what? You're too much of a lady to make a scene?"

"Guess so."

Denver snorts. "Never heard a taller tale."

"You gonna listen, or what?"

When I'm done, Denver's bent at the middle, head in his hands.

"Tullers," he says in a hollow voice. "I thought we were done with them."

"You really think they'd do something to him?"

"Wouldn't put anything past them, especially if Dad really did have some deal with Redbreast. Stupid bastard. He knows better than that."

Denver pounds a fist on the arm of the couch, sending up a cloud of dust.

"What kind of deal would Dad make with Redbreast Tuller?" I ask. "Not drugs."

I wanna be sure of that, but I ain't. And if Dad's using again, we got more problems than I thought. We lost everything last time, except each other and what's left of the land. Rainne finds out Dad's off the wagon, that's it. We'll never see Decca again, and Dad'll slip away, too, somewhere we can't save him.

Denver don't speak for a while. He just stares at his hands like they got answers written on them.

"We have to retrace his steps," he says finally. "When's the last time you saw him?"

"This morning. Rainne came and got Decca, then Dad headed out. To work, supposedly."

"Jerry says he showed. They quit for the day a little after six. I called him 'round then, about dinner. Said he'd be home by eight, had to take care of something first. After that, nobody saw him."

"I got a text about ten," I say. Denver nods. We been over that already.

"Wish he'd said where he was going." Denver rubs his face. "Wish I'd asked."

Takes me a minute to remember, with how tired I am, that *I* know where Dad was going.

"Rainne," I say. Denver lifts his head, narrows his eyes at me. "Decca forgot Waldo here, and Dad took him, said he'd drop him off at their house after he got off work. Must've been what he meant."

"You knew he was going over there and you let him?"

"*Let* him? Be real, Denver. I told him not to go. Can you imagine what would've happened if I tried to stop him?"

"Yeah, never mind. Just there's too many Bofords in this story for my liking," Denver says.

He leans back, lets his head fall, closes his eyes. With this heat wave, nights ain't no cooler than days, and we both got sweat pouring down our faces.

We're exhausted, too, but we probably couldn't sleep if we wanted. I think about how easy I dozed off with Brayton earlier and feel guilty.

Denver opens his eyes and hands me the cordless phone. "Call her."

"Why me?"

"I call her at five in the morning, ten to one she hangs up. Bitch hates me."

"Hates me, too."

"You don't got enough brains in your head to go 'round acting stupider than you are," Denver tells me.

I laugh, in spite of everything. It's a family joke, one of Granny Lester's favorite burns. Denver gives me a weak smile.

"Rainne always liked you best," he says. "Still does."

Don't know about that, but I take the phone anyway and dial Rainne's number. I gotta call three times before someone picks up. I roll my eyes.

"What?" Denver asks.

"Duke," I whisper. Then, louder: "Hey, Duke, sorry to wake you."

"Fuck you want, Sammy?"

Whether or not Rainne likes me, her new husband never did.

"I need to talk to Rainne." When he don't say nothing, I tell him, "It's about Dad."

"Yeah, I heard you were calling all over the county, asking after him," Duke says.

"How?"

"Text from Sybil," Duke says.

Sybil Little, that traitor. She does hair for half the women in the county, including Rainne, and she never did know how to keep her big trap shut.

"Rainne's sleeping," he says. "Call back later."

"Can't. It's urgent."

A waterfall of panic floods through me. We're having a family emergency.

"I need to talk to Rainne, right now," I tell him. "You don't put her on, I'll keep calling every five minutes, and if you unplug the phone, I'll come banging on your door, you know I will. So *put her on*."

Denver gives me a tired thumbs-up.

"Sammy," Rainne says, a few seconds later. "What's wrong?"

At the sound of her voice, my lip starts trembling. Funny what times like this dredge up: a memory of Rainne patching my knee after I scraped it in a fall.

I pinch the bridge of my nose to keep from tearing up. "Do you know where Dad is?"

There's a pause, and I can just see her shoulders stiffen like they always do when someone mentions Dad.

"No," she says, in a harder voice. "I don't. Why?"

"Ain't nobody seen him since he got off work. He ain't been home, and we can't get a hold of him or track down anybody who saw him last night. He told me he was gonna stop by your house to drop off Waldo for Decca. You know where he went when he left?"

"Bobby Ray didn't come by last night," Rainne says. "Didn't even know he was fixing to. We never saw him."

"You didn't?" Denver wrinkles his brow and I shake my head at him. "But he said…"

"Guess he changed his mind. The man does that. And he shouldn't be coming by here, anyway, with all the court stuff. Maybe he was planning on it, then figured he better not."

"Yeah," I say.

But if Dad did change his mind about going to Rainne's, what was the errand he mentioned to Denver?

Rainne sighs. "I don't wanna scare you, Sammy, but I been hearing stuff about Bobby Ray, and it's making me worry. You know anything about him working with the Tullers again?"

"Who told you that?"

"MaryEllen," Rainne says. Her mama, MaryEllen Boford, meanest woman in six counties. "But she might've heard it from Ash."

"Think he'd make something like that up?"

"I think Ash is capable of a lot of things. Wouldn't be much use to the Tullers if he wasn't."

There's sadness in Rainne's voice. Of her seven siblings, Ash always was her favorite, till he grew into the meanness he inherited from MaryEllen and found a new family, one that prized him for it more.

"Sorry," Rainne says. "Wish I could be more help."

"Me, too."

I'm about to hang up, but then I hear her say, "Sammy?"

"Yeah?"

"Bobby Ray and I had our differences. But I really hope you find him."

CHAPTER SIX

"We gotta call the sheriff," I say, squeezing the phone like I'm trying to choke the life out of it.

Denver raises his eyebrows. "How much of a shit you think Olina gives about Dad these days?"

"Well, we gotta do *something*." Maybe we're overreacting. Maybe Dad's gonna walk through the door any second. But I can't just sit here worrying. It'll make me crazy.

"He's a grown-ass man. We can't file a missing persons report after less than twelve hours."

"So what, we wait? How long? A day? *Two* days? Anything could've happened to him by then."

Denver picks at a worn patch on the sofa cushion. "Like as not, nothing *has* happened to him. He probably just up and left."

"You don't mean he left *us*?"

"Before he went to prison, he disappeared all the time. Day

or two here or there on a bender, sometimes a week on a job." He means a job for Redbreast.

"*Before.* He's different now. He'd never leave Decca. He's gotta be in court on Wednesday."

"Sammy," Denver says softly. "You know he isn't going to win, right?"

"I don't know that, and neither do you, so don't you go on saying it. Thoughts are things."

That was one of Granny Lester's favorite sayings: *Thoughts are things. They matter just as much as doings.*

"You know what else are things? Facts. Dad's an ex-junkie-slash-ex-con with a temper and a bad reputation. No court in this county's going to say Rainne can't move Decca out of state on account of his so-called *rights.*"

Denver drifts over to the window. Any second, the sun's gonna rise over the hilltops and it'll be morning. Morning, and still no Dad.

I put on a pot of coffee, like I think the smell of it might waft out the door, find him wherever he is and lead him home.

Neither of us has spoken for a while when I say, "He could be with a woman."

"I called all his women," Denver says. "Before you even got home. None of them saw him tonight. Where were *you*, by the way? I called you like a hundred times."

"I was out."

"Pick up your phone next time."

I attack this morning's dirty dishes with a scrub brush to keep from throwing one at Denver's head as he walks out of the kitchen. But I ain't even mad at him. I'm mad at me. For not taking Ash's warning serious enough. For being with Brayton when I should've been looking out for my family.

What'd I think I was doing, anyhow, messing with a city boy? They're always more trouble than they're worth.

Don't matter, I tell myself. Probably won't see him again after tonight.

Denver stands on the porch, staring at the sky as it lightens. I can see him out the kitchen window, and I think about how, when we were kids, there was but one ice-cream truck down in Tehlicoh. Couple of weekends every summer, the driver trekked up the bluff so us hill kids could have a treat. We'd wait at the end of the driveway with our scrounged-up change, coins slippery in Denver's sweaty grip, never knowing for sure if the ice-cream man would show or not.

Denver's a dozen years older now, but he's got that same look on now: expecting disappointment, but still desperate with hope.

The screen door whines, then slams shut.

"You saw Ash at the Deck. Where'd you go after that?" Denver asks from the doorway.

"Just over to Kenley's," I say, which is stupid—as Dad says, lies die in the details. But I don't wanna talk to Denver about Brayton.

"I called her, dummy. She was on shift, and she said you left early. With some guy. A new one?"

"It's none of yours where I was, or who I was with," I say. I throw the dish towel in the sink and brush past him.

Denver grabs me by the wrist—not hard, but firm enough to stop me.

"Are you okay, Sammy?" he asks.

My throat tightens. "Not just right now."

"I mean, outside of whatever's going on with Dad. I worry about you."

Now he's worried. This past year was the hardest of my life, with everything that happened between me and Reed. Denver knew about all of it, every terrible thing. But I barely heard a word from him after he went back to college last fall—where was all this brotherly concern when I needed it?

"Well, I'm fine," I say, pushing all thoughts of Reed back into the dark cellar of my heart where they usually live. "So don't."

Denver takes a deep, shaky breath. I look down at his hand on my wrist, thinking of Gypsum's bony doll fingers wrapped 'round it like cables.

In all my worry over Dad, I forgot I even saw her. The timing of our run-in, so soon after Ash's threat, seems off. Like rain brings worms up out of the earth, trouble brings Tullers. Gotta wonder if she's as clueless as she claims to be.

Like he's reading my mind, Denver asks, "You really think something bad's happened to Dad?"

I nod.

"Then I guess we better gather some folks up once it's a decent hour and start looking."

"Yeah," I say. "I guess we better."

My room's so stifling I can't fall asleep, so I lay down on the couch, in front of the crotchety old AC unit, turning everything over in my head. I guess I doze off, 'cause I wake with a start to Denver whispering, *"Dammit."*

I sit up, shading my eyes from the sunlight streaming through the grimy windows. He's standing over by the falling-apart bureau where Dad keeps his clothes. He gave up his bedroom to Denver for the summer.

"What's wrong?" I ask.

Denver jumps at the sound of my voice and whips around, shutting the drawer with a bang.

"I was just looking for something of mine. Thought Dad might have it."

I yawn. "What is it? Maybe I know where it went."

"Doesn't matter. You should get dressed. People are going to be here soon."

"You called everyone?"

"While you were sleeping, yeah."

"Sorry." I rub my eyes. "I could've helped."

He shrugs. "No problem. Mom's coming."

"What?" I snap.

"You know I had to call her."

"Yeah, but…"

I ain't talked to Mom since—well, it's been a while now, and she don't live 'round here anymore. She moved from the lake to her second husband's family farm outside Checotah a few years ago.

"Come on. I put a pot of coffee on for you."

I change quick, then trudge to the kitchen for my morning caffeine fix. I never touched the stuff till I moved in with Dad, but I guess he rubbed off on me.

In the daylight, the whole trailer seems shabbier than ever. The window glass is grimy with fingerprints, the curtains are faded and full of little holes, the couch is sagging and the carpet is covered in light, unidentifiable stains. Can't remember the last time a stranger stepped foot in here, and the state of it makes me ashamed, but it's too late to do anything about it—Karen and Wayne are at the door.

"We're here to help," Wayne says as Karen hugs me. I'm

board-stiff in her arms. It hits me all over again, what's happening. The truth of it damn near knocks the air out of my lungs.

I wonder what Decca's doing. Wasn't but yesterday she was here with me, and now I don't even know when I'll see her next. Funny how things that feel so solid one minute can vanish into thin air, like they were never there to begin with.

Karen smooths my hair back from my face. "You sleep at all, sugar?"

"Some," I say. She sighs and pulls me closer.

I known Karen a long time, and it's in her nature to comfort, but I feel like I'm betraying my own mama by letting her, for being grateful she's here instead of Mom. At least I know Karen's not thinking what a disappointment I am.

Mom shows up half an hour later, gray in the face, with her husband, Polk, in tow. I expect her to go straight to Denver, but instead she walks up to me and wraps me in her arms just like Karen did.

I melt into her, tears pricking my eyes, half hoping this means all the fighting of the past year is forgiven, but she don't say nothing to me and moves on to Denver after a couple seconds.

"We'll find him," she says, like Denver's not the one who thinks Dad deserted us.

"It's all right, Mom," he says.

She takes his face in her hands and strokes his cheeks with her thumbs and goddamn, it makes me wanna sob my guts out, but I bite my cheek and walk out the front door into the blazing sun.

There's a sea of people loitering on our front lawn. Seems the whole lake has turned out to search for Dad. From the porch where I'm standing I see longtime friends, relations close and distant, neighbors, some of my own classmates even. Dad's boss, Jerry, is here.

"Knew something bad must've happened soon as Denver called," I overhear him say to my cousin Ronnie Lipton, who manages the supermarket down in Tehlicoh. "Bobby Ray's one of my most reliable guys. Never known him to flake, but he didn't turn up to work this morning."

"Shit," Ronnie says, dropping his cigarette and grinding it into the dirt with the toe of his boot.

Kenley joins me on the porch, hands me a bottle of water. I gulp down half of it, throat so parched it's like a strip of salt pork left to dry in the sun.

"Thanks," I say, wiping my mouth with the back of my hand.

"Anything you need," Kenley says. She means it, but still I look away, embarrassed.

Word about Dad must've spread farther and faster than I thought, 'cause who should come walking right out of the shadowy tangle of the woods right then but Gypsum Tuller, casual as you please, like she's stopping by for a friendly visit. She zeroes in on me right quick.

"What are you doing here?" I ask. Bold of her, seeing as the best lead we got on who might be responsible for this nightmare is her own kin.

"Heard about what's going on. Thought I'd come by and lend a hand is all."

"And what exactly did you hear?"

She squints at me. Sun's right in her eyes.

"That Bobby Ray Lester's missing, and y'all are fixing to track him down yourselves."

"Who'd you hear it *from?*"

"Denver posted about it on Facebook this morning, asking

for local folks to help with the search. People been sharing it, and I saw. I can leave if you want?"

I can tell I hurt her feelings. Like that ought to matter right now, but I guess it does, 'cause I say, "Do whatever. Stay if you want."

Kenley shoots me a look of surprise. It ain't rational, but I got this terrible hope Gypsum knows more than she's saying and she'll lead us right to Dad. Wouldn't put it past a Tuller, even a twig off the family tree like she is. They got ways I'll never understand.

Denver comes outside and says, "Guess we better start."

He puts on some cheap Dollar General shades of Dad's and hands me a pair of my own. I tuck them in my pocket, knowing I'll want them later, when it's high noon and the sun's tearing up my eyeballs as I wade through muck creeks and knee-high weeds. Searching for the body of my father.

"Yeah, let's go," I say, but then I spot Brayton coming up the driveway.

I watch his face as he takes in all the people and it dawns on him something's off, but when he sees me he smiles, hesitant, like he's not sure it's the right thing to do but he can't help himself.

"I'm riding with Mom and Polk," Denver says. "You should come with us. You, too, Kenley, if you want."

He ignores Gypsum, don't even think he registers she's there. She watches us with those beady eyes of hers.

"Okay," Kenley says. She taps me on the shoulder and whispers, "You see him?"

I nod. "I'll catch up with y'all. Just gotta take care of something real quick."

Brayton smiles again when he sees me coming, bigger this time.

"Hey," he says. Looks pretty pleased with himself, the way only rich boys can.

"What are you doing here?" I ask.

"You said if I wanted to see you again to come find you. I woke up wanting to see you, so here I am."

The smile widens into a grin, like he's expecting a reward for his cleverness. "You weren't hard to find. I know where you live."

He looks around. "What's going on here? You having a birthday party?"

"More like a search party. You should probably leave."

The smile disappears as it sinks in, what's happening. "Your dad never came home last night."

I shake my head. "We're gonna go look for him."

"Okay. What can I do?"

"Nothing," I say. "*I* don't know what to do. I'm going with my brother. I gotta—"

Denver whistles to get my attention. I turn in his direction and that's when I see Rainne. Standing there, talking to Mom, bent head and frowning mouth, pale like someone drained the blood out of her body.

I don't much believe in miracles, but if they exist then this is one for sure: Bobby Ray Lester's two ex-wives turned up to look for him.

"Come on," Denver says, steering me by the elbow toward Mom's old sedan. I'm so distracted I don't even say goodbye to Brayton.

"Rainne showed?"

"Yeah, but don't go getting your hopes up she's had a change of heart about Decca."

"I won't," I say. But I always been the hopeful sort.

As Polk pulls away from the house I see Brayton standing where I left him, staring after us. Right before he fades from sight, he turns to speak with a person I can't see.

My heart drops to the floor. He ain't going nowhere. Must fancy himself some kind of white knight, coming to the rescue.

But I got plenty white knights here, and to a one they all got better armor against the truths of this place than he does.

It's nice he wants to help. I ain't so heartless I can't see that. But I'd rather push him off the cliff at the edge of the bluff than let him. I don't want him knowing how bad things can get. 'Cause I got a feeling things are about to get very, very bad.

We look for Dad till the sun goes down, over seventy of us searching streams and ponds, back roads and abandoned properties, burned-out houses and junked trailers. We knock on every door we see, walk as far as we dare into every cave, shouting his name. We make calls and cash in favors for tools or extra manpower in certain places, like the big field out behind Mrs. Carmichael's place, where we hold hands and form a dragnet to cover it inch by inch.

Through it all, I stick to Denver's side like a burr, out of fear we'll get separated and one of us will have to come across Dad alone.

Gypsum won't leave me be. She's a shadow at my heels, trailing me, bugging me with stupid questions, like who cuts my hair and do I think the Ozark Howler is real. And much as I don't like to admit it, she's a help. She knows the land better than even I do, pointing us down roads that don't look like roads at all, suggesting places I didn't even think to check.

"How do you know all this?" I ask her after she reminds me there's a ruined cabin someone left to rot up on the bluff head at the mouth of the river.

Gypsum pokes the ground with a stick she picked up somewhere. It's almost as tall as she is.

"I've looked for people," she says.

"Like who?"

Instead of answering my question, she says, "You ever think about the future, Sammy?"

I rub my dry, itchy eyes. "Not really."

Gypsum sighs. "Me neither. Sometimes I try, but it makes me so tired."

She sits on a log. I hand her my bottle of water and she takes a few swigs.

"Your family ever give you shit about it?" she asks.

"My future? Only Denver. Why? Does yours?"

"No. Not any of them. I ain't gonna be like that with my kids." She says it with a fierceness that makes me believe her. "I'm gonna tell them to get gone from this place first chance they got."

"You don't like it here?"

"It's a fine place. Pretty. It's my home. But I don't like feeling trapped. And I am. Just like you."

She looks even smaller in the woods, with the trees looming over her.

"You barely know me," I say.

"That's what you think."

"Why are you even helping look for my dad?"

"Just returning the favor, I guess. You helped me once."

"I did?"

Gypsum nods. "When we was younger. Ash tried getting all the boys in school to call me 'Jizzum' and you told him you'd never kiss him again if he was gonna be such an asshole."

The thought of kissing Ash Boford makes me gag now, but there was a time it didn't. So, so long ago.

"I don't remember that."

"Folks tend not to remember things to do with me," she says. "It's my gift."

The day is long and exhausting, but I always got one eye on the sun, tracking its position in the sky. Feels like every second that passes without finding Dad makes it less and less likely we will.

In the early evening, a group of us come down on the old Collins farm like locusts, slashing through knee-high grass and crawling over rusted equipment on the lookout for a flash of red plaid, a shock of Dad's dark hair shot through with gray. Denver and I are investigating a falling-down shed when a cry comes from our left, near the bank of a small creek that winds its way through the property.

"I found something!" Rainne shouts.

We all hurry over to look, hearts in our throats. But it's just a pile of fabric, what might've been clothes once but is so rotted it don't look like anything anymore.

Denver sits on a rock. He rubs his face with his dirt-red hands and groans. "This isn't *working*."

I look out over the group of searchers, once hopeful, now weary. "Maybe I was wrong."

The hot day has sucked the hope clear out of our bones. By the time we make it home, our backs are bent like tallgrass in a twister. Gypsum vanishes, as quick and quiet as she ap-

peared this morning, leaving me to wonder how she comes
and goes like magic. Her gift.

The others slough off like dead skin in great chunks, disappointed and full of apologies. Rainne says she'd stay, but she's
gotta pick up Decca from MaryEllen's.

"When can I see her again?" I ask. Rainne rubs her tired,
sun-blind eyes.

"I don't know about that, Sammy," she says. "We gotta see."

"But—"

"I'll call you when I think it's right," she says, then walks
off without letting me get another word out.

I go to follow her, but Denver holds me back, shaking his
head.

"Don't push it," he says. "Now ain't the time."

Mom and Polk stick around through the dinner Karen and
Wayne kindly feed us. I ain't hungry, so I chain-smoke on the
steps of their deck while everyone else stuffs their rumbling
bellies.

When it's time to go, I pull Mom aside. Ain't sure what I
was planning to say, 'cause both of us want apologies, tearful
confessions of sin, and neither of us believe we're in the wrong.
She stops me before I start.

"I don't wanna talk about all that right now, Sammy," she
says.

Been a while since we last fought and my angry heart used
the time to calm itself, to soften toward her, but it hardens
again. Shouldn't a mother ought to love her child uncondi-
tionally? Shouldn't a Christian like she says she is ought to
show her own daughter kindness?

When they're gone, Denver and I trudge back to the house,
looking low and feeling lower.

"Who's that?" Denver asks. His voice breaks, dry from hunting all day in the hot sun.

There's a dark figure lounging on one of our porch chairs. It shifts, and I feel like someone's reached into my chest and closed a big meaty fist 'round my heart. *Dad*.

But it ain't. It's Brayton, and he's asleep.

"Hey!" I shake him till he wakes. He blinks up at me. "What are you doing here?"

"Waiting for you," he says.

He sits up and drags a hand across his eyes. Granny Lester used to say sleep steals years from you, and Brayton looks like a kid for a second, pawing at his face, mouth half-open in a yawn.

He's so goddamn handsome I wanna smack him, or myself, 'cause desire curls in my belly just looking at him and now's not the time for such things.

"Have you been here all day?"

"No," he says, insulted. "I was out there searching with everybody else. I came here when they scattered. Wanted to know if you found anything."

Denver comes up the steps like he's creeping up on a wild animal deep in the woods. He must see how agitated I am, how I can't stop moving. I'm fixing to burst with powerless rage.

"Nothing," I say. "Half the county turns out on a Sunday to look and *nothing*."

Brayton gets to his feet and offers Denver his hand to shake. "Denver, right? Big brother?"

Denver eyes Brayton, wary. Dad says that of all of us, Denver's the true Ozarker. He's got our pioneer ancestors' work ethic, and he keeps his trust in a bear trap, right alongside his heart.

He's polite, though. "Nice to meet you…"

"Brayton. Foster."

"Which is it?"

"Brayton."

"Not from around here, are you?" Denver asks. Brayton shakes his head. "Welcome. It's a fucking paradise."

He shoots me a look as he goes into the house.

"You can't be here," I tell Brayton.

"What do you mean? Why not?"

"I don't know you," I say. "This is family business."

"But Sammy—I want to help."

He tries to take my hand but I pull away. Boys. They're all white knights, till they ain't. More like than not, he's just curious, but I ain't no zoo animal, put on display for him to gawk at. This is my life.

"What makes you think I want you to help? Or, if I did, that you even could?"

The sky's darkened so fast, I can hardly see his face. He shoves his hands into his pockets, shrugs his shoulders up to his ears.

"Guess I can't argue with that," he says.

A sharp splinter of guilt stabs at me. He did spend all day doing what he could.

"Thanks," I say. "For looking with us."

"No problem. Guess I'll go then."

He stares at the porch boards, scuffs at the weathered gray wood with the toes of his sneakers. I don't say anything, 'cause I'm afraid if I speak I'll stop him leaving. I don't want him gone. I wish things were such that he could stay, but they ain't.

Brayton takes his time walking away, giving me the chance to change my mind. I almost smile.

At his car, he turns and says, "Sammy? You might want to take a good look at your front door."

There's almost no light left, save for what the moon is throwing down, so at first I don't know what he's talking about. But then Brayton climbs into his car and switches on his brights for me to see by, and my stomach juices rise like a wave in my throat.

"Denver!" I shout, pounding on the door. "Come out here right now! You gotta see this!"

CHAPTER SEVEN

The words are scrawled on our door in black spray paint: "WHERES THE MONEY?" Not a bit sure what that's all about, but from the look on his face I think Denver might have an inkling.

"You know what this means?" I ask.

Denver stares at the door like it's a rattler fixing to bite, and him within striking distance.

"Sammy," he says, his voice weak and crumbly. "We got a problem."

"You think?" I snap.

I follow him into the house and fall like dead weight on the couch while Denver paces in front of me, tugging at the roots of his hair.

"I'm pretty sure Dad stole some money from Redbreast Tuller," he says.

"*Stole?* He ain't that stupid."

"Maybe not stole. Maybe borrowed. But now he's gone, it's the same thing, isn't it?"

"How—"

"I saw it! Right there in that drawer."

He points to the bureau he was rummaging through this morning.

"I was looking for a T-shirt of mine and I thought you might've put it in with Dad's by mistake, and that's when I found it. A big wad of cash tied up in rubber bands."

"What makes you think he got it from the Tullers?"

"I didn't count it out, but looked to be about ten thousand dollars. Who else around here you think's got that kind of cash to lend? Where else you think Dad would go to get money like that?"

"And now it's gone?"

Denver nods. "I went looking this morning and it's not there."

I push all the air out of my lungs in a long, hot stream through my nose, an old anger management trick to calm down.

"This is bad, Denny."

"I know."

"That cash must've been part of whatever deal Ash Boford was talking about at the Deck," I say. "He said Dad's been avoiding Redbreast. If they caught up with him—"

"Best case, he's run off," Denver says. "Maybe we'll be doing him a favor if we let him go."

"So they come after us instead? Don't know about you, but I don't got ten thousand dollars, and the Tullers ain't gonna stop chasing down their money just 'cause they can't find Dad."

All of a sudden, I can smell the smoke of burning tires from the night the Tullers set our car on fire in our own front yard. The sweet metal tang of Kibble's blood on an ashy breeze.

Decca. They could hurt her. They could use her to lure Dad back, or to punish him.

"We gotta go to the cops," I say.

Denver looks miserable, but he don't argue. "We'll call the sheriff in the morning."

"I gotta work in the morning. We gotta go now, before it gets too late."

Denver agrees to go with me to see the sheriff. He's just as suspicious about cops as I am, but it's the only option. We drive down to Tehlicoh in a car I borrowed off Karen and Wayne.

On a Sunday night in the middle of nowhere, ain't too much sheriffing needing to be done, so there's a bunch of deputies milling about the station, talking low on their cell phones or pushing papers around on their dented metal desks. Thankfully I spot one I know and don't hate: Pete Pourret, my ex-boyfriend's brother.

"Hey there, Sammy," he says. He don't seem too surprised to see me. "How can I help you?"

"Hi, Pete," I say. "Saw Sarah in town not a week ago. When's she having that baby?"

Pete beams. "She's huge, huh? Doc says any day."

"Boy or girl?"

"Sarah don't wanna know," he says. "But me? I'm hoping for a boy."

"You boys always do," I say. "Pete, I need to file a missing persons report. On my dad."

The light dies in his eyes right quick. "Heard about that, and I'm sorry. I can help you."

Denver comes in from parking the car and Pete leads us into a small room off the bull pen, armed to the teeth with forms. We spend the next hour telling him everything we know. We give a detailed description of what Dad looks like, what he was last wearing, the make and model of his car, what he might've had on him: wallet, watch, keys, sunglasses, cigarettes and matches.

"Identifying marks?" Pete asks.

A scar on the very top of his brow from a prison fight, and more in a patchwork on his hands and arms from the same. The ink we know about.

I hand over three current photos, and together Denver and I list every place Dad's been known to frequent, every person we know he knows. Everyone except the Tullers. I'll be saving that information for Sheriff Olina.

"Thanks for all this," Pete says. He rolls his neck to get a crick out.

Denver's jumpy, bouncing his leg up and down like he's fixing to run. I wring my hands under the table.

"What about the last time you saw or spoke to Bobby Ray?" Pete asks. "There anything else you know about where he might've been the night he disappeared?"

"I saw him morning before last," I say. "His ex-wife came over to grab my little sister, Decca, and then Dad went to work."

"That'd be Rainne Boford? His ex-wife."

"Rainne Tremont now," I say. "She married Duke Tremont two summers ago."

"Right." He straightens. "Anything else? He call you that day, or talk about going somewhere after work?"

"He was gonna drop Waldo off at Rainne's on his way back

into town." Pete squints at me in confusion. "My sister's stuffed elephant. She left it at our house, and Dad was gonna return it 'cause Decca can't sleep without it, but Rainne says he never showed. You can ask her."

"We will," Pete assures me. "Denver, what about you?"

"I went fishing with Holler Groom before Dad got up that day, so the last time I saw him was just after dawn, sleeping on the couch," Denver says. "I called him after I got back, asked if he'd be home for dinner and should I throw a crappie on the grill for him. He said hold off on cooking 'cause I can't grill for shit, he'd do it. He planned to be home by eight, needed to take care of something first."

"He say what it was?"

Denver shakes his head. "Didn't ask. Maybe it was the Waldo thing."

"I got a text from him a little before ten o'clock," I say. "I'd been calling...but if he never went to Rainne's, not sure what he did between the time Denver talked to him and then."

"This is good," Pete says, setting down his pen and sitting back in his chair. "Helpful, I mean."

"Now what?" I ask.

"I gotta type up a formal report and put it into the system. Normally you'd have to wait to talk to someone, but Sheriff Olina's still in her office so I'm gonna ask if she'll see you now. Personal favor," he says, giving me a smile.

He's being kind, 'cause we used to be almost family. I'm just glad he ain't tried to talk to me about Reed.

Sheriff Olina don't look too happy to see us, but I never seen her look happy about anything in my life. She busts into the interview room trailing Pete, waving a file folder in the air.

"Now, what's this about Bobby Ray gone missing?" she asks,

slapping the folder down on the table like an accusation, like we're wasting her time just by coming 'round.

Olina's been sheriff of Bittersweet County about ten years, practically inherited the position from her daddy, though technically she keeps getting elected. She looks just like her daddy, too—short and stocky with the grumpy expression of the mean old bulldog mix Kenley's bleeding-heart parents been fostering.

Denver ducks his head, like the whole thing's an embarrassment.

"He's been gone a day," I tell her. "We can't find him."

"Don't tell me this is the first time he took off without warning. And a day ain't that long. What makes you think he won't be back when his drugs done run out?"

"It ain't drugs," I snap. "He's been clean for years."

"Yeah, well, forgive me if I don't take your word for that, Sammy," Olina says. "Man's got a rap sheet a mile long, half drug-related, half fighting. Maybe he mouthed himself into a bad situation."

"You heard something about him fighting?"

"No, but he's been known to."

She gives me a hard look. Dad went to prison for fighting—well, fighting and drugs. Back then he was serving as muscle for Redbreast, collecting debts any way he could and racking up his own. He was rolling hard the night he beat a Tuller client named Arthur Comstock near to death, and he got sent down to McAlester, seven years for aggravated assault.

"I think I know what happened to him," I tell the sheriff.

"Oh yeah?" Olina sits across from me, pen hovering over a pad of lined yellow paper.

"The night Dad disappeared, I was at the Deck, minding my own business, when Ash Boford came at me with a message from Redbreast Tuller, saying Dad better not be backing out on their deal."

"So?"

Olina puts the pen down without writing anything and leans back in her chair, arms folded across her chest. For a big woman, she's got tiny breasts, like a twelve-year-old. It always did make her look strange, like in some ways she never grew all the way up.

"*So*, Ash made it sound like if Dad didn't come 'round and give them what he promised, they were gonna…do something to him," I say. "He didn't come home that night. They must've found him before I could warn him."

"That's a big accusation," Olina says. "You got proof to back it up?"

I elbow Denver. He shakes his head like he's coming out of a fog, then hands over his phone with a photo of our front door, the message scribbled in spray paint.

"What makes you think it was the Tullers did this?" Olina asks.

"Who else would it be?"

She tosses the phone back. "No reason to believe it wasn't the pair of you who wrote those things."

Denver comes to life all of a sudden. "Why would we vandalize our own house?"

"To make it look like there's been foul play when you know your daddy ran off somewhere," Olina says.

She leans forward and looks us straight in the eyes, that old cop trick to make you feel like they're your friends.

"I get it—you love him, and you're worried."

Denver snorts. Even he ain't falling for this.

"But Bobby Ray's a bad sort, he always was, and the last

thing two young kids like y'all wanna be doing is taking on his troubles."

"You mean you're not gonna try to find him?" I ask.

Olina spreads her hands. "Can't find a man don't wanna be found."

Not five minutes later, Denver and I are sitting in the car, minds spinning, guts churning with rage—or, anyway, mine is. Won't say I expected them to pull out all the stops, but we just got tossed out of the station on our asses. Old Sheriff Olina would've at least *pretended* to look for Dad.

"You see her face when I brought up the Tullers?" I say, twisting my seat belt in my hands. "She must be mixed up with them, somehow—her daddy was always in Redbreast's pocket, too."

"Could be she's right. All that money could take him a long way from Lake Bittersweet."

"He ain't *running*," I say. "He's in trouble and we gotta help him."

"Oh yeah?"

My brother's eyes are burning with something, all that anger he keeps tamped down inside, anger at the world, at Dad for never giving him a better life. Denver's lashes are so long and dark. I know girls think them pretty, but now they're dozens of sharpened spearheads guarding pools of blue, deep as the lake, with just as many secrets.

Denver don't tell me nothing about what he's feeling or thinking, not ever, always miserly with his realest self, but for a second he slips and I can see it, the accusation: *Why should we help him when all he's ever done is hurt us?*

"Well, the police won't do anything," Denver says. "And all our searching turned up squat. The Tullers probably know something, even if they aren't responsible, but how do you suppose we're going to find out what it is?"

"Easy," I tell him, coasting on a rush of courage that probably ain't nothing but foolishness. "I'm gonna ask them my fucking self."

FROYGAR OF THE LITTLE WATERS

People say giants weren't capable of love, but that just ain't true. Just 'cause a person likes being alone don't mean they don't got a heart that beats for someone besides themselves.

Don't believe me, Decca? Well, I guess I gotta tell you another story then, to prove it. This one's about a very special giant. Her name was Froygar of the Little Waters, and she was a hero.

Froygar was a lady-giant, about thirty-five or so, which was like a teenager in giant years. She'd been on her own for a while—giants don't keep their cubs long—and she lived about an hour north of here, up at Dripping Springs, which giants called the Little Waters 'cause of how small the falls looked to them.

She was young, but she was a fierce sort. By the time of this story, humans done took over the flatlands, driving the giants into the mountains. I told you before that giants were nomads, but Froygar was different. She was born at the Little Waters, and left there by her mama, so that's where she raised herself up. It was *her* land, and she wasn't gonna let anyone take it from her.

That ain't to say other giants didn't try. Big scary boy giants were constantly threatening Froygar's peaceful paradise, thinking she was just a girl, how could she possibly stop them from taking whatever they wanted? And Froygar, being smaller than these boy giants, sure did worry at first, but she wasn't just fierce, she was also clever.

Froygar couldn't beat the boy giants in a fight, but she *could* trick them, so that's what she did. One time, she promised to give up the Little Waters to a boy giant if he'd be her husband. Boy giants weren't good husbands, but this one was exhausted from battling humans, so he agreed, then told Froygar to fix his dinner. She fed him two freshly killed deer stuffed with thornapple berries—which are toxic, you know—and he fell into a deep sleep.

That boy giant ate so much poison he would've died no matter what, but she tore out his heart with her teeth and spat it into the pool at the foot of the Little Waters, where it fed the fishes for weeks.

Another time, she hid among the white oak trees, covering herself with dogwood branches so she couldn't be seen, and waited until a boy giant with designs on the Little Waters was standing at the very edge of the cliff. Then she lunged out of the forest and pushed him over the falls. He dashed his head on the rocks below, and, well…he died.

I ain't trying to scare you, and you *know* you're never supposed to hurt nobody if you can help it, but Froygar didn't have a choice. You understand how important it is to protect your home, right?

But this story ain't about killing. This story's about love.

One day, Froygar was patrolling her land, checking her traps, when she heard high-pitched crying coming from one of the holes she'd dug to menace intruders.

Now, these holes were too small to hold giants captive, but they were plenty big enough to cause them to trip and fall and break a leg. Froygar realized pretty quick that there was something *in* the hole, something that couldn't get out. Curious, she peered into it, and there, moaning and wailing and sobbing its eyes out, was a little giant cub.

Now, giants tend to abandon their cubs young, but this one was still a baby. Even Froygar's mama had kept her longer. The cub would starve to death in Froygar's hole if she didn't do something to help it. Froygar knew she should walk away. If she freed the cub, then left it on its own, it would die in the woods with no one to feed or protect it.

But if she kept the cub with her, then *she* would have to feed and protect it. It was enough work to keep the Little Waters safe from boy giants who wanted to steal it, and Froygar was in plenty of danger already.

People say giants weren't capable of love, but that just ain't true. 'Cause even though she knew it might give her all kinds of terrible grief, Froygar reached into that hole, gathered the giant cub into her arms, and pulled it out.

When she cried—the cub was a girl—Froygar comforted her. When she was hungry, Froygar gave her the food she was saving for herself. When she was tired, Froygar laid down next to the cub in her own bed of pawpaw leaves and soft green moss and rocked her to sleep.

And when the cub told Froygar she didn't have a name, Froygar called her Lubel, which was the word in their language for Froygar's favorite forest flower.

Before she knew it, Froygar couldn't imagine her world without Lubel in it, and she knew she'd sacrifice anything to protect the little cub—even her very own life.

CHAPTER EIGHT

For a chick who's always turning up places she ain't wanted, Gypsum Tuller's a tough person to find. Nobody I know knows her proper, and I ain't got a clue where she lives.

I ain't even sure what branch of the Tuller family tree she belongs to. Possibly she's Haran Tuller's get, a granddaughter or even great-granddaughter—Tullers breed young. Her nose brings to mind Vance Tuller's third wife, who looks like a hawk with a broken beak.

From school, I know Gypsum is cousins with Pettit and Rosemaree Tuller, but how far removed I couldn't say. And anyway, I don't know how to contact them, either.

My original plan was to go up to Rock Creek, the Tuller homestead, and confront Redbreast myself. Redbreast and his closest kin live all together, in a rambling stone house with extra rooms and wings and lean-tos that sprout off the main house like tumors.

But I can't get there on my own. Rock Creek is somewhere back in the deep Ozark hollers, and I don't know the way. Gypsum could tell me, but I can't smoke her out, so I gotta come up with a new way to get the answers I need.

In the meantime, I gotta work. Every summer since I was fourteen I've waited tables at Barnacle Bill's marina restaurant, and this one ain't no different. I meant to call out sick yesterday, but by the time I got 'round to phoning up the restaurant, Dora had already heard.

Take however long you need, and when you find Bobby Ray, you tell him we love him, all right? she'd said.

But I ain't found Dad, and I don't got much to do now but wait. Might as well earn a few bucks while I'm at it.

After a whole morning on my feet, dodging sympathetic looks from Dora and the rest of the staff, I'm aching to see a friendly face. Kenley strolls in wearing a pair of plastic orange flip-flops and a yellow bikini under a see-through white tunic, looking like a bird of paradise with her blue-tipped hair all frizzed up and rumpled like feathers.

I finish with a customer and I tell Dora I'm taking my ten.

"Here." Dora grabs a burger off the kitchen counter and hands it to me. "Eat this. You look like you're fixing to faint."

Kenley follows me out the back door. There are two plastic chairs where Dora and the cook smoke after closing. We sit and I take a bite of the burger, chewing slow. Tastes like a rubber tire.

"How're you doing?" Kenley asks, scratching at a mosquito bite.

"About as well as you'd expect."

Kenley lights a cigarette and blows the smoke straight up to the sky. It looks like a tornado forming backward, reaching and spreading the farther it travels. A summer storm is moving in from the west, drawing a lumpy gray blanket over the sky.

"I'm sorry we didn't find Bobby Ray," she says. "I really thought we would."

"The Tullers are smart. If he's dead, they hid him someplace we'd never think to look."

"You think this is the Tullers' doing?"

I tell her about the graffiti note on the door and Ash's threat. The wind picks up, scattering flecks of ash across her thighs.

"You gotta go to the sheriff," Kenley says.

"Already done that. Olina kicked us out of the station like we were contagious."

"Her daddy had ties to the Tullers." Kenley brushes the ash off her legs.

I nod. "Nothing ever changes 'round here."

Kenley lifts her head, gives me a hard look. "What are you gonna do? Nothing stupid, I hope."

"I gotta talk to them, Ken," I say. She groans like she just got punched. "Gotta straighten this whole thing out with Redbreast."

"Are you kidding? You want them to kill you, too?"

"Maybe he ain't dead," I say. "Denver thinks he ran. From what Ash said Saturday, seems like Dad had good reason to fear what Redbreast would do if he found him. But also like the Tullers hadn't caught him yet. Whatever happened, as of yesterday they ain't got their money back. Reason enough to think maybe he slipped out of town before they could grab him."

"Then maybe you ought to let him stay gone."

"That's what Denver said. But Redbreast Tuller ain't gonna just write off a debt like that. I gotta figure out what went down before his boys start coming 'round looking to do more than just spray-paint my house."

I sigh deep. "If the cops won't help, what choice do I got but to do it myself?"

"You got a plan? A real one?"

"Guess I gotta get a Tuller to talk to me. Thought of Gypsum first, but I don't know how to find her. I don't reckon you know where she's at?"

"Nope. What about Ash?"

"What about him?"

"He's a Tuller groupie, and he gave you that message—he must know something."

My laugh is harsh, joyless. "Think he'd tell me?"

"No…" Kenley stubs out her cigarette in the dirt. "But you could follow him."

I never thought of that. My compass is usually set to point me away from wherever I might likely stumble across Ash Boford. But it shouldn't be too hard to track him down.

"Speaking of Bofords," Kenley says. "Any luck getting the hearing moved?"

"No," I tell her. "My dad's lawyer put in a petition, but the judge ain't having it."

"So if Bobby Ray don't show up in court on Wednesday…?"

A fly lands on my knee. I swat it away.

"That happens, I guess I gotta come up with a plan to kidnap Decca right quick."

"Oh, Sammy." For a second, Kenley looks like she's gonna cry. She's softhearted, that one.

Two fat raindrops land on my shoulders. I squint up at the sky like it's betrayed me, like it's to blame for my troubles.

Anger swirls and boils and gathers like a pressure system inside of me. Being pissed off makes me feel strong.

"Let's talk about something happier." Kenley nudges my foot. "What about Mr. Texas, huh? I saw him hunting after Bobby Ray on Sunday. Must be into you if he's willing to do that."

"I got rid of him."

I slump down in my chair. The burger is like a boulder in my stomach. My crappy plastic watch tells me I got two minutes left in my ten.

"Why?"

I pick at the frayed edges of my cutoff shorts.

"When we got back to the house last night, he was waiting on the porch. First I thought he was my dad, which freaked me right out, but then I saw it was Brayton and I got this flash, you know, of what it'd be like if I kept hanging out with him. How much I'd have to hide so he wouldn't think I was…"

"Trash?"

I nod.

Kenley squeezes my hand. "You ain't trash, Sammy Lester." But she gets what I mean.

"Anyway. Figured now's the time to run him off, before I get attached," I say.

"I ain't seen you get attached to a guy since Reed," Kenley says. "Tex must be a great lay."

"He is."

I smile to beat back the steady pulse of heartache blooming in my chest. Reed left a gap in me when he went, a space that stays empty no matter how many guys I'm with.

"He ain't Reed, though," I say.

"Nobody's ever gonna be just like Reed," Kenley says. "Not

even Reed anymore, I don't think. I bet he's changed over there. I bet we've all changed in ways even we don't see yet."

I wipe my greasy palms on my shorts. "Let's go in. It's gonna pour."

But Kenley ain't done talking at me. "If Reed were still around, would you drive him off, too?"

"He wouldn't let me," I tell her. "He's stubborn, and he already knows what shit's like, anyway. It'd take more than a couple mean words to run him out."

"You think?" Kenley angles her head like a dog that's just heard its name called. "He enlisted soon as he graduated without even telling you. Reed's not real good at sticking 'round, you ask me."

The missing him comes back all of a sudden. Not the dull, throbbing kind I've felt recently, like a bruise healing, but the sharp kind I felt right after we broke up, like getting sliced through the gut with a knife.

"Don't matter. He ain't here, and Brayton ain't him."

"I bet he comes back," Kenley says.

"Reed?"

"Brayton."

"Doubt it."

"Probably just needs a minute to adjust. Bet he's never met a real country girl before. I hear we take a little getting used to, but you're easier to love than you think."

"Nobody's falling in love. If he's got any sense, he'll stay away from me. I'm a disaster."

"A total mess," she agrees. "It's part of your charm."

Ash lives with his mama in a small squat house on the outskirts of Tehlicoh. I never been inside it, not even back when

Dad and Rainne were married, but I know where it is. Rainne moved back in when she and Dad first separated, and this was where we came when we needed to fetch or deliver Decca.

The lawn is dead and the paint is peeling, 'cause MaryEllen Boford don't give a shit about the house. She don't give a shit about most things, least of all her seven kids.

"I don't like this," Kenley says.

The two of us are hunkered down in the trunk of her old hatchback, parked across the street from the Boford house.

"It was your idea," I remind her, though I don't much like what we're doing, either, mostly 'cause it feels stupid, the sort of bumbling scheme Lucy and Ethel might get up to.

"He's gonna see us."

"It'll be dark soon."

I shift to give my shoulder blades a break. They been digging into the tinted glass of the hatch all afternoon. My knees press into the back seat. We been watching Ash's white Chevy truck sit in the driveway for three hours now.

"How long are we gonna be here? What if he stays home tonight?"

"He won't. MaryEllen'll be home from bingo soon. That'll smoke him out right quick."

Can't nobody say I don't know the Bofords, 'cause sure enough, soon as MaryEllen's car pulls up in front of the house, Ash is on the move. He rounds the corner from the back-yard the second she puts her key in the front door, hops in his truck and screeches into the street before she can notice he ain't inside.

Kenley and I scramble into the front seat and pull away from the curb.

"Stay back a ways," I tell her.

Ain't hard to figure out which way Ash is headed. There's just not a lot of places to go 'round here.

We follow him south out of town via Route 82, across the low bridge that straddles Copper Creek, down past the unmarked spot where 82 turns into Route 100 and runs along the eastern foothills.

Ash signals left just before Nighthawk Cemetery and pulls into a half-empty parking lot in front of a low-slung brown building. There's a sign near the door with no name, only a line drawing of an angry bull with fire pouring out of its nostrils.

"Should I turn?" Kenley asks.

I shake my head. "He'll see us if we do. Keep on going."

Now ain't the time to confront the Tullers, not with Ash there. But I got a pretty good idea where to find them now, 'cause while Ash parks, a shadow near the door shifts and a man steps out into the last rays of sun: Luger Tuller, dressed all in black, with a gun strapped to his belt.

It's called the Snortin' Bull Roadhouse, but most people just call it the Bull.

"You stay away from that place, Sammy," Dora says when I ask her about it at work the next day. "Only reason people go to the Bull is they're looking for trouble."

After my shift I climb into Kenley's hatchback again—alone, this time—and, after a quick pit stop at the Boford house, drive down to the Bull.

I thought hard about this all day and decided not to bring Kenley or anybody else along, for reasons that made plenty of sense to me at the time. But on the way, my mind wanders and I start thinking about something Granny Lester once said: *Ain't never known a Lester didn't carry a death wish in his pocket, just in case he needs it.*

Guess Tuesday's a big night for the Bull, 'cause the place ain't so deserted as it was yesterday evening. There's about a dozen cars and trucks in the lot. Most of them seen better days, so the hatchback fits in all right—I'm lucky Kenley let me borrow it.

I park in the shadows closest to the door and tuck my long blond hair into a gray baseball cap that used to be Reed's, pull on a dark shapeless jacket of Dad's and slip a switchblade up the sleeve, just in case. I'm wearing a baggy old pair of jeans that don't hug my curves and a black T-shirt of Denver's. Ain't looking for the usual attention tonight.

Inside the Bull, the smell of liquor's like a punch to the nose. My shoes stick to the floor. The place is all-over grimy.

The skin on the back of my neck prickles as heads turn my way. Ain't seen a Tuller yet, and already I'm sure these folks have figured me out, but their eyes slide right past me like I'm invisible and they go back to whatever they were doing before I walked in. The breath I been holding leaks out of me slow. Starting to wish I brought someone with me, but it's too late for regrets.

There's an open stool at the end of the bar. I make a beeline for it at the risk of looking too eager 'cause I like the idea of having my back to a wall, so nobody can sneak up behind me.

Once I'm sitting, I take a look around. The Bull ain't that big, so it's pretty crowded tonight, but the Tullers are easy to spot among the Devil's Guardians biker gang in their black leather kuttes. I count six, a variety pack, some tall and big-shouldered with arms and chests so tight with muscle it looks like their clothes been vacuum-sealed on, some smaller or skinnier, some grizzled, some baby-faced, some hawk-nosed like Gypsum—a brother? Never heard of her having one.

Like before at the Deck, there's only two I recognize: Johnny, the biggest, and Luger, the meanest. Johnny's leaning against the wall, clutching a cue, sucking on a longneck while he waits his turn in the game of five-way cutthroat they got going. Luger's nearby, sitting in a booth across the table from an old guy dressed kinda like me: Carhartt and Wrangler and Stetson, oh my.

I watch them from under the brim of my cap while I shred a napkin to keep my hands busy. The pieces float onto the sticky bar like snow.

The sound of someone clearing their throat nearby gives me a start.

"Get you something?" the bartender asks.

"Coors," I mumble, digging around in my pocket for a couple dollars.

But the bartender don't move. "Sammy Lester?"

Shit.

Of course I know this guy. I know *fucking everybody* on Lake Bittersweet, and fucking everybody knows me. I put my finger to my lips and give Norris Nills a flirty smile. Always suspected he had a little crush on me. Maybe I can use that to my advantage.

"Shh," I whisper. "Don't blow my cover."

Only way I got the slightest chance to make a Tuller talk to me is if I can control the situation, and having them catch on I'm here before I'm ready would give them the upper hand. Gotta be the exact right moment, else I might as well not try at all.

At least Ash ain't here, otherwise I wouldn't have a prayer of talking to Luger and Johnny.

A grin creeps over Norris's face.

"Wouldn't dream of it," he says, grabbing a Coors from a nearby cooler and twisting the top off with his forearm. "On the house."

"Show-off," I tease.

Norris leans across the bar. My eyes flicker over to the Tullers to see if they're watching, but Johnny's bent over the pool table and Luger's finishing up his meeting. They shake hands and the old guy leaves, but friendly as they looked, Luger don't seem sorry to see him go.

I relax a bit. Very least, Norris won't let me get hurt. I don't think.

"Been a long time," Norris says. "Since before Reed left, gotta be."

I nod and take a long pull on my beer.

"You heard from him lately? Nah, me neither." Norris grabs himself a beer, opens it, clinks it against mine. "Cheers to Captain America, that traitor. Too good for us lake rats, huh?"

"Guess so."

"So what are you doing here, anyway? Spying on your new man?"

I shrug. Thing about people like Norris Nills is that you don't gotta do much talking. Ain't like they're listening to you anyway.

He starts sizing up all the guys. "Let's see if I can guess which one is him. Never figured you for the old lady type, so it probably ain't one of them Devil's Guardians. Messing around with a biker'd be the best way to piss Reed off, though."

I just shrug again.

"Nah. Let's see. You're too smart to screw a Tuller," he says, glancing at me out the corner of his eye. My beer tastes skunked. I push it away. "Ash Boford? That who you're waiting on? You guys back together?"

I shouldn't say nothing, but I can't let *that* go.

"I'd die before I let Ash Boford touch me," I say. "And we were never *together*."

Norris holds his hands up like he's surrendering.

"Okay, all right." He goes back to his game. "All the rest of these thugs are twice your age. This mean you're single and looking?"

Flash of memory: Brayton's head between my thighs. *No.*

"Just single. Not looking."

"Ouch," Norris says, slapping a hand to his chest.

I toss him another flirty smile. "Ain't ready yet. When I am, you're the first guy I call."

"Deal," Norris says. "Tell me why you're here, then. Never seen you at the Bull before."

I stare at Norris. How much can I trust him? He's an old school friend of Reed's, and we always got along. Ain't too smart, but ain't no fool, neither.

"Norris," I say, lowering my voice so he has to lean in even closer to hear. He smells strong of beer and BO. Gotta fight not to wrinkle my nose. "You seen my daddy in here lately?"

"Bobby Ray?" Norris's big old forehead pleats like an accordion. "The Horsefeather's more his speed these days, ain't it?"

"Usually," I say. "But I got reason to think he's been hanging with the Tullers."

"Heard he's gone missing. This got something to do with that?"

Norris's face goes blank like someone wiped it with an eraser.

"Might be."

"Sorry, Sammy. I don't know nothing about it."

"So he was here," I say. "With them. Thanks, Norris."

"Whoa." He grabs my arm. "I didn't say nothing. Don't you go telling them I did."

"Telling who? Norris." I say his name soft and gentle. "It's—"

The hard slap of the front door banging open drowns me out. I force myself not to turn, just peek out from underneath my cap. I freeze. Ash is here, his best friends Ty and Skinny Ray in tow. He stalks up to Luger with a face full of fury, and I bet I can guess why.

"Gotta go," I say, slipping off my stool. Leave it to Ash Boford to find a way to ruin all my plans. Like I didn't hate him enough already.

"There's a door past the bathrooms that lets out in back," Norris says, catching on. He throws the Tuller corner a glance then turns back to me with panic in his eyes. "Hurry. They seen you."

I can't help myself looking. My eyes crash into Ash's, and he yells, "Don't you dare run, Sammy Lester! What the fuck did you do to my truck?"

Blood pounds through my head and my vision fills with sparklers. I take off, half-blind, toward the neon sign that says Toilets and the unmarked door on the other side. I can hear heavy footsteps behind me—I ain't gonna make it—but just as I'm passing the women's bathroom a hand shoots out and yanks me inside.

I stumble into the bathroom, fall against the dirty, cracked sink. The sound of a lock sliding into place makes me whirl around.

"Gypsum?" I croak. She shoves me backward toward the wall.

"Ain't got no time for chitchat," she says in a steely voice, pointing over my head. There's a window near the ceiling.

Something cracks against the door—a shoulder, a boot heel. I'm fucking dead.

"Come on," Gypsum says, "I'll give you a boost."

"I ain't gonna fit through there!"

"Not in this," she snaps, yanking my jacket off. The switchblade falls out. She picks it up, and for a second I'm scared she's gonna use it, but she just tosses it to me. "Now *go*."

Gypsum cups her hands in front of her and even though I know this is a crazy idea, even though I know it ain't gonna work, it's the only chance I got. I step into her hands and haul myself up, shimmying through the tiny window.

My shirt catches on a sharp piece of metal, but I don't pay it no mind. There's a Dumpster under the window. If I fall right, I might not crack my skull open. I rip myself free and tumble through.

The Dumpster's full of all kinds of nasty shit. The fall knocks the breath out of me, but I don't stop to get it back. I scramble out of the Dumpster like my ass is on fire and drop to the asphalt. A muffled thump sets my heart racing. Takes a second to realize it's Gypsum.

"What are you doing?" I hiss, flicking the switchblade open.

"Watch where you point that," she mutters, crawling out of the Dumpster. How'd she boost *herself* up to that window?

"I gotta get out of here, too. They can't know I helped. Where's your car?"

"In front."

"Figures."

She creeps along the wall and peeks 'round the corner. Then she waves me forward.

"Hear that?" There's shouting in the distance. "They're coming 'round the other way. When I say go, you run till you get to your car. Keep that knife out."

I nod. I think I'm gonna faint. "What about you?"

"I can handle myself. *Go!*"

I'm so high on adrenaline I don't feel nothing—not the ground under my feet or the burning in my lungs or the stitch in my side I know is there. Never been much of a runner but I'm flying now, dodging parked cars and bikes and smoking poles like I was born to it.

Someone shouts, "Stop!" But I don't.

I reach the hatchback, fumble with the keys. My hands are shaking so bad I can barely get the door open, almost cut myself with the knife. I fling myself in and jam the automatic lock with my elbow. The car shudders as a body slams up against it. Ash screams at me, but I don't hear him. My head is full of thunder.

The car rumbles to life and I throw it into Reverse. Two Tullers in the rearview, Luger and one I can't name, but I bear down hard on the gas pedal, tires throwing up gravel.

The Tullers scatter. Ash lunges for the car, but Luger pulls him back by the collar of his T-shirt like a mama cat seizing a kitten by the scruff of its neck.

'Cause I'm a dumbass with a death wish—a Lester through and through—I roll down the window and toss out a plastic grocery bag full of spark plugs. It lands at Ash's feet.

Hard left out of the parking lot onto Route 100.

I don't let myself breathe till I'm halfway home.

CHAPTER NINE

If I was smart, I'd never leave my house again. That first night, I sit up till dawn with my back against the front door and Dad's hunting rifle in my hands, picturing all the ways Ash and the Tullers could put the hurt on me.

Or, worse, on people I care about. I list them in my head like a prayer: *Decca Denver Dad Kenley. Decca Denver Dad Kenley.* And so on through the night.

At least Reed is safe from the Tullers halfway 'round the world. I don't even let myself think about Brayton.

But Gypsum—what hell will she catch if they figure out she helped me? Why'd she even do it in the first place? She's their kin, not mine. Worst part is, I never got to ask my questions. I'm right back where I started.

'Round about 3:00 a.m. I realize the person I most wanna talk to about this is Rainne. She knows Ash, what he's capable of, more than I do. Maybe she could help me fix it so he doesn't come after me or my family, my friends.

But I can't go to Rainne for help. In a couple hours, the courts are gonna take Decca away from us, and that's all her doing.

The days of Rainne protecting me are over.

I had to return Kenley's car, so Denver's buddy Holler drives us to the county courthouse for the hearing.

We ride the whole way in silence. I told Denver about the Bull, so he's pissed at me, and Holler pretty much quit talking full stop when his mama and daddy passed last year.

He's different in other ways, too. Holler always slumped, embarrassed by his bigness, but now his shoulders are weighed down with the burden of his loss. He got aimless. Stares into space like he's seeing something none of the rest of us can see.

Gotta wonder how losing Dad will change me. Maybe it already has.

Denver almost wouldn't let me come to the hearing. Said it wasn't safe to show my face in town, and it ain't like there's anything I can do. But I can't let Rainne walk out of that courtroom without having to look me in the eye.

And, foolish as it is, I'm still hoping Dad will show. Granny Lester always said hope is heartbreak waiting to happen.

Dad's lawyer tries one more time to get the hearing delayed. But the judge is out of patience. He says if Dad don't care enough to turn up, he clearly don't care enough about his kid to compel the court to stop Rainne taking her out of state.

Holler puts an arm across my shoulders and squeezes tight, like he thinks I'm gonna break down, but Denver and I are twin blank-faced statues at the front of the courtroom. I can't even scrounge up the energy to feel betrayed. We lost Decca the second Duke took that new job in Arkansas.

Thank God the whole thing is over quick. When the judge dismisses us, I look to where Rainne is standing with Duke. Their lawyer, an oil slick in scuffed cowboy boots and a cheap suit, shakes their hands and pats them on the back. Congratulating them. For stealing my sister from me.

I catch Rainne's eye when she turns around. She gives me a sad smile and a weak shrug.

"I hate her," I tell Denver.

"I know. Let's leave now."

Rainne catches up to us on the courthouse steps.

"Sammy," she calls out. "Denver. Wait!"

"Keep going," Denver says. "Don't stop for her. It'll only make you feel worse."

But I do stop for Rainne, 'cause I'm itching for a fight. When Denver realizes I ain't with him, he doubles back to get me, irritated.

"This is a bad idea," he hisses.

"I didn't want it to be like this," Rainne says. "I'm trying to do the right thing for my family."

"Whatever helps you sleep at night."

"It does help me sleep. You really want Decca growing up here? You know what it's like. We stay in this place, she'll turn out just like—"

"Me?" I snap.

Rainne shakes her head. "I was gonna say *me*. I wanna give Decca chances I didn't get. Between the Bofords and the Lesters, that girl's got more than enough bad blood in her veins to make her life hard no matter where I take her, but at least out there she'll have a fighting chance."

"She steals stuff. Six years old and she's already lifting things. What makes you think it ain't already too late? That's about the age I started doing it."

I think, *That ought to scare her.* I never seen Rainne so furious with me as the night she got the call to pick me up from the Tehlicoh police station the first time I got caught shoplifting.

I was with Ash, and we were both thirteen. I tried to sneak a bottle of Malibu out of the liquor store under my shirt. She never looked at either of us the same after that. I grew out of my petty crime phase, but Ash graduated with flying colors.

"It's done," Rainne says. "I'm sorry."

It ain't an apology. It's pity. I can't believe I used to wish she was my own mother. A memory: us together on the floor, watching TV while Rainne, belly big with Decca, braids my hair. But whoever that woman was, she don't exist anymore. Something hollowed her out, made her desperate, and all that's left of the Rainne I loved is a torn husk full of fear and cunning.

Only a small part of me is willing to entertain the notion that what hollowed her out was Dad.

"Rainne," Duke says, at the same time Denver says, "Sammy." They each take a squabbling woman by the arm, try leading us away. But we ain't finished yet.

"You promise not to make this any harder than it has to be, I'll let you see Decca as much as possible before we move," Rainne says. "But you cause trouble, Sammy, I swear to God, you'll never see that little girl again. You hear?"

I gotta force myself to nod. Goddamn bitch.

Duke tugs on her hand. Rainne says, "I really am sorry."

"Me, too," I say. "Sorry Dad ever fucking met you."

* * *

After the hearing, I stick close to home. Denver's so freaked out about what happened at the Bull it's starting to freak *me* out, too. I start at the sight of my own shadow. Every unexpected sound makes me jump half out of my skin.

I don't even walk to work, though it ain't but a stone's throw away. Denver recruits Holler as my chauffeur and bodyguard, driving me to Barnacle Bill's and back, walking me everywhere else. Thank God Holler don't talk much—makes it hard to get sick of him.

But they don't come. Not even Ash, who's got just enough screws loose to think he can roll up and start something right where I live.

I'm afraid to put my guard down, but by Saturday it's been over half a week. I'm starting to get restless. If I gotta be stuck in this sardine can for one more day, won't be anything left for the Tullers to mess with, 'cause Denver and I will probably kill each other.

When the doorbell rings Saturday morning, I hide like a coward in the bedroom. Doubt the Tullers will be as polite as that when they come to beat me to powder, but no point taking the chance.

"Sammy!" Denver calls. "Door's for you."

Not sure who I'm expecting, but it ain't Norris Nills.

"Hey there," he says, flopping down on the couch like this is his own house and taking the beer Denver hands him with a nod of thanks. "Nice to see you're still alive."

"Funny," I say. "What's this about?"

"That was gonna be my question. What are you up to, messing with the Tullers like that?"

"I been wondering the same thing," Denver mutters.

"Were they pissed?"

"Fuck yeah, they were pissed," Norris says. "Ash Boford came back in after you left, shouting and swinging, kicking chairs and smashing bottles. Thought I was gonna have to call the cops till Luger knocked him upside the head and told him not to let some Lester bitch rile him up so easy."

"What a sweetheart."

"You think this is a joke?" Denver snaps.

"No."

"Good, 'cause it ain't," Norris says. "I told them you were there to see me, but they weren't having none of it. Luger just looked at me with those dead eyes of his and said, 'Then why'd she run?' Didn't have an answer for that one."

"I was being *chased*. Seems like a good enough reason to me."

"Okay, but that don't explain why you stole the spark plugs out of Ash's truck."

"You *what*?" Denver shouts.

"Didn't wanna risk running into him at the Bull."

Denver looks like he wants to throttle me.

"I thought it'd slow him down. Which it did. For a while."

Norris shakes his head, but I can tell he's impressed.

"You gonna tell me *why* you caused all that commotion?"

"I think the Tullers disappeared my dad," I say. "Or if they didn't, they're the reason he left. We been friends a long time, Norris. You know something, you gotta give it to me straight."

"Technically, I'm Reed's friend." Norris slurps his beer.

"Whatever," I say, getting up to leave.

"Wait, wait, Sammy, I'm joking. 'Course you and me are friends. But look, I don't know nothing about Bobby Ray or where he went. He started coming 'round the Bull about two months ago, but far as I could tell he just sat there shooting the shit, or playing pool with Johnny and Luger."

"No drugs?"

"Didn't see none."

"And they were friendly? My dad and the Tullers?"

"Friendly as those guys get."

I sigh. "Okay. Thanks."

"There was another guy, one time. Came to see Luger like he usually does, but Bobby Ray was there, so Luger introduced them. Everything seemed all right, but the other guy didn't stay long enough to finish his beer. Thought that was weird. Usually ties up Luger for at least an hour."

"This guy got a name?"

"None I ever heard, but he was there last night—you might've seen him. Carhartt jacket, Wranglers..."

"Stetson boots. I remember." The man was dressed like a cowboy paper doll.

"He and Luger got some sort of regular business going. Which is kinda weird, actually, 'cause I think he's got money. Real money, not the Tuller kind."

"Why?"

"Paid for a round at the bar one time and I got a good look at his hands," Norris says. "Smooth as a baby's bottom, like he never did an hour of hard labor in his life. Not like these puppies."

Norris holds up his cracked, calloused paws. Denver glances at his own hands, which are just about the same. Dad's were like that, too.

Norris stays through his beer.

"Don't come back to the Bull," he tells me on his way out.

"If the Tullers ain't been by yet, they ain't coming, but I don't expect they'll be so kind the next time."

Kenley shows up on my doorstep later that night, sucking on a slushie from the Fuel 'N Fun. Darkness is settling over the lake. The light has suddenly gone out of the sky, like someone pulled a plug and all the color circled right down the drain. I gotta turn on the porch light to really see her.

She's wearing a slinky summer dress with her hair and makeup done. She hands me a Strawberry Summer Sammy and lets herself through the door without so much as a hello.

"Come on in," I say to her back as she stomps down the hallway in three-inch heels.

I find her in my bedroom, rummaging through my closet. "Looking for something?"

"That dress you bought at the mall in Muskogee," she says. "The blue one with the sequins."

"What's wrong with the dress you're wearing?"

"It's not for me, dumbass, it's for you. We're going to a party."

"Pass," I say, slurping my drink.

"We ain't hung out in days. What've you been doing? Never known you to stay home so much."

I almost tell her about what went down at the Bull, but I didn't say nothing about it when I returned her car that night. She'll be pissed, and scared for me. Not worth upsetting her.

Besides, Norris is right: the Tullers ain't known for biding their time. If they wanted to strike back at me, they'd've done it by now. Maybe they've decided to just let me be.

Seems like a foolish hope, but I'm damn sick of being cooped up in this trailer.

"What party?"

She smiles. "The one Brayton Foster's throwing."

"No way. Not happening. I don't wanna see him."

"Bullshit."

"He probably don't wanna see me, either."

"You're a hot girl," Kenley says. "Guys *always* wanna see hot girls."

"Then he can look at you. Have fun." I flop down on my bed.

Kenley stands over me with her hands on her hips, frowning. "I know you're worried about Bobby Ray. But moping around this house waiting on news ain't gonna make it come any faster."

"Is that what you think I'm doing?"

"It's my going theory."

She crawls into the twin bed and shoves me till I shift over. We stare at the ceiling, the glow-in-the-dark constellations I helped Dad put up for Decca. They been peeling off for about a year now. I keep finding fallen stars in my sheets.

A couple minutes pass in silence. This is one of the things I like most about Kenley: she knows when I need someone to make me talk, and she knows when I don't.

"I miss Reed," I tell her.

"Yeah?" She don't sound surprised.

"People keep asking me about him, like I'm supposed to know how he's doing or when he'll be back on leave or what the hell he's up to out there. Feels wrong I don't got any answers, but I don't even know why he left in the first place."

"You don't?"

"He never said."

"Did you ask?"

"I was too busy begging him to stay."

I laugh at myself, at stupid last-year-Sammy, for ever thinking she could change his mind.

"Did *you* ask?"

"Well…yeah."

"And what'd he say?"

"That he wanted to go someplace new," Kenley tells me. "That he wanted to see just how big the world really was. He lived his whole life here, Sammy."

"So have I. So have you."

"Why do you think I'm leaving at the end of the summer? You think we don't got beauty schools in Oklahoma? I don't gotta go all the way to Kansas City to learn how to cut hair."

"Thought you picked that school 'cause it was the best."

"I picked it 'cause it ain't *here*." Kenley rolls onto her side to look at me. "You could go somewhere, too. Denver did it."

"In his head, Denver was always far away. Going to college just made it official." I close my eyes. "I like it here. I know who I *am* here. This is my home."

"You talk like you're gonna disappear if you step over the county line. That ain't gonna happen."

"Happened to my dad," I say.

"We don't know what happened to Bobby Ray." Kenley sighs. "Look, you don't gotta go to this party. But if you keep using the things you lost as an excuse for not going after the things you want, pretty soon you're not gonna have nothing at all."

She gets out of the bed and grabs the blue dress with the sequins from the closet, holds it up to the light.

"So what do you say? In or out?"

I take a deep breath and sit up. "In."

CHAPTER TEN

"This was a mistake," I say, staring up at Brayton's fancy lake house from the foot of a small rise. The thing is huge, all lit up like a jack-o'-lantern. "I shouldn't've come."

"Stop that right now," Kenley says, dragging me up the driveway. "Go in and show Tex what he's been missing."

"He don't wanna see me," I insist.

"Well, he's *gonna* see you, and then he ain't gonna be able to take his eyes off you. I mean, look at yourself."

Kenley eyes me with approval, like she's a painter and I'm her masterpiece. The blue sequined minidress is loose and tight in all the right places. It stops midthigh and sets off my tan. Kenley did my hair in big waves and gave me a smoky eye. Practice for beauty school, she said.

I know she's right. But *I'm* the one who ran *Brayton* off. It don't even seem fair.

"We're going inside. No more excuses."

"Won't showing up at his party uninvited make me look crazy?"

"The whole lake was invited," Kenley says. "Might be his party, but these are *your* people."

"That's kinda what I'm afraid of."

"Just don't freak if you see him all up on some other girl, 'cause I got no idea how this is gonna go, and that's low-rent."

"Ugh. Forget it, I'm going home."

"Nope," Kenley says, nabbing me by the shoulders. "You're going in. It's Saturday night, we both look amazing and we ain't wasting these outfits at the Waffle House, so *move*."

Soon as we step through the front door, the party rolls over us like a rogue wave. It's so loud, full of shouting and music, I can't make out any individual sounds—just pounding noise, like being inside a human heart.

The halls and rooms are packed with people. The porch overflows with bodies—they drip off the railings and tables and deck chairs—and everyone's got a red plastic Solo cup or two in their hands. I see faces I recognize everywhere, some I barely know, some I've gone to school with since I was in diapers.

Kenley gets busy hugging everybody like she ain't seen them in years.

At first, I don't think anyone even notices me. They're too drunk, or distracted, and I slink on past them in the wake of Kenley's whirlwind friendliness.

But then I see heads start to turn. They glance at me out of the corners of their eyes, hands cover mouths and people lean in to each other to make themselves heard. I know they're talking about me. And my family. And our ugly, mysterious tragedy.

What's she doing at a party, with her daddy missing? I bet they're thinking. *What kinda grieving daughter goes out in such a slutty dress?*

Bad things happen, folks need someone to pity, but right now I don't look much like the sort of victim they wanna see.

Kenley grabs my arm like she's afraid I'll bolt, which I still got half a mind to do. But I don't want them thinking I'm scared of their gossip. Running would only give them more to talk about.

"I think we both need a drink," Kenley says. She spots a keg of Coors Light in the kitchen and runs off to fetch us some beer, so single-minded she don't realize I ain't following.

Overwhelmed, I seek out a dark corner of the hallway where I can be alone. I press my back against the wall and breathe deep, tell myself this ain't so bad.

I tug at the hem of my dress. Looked cute at home but now it seems too short in Brayton's huge, airy home, with its fresh white paint and hothouse flowers in big milk glass vases.

The place ain't clean—there's party trash everywhere—but it's still the nicest house I ever stepped foot in, one of those cookie-cutter mansions that looks like it's been hauled straight up from the suburbs. No personality. No character. Like the set of a TV show.

There's a door across the hall, and I try opening it, figuring it for a bathroom. I should probably check to see my dress at least covers my crotch.

But the knob won't turn, and I hear water running inside. I step back when the door swings wide open and find myself face-to-face with *the* Brayton Foster.

He freezes, like he thinks if he don't move, I won't manage to notice him and take off running.

"You came," he says. He shoves his hands in his pockets and casts his eyes to the floor, daring a glance at me from beneath dark lashes, like I'm some mirage he can't trust is real.

"I came," I say. "That okay?"

He nods and steps closer. "I didn't think you would."

"I know I wasn't invited."

"Everybody was invited."

He's trying real hard not to smile, not quite sure if he should. Looks like he's bracing himself for a punch.

"I was hoping you'd show." He laughs. "Pretty sure I threw this party on the off chance you would."

"Awful lot of effort to go to for a girl who ain't that hard to get," I joke. "According to rumor."

"I don't know about rumors, but in my experience, when it comes to you, objects in the mirror are farther away than they appear. You like a good party. I figured if I had one, there was a possibility you'd check it out."

"Guess I don't get why you bothered."

"Yes, you do."

I smile. "Maybe I just wanna hear you say it, then."

"Because," he says in a low voice. Sends a tremor down my spine. "I don't have your phone number and I got the sense I'm not welcome at your house."

"And?"

"I wanted to see you. I keep wanting to see you, even though you don't want to see me."

He finally looks me straight in the eye.

"Brayton..."

How do I explain? I didn't wanna drive him off, but that's how you protect yourself. You hunch your shoulders and coil your muscles and curl up to hide your softest parts, the ones that are weak. The bits that shame you.

I miss him, and I wish I didn't. Ain't like missing Reed, which feels like being homeless. Missing Brayton's like knowing you got a home but you don't remember how to get there.

I don't wanna seem needy, or foolish, but he looks so good standing there in a bright white shirt, tanner than he was a week ago, in another pair of ugly shorts, leather flip-flops, hair a mess. He's summer. It's like he just stepped out of the sun.

"So. You're here. And you're staying?"

"For now."

"Okay, then." He holds out his hand. "Welcome to my house, Sammy Lester. Let's party."

Brayton sticks close by me as we make our way through the crowd, don't take his eyes or hands off me a second longer than he has to. We hang out with friends of mine in the kitchen near the keg, dance to eardrum-busting music in the cavernous living room, lose at flip cup on the backyard patio. He fetches me drinks and whispers in my ear and takes every opportunity to have me all to himself, even for just a minute or two.

I'm having a good time, but I gotta stay watchful, on the lookout for Tullers or—maybe worse—Ash, but I never do see them. I try to relax. I'm safe here in Brayton's home, shielded by my friends.

Finally, Brayton gets tired of sharing me.

"Can we, um…?" He clears his throat. "Can we go somewhere? And talk?"

"Where?" I look around. There are people everywhere.

He takes my hand and drags me down the hallway to a door half-hidden in shadow.

"Jack's study," Brayton says, pulling a key out of his pocket. "Only room in this house with a damn lock on it."

Like every other room in this too-big house, the study's got a not-quite-lived-in look about it, but there is a couch, and a desk covered with papers. Brayton leans against it and smiles.

"It's been three hours and you're still here. I want to take that as a good sign," he says.

"What do you mean?"

"The way I figure it, you wouldn't've come to my house if you didn't want to see me, and you wouldn't've stayed if you weren't enjoying yourself."

I sit down on the couch. Even with the AC going full blast through the whole house, it's hot and stuffy in this room. I'm light-headed.

"I'm glad you're here, if it makes any difference. And I'm so damn happy you stayed."

I smile.

"How are you?" he asks. I wrinkle my nose. "I mean, really. Don't tell me you're fine."

I glance down at my dress, which is riding up my thigh. "I think I look pretty great."

"You look hot, but that's not what I meant."

"Everything's a mess, if you really wanna know. Pretty sure my dad ain't never coming back."

Brayton sits down next to me. He leaves a space between us, but I can feel him there, a column of warmth. Maybe he thinks I don't want him near me. And I don't. I want him on top of me, around me, all over me. Near wouldn't be nearly close enough.

But I don't move. I barely breathe. There's a spell on us, like in the stories I invent for Decca, and I'm afraid of breaking it.

"Sammy?"

"Yeah?"

"I'm very, very sorry about what happened—"

I cut him off with a kiss—screw the spell. I don't need apologies. Rather have his mouth instead.

Brayton kisses me back, urging my lips apart and grazing my tongue with his—soft at first, softer than he's holding me, softer than anything I've felt in a long, long time. We ease into each other and the kiss gets deeper, hungrier, more demanding, like he's trying to get at why I pushed him away and make me see he ain't gone nowhere at all.

Then he shifts so he's bending over me, shoving me against the slick-cool leather by my shoulders till I'm lying down. His hand whispers up my thigh, pushing my dress all the way to the line of my underwear. He groans in the back of his throat. The sound echoes in my bones.

I put a hand against his chest and push till he sits up, panting and rosy-lipped, so I can yank his shirt over his head. I want his skin on my skin, everywhere I can get it.

He smells like soap and heat and his fingers stroke, stroke, stroke that tenderest part of me till I gasp and he smiles. His mouth lands on mine and I struggle, I do, to see anything but him, but I can't. He's everywhere—around, without, within. His muscles soften where I touch him, like he trusts me. I can feel my own armor falling away.

My hand drifts down his back, pushing his shorts off his hips, skating past the band of his boxers. When I touch him, he shudders. He presses his face to my neck and mutters something I can't make out.

"Hmm?"

I let my touch get lazy. He presses closer, puts his mouth to my ear: "I said it feels so much better when you do it."

I kiss the curve of his jaw, nip him softly with my front teeth. "Opposed to who?"

"Opposed to *me*."

I feel mighty, and unbelievably calm. The slow movement of my hand has tangled Brayton's brain into knots. His fingers are working their own magic on me, knuckles brushing in a light-cruel way. My throat's so tight I can't swallow.

"Oh, Sammy," he says. "Sammy, Sammy, Sammy…"

Little fireworks shoot through the core of me. My feet are tingling like they done fell asleep. It's so joyfully simple, being with Brayton. I want him. He wants me. Ain't trying to hide it from each other, if we even could.

"I missed you," he says. His nose and mouth and free hand are in my hair, tugging with every inhale.

We're both so riled, it'll end right quick if we keep this up. He sits back and I let go, just look at him. It's beautiful, the sight. His body so fine, his face so flushed and happy. I need this to last and last, 'cause as long as it does, it's all I gotta think about, and it really don't require much thought.

"You really wanted me to show up here tonight?"

He takes my hand, and I'm so surprised I almost jump, both 'cause I didn't expect him to be so gentle, and 'cause it don't matter how gentle he is. Every time Brayton touches me, my body responds the same way: combustion.

"Wanted, hoped, yearned."

I smile. "Yearned?"

Brayton kisses my neck, pressing his lips softly against the fading bruise he gave me the first night we met.

"Definitely," he murmurs against my skin. "Absolutely."

I close my eyes, hitch in a deep breath. Was I ever so lust-sick for a boy as this? Not with Reed. That was different. And Brayton wants me so bad.

"Don't leave after this," he says, kissing my open palm. "Stay with me for a while."

I touch his face, fingers soft against pink skin, from the top of his forehead to his chin. I ain't felt a lick of tenderness to-ward any boy since Reed, but I can recognize it in me now. It's a danger, but it's also a relief.

"What about the party?"

"Screw the party," he growls, grabbing my hips and pulling me forward so I'm straddling him.

I laugh, planting my elbows above his shoulders, bending to kiss him, and kiss him, and kiss him with my hands on his cheeks. They burn against my palms.

Suddenly, we hear a loud crash, yelling. Brayton sits up, gripping my waist, holding me tight.

"What was that?"

"Don't know," I say, pressing my lips to his shoulder. "Don't care."

"It's a fight."

Brayton sets me aside. He stands and pulls his shirt on. Then he braces his hands against the edge of the desk, not looking at me, thinking whatever thoughts he needs to calm down.

"What are you doing?" I'm irritated. I ain't some toy he can toss away when he's finished with it.

"Wait here," he says. "I'm going to look into it."

"Seriously? Right *now*?" I glare at him.

"Should I let them destroy the house just so I can get laid? Sorry. But—"

"Fine." I adjust my rumpled dress. "I'll come with you."

"No. Don't worry about it. It's my house, I'll handle it." He pauses at the door. "Five minutes, I swear. Don't go anywhere, okay? Stay right here."

"And do what?"

"Think dirty thoughts about me," he says with a wink. I roll my eyes.

He ditches the playfulness. "Sammy, promise you won't leave."

"Yeah," I say. But I don't promise him a thing.

Figures Brayton leaves me behind in a room with nothing to keep me occupied. The way I see it, I ain't got no choice but to snoop around a bit—ain't good at being idle.

Unfortunately, there ain't much to look at in here. Besides the couch and the desk, only furniture is a couple floor lamps and a low row of bookshelves with barely anything in them.

I take a stroll 'round the room, casing the joint, till my eyes land back on the desk. A cup full of miscellaneous pens and pencils, a phone, and a laptop dock with no laptop. The rest of it's got maps spread all over it. Don't take long to realize they're maps of Gibson Bluff—*my* bluff.

I walk over to the desk to get a closer look. At first I ain't quite sure what I'm seeing, till I notice two words printed in the upper left: "Sweet Home."

What's Brayton's stepdaddy doing with maps of the Sweet Home development?

This map on top is recent—dated just about a month ago— and it shows all the land the developers managed to collect from the government and good old Bittersweet folks, my neighbors, the ones they convinced to sell up.

I spot Louis Long's place, and Sally Kendrick's, goofy Bill

Thompson's acre and three-quarters halfway down Gibson Bluff road. My finger follows the lines from one parcel boundary to the next, counting it all up.

I expect a fat black border when I get to the edge of the forest that separates our acres from corps land, but it ain't there. Instead, it snakes around our plot, hugging it like a python that's got its prey in a death squeeze.

What the hell is going on? What right do the Sweet Home folks think they got to put *our land* on their maps like it's theirs?

I reach for my phone, but it ain't in my dress pocket where I put it. I find it under the couch and see I got a text from Denver.

Ash & his boys just came by looking for you. They think you're at that rich kid's party. Hope you're smarter than that but if you're not gtfo!!!!!

My heart starts beating like crazy, and I don't waste time. When I open the office door I hear Brayton yelling, probably at whoever's trashing his house. I gotta get out of here before Ash and his friends arrive, but I don't want Brayton catching sight of me leaving. He'll only try to stop me.

I slip out the door and shut it quietly. The hallway's empty— everybody's in the living room watching the circus. A guy who ain't Brayton starts shouting at him—*"Where's your slut?"*— and my blood freezes.

Denver's text was from half an hour ago. While I was getting it on with Brayton, Ash Boford was driving up here to find me.

"Sammy," someone hisses from the shadows. Gypsum. I ain't even surprised anymore.

"There's a door over here, leads to the garage. You can get out that way."

I got a million questions for this strange little Tuller, but now ain't the time to ask them. I follow her into the garage and out the door that dumps us in the darkness of the side lawn. Our movement trips a sensor and floods the lawn with light.

"Better get a move on," Gypsum says. "Ash sees you, I don't know what he'll do."

"Did you come here with him?"

"No way. Ash Boford is Luger and Johnny's pet. I ain't got nothing to do with him and I don't wanna. I'm here to help *you*."

She shoves me toward the front of the house. "You go on and get. You got a ride?"

I shake my head. My house is down the hill a ways so Kenley and I just walked. "My friend—"

"I'll tell her," Gypsum says. "Can your brother come get you?"

"No car."

"Then you better start walking. Don't stop for nothing or nobody till you're safe in your bed."

"*If* I'm safe in my bed."

Gypsum glances back toward the house.

"If that. Sammy, I don't know what you think you're doing, spying at the Bull and making Ash Boford so mad, but you better call it quits before something bad happens."

"Something bad's already happened."

"Before something bad happens *to you*."

"Why are you *helping* me?" I ask. Feels like the millionth time, but she ain't never given me a good enough answer.

Can't really be 'cause I protected her once long ago. I don't even remember doing it.

Gypsum's eyes get big with surprise. "We're friends, ain't we? Helping is what friends do."

"Gypsum," I say. "What did your family do to my dad?"

"I don't know what happened to your daddy, but don't be so sure it was them."

Brayton's front door pops open, spilling light. I hear Brayton's voice again, and a flood of loud, drunk male cackles and cursing from Ash Boford and his buddies.

"Go!" Gypsum whispers, pushing me forward.

I take off down the drive without a backward glance. Ash, Ty and Skinny Ray are too busy pissing on Brayton's lawn to notice me, but as I round the hedge, I think I hear someone call my name. I speed up.

The bluff road is dark and quiet, and though I've lived here all my life, I'm nervous. Even without Ash on my tail, it's too late at night to be so alone and exposed on this road.

I think to call Denver to come pick me up in the Mule but reception is spotty up here and I don't have enough bars on my cheap-ass prepaid phone. I just gotta be quick and smart and hope nobody mean or stupid drives past. Hope Ash takes the other way back into town.

When I feel the heat of the headlights on my back, I know it's them. The white truck swerves and pulls up next to me, driving slow enough to match my pace. Ty leans out the passenger door window, leering.

"Where you going, baby?" he asks. "Need a ride?"

I ignore him and keep walking, head up, eyes straight ahead.

"Didn't like the party? I hear you're fucking that douchebag, what's his name, Brandon?"

"Brayton," Skinny Ray says. He's sitting bitch, as always. "You really fucking him, Sammy? Wouldn't think he'd go for a poor-ass redneck slut like you."

Nobody's more redneck than Skinny Ray Loomis, except maybe the Tullers, and I've got half a mind to tell him so. But ain't no use making them madder than they already are.

"Sammy!" Ash calls. His friends sit back so he can get a good look at me from the driver's seat. "Get in. We'll take you home."

"No thanks," I say. "I'm just fine."

"Get in right now," Ash says. "Guys, make room for my niece." He laughs.

"I ain't your niece, and I don't need a ride from *you*," I snap. "Go bother somebody else. Or go home. I bet your mamas are worried sick about their baby boys. Especially yours, Ash."

Ash sneers at me—all MaryEllen Boford's kids hate her rotten guts.

I wish Gypsum were with me. She'd know how to manage this the smart way. Girls like that spend their lives learning to survive around boys like Ash Boford. I never did get the hang of handling him.

"Get in the goddamn *truck*!" Ash yells. I flip him off. It's like I can't help myself.

Ash pulls the truck over and the three of them tumble out of the cab. I turn and run back up the hill fast as I can, but they catch up to me in seconds. Ash grabs me by the arm. I wrench away and try to knee him in the balls, but he holds me at arm's length, fingers digging so deep into my flesh I yelp.

"Get off me," I shout.

"Calm down," Ash says, mocking me. "I just wanna talk."

They've got me surrounded, trapped. The sharp taste of bile

hits the back of my tongue but I clench my jaw and swallow it down. I won't throw up, or cry, not in front of them.

"About what?"

I step back, stumbling into Skinny Ray's chest. He clutches my hair by its roots and pulls my head back so Ash can look into my face as he leans over me. He's so close I can smell booze on his breath, and something else, cologne I guess.

Ash always smelled good. I sat behind him in the sixth grade and spent the whole year sniffing him, nursing a crush that died when he took my virginity.

I think about spitting in his face, but my mouth is dry as a desert.

"I wanna know why you were at the Bull," Ash says. "You missing on me, that it? Wishing you never broke up with me now that Reed Pourret dumped your ass?"

"We were never together," I choke out. My chest's so tight I can hardly breathe enough to speak.

"Be real careful what you say," Ash warns me. "You'll go straight to hell for telling lies."

"Guess I'll see you there, then."

Ash grabs my ear and twists hard. I bite my lip to keep from crying out, and draw blood. My mouth tastes like old coins.

"Don't you get it? I could kill you right now, and I got half a mind to. One less whore in the world—maybe I'd be doing everybody a goddamn favor."

"Then do it!" I snap. "You want your boys thinking you're all talk? What about the Tullers? Bet they always make good on their threats."

Some emotion I can't read flickers over Ash's face. Then he smiles.

"That's right, they do. Speaking of the Tullers, how about

you tell me what you were doing spying on them? Luger and Johnny weren't too happy about that."

"I was there to see Norris."

"No you weren't. That loser ain't your type. This about Bobby Ray, huh? This about that no-good wife-beating thief you call a daddy? *Huh?*"

I fly into a rage, struggling against Skinny Ray's grip on me like I don't even feel the pain.

"Where is he?" I scream.

"Ask me real nice," Ash says, putting his palm against my face. "And maybe I'll tell you."

"You don't know, do you? The Tullers don't tell you nothing! You're just a pet to them, Ash," I tell him, thinking about what Gypsum said. "Like one of those dogs they breed to be mean. You ain't one of them, you ain't never gonna be one of them."

His face goes blank. I must've hit a nerve.

"Now, you listen to me. Are you listening?"

He shakes me by the ear. I whimper. It hurts so much more than I ever would've thought it would. He might tear it clear off my head, he yanks any harder.

"Are you listening, Sammy?"

I nod.

"You're gonna stop poking your pretty little nose into what ain't none of your business. Stop looking for your daddy. He ain't here, and that's all you gotta know, okay?"

"Fuck you."

A slow smile spreads across Ash's face. It's a terrible sight. "Funny you should mention that."

He grabs me by my shoulders and shoves me to the ground. I land face-first in the dirt, but when I try to get up, Ty knocks my feet out from under me and I fall again.

My shoes are gone. I don't remember losing them. Skinny Ray kicks a spray of dirt and gravel at me just as I'm taking a breath. I sputter to get it out. My lungs ache. For a second, I hope they kill me, and I hope they do it fast.

"Get on your knees," Ash says.

I rise up on my hands and cough and spit some more. There's dirt in my mouth, in my throat. My saliva's red, but I can't tell if that's the dirt or my own blood.

"Ty, make her kneel."

Ty pins my arms to my side and hauls me to my knees. I slump to make it harder but Skinny Ray grabs me by my hair again and pulls till I got no choice but to sit up straight unless I want him to tear big hunks of it right out of my head.

Ash starts unbuckling his belt. I do some quick math: two things could happen with that belt. For the first time in my life, I'm desperately hoping for a whipping.

"You got one thing right," Ash says. "We ain't family."

He's playing this all calm, like the big men do when they're about to dole out some country justice, but he can't hide how much he's enjoying this. My eyes burn. I wanna tear his face off with my fingers.

The buckle's undone now, but he don't slip the belt from its loops, so it ain't a whipping.

I squeeze my eyes shut. I should scream for help, but it's like one of those horrible dreams where every time you open your mouth, you can't say a thing, not a single word.

Ash unbuttons his fly slowly. "Means this thing we're about to do, it ain't incest."

He pats my head. "I bet you'll like it. You done it before. One last time to remember you by?"

I hear a tiny *click* above my head, next to Ash's ear. I open my eyes and see Brayton standing behind Ash with a gun's muzzle pressed to Ash's close-shaved scalp.

"I told you to get on home," Brayton says.

Skinny Ray lets go of my hair. He and Ty back away. I pitch forward and heave, but ain't nothing in my stomach. Relief and shame slosh through me.

Ash raises his hands and the pupils in his wide eyes get big.

"Don't be an idiot," Ash says. His voice wobbles. Not such a big man now.

"Shut up," Brayton says.

He shoves Ash, who stumbles past me. Skinny Ray and Ty grab him to keep him from falling. I scramble away.

"Get into your car and fucking *leave* before I shoot you."

"You ain't gonna shoot me, rich boy," Ash sneers. "Bet you don't even know how to use that gun."

"You want to test me? Go ahead."

Brayton's calm as a spring morning holding that gun, like he was born with it in his hand. Maybe we all underestimated him.

"This ain't over," Ash says. He spits at me, then gets into his truck through the open passenger door.

Skinny Ray and Ty follow in a hurry, and before I can count to ten they're gone.

Brayton gets on his hands and knees and crawls over real slow, trying not to spook me. But I'm blank inside. Don't think I could react if I wanted to.

"Sammy," he says, wiping Ash's spit off my forehead. "You okay?"

I shove him so hard he falls back on his ass. The gun thumps to the ground.

"What the hell?"

"That was so stupid, Brayton. Where did *you* get a gun? Do you even know how to shoot it?"

"Of course I do! My old stepdad Rich taught me. Said you can't call yourself a man if you can't protect your family with deadly force."

He lays the gun in his lap. "This one's Jack's. He keeps it in his nightstand for, you know, intruders. It's not loaded. See?"

He opens the barrel and shows me the empty chambers, but my eyes aren't working now Ash's headlights are gone. The light from the house is very faint.

"I didn't load it," he says.

My breaths start coming hard and fast and I know what's about to happen, that I'm gonna cry. The numbness is fading and fear, raw and razor-sharp, floods in.

Don't wanna cry, don't wanna shed a single fucking tear over Ash Boford, but I don't got a choice, the sobs are rolling up through my chest and any minute now they're gonna burst right out of me.

I cover my face with my hands and bawl.

"Sammy, Sammy," Brayton says, wrapping his arms around me. "I'm sorry if I scared you."

"*You* didn't scare me." I feel like I'm choking.

"I know," he says. "But I'm sorry if I made it worse, with the gun. I didn't know what to do."

I shake my head. My family's always had shotguns and hunting rifles, Oklahoma's an open carry state and everyone I know's got some kind of heat on their property. What scared me was how I was at those assholes' mercy from the minute they pulled up in that truck.

"I wish I could've shot him," Brayton says—to himself, I think, more than me. "Just a little bit."

There's a sound you make when you're tired and afraid, when you can't quite breathe and you can't quite talk, but then a thought hits you, and even though your mouth is full of your own spit and blood and your eyes burn, it strikes you as funny and you laugh. It don't sound like a laugh. It sounds more like a cough, and it hurts, and it seems stupid you're laughing after what you been through.

I don't know the word for that sound, but it's the one I make.

"Shot him a little bit? Who are you?"

Brayton cradles the base of my skull in his palm and I press my face into his shoulder. We go quiet, just sit there, half on the road and half in the brush.

A pair of bullfrogs groan to each other in a pond somewhere, and a cheeseburger bird sings for his supper in a nearby tree. The house is a dim, faraway glow, and the forest is dark, the night aggressively alive, looming over Brayton and I, pressing in while we cling to each other in the dirt.

Finally, Brayton says: "That was the guy from the Deck. Who is he?"

"My ex-stepmother's younger brother."

"So all...*that*...was about protecting his sister?"

I shake my head. "Ain't got nothing to do with Rainne. Ash's hated me for years, and those thugs he hangs with—I think they did something to my dad."

"Why would he hate you?"

"We were friends sorta, long time ago. We had sex once when we were fourteen and it was awful and I didn't wanna do it with him no more. He's always held that against me."

"You slept with that guy?"

"Not on *purpose*," I snap.

He hesitates. "Do you...want to tell me about it?"

"No," I say. "My shoes. I can't find my shoes."

Brayton fetches them for me. I put them back on and get to my feet, ignoring the pain in my muscles. I brush my hands off on my dress, which is ripped and ruined. At least I'm still wearing it.

Soon as I feel steady enough, I start walking back down the hill. Brayton scrambles after me.

"Where are you *going*?"

"Home."

"Let me drive you."

"It's okay." Ash is long gone now, and he won't come back, not tonight. Redneck bravado aside, I think Brayton scared him for real.

He steps in front of me, blocking my way.

"Move," I say.

He don't get it. He don't see how he's just another guy telling me what I can and can't do, where I should and shouldn't go.

Brayton thinks he's different, 'cause he *cares*. 'Cause he's rich and has those nice fancy manners and he rescued me, he thinks that gives him the right to stop me doing what I want and say it's for my own good.

"Okay. But will you please tell me why you left? Did I do something wrong? I didn't want to leave you, but those dicks were breaking all my mom's expensive shit and I—"

"What does your stepdad really do for a living, Brayton?"

He looks confused. "He's in real estate development."

"I thought he worked for Chesapeake. You said he's in oil."

"I said he *was*. He quit around the time he married my mom, started his own company. What's Jack's job got to do with anything?"

"Is that why y'all came up to the lake this summer? His company's building Sweet Home and he wanted to be nearby?"

"Basically. Is that a…problem?"

"Yeah, it's a problem. Your stepdad and his company done bought up half the bluff I live on!"

"So?"

"So they're gonna tear it all up and build some 'luxury recreational complex' so rich people like you can *relax* from all the *stress* of your lives in the big city while us poor country folk lose the land that's been in our families for generations."

"I still don't know what this has got to do with you and me right now. As far as I know—and, really, I know next to nothing—that land was bought and paid for, fair and square."

"Yeah, and how many of those people really wanted to sell? How many got bullied into it?"

"I bet they were happy enough to leave. Jack said everybody who sold up got twice or sometimes three times what the land was actually worth."

"So they didn't do nothing shady to get that land?"

"I have no idea! But Jack's not a bad guy. I can't imagine him trying to trick anybody out of land they didn't want to sell."

"Then why's there a map of the development in his office right now that includes *my* land? We didn't sell up to Sweet Home."

Brayton drags his hand down his face. "I don't know. It was probably a mistake."

"Didn't look like a mistake."

"What do you want me to do?"

"Ask him, for starters."

Brayton deflates. "I…can't do that. I'm sorry."

"Why not? It's a simple question."

"Because I just can't, okay?" he snaps. "Jack's not my dad. He doesn't like me or trust me. He's not going to tell me anything. I pretty much just try to stay out of his way. Maybe you think I'm a coward, but— Maybe that's what I am."

A long silence stretches between us while I work out what to say.

"Putting a gun to Ash Boford's head don't seem too cowardly to me. Stupid, yeah. But you ain't no chicken, Brayton Foster."

"I should've called the cops," he says. "But I didn't want Jack to find out I threw a party in his house and he *definitely* would've if I'd done that."

"You shouldn't've thrown the party at all. I'm not worth making your stepdad mad if you're really that scared of him."

"I'm not scared of him," Brayton insists, but it don't quite ring true. "I'd just...rather not provoke him. But I wanted to see you. I like you. A lot."

"You only think you do 'cause I'm really good at blow jobs."

Brayton laughs. "That is definitely part of it. But I've got a hunch there's more to you than that."

I give him a hard look. "You really wanna be with me."

"I really do."

"For how long?" I ask.

He smiles unsurely. "As long as we want."

"You gotta be heading back to the city in the fall."

"Off to college, but yeah."

I shake my head. "Don't waste your summer chasing after me, Brayton. I'm sure there's plenty of girls in that big fancy house of yours right now who won't give you half the trouble."

"Probably." He puts his hand on my cheek, light as the brush of a moth's wing. "But I don't really mind trouble."

"Trouble like tonight? You like that?"

He frowns. "If you're trying to scare me, it's not going to work. If you're trying to test me, I think I pass. We're not so different, you and I, and once you get to know me better you'll see that. I'm not what you think I am."

"What are you, then?"

"Well, for one, I'm not rich. Any money you think I have is Jack's."

"Same thing."

"I didn't grow up with money, either. My dad ran off when I was a baby and my mom raised me by herself in a one-bedroom apartment for eight years. We never had anything before she married my first stepdad, and she got nothing from him in the divorce. Without Jack...well. My mom's gotten pretty good at finding herself rich husbands, so maybe we'd be all right in the end."

He stares at me. "Does that change anything?" he asks.

"A little bit, actually."

"That's crazy," he says. "What do you care how much money my parents have got?"

I shrug. "Maybe I'm kind of crazy."

"Don't play with me. Are we going to try this or not?"

"I guess," I say, after a long pause.

Brayton laughs. "That's the sort of apathy I was hoping for."

He brushes his lips against mine, the softest touch, like a dragonfly skimming across a pond. He whispers:

"I *am* going to spend my summer chasing after you, Sammy, unless you tell me to stop. Lead me on if you have to, run when you're scared and come back when you miss me, push me away, pull me in, screw me, leave me, use me. I'll take what you've got to give and try not to ask for more. I promise."

"Don't make promises."

His warm mouth travels down the length of my neck. I close my eyes and put my hands on his waist. The knots inside me start to loosen and unravel. Brayton hugs me.

"Too late," he murmurs. "Already done."

"Brayton." He stops what he's doing and looks at me. "What if I am crazy?"

"You might be," he says. "But if you are, you're exactly the sort of crazy I like."

CHAPTER ELEVEN

"We have to go to the cops," Brayton says. He puts his arm 'round my shoulders and holds me tight against his side as we walk slowly up the hill toward his house.

"No. No way."

"Sammy, they kicked the shit out of you. Ash was going to—" He can't even say it: *rape you.*

"Reporting him will only make everything worse. The police won't do anything."

"You could get a restraining order."

"A piece of paper's not gonna keep Ash Boford from harassing me if he wants."

We've reached the edge of Brayton's long green lawn. I look up at the house.

"I don't want to go back in there, do you?" Brayton asks.

I shake my head but then I think of Kenley. She's probably wondering where the hell I've gotten to.

"I should make sure Kenley knows I'm all right."

"Text her, then. I say we take *Stella* for a drive."

"Okay." Can't think of nothing better to settle my nerves than a ride across the dark, empty lake in Brayton's hellcat of a speedboat.

He smiles. "I have to go inside for a second, get my keys and put the gun away. Be right back."

He starts up the driveway, but I grab his hand.

"How'd you know to find me?" I ask. "How'd you know to bring the gun?"

"That girl who helped look for your dad," Brayton says. "I can't remember her name, but she had red hair, kind of a boxer's nose?"

"Gypsum."

"That's right. I went to find you after Ash and his friends left, but I found her instead. She said you were in trouble and if I wanted to help you before something really bad happened, I should head on down the hill road and bring a weapon if I had one. Jack's gun was the first thing I thought of."

Brayton runs his fingers up and down my arm. I lean into him, wanting him to keep touching me and never stop. It's a comfort, the slide of his skin against mine.

"How'd she know?" Brayton asks. "You don't think she sent them for you?"

"Why tell you to help if she did?" I ask. Brayton shrugs.

He goes inside and I climb into *Stella*. While I wait for Brayton, I shoot Kenley a text:

Left party with Brayton. All ok. Talk tomorrow?

I put my phone aside and lean my head back. There's a patch

of sky above my head, pitch-black and dusted with stars like fine grains of sugar.

I inhale deep and taste the country air. Breathing up here, where the forest is old and endless, is like drinking from a mountain stream.

I jump when I hear a rustle in the nearby trees. My head whips around and I see a small figure disappear into the brush, what looks like a frizzy red ponytail bobbing between the branches.

"Gypsum?" I call out, but if it's her, if she hears me, she don't turn or call back.

Dad was fond of folklore. He told me stories of woodland sprites and green fairies that live in the Ozark hills, said they're not native to these parts but came over in the pockets of the European peoples who settled these lands. Sometimes I wonder if Gypsum ain't a Tuller at all, but some kind of backwoods brownie fixing to cause mischief. Or give a helping hand.

Brayton drives us to the boat launch with me riding in *Stella*. The wind tosses my hair and runs across my face as my heartbeat finally steadies. I can see bruises forming on my arm in the moonlight, my head aches something fierce and I can't stop thinking how much worse things are gonna get before they get better, if they ever will.

Stella's on the lake in no time, skimming across the water. Brayton holds my hand. He parks us near the mouth of a dark, empty cove and we move wordlessly into the back of the boat, where we curl up together and he touches me sweetly. I miss the electric, pulsing greediness of before, but I also don't know if I can handle it now, all that raw, naked need.

We kiss and kiss and kiss until the sun comes up.

* * *

Later in the morning, I insist Brayton drive me into town. When he asks what for, I tell him there's somebody I gotta see.

I only been to this house once, a long time ago, right after they first bought it, back when I was still with Reed. Feels weird driving up to it with Brayton, like the house, and anything to do with Reed, exists in a totally different universe than the one I live in now.

It's just about seven in the morning, so I knock softly on the door at first. I don't wanna wake Sarah—women that pregnant need all the sleep they can get. But a couple minutes go by and I think probably nobody heard me, so I press the doorbell and a few seconds later there's the sound of footsteps inside, the door unlocking.

"Sammy?" Sarah blinks at me. Her belly's so round it's like she's got a watermelon stashed under her T-shirt. "What are you doing here?"

"I gotta talk to Pete," I say.

"Who's this?" Sarah's eyes slide from me to Brayton. Typical cop's wife, always on high alert.

"Brayton Foster," he says, giving her a hand to shake. She don't seem too sure about him, but she takes it and smiles politely. "Friend of Sammy's."

"What's this about needing Pete? Did something happen?"

"Sort of. Can we come inside? I don't want nobody seeing me."

"Seeing you? Sammy, what's going on? Are you in some kind of trouble?"

Sarah puts a protective hand on her belly, looks me up and down. It's a bright morning, and I got bruises and scrapes all over my arms. I look a mess, and she must be wondering if I'm about to pull Pete into whatever it is I've gotten myself into.

"Sarah, who's at the door?" Pete calls, wandering into the front hallway from a room beyond, tucking his uniform shirt into his pants. His face drops when he catches sight of me.

"Oh, hey. Why don't y'all come inside real quick? Get out of that sun."

When the three of us are sitting at their breakfast table, nursing cups of hot coffee, Pete asks, "You here about Ash Boford?"

Sarah's in a laundry room just off the kitchen, folding onesies and cloth diapers fresh from the dryer.

"How do you know about that already?" Brayton asks.

"Word travels fast 'round these parts," Pete says, glancing at me. "He hurt you bad?"

I shake my head. "Just a little dinged up is all. Mostly he scared the shit out of me. Think Olina will let y'all do anything about it if I file a report?"

Pete hesitates. "Don't know. I tried bringing up the fact your daddy's still missing to her the other day and she just about bit my head off. Said if I uttered the name 'Lester' in her presence one more time she'd have my badge."

"But this doesn't have anything to do with Sammy's father's disappearance," Brayton says. "This is straight-up assault and attempted rape!"

"Rape? Ash Boford raped you last night?"

"No. Brayton, hush," I say, putting my hand on his arm.

"How can you be so calm about this?" Brayton asks. "I want to kill somebody."

"I'm gonna go ahead and suggest you not do that, son," Pete says.

"Son? You're like five years older than me."

Pete ignores him, and so do I. I'm all about getting justice for myself and my family, but I'm long past trusting the Bittersweet County Sheriff's Department to deliver it.

"What'd you do to make Ash Boford so mad?" Pete asks.

"What makes you think I did something?"

"Remember we grew up together, Sammy. You always had a way of ticking that kid off."

I tell him what went down at the Bull. He stares at me, wide-eyed.

"You *are* bold," he says.

"Thanks."

"It's not a compliment. Reed would tear me limb from limb if he found out I knew anything about you putting yourself in danger like that and didn't try to stop you."

"Yeah, well, Reed dumped me, so I think he's beyond caring what I do."

"You know that ain't true."

"Ash hates my guts, but what he did last night was more than a little teenage romance gone sour. I think it was my last warning—stay away from the Tullers and stop trying to pin Dad's disappearance on them, or else. Which is why I need your help."

"I already told you, Olina's folding this hand. She don't want nothing to do with pissing off the Tullers. Their money keeps getting her elected, and for the most part she leaves them alone."

"I'm done with Olina. But I bet if you think real hard you can come up with a name. Someone who'll help me. Someone who *ain't* in Redbreast Tuller's pocket."

"What, like a PI?"

"Can't afford a PI. Think of someone else."

"Well—I do know a guy, used to be a sheriff's detective under old man Olina. They forced him out when he tried to get some Tullers on a bunch of charges few years back. Had a conniption when Olina told him to turn them loose. Made a huge stink about it. Real boat rocker."

"Old man Olina—that long ago? How do you even know this guy?"

"My dad was kind of a mentor to him—you know, veteran cop takes on newbie deputy, that sort of thing. He used to come 'round the house, for dinner and stuff. Family parties, sometimes. I ain't seen him in a while, not since the funeral, but I got his card around somewhere."

Pete gets up, but Sarah's already searching through a drawer.

"Here, this it?" She hands the card to Pete. Sarah seems eager to be rid of us.

"Yeah, that's him. He's at the Bureau now, special agent."

"The…*Federal* Bureau?" Brayton asks. "Of Investigation?"

Pete scowls. "No, man. OSBI. Here."

Brayton looks at the card over my shoulder. *Special Agent Mark Pilson*, it says. *Oklahoma State Bureau of Investigation*.

"You really think he'll help me?"

"Lord, Sammy, I don't know. Could be he won't even answer the phone. But I'll tell you what—he ain't got no love for Bittersweet County law enforcement, and he sure as shit hates the Tullers. Be sure to mention them when you get in touch. It'll get his attention."

"Thanks so much, Pete. I really appreciate this."

"Yeah? Then do me a favor."

"Anything."

"I don't wanna have to say this. I always liked you. But I got a family to protect."

"What's the favor?" I ask, feeling cold all of a sudden.

"If you're really grateful—if you really wanna do right by me on account of this—then make this the last time you come knocking on my door."

"That guy's a dick," Brayton says, soon as we're out of there. "It shouldn't take you getting beat up to make people help you, especially people you've known your whole life."

I turn the card Pete gave me over in my hands.

"He's just scared. Everybody's scared of the Tullers 'round here."

"I'm starting to get that impression. Hang on. What's this?" Brayton says as I get into the car. He holds up a bundle of leaves and sticks fretted with a tangle of red yarn. "Found it under my seat."

"I don't know. Probably something you dragged in on your shoe."

He shrugs and tosses it in the bushes lining the driveway.

"Ain't for no reason, neither." I let my head fall back against the seat as Brayton pulls away from the curb. "People being afraid of the Tullers, I mean."

"Sammy, are you sure you want to keep doing this? You've got to know what happened to your dad, I get it. But are the answers—which you're probably not going to like—worth all this?"

Brayton rubs at his eyes. He looks exhausted. We didn't sleep much last night.

"I can't get the sight of those guys hurting you out of my

head. It makes me sick, what they did. I'm scared, too. Scared for *you*."

"I'm scared for me, too," I whisper.

"Then why?"

"'Cause 'round here, the only justice most folks get is the kind they go out and take for themselves," I tell him. "Somebody's gotta fight for my dad, and if I don't, ain't nobody gonna. I don't think I could live with knowing I could've done more but I didn't 'cause I was too chickenshit to try."

Brayton nods. "When are you going to call that special agent guy?"

"Right now."

"You dial, I'll drive. Where do you want to go?"

"I don't know. Not to my house. Can't face another lecture from Denver at the moment."

"Then what about mine? God knows what kind of state it's in. I've got to clean up after the party before Jack comes back. Want to help?"

"Sure."

Brayton's staring at the road, worrying his lip so hard I'm afraid he's gonna chew all the way through it.

Reaching over to brush a lock of hair off his forehead, I say, "What happened last night ain't gonna happen again, okay? I ain't in a habit of making promises, but I'll promise you that. I made some mistakes and Ash got the drop on me. Next time, I'll be ready."

"I'd rather there wasn't a next time."

"Can't say there won't be. You *sure* you like my crazy? Wasn't kidding when I said being with me ain't all two-stepping and blow jobs."

When he don't laugh at that, I poke him in the ribs, which gets me a half smile. Better than nothing.

There's a long silence, and then: "There will still be *some* blow jobs, right?"

I grab his hand and squeeze. The half smile widens into a full one, though he never does take his eyes off the road.

I pick up my phone and dial Special Agent Pilson's number.

"We should forget cleaning and just call FEMA," Brayton grumbles as he pulls trash bags out of a cardboard box and tosses them to me. "Or maybe set the house on fire."

"I got matches," I say. He smiles.

The place is a disaster: the coffee tables and windowsills of the living areas are covered in Solo cups and empty beer bottles, cigarette butts and the bud-like corpses of someone's joints.

The kitchen looks like it got hit by a tropical storm, and a search of the bedrooms coughs up discarded condom wrappers and stiff, wadded-up tissues, among other things. Takes us hours to clean, and by the end we're covered in sweat. The sun streams through big picture windows, roasting us like chickens.

Brayton suggests a shower. The cold water feels like needles. It clears my head with painful pinpricks, like the ones you get when blood rushes back into a sleeping foot.

Once we're clean, we lie down side by side in Brayton's unmade bed, limbs braided, damp hair making wet spots on the pillowcases. We sleep a long time.

First thing I'm aware of when I wake, before I even open my eyes, is the sound of a phone buzzing. Takes me a second to realize it's mine.

I fumble for it, find it under my dress, which is in a pile with Brayton's clothes on the floor. I look at the screen: it's Rainne.

"What happened? Is Decca all right?" Rainne don't just call me for no reason.

"What? Yes, of course. She's fine."

I let out a deep breath and flop backward onto the bed. Brayton stirs, reaches for me, nuzzles his face into the crook of my neck. I relax against his body, enjoy the tickle of his warm breath on my skin.

"So what's going on?" I ask Rainne.

"You said you wanted to see Decca."

"Uh-huh."

Brayton's hands skate up under my shirt. I tense, like Rainne can somehow see us through the phone.

"Well, I need someone to pick her up from day care. Vera's mother took a nasty fall so now I'm stuck covering her dinner shift and Duke's in Arkansas for the week and MaryEllen's not speaking to me at the moment for some stupid dumbass reason I don't even know and Lally can't 'cause—"

"You want me to get her?"

Rainne sighs. "Yes, can you?"

I glance over at Brayton, who's looking at me sleepily through half-open eyelids.

"Yeah. I'll pick her up. Just gotta figure out a ride, but I'll be there."

"By five thirty, Sammy," Rainne says. "The woman who runs that day care gets cranky when you're late."

"Okay." It's four thirty now, plenty of time. "I'll just take her to our house and you can pick—"

"No," Rainne snaps. "My house. There's a key under the

flowerpot farthest away from the front door. You take her *straight home*. Don't you be bringing her by that trailer."

"Fine." No use arguing. I'm lucky she's letting me see Decca at all.

But the way she says *trailer* makes me feel ashamed, and I realize it's possible Decca will never step foot in our house again.

"Thanks." Rainne hangs up.

"Where are we going?" Brayton asks, stretching and yawning.

"We?"

"You said you needed a ride. I've got a car."

"I need to pick up my sister from day care."

"Okay."

"Don't you got shit to do?" I ask, pulling my dress on and raking my hair into a ponytail.

Brayton sits up. "You helped with my chores, I'll help you with yours. How old is your sister?"

"Six. And she ain't a chore."

"Noted. Hey."

He catches my hand and reels me in so I'm facing him. He brushes his fingers over a constellation of fresh bruises on my arm.

I got scratches up and down my body, too, from falling. My scalp aches from Skinny Ray pulling my hair and my ear is tender from Ash twisting it.

Brayton frowns. "You okay?"

The look on his face tugs at something inside me and I feel the sharp sting of tears in my eyes. I force them back.

"Just dandy. How about you?"

He keeps staring at me like he wants more, but what am I supposed to say? I kiss him instead.

"Get your keys," I say. "We gotta go fetch Decca."

I can't shake the terrible feeling this might be the last time in a long time I get to see my sister.

CHAPTER TWELVE

Decca's running around the playground when we pull up to her day care. I can see her through the barred fence, swinging on the monkey bars like gravity don't exist.

"Hey, beastie!" I shout through the window. "Ready to go home?"

"Sammy!" she shrieks, dropping to the wood chips and waving her arms like I'm a plane she's trying to flag down.

We gotta walk through the day care's main building to get to the back. There's a woman inside stacking tiny plastic chairs on top of tiny round tables. Everything in here's kid-size. The woman looks dead tired.

"Can I help you?" she asks.

"I'm here to pick up Decca Lester," I tell her. "I'm Sammy Lester, her sister."

The lady narrows her eyes on me, puts her fists on her meaty hips.

"I don't know about *that*. Rainne's gotta tell me these kinds of things—I can't be handing these kids over to just anybody."

"I been here to pick her up before. I gotta be on some kind of approved list or something."

The woman shakes her head. "Only people on that list are Rainne and Duke."

I sigh. This is so like Rainne. Brayton wanders off to look at a wall of kiddie art. Bet he wishes he'd waited in the car.

"I'll call her. She asked me to pick Decca up for her—she'll tell you."

"How about I call her?" The woman juts her chin toward a door in the corner. I can see a smaller room beyond through a window fitted with safety glass. Looks to be an office. "Won't be a minute."

When the day care woman comes out of the office. I put a smile on for her. "All set?"

"No. Couldn't get a hold of her."

"You try Mr. Whiskers? She had to pick up someone's shift. That's why she ain't here."

"I called there first. They said she left an hour ago."

"What?" Where the hell could she be? And what about Vera's mother, the whole sob story she told me?

A sudden banging gets our attention—it's Decca, knocking on the sliding glass door.

"Sammy, you gonna take me home or what?"

"Can I at least go outside and be with her while you figure this out?" I ask the woman.

She throws her hands up. "What do you want me to do? She's not answering."

"It's just about time for y'all to close up shop, right? Ain't she the only kid left?"

Don't see nobody but Decca outside, except a mopey-looking teenager wearing headphones and playing on her phone. She don't seem to be watching Decca very well. Must be the day care woman's kid or something.

"I'll call Duke," the woman says. "You can go out there, I guess. There's a lock and an alarm on the back gate so don't you even think about taking her. Cops are right down the street."

"You think I'm here to steal her or something?"

The woman pauses at the door.

"There's a note in Decca's file from Rainne, says watch out for anyone coming in here calling themselves Lester. Kellie's got her eye on you, so you best behave."

Doubt Kellie's got her eye on anything but the dumb game she's playing on that phone of hers, but whatever.

"We'll be outside. Come on, Brayton."

Decca throws herself at me soon as we step through the sliding glass doors.

"Who's this?" she demands, frowning at Brayton.

I crouch low so we're at eye level.

"This is my friend Brayton. He's nice. Can you be friendly, or do I gotta resort to tickle torture?" I ask, reaching for her sides with wriggling fingers.

She squirms away, laughing. "No tickle torture!"

"What?" I start tickling her and she doubles over in a fit of screaming giggles.

"No tickle torture! I'll be friendly!"

I stop, smiling, and pull her in for a hug. "That's what I thought. What do we say to Brayton?"

Decca puts out her hand. Brayton, who looks like he just landed on an alien planet—don't think he's very used to kids—shakes it politely.

"Nice to meet you, Miss Decca," he says.

"Nice to meet you, too." Then she whispers in my ear: "Is he your *bo*yfriend, Sammy?"

"That's a very personal question, beast. What do you know about boyfriends, anyhow?"

"A boyfriend is something a big girl has," Decca explains, like I'm some kind of idiot. "And he kisses her and sometimes he gets to sleep in her bed."

"Who taught you that?"

Decca looks at the teenage girl, sprawled out on a bench. She ain't looked at us once. "Kellie."

"You don't gotta worry about boyfriends right now. They're for big girls, like you said."

"I'm a big girl." She pouts.

"Not that big. Now how about you show me the way you swing on those monkey bars?"

But Decca ain't interested. She's still giving Brayton the once-over. Reminds me a bit of Dad.

"You ain't Sammy's boyfriend," she tells him.

Brayton smiles at her, then me. "I'm not?"

"Uh-uh. *Reed* is Sammy's boyfriend."

"Let's go check out those monkey bars now," I say, grabbing her hand. She resists, dragging her feet so I gotta pretty much pull her onto the playground.

Brayton strolls along after us. At least he looks amused.

"Decca, you don't want to swing on the monkey bars, do you? How about you tell me about this boyfriend of Sammy's?"

"Well, he—"

I put my hand over Decca's mouth. "Hush, you. Don't go talking about things you don't know nothing about."

I glare at Brayton. "Both of y'all. Reed ain't my boyfriend."

Brayton shrugs like he don't care one bit, though I know he does. Decca licks my hand and I pull it away.

"Yuck, Decca. That's gross."

"That's what you get," she says. Then her eyes light up and she calls out, *"Daddy!"*

My head whips around so fast I'm surprised my neck don't snap.

"Dad? Where? Where'd you see him?"

For a second, my stomach swoops like in all those dreams I have where the floor goes out under my feet and I'm falling, falling forever. Dad's here. He's fine. Everything's gonna be okay.

But I don't see him. Don't see nobody at all.

"Where, Decca? Where do you see Daddy?"

"Not *Daddy*," Decca says, laughing at my stupidity. She points. "I said *Johnny*."

"What?"

Sure enough, there's Johnny Tuller across the street, leaning against a battered black truck with one white door, smoking a cigarette, watching us.

When I was five I stuck a fork in the toaster to rescue half a PopTart and got a nasty shock. Seeing Johnny Tuller not fifteen feet from Decca gives me that same feeling, like I been hit with two hundred volts.

"Hey!" I shout, going for the gate, but it's locked, just like the day care woman said. Brayton puts a hand on my shoulder.

"There's an alarm," he says.

"You wait here with Decca."

I run through the day care and out the front door, but by the time I reach it Johnny's flicked his cigarette into the street, climbed into his truck and driven off.

I stare after him, watching his taillights disappear around the corner. This can't be the first time he's been here. Decca knew him on sight.

"We going home now?" Decca asks when I get back to the playground. "I'm hungry."

I grab her by the shoulders. "Do you know that man? He ever talk to you?"

"Who, Johnny?" She nods. "He's my friend. Sometimes he comes to the fence during playground time and talks to me."

"That lady in there lets you talk to strangers?"

Decca picks up on my anger right quick and I think I scared her, 'cause her lip starts trembling.

"No, but sometimes Kellie is supposed to watch us."

"Sammy," Brayton says in a warning tone, but I shove past him, stalking up to Kellie, who's still lounging on her bench. I rip her headphones off and throw them to the ground.

"What the hell?" she cries. "Who are you?"

"Did you know there's some thug been coming around here, chatting up Decca?" I demand. "Do you even pay attention to these kids when they're out here?"

"What do you mean? What thug? I don't know what you're talking about."

The day care woman opens the sliding glass door and pokes her head out.

"What's going on? I heard shouting."

"You let this loser sit out here by herself with other people's kids and she don't even watch them! Johnny Tuller's been talking to Decca through the fence and nobody even knew about it."

The woman is horrified. "Decca, is that true?"

Decca nods, wailing, "But Johnny's my *friend*."

"He ain't your friend," I tell her. "He's a very, very bad man and you shouldn't be talking to him. Next time you see him you gotta run and get help, you hear? What does he say to you?"

"He don't— He don't—"

She's sobbing so hard by now she can't hardly get the words out. So much for making these last moments with her count. All I done is upset her.

If this is the memory of me she takes with her to Arkansas, I ain't never gonna forgive myself.

But then I think of all the bad men I met in my life, the bad things bad men do to little girls. Somebody's gotta protect her. Somebody's gotta teach her how to look out for herself.

"It's okay, sweetie," the day care lady says. "You take a deep breath and tell us when you're ready."

"He don't say *nothing*!" Decca cries, stamping her foot. "He asks me questions."

"What kind of questions?"

"Like about Mommy and Duke. I don't remember."

"Does he ever ask you to go with him places, or…do things you don't wanna do?"

Decca squints at the day care lady. "No. He just wants to know about Mommy."

"What things about Mommy?"

"I don't know. Like when she's at home and where she goes and stuff. I don't remember."

The day care lady nods. "Okay. Thank you, sweetie. That was very helpful."

Then she says to me, "I'm gonna talk to Rainne about this, and maybe someone down at the sheriff's office, too. But you better tell her soon as you see her tonight. I'm so sorry. Kellie's sorry, too."

"Not half as sorry as you're gonna be if something happens to Decca," I say. I grab Decca's hand. "I'm taking her home, *now*."

"Yes, all right. I got a hold of Rainne. She says she called earlier, left a message with Kellie. She didn't write it down. I apologize for the misunderstanding."

"Fuck you, lady," I say.

"Are you okay?" Brayton asks. We're sitting in his car, but I got no idea where we're headed. Maybe nowhere in particular. I'm too tangled up in my thoughts to bother asking.

"Fine," I say, not turning my head from the window. Clumps of trees and softly rolling green-as-dollar-bills farmlands fly past in a blur.

Angry tears sting the backs of my eyes and my head aches from keeping them in.

Rainne was pissed when I told her what happened and she banned me from seeing Decca anymore, saying it was my fault, that I brought the Tullers down on Decca by messing with them. She said if I kept my distance, she'd think about letting me visit them in Arkansas when the move was over.

Screw that, I said. *You better believe I'm gonna do whatever I can to stop you from taking her away from us. And when Dad comes back, he's gonna help me.*

Don't be a fool, Rainne said sharply. *Your good-for-nothing daddy ain't never coming back.*

The thought of Decca gone from the lake turns my stomach. Rainne's certainty Dad's gone for good breaks my heart. I'm gripping the door handle so hard the fingers of my right hand are stiff.

"Can I smoke in here?" I ask.

Brayton rolls down all the windows. A blast of hot air slams against my cheeks.

I light up and take a long drag. "Sorry. I know how you are about this car."

Brayton shrugs. "It's just smoke. It'll clear."

I turn back to the window. The wispy gray-white tendrils curl till they disappear on the breeze. My chest feels tight and I realize I been holding my breath.

"I hate her," I tell Brayton.

"I know," he says.

My phone rings in my back pocket. "Sammy Lester?" a man's voice asks when I answer.

"Yeah, that's me."

"This is Special Agent Pilson, OSBI. You left me a message this morning."

"I did. Thank you for calling back."

"I've been looking into your father's case—got the missing persons report from the Bittersweet County Sheriff's Department, did some digging into his background. How long did he work for the Tullers?"

"Little over twenty years. Since he was seventeen."

There's a pause on the line, like Pilson's writing this down. Then he says: "I'd like to meet with you, have us a long talk about your dad. Are you available tomorrow?"

"Yes! Just tell me when and where."

Agent Pilson names a diner about an hour away from Lake Bittersweet on the outskirts of Tulsa. No clue how I'm gonna get all the way out there—seems like taking advantage to make Brayton haul my ass every single place I wanna go—but Denver and I can figure that out. We're pretty resourceful.

Money's a whole other problem, as in I need some and got none. I'm supposed to work tomorrow, so I gotta get someone to cover for me. Been doing a lot of that lately. Dora's been understanding, but missed shifts mean no tips.

"Agent Pilson," I say. "Are you really gonna help find my dad?"

"Well," he says. "We're just going to have to wait and see."

LOSING LUBEL

Froygar never thought she'd much like sharing her land with another of her kind, but Lubel was a good companion, a sweet cub with not a lick of meanness about her. Together they hunted and fished and tended to the Little Waters, happy and free.

At night they lay on their backs and looked up through the trees at the stars, marveling at the beauty of this little patch of forest they lived in until they fell into a peaceful sleep.

Sometimes, Froygar wondered what happened to Lubel's mama, if she up and left her cub one day, or if she got herself killed somehow. She never wondered what would've happened to Lubel if Froygar hadn't found her, 'cause that was just too sad a thing to think about.

But all the time, Froygar worried about the future and what it had in store. She kept running across signs of human activity on her forest patrols. The more time passed, the closer they got to the Little Waters, and Froygar never heard of a giant—boy or lady—who'd escaped or beaten the human foe.

Froygar figured the best way to keep her and Lubel safe was to move on from the Little Waters, press back farther into the mountains where the humans ain't yet settled. But Froygar was afraid to leave the only home she ever had for a deep wilderness full of who knew what dangers, belonging to who knew what creatures. So they stayed put and protected their land best they could, till—one hot day at the beginning of summer—the humans finally found them.

Hard to say what would've happened if Froygar had been at the Little Waters the morning those ten pale-skinned men carrying hunting rifles crashed through the trees at the base of the cliff, near the pool right beneath the falls. Maybe it would've gone down different. But Froygar was checking her traps in the forest, higher up beyond the bluff, and Lubel was alone, bent over the water catching fish for their supper with her bare hands. Giants had pretty sharp ears, but the roar of the falls made Lubel near deaf, so she didn't hear the men till they were almost on top of her.

Before Lubel knew what was happening, she'd been shot—not enough to kill her, but enough to make it impossible to run—and tied up by those men. Drawn by the commotion, Froygar hurried to the lip of the bluff. Lubel cried out in hurt and rage and fear as the men dragged her off. The pounding water drowned her voice out, but Froygar didn't need to hear Lubel's screaming to feel her heart breaking.

Froygar chased after them, half sliding, half falling down the cliff's steep slope and tearing into the forest on the men's heels. But giants weren't as quick as humans and she was too far behind to catch up. She followed the trail of Lubel's blood through the woods by scent. At the place where the trees stopped and the flat, wide-open plains began, Froygar stopped and shivered. She'd never wandered so far from the Little Waters before, never stood so close to a human camp.

She ought to go back to her land. Some other giant could be laying claim to the Little Waters, and after all she done all those years to keep it safe, leaving it unprotected seemed like a mighty stupid thing to do.

Froygar turned and started back home the way she came, but then she heard a shout, a high-pitched shriek of pain that couldn't be nothing or nobody but Lubel. Tears sprung up in Froygar's eyes. She couldn't leave the cub to whatever fate the humans had in mind for her, even if it meant losing the Little Waters forever.

Weary and light-headed, Froygar sat down on a nearby rock, making sure the trees hid her hugeness, and started to plan. The humans had guns, and Lubel. All Froygar had were her wits. But she'd used them to keep enemy giants off her land, and she was sure if she thought long and hard she could come up with a way to rescue Lubel.

With her keen giant eyes, she could see the camp well enough from where she sat, even though the light was failing and there wasn't no moon.

Just about midnight, Froygar stood back up, stretched her long, powerful limbs and walked out of the trees, making for the human settlement in the big field beyond the forest.

She was gonna free her cub, even if it was the last thing she ever did.

CHAPTER THIRTEEN

"You really think this guy can help us?" Denver asks.

"I don't know." Yesterday, I started to feel something like hope, but now I ain't so sure.

Denver and I are driving to Tulsa in a junky old car Holler lent us. Took a bit of convincing to get Denver to come along, but I don't wanna do this without him. He's the only family I got at the moment, and we can't be turning away from each other now.

"Thought you had to work today," Denver says.

"I did, but I begged off."

"Dora's cool with that?"

"Yeah," I lie.

When I called Dora yesterday to tell her I couldn't make my morning shift, she sighed and said that was fine, but if I didn't come in this morning, I shouldn't come in again—ever.

I'm so sorry, Sammy, she said. *I know things been hard for you*

*lately, and you can't help but be distracted, but I got a business to
run, and I need folks I can count on to be here. I'll mail your last
paycheck to your house. I'm really sorry.*

I'm sorry, too. Sorry this whole shitty thing is happening,
that it's ruining my whole life. But I can't stop looking for Dad,
not now there's a slim chance the law might pitch in with the
search. I can get a new job, but this opportunity might not
come 'round again.

"Why do we gotta go all the way to Tulsa to meet with
him?" Denver asks.

"He don't wanna be seen in town, I guess. Used to work for
old Sheriff Olina, so he figures some people might still know
him. He don't wanna spook the Tullers."

"When we find Dad, I'm gonna kill him for putting us in
this situation."

If we find Dad—and we gotta find him, we *gotta*—I'm gonna
throw my arms around him and sob like a baby. I'm pissed at
him, too, but that ain't nothing compared to how scared I am
for him.

The diner's shitty and falling apart, but I can see why Pilson wanted to meet here: it's nearly empty, and there ain't no
chance we'll see anybody from the lake.

It's a relief to be away from that place for a little while. I
can't stop looking over my shoulder, can't take a deep breath
without worrying somebody's gonna jump me before I can let
it out again.

Agent Pilson ain't what I expect. Guess I been trained by
movies and cop shows to think someone in his position should
be handsome and charming, but he ain't none of those things.

He's a plain man, and pretty quiet. We find him in a booth
near the back of the diner, where he's nursing a fresh cup of

milky coffee. There's a plate of leftover bacon and eggs balanced on the edge of the table. My stomach growls at the sight. I ain't eaten today.

Pilson waves the waitress over and asks for coffee for Denver and I.

"My treat," he says. He stares like he can figure us out just by looking. If we ain't what he expects, either, he don't let on.

"Sammy says you're going to help us track our dad down," my brother says.

"We'll see," Pilson says.

He's got a couple of file folders on the seat next to him. He puts aside his coffee and starts flipping through them.

"He's been missing since the first week of June, the report says. You think the Tullers had something to do with it?"

"It's looking that way," I say.

"What gives you that impression?"

I tell him everything we know: Ash's threat at the Deck the night Dad disappeared, the graffiti note on our door, Johnny Tuller showing up at Decca's day care. I ain't gonna mention the Bull, seeing as I didn't really learn anything there, but Denver blows up my spot. The tale annoys Agent Pilson.

"Don't you ever pull anything like that again," he says. "That's a good way to get yourself killed, whether they had anything to do with your father going missing or not. The Tullers don't take to being spied on, or threatened, and showing up at their hangout with an obvious agenda is definitely something they'd see as a threat."

"That's what I told her," Denver grumbles. "What do you know about the Tullers?"

"More than you probably ever will. *Dangerous* gang. The Bittersweet County Sheriff's Department is beholden to Red-

breast somehow, and they don't lift a finger against the Tullers unless they absolutely have to. So there's no hope of them
interfering until there's evidence they can't ignore."

"Like what?"

"Like a body."

I been refusing to let myself think that way too much, so
the idea of Dad as a *body* is a shock.

"We don't know he's dead," I argue.

"We've got to take every possibility into consideration."

"Why are you interested in this case?" Denver asks. "Do
you even have jurisdiction?"

"Depends on how you look at it. If this were a cut-and-dry
missing persons case, or even a homicide, the sheriff's department would have to request our help with the investigation
for the OSBI to get involved."

Shit. Olina ain't never gonna do that. I feel all that hope
from yesterday start to leak out of me like air from a punc-
tured tire.

"*But*," Pilson continues, "the OSBI's got original jurisdiction over organized crime and criminal conspiracy cases. We've
been looking into the Tullers for years, trying to get them on
something. If I can find any concrete way to tie your father's
disappearance to their ongoing illegal activity, I might be able
to go over Sheriff Olina's head."

"That's a big if," Denver points out.

"Sure is, and everything you told me so far, while suspicious,
is weak and circumstantial."

"So you can't help us."

"I didn't say that. Today, we're going to have a chat. You're
going to tell me everything you know about your father's con-

nection to the Tullers, going as far back as that relationship goes, through the day he disappeared."

He pats the file folders. "I was still a detective with Bittersweet County when Bobby Ray Lester went to prison for aggravated assault. I wasn't assigned to that case, but I've been going through the records. Your dad was muscle for Redbreast's drug operation, and he was supposed to collect on a big debt from Arthur Comstock that night. Comstock didn't have the money, and your dad was high. He beat the man into a coma."

Denver and I don't say anything. It's all true.

"Bobby Ray never rolled on Redbreast, though," Pilson says. "The ADA offered a deal if he would but he just pled guilty, did his time. Know what that says to me? Says he might've decided, after seven years in the joint and a couple more of clean living, to finally unburden his conscience."

Denver and I glance at each other.

"I don't think Dad would turn on Redbreast," I say.

"Even if he wouldn't, maybe Redbreast was sick of taking the chance."

"Don't explain the money."

"Ten thousand, you said? Any chance it could've come from somewhere else?"

"Doubtful. And I been wondering if he even meant to keep it."

"What do you mean?" Denver asks.

"The money ain't in our house, so he must've had it on him. But he borrowed money from me that morning. If he had ten thousand cash in his pocket, why'd he need mine?"

Especially when he knows I got none to spare.

"Could've just been trying to get all he could before he bolted," Pilson says.

"I guess. Maybe."

"Could've been hush money," Denver says. "Get-out-of-town money, to ensure he wouldn't have a change of heart and go to the ADA, like you said."

"No way," I say. "He wouldn't take off like that without telling us, at least. Then there's Decca."

"Yes," Pilson says, leaning forward. "Tell me about the situation with your sister."

That night, Denver's hanging out with Holler, so I invite Brayton over for no reason other than I wanna see him—so much I'm willing to let him into my house. I ain't brought a boy here since Reed.

"It's a trailer, okay?" I tell Brayton over the phone. God, I hope I don't regret this.

"I've seen it, remember?"

"I know, but inside it's—small. And messy. I just gotta warn you not to expect a whole lot."

"Noted. I'll leave my tails at home."

"What?"

"Nothing. As long as you're there, I won't have anything to complain about," he says.

Soon as he gets here, I drag him into my room. He stumbles over a pile of clean laundry, steps on one of Decca's plastic toys and yelps.

"Did that hurt?" I ask. He grimaces. "Want me to kiss your foot to make it better?"

"My foot'll be just fine," he grunts. He sits down on the edge of the bed and pulls me into his lap. We both fall back against the pillows. "But I'll take that kiss somewhere else if you're offering."

I press my lips to the underside of his chin, cupping his cheek with one hand and working the button of his jeans open with the other. "Here?"

"Lower."

I trail the tip of my tongue down his throat, then brush my mouth along his collarbone. "Here?"

"Lower."

I pull his shirt over his head and spread my fingers over his chest, feel the beat of his heart in my palm, the slight rise and fall of his body as he breathes, rustling the hair near my face. I kiss his stomach, right above his belly button. "Here?"

He lets out a shuddering sigh. *"Lower."*

I'm about to unbutton his jeans when the doorbell rings. Brayton throws an arm over his face and groans. "Don't answer it."

"I'll be right back," I say. He puts his hand on my neck, traces my jaw with his thumb.

"Hang on a second, I'll come with you," he says.

Brayton holds my hand on the way to the door. I peek through the peephole and frown, not sure what to make of who's on the other side.

"Pete? What's wrong? Is it Dad?"

But I can tell just by looking at him it ain't. Pete's shoulders are slumped and his eyes are rimmed with red. He shakes his head. "Can I come in?"

I step aside and he lumbers into the front room, collapsing into the armchair that belonged to my grandfather. It's yellow with tobacco stains, tattered and pockmarked with cigarette burns, but it's an heirloom, and I can almost hear Grandpa Lester turn in his grave when Pete's butt hits the cushion. He wasn't such a big fan of cops.

Pete picks up an ashtray off the coffee table, turns it over, staring like he's mesmerized.

Brayton glances at me, mouths, *He okay?*

I shrug. Pete looks poorly. I offer him a drink and he asks for juice.

"What's going on?" I ask, handing Pete a cup. "It ain't Sarah, is it?"

Pete puts down the ashtray. "No. It's Reed. He's…hurt." Pete's eyes well with tears. "Bad hurt, Sammy. Got his fucking leg blown off and I—"

He gulps back a sob and buries his face in his hands. Pete always was the emotional one of the Pourret family.

But the sight of Pete crying now makes me wanna toss him out of my house. 'Cause when he says it—when he plants the image in my head of Reed wounded and alone in some foreign desert—it's like I been blown up, too. All that unmanly blubbering just makes it worse.

"Whoa!" Brayton tries catching me, but he ain't quick enough. My knees give and I'm on my ass before I realize I've fallen down.

I blink hard to bring the room into focus, but it keeps tilting. Pete bawls into his hands. I can't take it. Can't concentrate with all the fuss he's making.

"Stop." I close my eyes. "Stop. *Stop!*"

"They were headed to base when the jeep he was riding in hit an IED," Pete says between sobs. "Killed three guys. Reed's leg is gone. The left one."

Like it matters which leg.

"*Jesus,*" I whisper.

When Reed left for boot camp, he had two perfect legs, and now he doesn't. A month ago, Dad was here and now he ain't.

For six months, a sinkhole was lurking under my whole life and I didn't know a goddamn thing about it. Now suddenly here it is, a dark pit I'm so close to falling into I can't hardly see anything else.

"Where is he?" I ask. "Where's Reed right now?"

"Germany. Flew him straight there once he was stable. My mom…" Pete takes a deep breath. "She's already gone. Wanted me to tell you. She thinks he might wanna talk to you."

"Why?"

Reed and I ain't talked since our breakup. Not since I told him. I tried calling him after, but I could take a hint and his silence was a red flag: *Stay the fuck away.*

He'll never forgive me. He even said that: *I'll never forgive you for this, Sammy.* But now Pete's saying Reed wants to talk to me, and it's like he's speaking ancient Greek for all I understand him.

"Why?" I ask again, when Pete don't answer.

"That's all she said. 'Go tell Sammy—Reed might wanna talk to her.'"

Pete's phone chimes with a text. "It's Sarah. She wants me to come home."

"Go," I say. *Get out. Take your tears and leave.*

When Pete's gone, Brayton reaches for me, but I shake my head. I'm not sure, right then, that I can stand.

"Tell me about him," Brayton says.

It ain't a question, or a suggestion, or a request. Hard to get a read on what Brayton's thinking. Might be he's jealous, or curious, or some combo of the two, but his face tells me nothing.

"Sammy. Tell me."

"We started dating during the summer after my freshman year, but we knew each other our whole lives," I say. "It lasted two years. Reed's a year older than me, and right after he graduated last summer, he enlisted in the Army. We stayed together through boot camp, all through the fall. He came home to visit a few weeks before Thanksgiving."

It'd been nice, having Reed back at the lake, but terrible, too, 'cause I knew something was wrong. He wasn't comfortable around me anymore. His heart wasn't in it. I knew, and it scared me.

"He called a couple weeks after he left and broke up with me," I tell Brayton.

Sounds so simple when I lay it out like that. Felt so tangled and foggy at the time. I almost can't remember it happening, except the way you remember a dream in the thirty seconds after waking up.

"Why?"

I stare at my hands. "I don't know. He just said it was too hard, we weren't right, he was different. At first I thought he was lying, hiding something from me. That there was someone else. But he ain't that way."

"What happened next?"

"Nothing. We broke up. End of story." Dad always said lies come easier the more you tell them.

Was Reed's leaving me the universe's way of trying to teach me about letting go? To prepare me for losing Decca, and Dad? If anything, it only makes me wanna hold on tighter.

"Do you speak?"

"To him? Not since Christmas."

He hesitates. "Do I have something to worry about here?"

"Are you worried?"

"The guy lost a limb fighting for our country." The tips of Brayton's ears are pink, and he won't look at me. "Of course

I'm worried. He'll come home eventually, and by then I'll probably be at school. Who's to say what'll happen?"

"Reed don't want me back."

"And what about you?"

"It was puppy love. And the puppy grew into a rottweiler."

"That's not an answer."

Reed don't want me. That's a fact. But if he called right now and said, *I need you, come back to me*, would I say no?

My mind's so sticky with Brayton, it's hard to imagine being with anyone else. I can't remember what Reed looks like naked, but I could draw a map of Brayton with my eyes closed.

But Reed's part of me, down to my roots. He sprouted from the same red dirt I did and we grew up side by side. Brayton's a shiny, fancy new thing you can't afford but buy anyway 'cause it makes you feel special, like more than you are.

Eventually, those things need returning.

"What do you care?" I snap.

The thought of losing Brayton makes me angry, and the only way to cover it is to be angry at him.

"You don't get it," he grumbles.

"What?"

"Nothing."

Brayton stands. "I want to stay. I know I should stay with you. It doesn't feel right leaving you alone like this. But I don't think you want me here."

He waits for me to protest. Begs me to, with his eyes. But I don't.

So he goes.

I'm still sitting on the floor when Denver comes home.

"What are you doing?"

The sun's gone down and it's dark in here. Denver switches on a lamp and sits next to me on the floor.

"Trying not to think."

"I heard about Reed."

"From who?"

"Gypsum Tuller. Ran into her down at the marina—or maybe she came looking for me, I don't know. Not like she's got a boat."

"What's up with her? It's like she's a reporter for the *Sammy Lester Daily News*. How does she know all this stuff about me five seconds after I know it myself?"

"Same way anybody in this town knows anything, I guess."

"Don't it freak you out there's a Tuller hanging 'round keeping tabs on us?"

"I thought you were friends. She seems to look up to you, though I can't figure why. Who told *you* about Reed?"

"Pete."

"I'm sorry," Denver says, and I can tell he means it. "For him, mostly, but for you, too. Imagine what it'd be like if—"

He stops, but I know what he was gonna say: *Imagine what it'd be like if you kept that baby.*

I stare at him. "You really think Dad ran off?"

"What's that got to do with anything?"

"You never talk to me anymore. Even in the car today, you wouldn't say what you really thought. I'm taking the opportunity, us being in the same room and all, and you feeling sorry for me."

"Well, you got Dad's manipulative streak, that's for sure." Denver don't open his eyes. "I don't know what to believe, but I'll tell you one thing—I don't buy for a second he'd stick around just for Decca. Maybe there was a time when he wanted to change, for her. But he doesn't have it in him. You want to fix the pattern of your life, make yourself into a different person, you've got to *try*. You have to cut all ties to the shit that makes you hate yourself and never look back."

"Like you did?"

Denver shakes his head. "I'm here, aren't I?"

Maybe in body. But in spirit, he's miles away.

"He's trying," I insist. "He's done everything to make sure he gets the chance to be a father to Decca. He spent all his money on that lawyer to keep Rainne from taking her away. If he got mixed up with the Tullers again, it's gotta be 'cause he had no choice. It's gotta be 'cause he needed—"

"*No!*" Denver shouts, lurching to his feet. "If he got mixed up with the Tullers again, it's 'cause he *wanted to*. Don't you see he doesn't care about anybody but himself? Not me, not Decca and not you. Why are you so stupid about him? You and Mom get in one fight, you haven't talked to her since, but Dad can hurt you again and again and you just let him. Why?"

"It wasn't just one fight! You know the things Mom said to me. But Dad understood. He helped me do what needed doing." I'm seething now. "If I'm stupid about him, then you're blind. You act like he's a stranger to you. He's your father, Denver."

"I know him better than you do. You don't remember everything that went on back then."

"I remember plenty."

"You were protected. We lied so you could sleep at night. Nobody told me any fucking lies. I know who Dad really was."

"*Is*."

"Whatever."

"I knew him. I'm his *daughter*."

"I don't give a shit what you think," Denver says. "It's not the same as being his son."

CHAPTER FOURTEEN

I turn on the overhead light and squint.

Dad's MULE, a golf cart–type contraption he bought secondhand a few years ago, has been gathering cobwebs in our shed for weeks. It always was a little dilapidated, but now, covered in a thick layer of dust, it looks sad and abandoned.

I wipe it clean with a rag and take the keys from their hiding place in Dad's toolbox. Not sure where I'm headed, but I figure I'll know when I get there.

I back the MULE out of the shed. Wayne and Karen's dog, Dolly, is waiting for me. She comes up to the driver's side, grinning and panting, and angles her head to be petted.

"Almost didn't see you there," I say, scratching behind her ear the way she likes. "Sorry, girl."

Dolly whines and sniffs my hand as Karen comes 'round the corner.

"There you are, silly dog," she says, relieved. "She bothering you?"

"Not a bit." I stroke Dolly's back, muss her fur with my nails. "You're no bother, are you, girl?"

"Where you going, honey?" Karen asks. She sounds worried. Probably heard about Reed, too.

"Don't know. Need to clear my head, is all."

"Come hang out with us instead. You hungry? I made too much food."

I shake my head. "Another time."

Karen hesitates. "All right then. Will you take Dolly with you? She'll run alongside if you want, but I'm sure she'd be happy for a ride."

Dolly whines. I pat her flank and she hops into the flatbed.

"Karen, what kind of witch is your dog, anyhow? Can't nobody resist her."

"I ask myself that every day," Karen says with a smile. "You girls take care of each other, now."

The MULE only goes about twenty-five miles an hour, so it takes a while to get anywhere worth going. I try not to think much as I cruise down empty, twisting roads. The air is sweet with the smell of hyacinths, and the breeze makes the heat tolerable for the first time all day. Feels like any other summer— they're all the same, boiling and sticky and endless, till they end.

Reed and I fell in love during a summer like this, hot and lazy. Sometimes I wonder if we did it just to have something to do. Sometimes I wonder if that's why Brayton sticks around, too.

'Round the next curve there's a cliff that overlooks a small cove where a local man, Bruce Coleman, takes his SCUBA classes for practice dives. I park the MULE on the side of the road and walk to the edge of the cliff.

This spot has an amazing view. Reed and I came here all the time when we were together. It's the spot where he told me about joining the Army. It's the spot where I stood when I called to tell him I was pregnant, and the spot where I stood when I called to tell him I wasn't pregnant anymore.

It's called Satan's Chin, this small sheltered overlook. Popular with local daredevils, it rises thirty feet above the water, but the banks on either side have gentle slopes, easy to climb back up once you've jumped. The cove is deep and there ain't a lot of rocks, though a moron could still get himself killed if he fell the wrong way.

Reed ain't reckless, but he is impulsive. He likes speed and adrenaline, probably the only thing he's got in common with Brayton.

He started every summer with a leap off Satan's Chin, yelling *Geronimo!* as he fell. I hated it, afraid one day he'd land wrong and that'd be it: lights out, Reed.

Every summer he told me not to be such a baby, but every summer I covered my eyes till I heard the splash, then peered through my fingers to watch his dark head surface. I'd climb down to give him a towel and cling to him with relief. It felt like a ritual, like if we both did things the exact same every time, he was invincible.

The last summer we were together, we did everything the same, but when I looked over the edge, he wasn't there. I waited for him to come up for air, too shocked to do anything but stare at that still stretch of water and pray, knowing I was too far away to help him, and that if the fall had hurt him, there was likely nothing anyone could do.

Please, I whispered. If Reed died, I'd die, too.

Please what? Reed said, covering my eyes with his hands, which were flecked with red dirt from climbing up the bank. I turned and smacked him. He grinned at me like an idiot.

Oh fuck *you, Reed,* I said, storming off.

He grabbed my hand. His hair was longer and darker wet. Made him seem dangerous, like the sort of boy who'd leap off a cliff called Satan's Chin. It had an effect on me, made my skin grow hot.

What did I do? he asked, all innocent.

You know how much that stupid jump scares me.

He was only screwing around, but even with him standing right there in front of me, alive and whole, I couldn't shake that horrible feeling of dread that came with the thought of losing him.

Sorry, baby, he said, wrapping his arms 'round me. *I'll never do it again.*

But he did. He joined the Army, which scared me, and then he left me, which scared me more. Now he's lying broken in a German hospital, and Dad's gone, and I might never see Decca again, and I realize I never knew what scared felt like till now.

I sit and dangle my legs over the edge of the cliff. Dolly plops down next to me, sighing as she settles.

I need a new job. I need to find Dad. And if I can't, I need a lawyer to help me fight Rainne. I ain't giving Decca up. That just ain't an option.

The thought of jumping snags in my mind. It'd be so easy to sail through the air, to feel that rush Reed always talked about, the one he was always chasing.

"What do you think, Dolly?" I ask, putting my arm 'round

her and pressing my cheek to the top of her head. Her fur is soft and silky.

Dolly woofs, but if she's got something to say, it's lost on me. I stand and look down at the cove. The water's black and calm, both frightening and weirdly comforting.

If Reed can do it, no reason I can't, too. Long as I do it right, I shouldn't be in any danger.

I'm airborne before I realize I've made a choice. Falling feels like a release. I hear someone call out my name as I leap off the cliff, or I think I do, but it's probably my imagination, or the wind, or the echo of a memory that won't let go no matter how desperate I am to be free of it.

I hit the water feetfirst, the way Reed always said was safest. The water is shockingly cold, thick and black like oil. For a brief lightning bolt of a moment, I think I might be better off just letting the darkness swallow me up.

The ruins of old Gibson are below me somewhere, waiting. My ancestor's shop and his neighbor's plow and the dishes someone used to serve Sunday dinner are all still there, like they believe their owners will come back someday. I imagine floating down, down, down and landing on my back in the old town square, staring up at the surface with unseeing eyes, like I'm looking at the stars.

My lungs start to ache, and I realize I got a choice: open my mouth and take on water, or kick toward air and life. Things are so bad, seem so unlikely to get better, the thought of giving it all to the lake and letting go is tempting.

But then I think of Decca, and Denver. Even if I could do it, could give up, they don't deserve to lose yet another person.

I swim toward the light of the moon, which shivers and

shines impossibly far away, and when my head breaks through I suck in a huge breath, thankful to be alive.

"Sammy!"

I turn to see Brayton scrambling down the slope fast as he can without losing his footing. He reaches me just as I'm hauling myself onto the rocky shore, crawling on all fours.

"What are you *doing?*" Brayton asks.

"Swimming," I say. "What are *you* doing?"

"I went for a run to clear my head," he says. "I was passing by the cliff when I saw you jump."

"Oh."

"You lunatic," he says, eyes wild with panic. "You scared the *shit* out of me. You were down there so long, I thought you were trying to drown yourself."

"I'd never," I tell him. "People jump off that cliff all the time. It's a local thing."

He's still pretty shaken.

"Sorry," I say. "It was an impulse. I never done that before."

Dolly pads up to us, wagging her tail and panting. I reach out my hand and she nuzzles it with her head, as if to say, *See? I wasn't worried.*

"What's Dolly doing here?" Brayton asks.

"She came along to keep me company."

"You could've called me if you needed company."

"I thought you were mad. About Reed."

I pat Dolly's flank and point at the top of the cliff.

"Go protect the MULE, Dolly. Denver will make me cut my own switch if someone steals it."

She trots off. Brayton sits next to me and puts an arm 'round my shoulders. I press my wet cheek into the fabric of his shirt.

Water streams off me in tiny rivers but Brayton don't seem to mind.

"I wasn't mad at you," he says. "Or maybe I was, but that's stupid. None of this is your fault."

"Could be it is. He joined the Army to get away from me."

"Plenty of ways to break up with a girl that don't involve combat duty. Seems extreme."

Not to me. Back then, the way things were between us, I'd've felt I had to move to a different planet to get away from Reed.

"Reed and I were friends since we were kids. Our families were friends, our friends were friends… When we got together, it was like everybody had a stake in our happiness."

"Sounds awful," Brayton says sarcastically, tightening his grip like he's trying to keep me from floating back to Reed on a current of memory. "People caring."

"It was a lot of pressure. For him. I was so happy."

I was a redneck girl, from a fucked-up family with no money, and here was this good boy, handsome and brave and sexy, and he wanted *me*. He loved *me*. Reed's family ain't rich, but they're close-knit and kind and they welcomed me. I was thrilled to get out from under the Lester shadow.

"I wanted it so bad I didn't read any of the signs he didn't. Even when he enlisted, he fed me bullshit about building a career so he could provide for our future family and I ate it right up."

"That doesn't sound like you, that girl who just wants to be somebody's wife."

"I know."

That girl feels like a different person to me, too, like her memories been planted in my brain, but I know I was her once. Or wanted to be.

"Reed was a life raft," I say. "So I grabbed him."

"What about now?"

"Breaks my heart to think of him in pain. But I don't think it changes things between us."

We sit there for a while on the cove's rocky shore, not talking, just holding each other. Then Brayton says: "I talked to Jack about your land."

"You did? I thought you said—"

"I know. Wasn't easy, let me tell you. But I didn't know what else to do to say I was sorry."

I put a hand on his arm. "Brayton, why are you really up at the lake this summer?"

He stares out over the cove. The water's a silver shiver in the moonlight.

"I got into some trouble with a couple guys at my school," Brayton tells me. "Jack told me I had two choices—spend the summer on my aunt's ranch down in Texas, or move up here where he could 'keep an eye on me.' I picked the one that sounded like less work."

"What kind of trouble?"

"Stupid shit. Partying and, like, drunken mischief. We snuck into the country club golf course one night and passed out on the eleventh hole."

I laugh.

"Yeah, the membership committee didn't find it quite as hilarious as you do."

"Sorry, I didn't mean to laugh. Keep going, I'm listening."

"I mean, there's really nothing to tell. My grades were in the toilet. I got kicked off the soccer team for failing a random drug test. We took one of my friends' dad's classic cars on a joyride and drove it into a ditch. That was fun—we got arrested for that one," he says, clenching his fist like he wants to throttle his past self.

"They press charges?"

"No, but Jack was so pissed I thought he was going to give himself a stroke. He'd pulled a bunch of strings to get me into the college he and my mom wanted me to go to and I was ruining it. My mom was a wreck, and because I'm an idiot, when she asked me why I kept doing these things, I said it was because I was bored. So Jack was like, 'You're bored? I'll show you bored.' And he sent me up here. Put a GPS tracker on my phone and car so he'll know if I try to leave. How's that for creepy and controlling?"

"Sounds like he cares about you, though. Least he wants you to be safe and go to college."

"He doesn't care about me. He barely even knows me. He cares about how what I do makes him look. I'm not denying it was stupid. Wasn't even fun most of the time. And those guys were dickheads."

I lay my head on his shoulder. "You didn't do it 'cause you were bored."

He sighs. "I did it because I was lonely. Isn't that pathetic?"

"No. I been there," I tell him, thinking of my friendship with Ash. One of the worst decisions of my life, ever giving that asshole the time of day.

"Joke's on Jack, because I met you practically the first night I got here and I haven't been lonely or bored since."

It surprises me how happy I am to hear that, so happy I blush a little. Good thing it's too dark for him to tell.

"So what did Jack say about the land?"

"Oh, right. He says they bought it."

"That just ain't true." Only person could've sold it to them was Dad, and he'd never.

"I kept my mouth shut about why I was asking, that I know you, because I didn't want to cause any trouble for you. Told him I was just interested in the business—he's always trying to bond with me over his work."

"He tell you anything else?"

"Not about your land. But Sammy," Brayton says, frowning. "I think the Tullers might have something to do with it. Jack said they were having trouble getting people to sell up, so they hired a local group to convince them. He was sketchy on the details, but he looked pretty pleased with himself. Said they were the type people'd think twice about saying no to."

"Sure sounds like the Tullers."

I can see it all so easy. Johnny and Luger show up at your place, offer you a hefty sum to pack up and go, then make threats if you refuse. They probably went after everyone, including Karen and Wayne—might explain why they were so twitchy on the subject.

But Dad's different. The Tullers *owe* Dad, for how he never ratted on them.

Except maybe they fear him, too, for the same reason.

So maybe their offer to him was special. Maybe he gives over our land, and they help him with something. A month ago, I would've said he'd ask to make this whole custody thing with Rainne go away. Now I got no idea what to think.

Maybe Denver's right. Maybe I didn't know him at all.

"Why are you doing this?" I ask Brayton. "Helping me, I mean."

"I think it's pretty obvious."

"You like me."

Brayton nods.

"But there's lots of people I like I wouldn't go out on a limb for. I don't want it to be 'cause you feel sorry for me."

"Of course I feel sorry for you."

My cheeks get hot. "Well, don't. I don't want your pity."

"It's not pity. Jesus, Sammy. How far are you going to go to prove you don't need anybody before you get that's not how things work? I know you're scared. I'm not going to pretend that just because I care about you means I should fix everything for you, or that I even can. But give me credit for being a decent enough guy to want to try my best."

Sometimes I wish Brayton wasn't so decent. Be easier to resist liking him so much if he was an asshole, easier to say goodbye when summer's over. Easier to wipe him right out of my heart once he's gone.

I stare across the water to the mouth of the cove, the joint where it meets the lake. Night falls hard here. When I was a kid I asked Dad where the sun went when it got dark and he told me it was his job to take it out of the sky at bedtime and keep it safe in his pocket till morning. I asked to see, not quite believing, and he refused to show me.

Then one night when it was time for bed, the pocket of his sweatshirt gaped open as he leaned in for a good-night kiss, smelling of smoke and chewing gum, and a stream of light burst out. I was amazed, but I didn't say anything, convinced now he was telling the truth and knowing I wasn't supposed to have seen.

After he went to prison, I made the mistake of telling my mother this story.

You know that was a flashlight, right? she snapped. *He tricked you, Sammy. He's always tricking people.*

"Why can't I seem to scare you away?" I ask Brayton now.

"Honestly? I have no fucking clue."

I grab him by the front of his shirt, leaning in close.

"Can't fool me, Brayton Foster," I say, brushing my lips across his. "You got a heart after all."

"Maybe once I did," he whispers. "But I think someone stole it."

"Now, who would go and do a thing like that?"

He grabs my mouth with his, drawing me into a kiss that deepens like the lake: slow and steady, sloping gently downward, then with a sharp and sudden drop that makes me feel weightless and weak.

He grips my waist and pulls me into his lap. I straddle his hips with my knees and wrap my arms 'round his neck. His hair is soft as corn silk. It falls through my fingers like fine sand.

Brayton's hands slide down to my hips and he plays with the hem of my tank top. I lift my arms and he slips the top over my head. It's a relief to be rid of my sopping-wet clothes. He eases my skirt up and runs his palms across the tops of my thighs. A happy sound rumbles in the back of his throat. I bend to kiss that throat, right above his collarbone.

"You," he says, tilting his head so our eyes meet.

Sitting like this, half up on my knees while he leans back, I got the advantage of height, looming over him like an ancient Ozark oak. Seeing the tenderness in his eyes, I realize I got the power to hurt him. Whatever it is he sees in me, he wants it, and only I can take it from him. Or give it to him.

I smile at him. "What about me?"

He shakes his head. "Just…*you*."

My skin is wet beneath his warm fingertips. Water runs off my hair and onto his shoulders, his neck, his face. There's some local lore about water sprites, fairies brought over from the old country who take the shape of women and lure men into the deepest parts of the lake to feed the ancient beast that lives there. That's what I must look like from far away, a spirit risen from beneath the waves to drag this boy down where no one will ever find him.

There's a feeling of power comes with it, but when he says *you*, I sense it flowing out of me, too, an alternating current that locks us together.

I put my hand on his chest, over his heart.

"*You*," I say. I cup the back of his head like it's something fragile.

"*You*," he says again, like it's the only word he knows. I nod and kiss his open, speechless mouth.

Brayton moves his face away from mine and presses his lips softly to the tops of my breasts. I shiver. He unclasps my bra and tosses it aside. I should worry someone will see us doing this, but I don't. The lake is large and full of secret places no one ever looks. Places to hide bodies, alive and not.

"You're so sexy," Brayton says, bracing himself on his hands to get a good view of me in the moonlight. The water laps right up to our feet, tiny waves licking our toes like kitten tongues.

"God, the things I want to do to you make even me blush," he says.

I laugh. "Don't think God'll like hearing you talk like that."

"What do you mean?" Brayton grins. "This is what He made us for. Now come here. Let me show you what I can do."

He tugs me closer, farther up his lap. I really feel I *have* seduced him, and got no regrets about it. We done things before, but never gone as far as I know we're gonna go tonight.

I don't want this to change nothing between us, but I think

it might just. I want this boy. I *like* this boy. I wanna make him feel less alone.

I lift my head for a second and catch glimpse of that cliff where I told Reed I was pregnant. I didn't know a thing about my body back then. Brayton's got a condom—we're being safe. When I remember the Sammy I was before, the one huddled over a toilet at the high school with a pee stick in her hand, disbelieving and terrified, I'm sad for her, and angry at the world that let her down.

But I'm also grateful to her. She went through what she went through so I could be different.

Just hope the Sammy I'm becoming will feel the same way about who I am now.

"How about you let me show you what *I* can do," I say.

I push him so he's lying flat along the pebbled shore and shift my hips. He groans and splays his hand against my stomach.

"I'm counting on it," he says.

CHAPTER FIFTEEN

I call Agent Pilson the next morning and tell him what Brayton said about Sweet Home, how they might've paid the Tullers to coerce local landowners into selling up.

"Are you going to give me some names?" Pilson asks.

"Yeah. I think I can do that."

"I've got some information for you, too. But you're not going to like it."

"Just tell me," I say.

"Better to show you. You going to be at home for a while?"

"I can be here whenever. You sure you wanna be showing your face in these parts?"

"I know how to be invisible when it suits me. I'll be there in an hour."

Agent Pilson shows up driving an unmarked vehicle, wearing jeans and a T-shirt. He don't look like a cop at all, which is a relief. People find out I'm entertaining the law up here, they're gonna have questions.

Denver was supposed to go fishing with Holler, but it's been fixing to rain all morning. I ask him to stay home and he does. We ain't talked about our fight, but we don't gotta. He's my brother. I love him no matter what, even if he can be a dick sometimes.

When we're all sitting at the tiny kitchen table, Agent Pilson pulls a crumpled file out of his back pocket and sets it in front of us.

"What are we looking at?" Denver asks, picking it up like he thinks it might explode.

"The red dots are all the cell phone towers in the area," Pilson explains. "You called your father fourteen times that night, and each time the call pinged off this tower here."

He points to a red dot on the razor's edge of Tehlicoh.

"If he was headed out of town, the calls should've bounced off other towers en route, but they didn't. They all pinged this tower right here in town till they stopped coming."

"So you're saying he was here the whole time. In town."

I ain't stupid. I know what that means. If Dad never left town, he's probably dead. All the hope I been holding on to bleeds right out of my heart.

Pilson nods. "Sure seems that way. Him, or his cell. He could've ditched that one somewhere in town and bought a burner somewhere. We've canvassed all the stores in the area that carry disposable phones and nobody remembers Bobby Ray coming in. No security footage of him, either."

"But he could still be all right. Right?"

Almost sounds like I'm begging.

"It's possible," he says carefully. "His bank account hasn't been touched, though. No activity on his debit card. And he hasn't made any big withdrawals in months—hasn't been anything to withdraw. If you're right about him having a lot of mystery money on him, that might be all he needs. But for a person to not show up electronically for weeks…these days, it's unusual."

"Here's another odd thing," Pilson says. He points to a line on Dad's phone records. "Sammy, that text you got came in near ten o'clock, but before that the last time he sent an outgoing message, or a call, or even answered a call, was a little after six when he and Denver spoke for three minutes."

"He call Rainne at all that day to let her know he was coming over?" I ask.

"No," Pilson says.

"So he never went," Denver says. "Never even planned to go."

"I don't know," I say. "If he'd told Rainne he was on his way, she wouldn't've been there when he pulled up. Best way to actually catch her at home would be *not* to tell her. He could've still meant to, but got…sidetracked, or something."

Except it was past eight when Ash cornered me at the Deck. If the Tullers had gotten to Dad before then, why bother? They must've nabbed him later, so where'd he go after he talked to Denver?

Denver thinks this over some. "Maybe. So where do we go from here?" He looks a bit green.

"Well, it's still not my case," Pilson says. "And while your information about LakeLife commissioning the Tullers as their negotiators is interesting, it's not enough for me to get involved at a more jurisdictional level. What we need is a crime scene."

A *crime scene*. Pilson thinks somewhere out there is a kill site, or a body dump where the Tullers disposed of Dad like so much trash.

My mind travels to some remote, deserted place, over-grown with weeds…plenty of places like that 'round here. We searched a lot of them, but I ain't fool enough to think the Tullers ain't got hidey-holes all over this county, known only to them.

"I do have some good news for you. I called in a favor, asked an old PI friend of mine to keep watch over your sister, make sure the Tullers aren't hassling her or your stepmom. Rainne's got Decca stashed at her mother's house, and there's been no sign of Johnny or anyone else who isn't supposed to be there."

I rub my wrist anxiously. "I wish I could see her."

"He took some pictures, if you want to look at those." Pil-son hands me a stack of glossy photos.

My heart aches at the sight of Decca. I'm glad she's safe, I am, but she looks so sad and lonely, playing in MaryEllen's front yard by herself.

"Denver, would you look at this?" I pass him a photo of Decca cuddling up on a stuffed animal.

He squints at it. "So?"

"Denver," I say softly. "I think that's Waldo."

"You sure?" He brings the picture closer to his face. "It's just a gray blur."

"No," I gotta admit. "I ain't sure."

Outside, a clap of thunder rolls and the sky opens up, spill-ing itself over the lake. The rain clatters down on the trailer's metal roof like a waterfall of glass beads.

"You believe Rainne about your dad never showing up at her house that night?" Pilson asks.

"I did, but how else would Decca have Waldo?"

"I can't question her yet," Pilson says. "But Johnny Tuller's got his eye on Rainne and her kid. Might mean she knows something more than she's saying about the reason Bobby Ray left town. Might mean she knows what the Tullers are up to."

"Her brother Ash runs with them," I say. "He could've told her what was going down."

"I'll look into it. As for where y'all should go from here, I think it'd be best if you tried to live your lives as normally as possible. It could take weeks or months to turn up any solid leads. Hopefully it won't, but experience tells me otherwise. These things take time, and I got my hands tied."

"We understand," Denver says.

"Sammy?"

I nod.

By the time Denver and I show the detective out, the rain has slowed to a steady drip and the sun's starting to peek out from behind the clouds. Pilson pauses on the porch and taps the doorjamb.

"Which of you's the superstitious one?" he asks, pointing to three short nails hammered into the wood in the shape of a triangle.

"Never seen that before," I say.

"Me neither," Denver says. The hair at the back of my neck stands on end.

"You know what that is, don't you?" We shake our heads. "Old backwoods conjure. You got a yarb doctor in the family?"

My brother laughs. "There's no such thing."

"Is it dark?" I ask. I ain't the type to believe in magic, but lots of things in life can't be explained, and there's nothing like growing up surrounded by deep forest and ancient rock to make you wonder what strange and supernatural secrets they might be hiding.

"Not this one," Pilson says. "If you believe the tales, it's supposed to ward off bad spirits, protect the people inside the house. Maybe your daddy put it there."

"I doubt it," Denver says. "Only spirits Dad believes in are the ones in the liquor cabinet."

I run my fingers over the nails. Could've been bought in any hardware store. If they got power, they ain't showy about it.

Dad might not've believed in spirits, but he *did* like legends and tradition. Just 'cause Denver and I never noticed the conjure don't mean it ain't always been here.

"If it's supposed to protect us, it's doing a shitty job," I say.

"That's the tricky thing about magic—it's got its own mind about things."

"You really buy this stuff?"

Pilson shrugs.

"My grandmother was a seeker, could find any lost thing you were searching for. Claimed she had a touch of the sight. Maybe it was just good intuition, but her knack for finding things was downright spooky at times, and you can't argue with results. I like to keep an open mind about everything. I suggest y'all think about doing the same."

I gotta get a new job, and I gotta do it fast. The bills are stacking up, and Denver and I don't got the money to pay them. I don't need luxury, but I like electricity.

Brayton and I spend most of the day driving around the lake looking for places that are hiring. It don't go too well. Eventually, I ask him to drive me home.

Halfway up the road that threads through the hills, right

where Satan's Chin juts out over the cove, something's happening. We see the lights as soon as we round the corner—red, white and blue, flashing soundlessly in the dark, which can only mean one thing: police.

Brayton slows to pass them, but instinct makes me scan the faces on the shoulder and I pick out Denver's.

"Stop, Brayton! Stop!"

I jump out of the car before Brayton can even put it in Park and run to my brother. My head is full of wild thoughts, but ain't no time to wrangle them into an idea of what's going on. I only know it's important, and possibly the start of everything, the beginning of answers.

"What's going on?"

"I've been trying to call you," Denver says. He sounds hurt, and angry. There ain't been a moment so far this summer when I didn't feel like I was letting him down.

Denver sees Brayton, and he looks at me like, *I see what you were doing.* I ignore him and turn to another familiar face: Pete.

"What's down there?" I ask.

"Coleman had one of his SCUBA classes out here this afternoon doing their final certification test and they found something in the cove."

"Found what?"

The image of Dad's bloated body floats through my head. Only yesterday, I jumped off Satan's Chin for the first time, had sex with Brayton, made promises to myself. The idea Dad could've been at the bottom that whole time, waiting for me to find him, but I chose to swim in the other direction, makes me feel so guilty.

Don't matter that, if it's true, he was already past helping.

"A truck. Don't get your hopes up, Sammy. There's all kinds of junk down there—"

"I wanna see."

Pete don't have the heart to stop me, which is how I know he's full of shit—it's Dad's truck, all right. It's gotta be.

"All right," he says. "But be careful."

Brayton grabs my arm. At first I think he's trying to hold me back, but when I look at him over my shoulder he nods and I realize he's holding on so I won't fall.

I creep toward the edge of the cliff. Thirty feet below, huddled in small groups on the rocky shore, dozens of men dressed in reflective gear and hard hats watch from under a spotlight as something enormous is winched out of the water.

It's Dad's red beater, covered in muck and scum, rising out of the lake like a baby being birthed.

"That's Dad's truck, Sammy," Denver says. He sounds like a drowning man. His breath glugs out of his lungs like he's taking on water.

Brayton's fingers tighten and he hoists me away from the edge. I press my face into his shoulder, too freaked out to keep looking.

"He's not in there," someone says. I look up and see Agent Pilson standing a few feet away.

"Are you even supposed to be here?"

"I put a BOLO out on Bobby Ray's license plate," Pilson says. "Convinced my superiors the disappearance of a former Tuller lieutenant in the position to inform on Redbreast merited OSBI intervention. Olina's not too happy about it, but there's not anything she can do now we've got the truck. His cell's in there."

This should feel like a win, but it don't. "He never made it out of town, did he?"

Denver squeezes his eyes shut and turns away from us. His shoulders heave, just once, with the force of a barely suppressed sob. Brayton puts his arms 'round me, but I'm too numb to cry.

"I don't know," Pilson says softly. "But it's looking less and less likely."

We all stand there in silence, watching the recovery team yank my father's drowned car from the sucking mouth of the lake.

As onlookers start to leave, I'm almost positive I catch a glimpse of Gypsum Tuller's frizzy red head bobbing through the crowd like a cattail in the breeze. But I blink and she's gone and I start to wonder if I even saw her at all.

CHAPTER SIXTEEN

"I don't have to go," Brayton says, putting his hands on my hips and pulling me to him. "I could make up some excuse to stay here."

I shake my head. "That's stupid. You been planning this trip since you got here. Wouldn't be fair for me to ask you to stick around just to watch me mope."

"But if you did ask, I would." Brayton makes a face. "I don't really want to go back to Oklahoma City, anyway."

"You gonna see any of those guys you got in trouble with?"

"No."

"Might be nice, then. Going home for a spell."

"Oklahoma City isn't my home. I'm from Texas, remember?"

"But you're going to Texas, too." Brayton's headed south to his aunt's small farm outside of Dallas for his grandfather's eightieth birthday party, then back up to the lake via OKC to drop off his mom.

"Middle-of-nowhere Texas."

"Look around," I say. "Lake Bittersweet's pretty much the definition of middle of nowhere."

"Yeah, but at Lake Bittersweet, there's you."

He squeezes my waist playfully and smiles. Then his expression darkens.

"I don't like the idea of leaving while all this stuff's going on."

"Except there ain't *nothing* going on."

It's been weeks since they found Dad's car and all Pilson will tell me is that the investigation is "in progress."

"I'm about to go stir-crazy myself," I say. "Can *I* come with *you*? I never been to Texas. Or Oklahoma City, for that matter."

"No way," Brayton says sharply. It hurts more than I would've expected.

"I was kidding."

"Sorry, I didn't mean it like that. I just… You'd hate it. And I like you too much to put you through ten hours in a car with my mom."

"Uh-huh."

I almost ask him if he don't want me along 'cause he's ashamed, but I'm too afraid of the answer to dare.

"You better get if you wanna make it to Dallas before nightfall," I say.

Brayton puts his arms 'round me. I resist at first, 'cause I'm feeling a bit stung, but he nuzzles my neck with his nose and presses sweet, soft kisses to my throat and I melt into him, can't help it.

"*You*," he whispers.

I take his face in my hands and press my mouth to his. "Don't be a stranger, now."

He nods. "Text or call me if anything happens."

We kiss one more time, then he tears himself away from me with a groan and gets in his car. I stand at the end of the drive-way until he turns the corner, then walk back up to the house.

When I went out to meet Brayton, Denver was napping on the couch. Now he's in the front room, throwing clothes into a battered duffel from a basket of clean laundry on the floor.

"What are you doing?" I ask him.

He tosses me a bag. "We're going to stay with Mom for a few days. Get packed."

"Oh *hell* no. Go by yourself."

I throw the duffel back at him. He lets it drop to the floor and kicks it so it lands near my feet.

"You gotta come with me. Mom just called—Polk took a spill off his tractor and broke his damn arm. She needs help around the farm, and I can't do it all on my own."

"She don't want me there, Denver."

"Yeah, she does, and you want to see her just as bad but both of you have that stupid pride holding you back. I'm sick of y'all acting like you can't ever forgive each other, and I am *sick* of sitting 'round this house waiting for God knows what awful news to come walking through the door, so *please* will you listen to me for once in your life and put some clothes in a goddamn bag?"

"How you planning on getting down to Checotah, anyhow?"

"You saw the car outside?"

"That's Holler's car."

"Not anymore. He sold it to us," Denver says.

"Sold? We don't got any money."

Denver shrugs. "He says I can pay it off in installments."

"What, like zero dollars a month? 'Cause that's about all we can afford."

"It's a pretty generous payment plan," Denver says. "Come on. We're losing daylight and I hate the roads around here at night."

These weeks since Dad's been gone have changed my brother. He's lost weight, let his hair grow out ragged. There are dark hollows under his eyes.

Before, Denver's nose was always in a book, but I ain't seen him pick one up in weeks, or listen to music, or watch TV. All he does is work at the marina, fish a little, sleep and worry.

"I know I been ornery," he says. "But I'm looking out for you, Sammy. That's what you do for family."

I lift the duffel bag in my hand. "This is you looking out?"

"She loves you. It'll be good for you to see her. Remind yourself what you've still got."

I shake my head. "I can't, Denny. Please don't make me face her."

He stares at me, like he thinks if he don't give me permission to stay I'll give in and go with him. But in the end, he's the one who gives.

"Fine," he says. "Do whatever you want. I'm not your minder."

I know it's my choice, and maybe I don't got a right to feel this way, but as I watch him walk out the door, I feel like he's turning his back on me. Like he's leaving me behind, just like Dad.

And I get so scared that, like Dad, he ain't never coming back.

The house is too quiet, too empty with Denver gone, and if I'm honest I miss him almost as much as I miss Brayton— almost.

Brayton calls a couple times, leaves a few messages, bombards me with a string of texts. He's bored out of his mind in Dallas. His aunt keeps chickens, exotic ones with bizarre plumage. He keeps sending me photos captioned Alien chicken!!! and Just waiting for one of these weird motherfuckers to lay a square egg.

I lay on my back in bed each night, dusty feet on clean sheets, typing at him with a stupid grin on my face. But every morning around sunrise, just as I'm about to doze off, thoughts of Reed flutter through my brain. I wonder what time zone he's in, if he's awake. How much pain he's in, and if anybody's holding his hand.

As the days march on, I hear from Brayton less and less. First I chalk it up to the distractions of family, but near the end of the week he heads on up to Oklahoma City and stops responding.

I scroll through our messages, looking for a clue as to why the boy who texts You at least once a day has gone silent. Maybe his battery died. Maybe he lost his phone. Maybe… something bad happened to him.

I push that thought away and keep trying, sending jokes I think he'll laugh at, silly stories about the lake, but as the time stamps get stale I realize there ain't nothing wrong. He just don't wanna talk to me.

Safe in OKC is the last thing he texts me, when I tell him, against my better judgment, that I'm worried. Nothing after that. Well, I ain't gonna beg him. Still got my pride.

Whatever you're up to better be worth it, I say in my last text. Cause this is bullshit.

Then I turn my phone off. Let him worry for a change.

One night, I wake up from a dead sleep to a loud crash. I

sit bolt upright in bed like somebody done smacked me awake and breathe deep to calm the frantic pounding of my heart.

Somebody's here, I think, panicked. Ash Boford's face flashes through my head.

I fetch Dad's shotgun from under the bed where I been keeping it and creep into the hall with a shaky finger on the trigger, making my slow way through the now-silent trailer.

Somebody pulled out the kitchen drawers, dumped them out on the yellowed, peeling linoleum. They've ransacked Dad's bureau in the front room, too, upended all the couch cushions, knocked the coffee table on its side. I try to make as little noise as possible, like I'm hunting deer in the woods, but the floors creak and every step I take sounds like it's coming through a speaker.

Denver closed his door when he left, but it ain't closed now. I nose it open farther with the barrel of the shotgun. I hear the sound of heavy breathing, but can't tell if it's mine or the intruder's.

"Who's there?" I call out, but don't get no answer.

A figure darts at me from out of the darkness, grabs the barrel with a big gloved hand and gives the gun a good hard shove. The stock clips my chin hard and I stumble back, tripping over a piece of loose carpet and accidentally squeezing the trigger, sending a shotgun blast straight through the ceiling.

The back of my head slams hard against the bathroom doorjamb and I crumple to the ground. Ain't no light to see by except the moonbeams pouring in through the window in the back door. Pain and shock pull a dark cloak over me, but before I black out, my terrified brain makes a list of everything I know I saw:

Big guy. Dark gloves. Ski mask over his face. Black combat boots that narrowly miss crushing my fingers as he takes off running.

And maybe the worst thing of all: a vulture tattoo on his right bicep, just like the one on Dad's.

Denver eyes the hole in the ceiling. "Well, next time it rains, we're screwed."

"Think if we patch it with a tarp and some duct tape, it'll hold?" I ask him.

He looks at me sideways and shrugs. Kinda doesn't matter. We got no money to fix it. Denver had to borrow off Holler just to get the locks changed.

"Here, Sammy," Mom says, dropping two aspirin in my palm. She came up with Denver soon as I called him.

She puts her hands on her hips, faking a stern calm, but her chin's trembling with the effort of keeping tears in.

"Y'all need to come back with me right now. Can't stand the thought of you living here, after what's happened."

"No way," I snap. Who does she think she is, telling me what to do?

She should know better than to think I'd ever leave my own home. Ain't the first time I've refused her.

I swallow the aspirin dry. Head's been pounding nonstop since I woke up on the floor this morning. Feels like it might split in two. Mom's hovering ain't helping.

Mom sighs. "Why you always gotta be so difficult? What if whoever broke in comes back?"

"Won't happen," I say. "What they're looking for ain't here. They know that now."

"They?"

"The Tullers."

Mom stiffens. She's more scared of the Tullers than she is of the devil, with good reason—she was here through the worst of it with Dad. And, unlike me, she remembers it all.

Police were here earlier to take my statement and dust for prints, do whatever it is that passes for investigation in these parts. Olina called this afternoon to tell me all the Tullers that fit my description had alibis for last night—a lie, of course, but long as they stick to their story it can't be disproved.

Plenty of people 'round here got that vulture tat. You ever think, Sammy, that it might've been Bobby Ray you saw? she asked. *He's got it, too.*

That made me so angry. Why would Dad rob his own house?

"What do you think it was they were looking for?" Mom asks, soft as a whisper.

Denver and I exchange a look.

"Money," he says.

He explains about the ten thousand. All the blood drains out of Mom's face.

"Bobby Ray," she says. "What've you gone and done?"

I keep waiting for Mom to go on home, but she don't. Instead she stays and helps us clean up the house, put everything back where it was. Then she performs a miracle in the kitchen, cooking us a real meal out of whatever random crap we got in the fridge and cupboards.

After dinner, Denver disappears into his room and shuts the door, leaving Mom and I alone together. She asks me about Reed. I tell her what I know, hoping that'll be the end of it, but she lingers on the subject, repeating questions I already answered like she thinks that'll change the story.

"It's fucking tragic, Mom," I say, lighting a cigarette to cover the shaking in my hands. It started this morning and ain't stopped yet.

"I told you everything I know. He's still being treated in Germany. Ain't heard nothing new."

"Don't smoke in the house," Mom says, but she fetches a saucer for me to ash in.

"He didn't have to go and join the Army, did he?" I stub out my cigarette and light another. "I'm sick of people treating me like some widow. He ain't dead, and we broke up anyhow."

Mom sits back in her chair and stares out the window. She never did know what to do with me after I reached a certain age, never understood how a daughter of hers could grow up so wild.

Probably why she always liked Reed so much. Thought he'd tame me. Broke her heart when he left me, in a much different way than it broke mine.

"Maybe this is a second chance," Mom says. "Maybe you can get back together."

Like she thinks what happened can be undone if I just hook up with Reed again. Like she thinks that'll save me from the special sort of hell her god's got reserved for teenage girls who get abortions.

"Mom, he dumped my ass. Dumped my *pregnant* ass."

She shakes her head. "Let's not discuss all that hard business again."

"Why? It's what you're thinking about. My 'mistake.'"

"Well, what am I supposed to do?" she snaps.

"Accept it! It was my choice to make, and I made it."

"Yes, you're so very *liberated*, Sammy."

She looks down at her hands. They're dry and scarred and calloused from years of farmwork.

"Don't you understand what a sin you've committed?" she asks.

"See, this is why I stayed at the lake when you moved." I seethe. "Dad ain't perfect, but he helped me when I needed help."

I couldn't afford the procedure, but I found a nonprofit that agreed to pay for it, and Dad drove me clear across the state to get it done.

He never said a word to me about it except to ask what I needed him to do. It's the sort of thing I think of every time somebody acts like I ought to give up on him. Like he ain't worth looking for.

"I would've helped you take care of the baby. You didn't have to do what you did."

I don't respond. Ain't nothing I could say that would make her understand.

"Did you ask him before you did it? Did he even know till it was done?"

I bite my lip and it starts to bleed. Remembering all this is so hard.

"No," I tell her. "I never asked him. And now he hates me, and you hate me...but I still think I did the right thing."

Mom's anger cracks then and her expression softens.

"Oh, Samwich, I never hated you. I was just really devastated for you."

I sink my cigarette into my water glass and rub my eyes with the heels of my hands. "Me, too. Like you said, it was a bad business."

"I know how worried you are about Bobby Ray," Mom says. "But these things you been doing, putting yourself in danger, spying on the Tullers, riling Ash Boford up...honey, you gotta be careful. Don't make the same mistakes your daddy did, getting involved with those people. They're more dangerous than you know."

I play with my lighter, passing it between my fingers like Dad used to do with coins.

"They found his car, at the bottom of Satan's Chin Cove," I say.

"I know. Denny told me."

"Mama," I say. My voice wobbles. "He ain't coming back this time."

"I know, baby," she says, stroking my hand. "I know."

In the middle of the night, I wake to an unfamiliar sound, and I think: *They're back. They're gonna kill me this time.*

I force the sleep from my brain and reach for the gun under my bed, but then I catch sight of a face at my window and sag in relief. It's just Brayton, tapping on the glass.

I throw up the sash.

"What are you doing here?" I ask him. "It's the middle of the night."

"I know," he says. "But I just got back and I had to see you. Can I come in?"

I almost tell him no—I'm so mad at him—but I'm freaked out, too, after what happened last night, and I know I'll feel safer having another warm body in the room.

I let him in through the back door and, after checking a couple of times to make sure it's really locked, I lead him to my bedroom.

Neither of us bothers to turn the lights on. Something about how late it is, how velvet soft the darkness, puts a damper on my anger. I'm so happy he's here. I missed him.

I sit down on my bed and watch him. He stays in the door-way, leans against the wall.

"I tried calling," he says.

I fish my phone out from under the covers and see he did—three times. Two voice mails. Five texts.

"It was on silent. What's your excuse?"

"Stupidity?"

The shadows in the room make it hard to read the expression on his face. He sounds tired, and sort of sad, though I can't think why.

What happened to you, Brayton, while you were away from me? I wonder.

"You gotta give me more than that," I tell him. "How busy you been that you can't send a text?"

Brayton walks to the foot of the bed and puts a knee down on my mattress. "I wasn't busy. I was just…confused, I guess."

"About me?"

He shakes his head. "You're like the only thing in the whole world I'm not confused about."

"Then what is it?"

"Texas was okay, but being in Oklahoma City for the first time in months was weird. Jack was there, and I wasn't expecting that. He found out about that party I threw and he was pissed. Said I hadn't learned a thing and I was ungrateful and maybe he should take away my car, ship me off to my aunt's farm until school starts up. I had to beg him not to—my mom got in the middle and it was a total disaster. Tons of yelling, my mom cried a *lot*—"

Brayton sighs. "I hate being dependent on him. And I hate even more that I'd rather put up with it than have him cut me off. Is that awful?"

"No. If I had the sort of dad who could pay for the things I need and *would* pay for the things I want, I think I'd put up with a lot," I say. "I just never had that option."

He rubs his arms like he's cold even though it's boiling in this tiny room. "I know."

I put my hand against the side of his face and trace the ridge of his cheekbone with my thumb. He leans into my touch.

"Thing is," I say, "parents are all up in your shit whether they pay your way or not."

"He's not my dad," Brayton says bitterly.

"You really drove all the way up here in the middle of the night? Those roads are dark. You could've gotten into an accident."

"I needed you," he says, and there's a roughness to his voice, tells me exactly how he means it.

"Come here, then." I shift back on the bed to make room for him.

He crawls over and pulls me close, kissing me hard and frantic. Feels like I'm being punished for something, and thanked at the very same time. He slips his tongue into my mouth and I sigh, which makes him bolder.

My nerves all fire up at once as he puts his hands on me. It's been too long since I seen him, since I felt his skin against mine. Think I'd be just as happy right now if all he did was hold my hand and not let go.

There's a voice in the back of my head, tells me to be cold to him, push him away, make him suffer for leaving me to doubt and worry so many days, but I want him near. And where's it written I gotta sacrifice everything, all the time?

Brayton threads his fingers through my hair, pulling it tight. Sends a bolt of pain down my neck.

"Be gentle," I say.

Worry flickers over his face. He strokes the back of my head softly, trailing his fingertips over the bump I got when I fell.

"Are you okay? What happened?"

"Not now. I'll tell you in the morning." Can't let anything ruin this, not now he's finally here.

"Sammy—"

I cut him off with a kiss, curving my body around his, wanting to get closer. He lifts my tank top off, throws it on the floor. I tug his T-shirt over his head and unbutton his jeans with one hand as the other skates over the flat planes of his chest, stroking his warm skin with gentle fingers.

Soon we're both naked, panting in the watery light, and he's on top of me, a welcome weight on my belly and hips.

"God," he says, gazing down at me with a dumbstruck look. "You."

Words are hard to find, so I don't try—or maybe I'm just beating back the words I wanna say. He trails kisses down my throat and between my breasts before meeting my mouth again. Every touch and gesture feels urgent, like he thinks if he stops, I'll disappear.

"Brayton," I say, putting a hand on his breastbone. "Condom."

He pauses, like he's gonna suggest maybe we don't need one.

"I ain't on the pill and we don't need no accidents."

He groans and rolls away from me, fetches a silver packet from his wallet and sorts himself, then sorts us both. I'm on my back and he's got himself propped on his elbows, hovering over me. I kiss the underside of his chin and my lips come away wet.

"Are you crying?"

Brayton shakes his head and adjusts his hips. A shock wave rolls through me. I close my eyes and arch my back and he buries his face in my shoulder.

"I love you so much, Sammy," he says.

"It's all right," I say, stroking his back. I can't say *I love you, too.* Can't imagine myself taking that leap just yet, not after what happened the last time I loved someone.

"I saw your text and I was afraid we were over. I can't take feeling like I let you down." His voice breaks. I kiss one corner of his mouth, then the other.

"It's okay," I tell him. "We're okay."

"I'm sorry I didn't answer your calls," Brayton whispers, his voice strung tight like a crossbow.

I gotta force myself to concentrate on what he's saying, 'cause all I wanna do is feel him.

"I had to take care of something," he says. "It was important. For us, it was important."

Whatever it is, if it's shaken him so badly, then I don't wanna know. I brush the tears out from under his eyes with my thumbs.

Seeing guys cry usually freaks me out, but my heart swells up like a tick. I was wrong about him. He ain't just a charming player like he comes off at first. His hidden pockets got some of the same worries and fears mine do. Our hollow places are shaped just alike.

I could've been anyone with him, that first night we met, played any part, but I was myself instead. I showed myself to him. Wasn't easy, but I think I made the right choice.

At least later, when he remembers, he'll remember *me*, not a person I never was.

CHAPTER SEVENTEEN

I wake up to the sudden jolt of someone kicking the bed. When I open my eyes, I find Denver glaring at me with one giant foot on the mattress.

"What the hell, Denver?"

I scramble to cover myself with a sheet, accidentally revealing a naked Brayton to Denver's angry gaze. I throw a sheet over him while he mutters something in his sleep.

He nestles closer. I put a hand on his head, sweeping back the hair that's fallen in his eyes, turn away from Denver.

Denver nudges Brayton with the toe of his sneaker. Brayton opens his eyes with a start.

"What're you doing here, man?" Denver demands.

"Get out," I say. "Get out of here *now*."

"Hey," Brayton says, rubbing his face. "What's going on?"

A hedge of bushy red hair bobs into view as Gypsum pokes her head into the room.

"I'm so sorry, Sammy," she says. "Didn't think he'd react this way, swear to *Gawd*."

"What the hell is this? Who the fuck do you guys think you are?"

"Who's Jennifer?" Denver asks.

"I got no clue," I say, but Brayton sits up straight and I realize Denver ain't talking to me.

"I can explain," Brayton says.

Everybody starts jabbering at once, but it's all noise, nothing sticks. Gypsum barges into the room and shoves a smartphone into my hands. It's hers, clearly, covered with a pink rhinestone-studded case and with a selfie set as her background.

"What am I supposed to do with this?"

"Press the blue square," she says, leaning over to show me, like I'm stupid, like I don't know how apps work or what the navy one with the white lowercase *f* on it does. I slap her hand away.

Brayton grabs at the phone and says, "Wait, Sammy, don't," but I push him back and press the Facebook icon. Now I'm curious, more 'cause of his reaction than anything Denver and Gypsum said.

Brayton's profile pops up. Don't see much worth making a fuss over, just a photo of Brayton in a Thunder T-shirt and black baseball cap, wearing those expensive sunglasses and grinning.

I look at Gypsum. "So?"

"Scroll through his photos," she says glumly, like she ain't getting no joy out of this, but she must be, otherwise why all the drama?

I wonder if she started this to get Denver's attention, if

that's why she keeps coming 'round, 'cause she's sweet on him. Wouldn't be the first Backwoods Betty to get moony beyond all sense over a Lester man.

Whatever her reason, it stops mattering when I see what she's getting at. Brayton's photo feed is full of pictures of him and some other girl, a preppy-ass-looking blonde.

In some pictures, he's kissing her—on her cheek, her forehead, her prissy pink mouth—and in others he's just got his arm slung 'round her shoulders, but in all of them she's wearing a strand of pearls that's gotta be real and a big pair of sparkly stud earrings that must be diamond.

Rich girl. Of *course*.

"Sammy—"

Brayton reaches for the phone again, so I get up, wrapped in a sheet, and move to Decca's cot. I keep thumbing through his photos. They go on *forever*, back at least six or seven months, and every time I stumble on one of them kissing I feel bile burn the back of my throat.

I switch to his wall, where there are plenty of messages from the girl, whose name is Jennifer Wiggins.

Miss u baby. Hope ur not having too much fun w/out me.

It's good Denver's standing between me and Brayton right now, 'cause I wanna punch him square in the throat. I'm wishing Denver had kicked him harder—in the balls.

"So," I say. "You got a girlfriend. Congrats. When's the wedding?"

Brayton looks like he's gonna be sick all over the floor. "It's not like that. It's not serious."

"Looks serious," I say, holding up the phone.

Denver watches me warily. Probably thinks he'll have to pull me off Brayton before I claw his lovely dark snake eyes right out of his head, but I'm not giving any of them the satisfaction of acting like I give a shit.

I think about last night and cringe. What I wished I could say. What I thought I felt for him. My cheeks are hot with shame.

"Not anymore," Brayton insists.

He starts to get up, but realizes he's only wearing a sheet himself and it's about to fall off. He tucks it 'round his waist and glares at Denver and Gypsum.

"Can we have a minute?"

"Nah," Denver says, tossing Brayton's clothes at his face so hard we all hear it when the zipper on his jeans hits his front tooth. Brayton rubs his mouth with a scowl. "You should go."

"Sorry, Sammy," Gypsum says again.

"Yeah, we're all sorry." I look at Brayton. "We're a real sorry bunch, I'd say. Were you gonna tell me about her, or were you just gonna leave at the end of the summer and never speak to me again? You know what? Never mind. Not like I fucking care."

We both look so stupid right now, like toga party rejects. I hate that Denver's watching all this, hate that he won't leave, hate that he brought this down on me 'cause he thinks I can't protect my own self. Like he thinks he's gotta do everything for me.

"Don't," Brayton says.

"Don't what?"

"Don't act like we're nothing."

"Don't *you* act like we're something. You been ch—"

I stop myself. 'Cause he *ain't* been cheating on me. He's been using me to cheat on somebody else. Which makes it worse, if that's even possible.

"Were you ever gonna tell me?" I ask.

"Honestly? I was hoping I'd never have to."

"So you're a coward."

"We've established that. But let's face it, Sammy, you're no saint."

"I don't see how that makes what you did any better."

"You're really going to look me in the eye and promise me there's not a part of you that's thinking I'm just a holdover till Reed comes home?"

It feels like he slapped me. I wasn't even thinking about Reed.

"I don't make promises," I say, cold as a winter storm. "And don't you dare talk about Reed like you know anything."

I can't believe this is happening. Last night feels like a dream.

Brayton looks like a puppy that's been kicked and I almost feel guilty. I knew this thing with Reed has been eating at him, and I ain't done much to reassure him. But that don't excuse what *he's* done, what he's been doing since long before Reed got hurt.

Denver loses his patience, grabs Brayton by the arm. "You gotta go, dude. You done overstayed your welcome."

That's how I know Denver's real mad, 'cause he never talks like he's from here if he can help it.

"Knock it off," I say. "Denver, get out of here. I mean it. Gypsum, you too."

Denver hesitates, but I must sound scary serious 'cause he backs out of the room and takes Gypsum with him. A second later, she peeks in again.

"My phone?" I toss it to her, glad to be rid of it, and she beats a hasty retreat.

Then Brayton and I are alone. The silence is heavy. This tiny room smells like heat and sex and sweat and dust.

"I broke up with her," he says. "That's why I had to go to the city. And also why I didn't want to. She knew it was coming. I probably didn't even have to tell her in person, but I felt like I should. I felt like—you'd want me to."

"'Cause I make you wanna be a better person?"

"I know you're being sarcastic, but…yeah. Except I've never been a particularly good person. But I'm trying."

"You broke up with her last night, didn't you?"

He takes a deep breath. "Yes."

"So that's why the tears."

"*No.* That was— I don't know what that was. Relief, maybe. That it was over. I just want *you.*"

I rub at my temples, trying to calm down. My head is killing me. I work on putting a distance between us, making it clear: he couldn't hurt me if he tried.

He sits on the edge of my bed and grabs my wrists. That's how small this room is. Everything's in arm's reach.

"I'm sorry," he says. "It's over with her. It's *been* over. It was just loose ends and now it's done."

"Too late, Brayton."

"Sammy, come on."

He gets up, clutching that sheet 'round his waist. It's white and thin and I can see all of him through it. I hate him, but I'm still so attracted to him, and that makes me hate myself.

"Sit," I say.

Brayton sinks back down onto the bed, balls his fists in his lap and gazes up at me with eyes full of heartbreak, which enrages me. Also makes me wanna put my arms around him. God, the both of us, we're so pathetic.

"Close your eyes."

When he does, I drop the sheet and dress quick.

"Okay, you can open them."

"You don't have to be shy around me."

"I ain't being shy," I snap. "I just don't want you looking at me naked. Now, you tell me everything, and don't you dare lie to me, Brayton Foster."

He takes a deep breath, stares at his bare feet, lets seconds pass in silence. Finally, he says:

"You know I moved to Oklahoma City last year, my senior year. I kind of had a hard time making friends."

"Oh, boo hoo. Maybe it's 'cause you're an asshole."

"It was a small private high school. Everybody had their cliques and they weren't interested in getting to know the new guy nine months before graduation. But one of the popular girls started paying attention to me. Jennifer. I liked her, and I latched on because I didn't want to feel invisible."

I roll my eyes. Like a boy as hot as Brayton could ever be invisible.

"Jennifer was a part of things, and I like being a part of things, too. The school revolved around her group of friends and she made me feel included. She was nice."

Must be paining him to tell me this, 'cause he's exposing his softest parts to me now, that lonely boy he tries to shield with charm—just like last night, except now I ain't exactly overflowing with sympathy.

If he thinks honesty's gonna save him here, he's an idiot. I got too much sorrow in my life right now to spare even a drop of it for him.

"I wanted to break up with her before I even came to the lake, but I didn't have the nerve."

"Well, I'm gonna save you the effort of breaking up with me."

"Sammy, please. I meant what I said last night. How can I make you understand?"

"I do understand. You got bored with your sweet, suburban real-housewife-in-training and you figured you'd get yourself a piece of rough to spice things up. Happens all the time. Hate to break it to you, Harvard, but you're not the first city boy to come up here looking for some side action."

"Yale," he says miserably.

"What?"

"I'm going to Yale. In the fall. Not Harvard."

I don't even know what to do with that.

"Perfect. Yet another reason why you and I were never gonna work. Know where I'm going to college? *Nowhere.*"

"You think I care about things like that?"

"I care."

"You care about the wrong shit." His face reddens. "I know I hurt you, and it *kills* me, it does. It's been killing me since I realized what was happening with us, how deep it was going.

"But you act like the problem is I think I'm better than you, when really it's the other way around. All that redneck pride you've got has you assuming I'm shallow because the man my mom married has money. I told you where I really come from. You know I'm not that guy."

"Not what guy? The kind of guy that can get into Yale? That can *pay* for Yale? Might be your mom that married rich but you're sure as hell living off the proceeds."

Brayton throws up his hands. "Fine. If that's how you want to see it, I can't stop you."

"Look," I say, mustering all my meanness and coldness and spite so I can put off feeling the painful slice of losing him till he's good and gone. "This was fun. You were a great distraction from all the bad things in my life. But I need to focus on my family now. I don't care what you did, Brayton. So you had a girlfriend you didn't tell me about. Big deal. Ain't like we were ever really together."

"That's not even true," he says quietly.

"I never asked you to be faithful to me, and you never promised to be. So it's fine."

"This is unbelievable."

"Did you tell her about me?" I ask. I can tell from the look on his face the answer's no.

"I didn't want to hurt her," he says.

"That's not why. It's 'cause you still want her to *like* you. That's all you care about. You'll do anything to get people to like you, even if it means pissing off your parents. Even if it means getting arrested."

I shake my head in disgust. "You're right. I ain't no saint. But at least I know who I am."

"I'm going to make this up to you," he insists. "I promise. What can I do? I'll do anything."

"Don't promise me nothing. Just leave, and never, ever call me again."

If he does, I know I'll wanna pick up, and I shouldn't. I can't. This thing with us will never not end badly.

"That's how you can make it up to me," I say. "By going the fuck away."

He pulls his phone out of his pocket, brings up my name in his contacts, holds his finger over the big red delete button.

"You want me to forget your number? You really want that?"

I take the phone and delete it myself, then toss it back to him—nobody calls my bluff. He stares at the phone like he's never seen it before. Shocked.

So am I. For a second, I worry I been too reckless.

But Brayton humiliated me. I can forgive a lot of things, but that ain't the sort of thing I could ever get over.

"Do better than that, Brayton. Forget you ever met me."

I sit on Decca's cot and press my face into her pillow, waiting for the sound of gravel crunching under Brayton's tires. The pillow still has Decca's smell on it, baby powder and no-tears shampoo and whatever Rainne washes her clothes in.

The room is hot and messy and I can't breathe in here, so I start cleaning, sorting clothes into piles and ripping the sheets off the bed for washing. I gotta get rid of all Brayton's traces, scrub him off my skin soon as I can.

I shake my own pillows out of their cases and something falls to the floor: a bundle of twigs and leaves fretted with red yarn. I snatch it up and crumple it in my fist.

"Gypsum," I growl, stalking out of the room.

I blow through the trailer like I got someone on my tail, sweaty and furious. I'm almost to the front door when Denver calls my name. He's sitting on the couch in the front room with Gypsum. She sees what I'm holding and makes a run for it.

"Oh, no you don't!" I block her path. "What the hell kind of hillbilly voodoo shit is this?"

She stares at the floor, doesn't answer me.

"It's yours, ain't it? You left this in my room. The one in Brayton's car, too. Those nails in our door—you put those there. I wanna know why."

"Sammy," Denver says. "Calm down."

"I won't calm down! What is your *deal*, Gypsum? Why do you keep coming 'round, messing with me? Messing with my *family?*"

"I was just trying to protect you," Gypsum blubbers. She's shaking like a tree branch in a bad storm. "There's people out there fixing to hurt you, and I was wanting to keep you safe."

"With what? Witchcraft?"

Gypsum crosses her arms. "Ain't no *witch*craft. Those are charms, made special for you by my great-auntie Tett, most powerful yarb doctor in three counties. After what happened to your daddy, and what Ash Boford did, figured we can't be too careful."

"We? What's any of this got to do with you? And who you trying to protect me from, huh? It's *your* people fixing to do bad to me!"

"It ain't," she snaps. "Your problem is you don't know danger when you see it. Could be the only reason you're standing here steaming at me and not dead in the ground is 'cause I been leaving those charms behind."

"I can't believe we're having this conversation. That shit ain't *real*."

"Who are you to say what's real and what ain't?"

"No more," I say. "No more sneaking 'round my house planting bundles of dried weeds in my bed, no more putting nails in my door, no more throwing spells in my boyf— *No more*, Gypsum! You get out of here now, and take this stupid charm with you."

I fling it at her, but she just lets it fall to the ground. I pick it back up, meaning to press it into her hands, but she steps away from me.

"You gotta keep it. I believe enough for the both of us, but you gotta let the charm do its work."

"Just leave it, Sammy," Denver says. "No use getting worked up over a little bundle like that."

"Don't even get me started on you, Denver." I step back, look at them. "Why'd you do that?"

My bad Lester blood is good and boiling. I feel it pounding in my throat. Mine are an angry people, and I never felt more like one of those that came down through the hills and scratched out a living in these unforgiving lands than right this minute.

"You'd rather not have known? I was just trying—"

"I know why *you* did it," I say to Denver. "You don't want me to have nothing to call my own."

He reels like I hit him. "That's not true at all."

I point an accusing finger at Gypsum. "*You.* Why'd you have to go and do that if you're really trying to protect me?"

"'Cause a boy like that only wants one thing from a girl like you and me," Gypsum says.

"You and me? We ain't the same girl. Don't you get that?"

My fist tightens around the charm. It sheds bits of wood and leaf all over the floor.

"You wish we weren't," Gypsum says.

"Why'd you do it, really? Huh? Why're you poking your big old honker up in my life? You went looking for that information—it sure as hell didn't seek you out. Then you scurried right on up here like a weasel to tattle to Denver. Why? Were you hoping he'd be grateful enough to hook up with you? Tell you what, Gypsum. Denver thinks he's way too good for the likes of you. That's just about the only thing you and I have in common."

Denver steps up to me. "That's enough. She was trying to help."

"I don't need help!" I shout.

To Gypsum, I say, "You been following me 'round all summer, asking after me, turning up places you know I'll be. What's your game? What do you want from me? 'Cause look around. Ain't nothing I got to give. Nothing at all worth having."

"I just wanna be your friend," Gypsum sniffles. "I just wanna make it so nobody else can hurt you. I told you about that two-timing rich asshole 'cause that's what friends do."

"We ain't friends," I say. "We never were. You need to leave, now, and you need to stay away from me and mine before I do something we're both gonna regret. You hear?"

"He tell you his daddy hired Redbreast's boys to scare folks off this bluff so he could buy up all their land?" Gypsum asks.

"What do you know about that?"

"Enough."

"You know so much, who broke into my house two nights ago and knocked me out cold? My money's on Johnny."

Her face betrays nothing. "I got no idea what you're talking about. All I know is my family didn't do nothing to your daddy. And I'm gonna prove it to you."

"Yeah? How?"

"You'll see," she says darkly.

If I gotta listen to one more word out of her sneaky, lying mouth I think I'll clobber her, so I take off running, let the screen door screech and slam behind me, and keep on going till I reach the woods.

I push past the tree line and follow a winding gravel path Dad put in. I take it all the way up to the Oklahoma rock, a piece of schist shaped like the state Dad found years ago.

Sitting on the rock, I take full, deep breaths, trying to get calm. Push all thoughts of Brayton out of my head and stare at the lake, that blue meanie what keeps me trapped here. That planet with the irresistible gravity whose orbit I can't escape.

There's a rustling in the trees close by and I turn to find myself looking into the big brown eyes of my pregnant doe. She's a late one, still carrying even though most her friends have dropped their fawns already.

She's huge in the belly, so close I could probably reach out and touch her. But she'd balk and run and I don't want her to. She's the only company I got and I don't wanna be alone.

"Sorry, but I got nothing for you," I tell her.

She angles her head. I put out some deer corn last week but it's all eaten up. I wonder if she depends on it, if she's still capable of feeding off the land.

When they build Sweet Home, what'll happen to my doe, to her family? Will she get run off, or die trying to keep her home?

All that shouting and running's got me feeling faint. I bend over with my head in my hands, take deep breaths in through my nose. Something catches my eye, sticking out from underneath the Oklahoma rock.

I grab at it, and it slips right out—looks like there's a cubby hole in the rock about the size of a piece of paper. I never noticed it, but then again, I never looked at the rock from this angle before.

It's a small stack of twice-folded paper sealed in a freezer bag. The paper ain't yellowed, so it can't have been here that long. It must be Dad's.

The sound of sticks breaking underfoot crackles like a weary gunshot and my doe is on the move, scampering into the dark of the woods faster than she's got any right in her condition.

Dad always said deer were magic, and even now I still almost believe him.

Denver appears from behind a big black walnut tree. He sizes me up, keeping his distance.

"You okay?" he asks.

"Never better."

"You were real mean to Gypsum back there," Denver says. "Damn near broke her heart, I think, tears running down that beak of hers like a waterfall."

"Don't know why you care. She's a Tuller."

"She's a kitten," Denver says. "Runt of the litter, that one."

He takes a seat next to me on the Oklahoma rock and drops something in my lap. The charm. I busted it up good.

"Tuller runts grow up to be hellcats, too," I say.

"She's just taken with you. Wants to be you, probably."

"That's her problem."

He points to the paper in my hand. "What's that?"

I pass it to him. He stares at it. "A purchase agreement?"

"For *our land*. Dad sold it to those Sweet Home bastards. Think Gypsum's backwoods holler magic can do something about it, or should I continue *losing my shit* over the fact that we're homeless?"

"Calm down, we're not homeless. Dad never signed this document. Look."

"So? Why does he have it in the first place? And why'd he hide it in the Oklahoma rock?"

"I think that's pretty obvious. He didn't want us to find it."

"Gypsum's right, you know—Brayton's stepdad is working on Sweet Home. I saw a map of their property in his office and our land's on it."

"How long you known that?"

"Couple weeks."

"And you stayed with him? The way you hate Sweet Home, I'd've bet you'd toss him out on his ass just for that."

"I should've. Would've saved me the complete humiliation of this morning. Thanks for that, by the way."

"Sammy, I'm sorry you're hurting—"

"I ain't hurting."

"—but you would've wanted to know. Isn't that what you keep telling me? You want to know everything, even the bad stuff?"

"About *Dad*."

"Well, you don't get to pick and choose. Either I protect you from everything I can, or I tell you everything I know. You better get your mind around which you prefer."

"Tell me," I say.

Denver takes a deep breath. "There's a lien on the property. Dad hasn't paid his taxes in years. Couple months ago, the IRS came around, said they were going to take him to court and get a judgment compelling him to pay up. Easiest choice he had was to sell the land."

"How come I didn't know any of this?"

"Dad didn't want to freak you out, after everything that happened, you know, with you and Reed. There wasn't anything you could've done about it anyway. He was waiting to tell you till after everything was final."

"You mean he didn't trust me. That why he asked you to come home for the summer? To help break the shitty news that I ain't got a place to live?"

"Part of the reason," Denver admits.

"And the other part?"

"He wanted me to convince you to go to college."

"With what money? And since when did Dad care about me going to college?"

"I don't know that he cares about the college part that much. He just thought you should get away from here. Did he tell you he came down to visit me at school this spring?"

"Why would he ever go there? He *hates* that you're living down in Norman."

Denver shrugs. "I think he wanted to prove to himself that I'm miserable there, or that the campus is terrible. But he actually seemed to like it. Kept saying it made him wish he'd tried living somewhere besides Bittersweet. That maybe if he had he wouldn't've gone to prison."

"You ain't done much to talk me into college."

"I've had some other things on my mind lately."

"Ain't we all."

I look out over the bluff, across the water to the forest on the other shore—the Tuller side.

"If he was gonna sell up our land, how come he didn't sign that contract? Why stuff it under a rock? And where'd that money you found in his drawer come from?"

"Maybe it was an advance."

"From Redbreast? What the hell for?"

"Who knows? Dad had plenty of secrets. He didn't share everything with me, either."

"Fuck those Tullers. Why'd he have to get involved with them again?"

"It's the life he knew."

"*Knows.* We got no proof he's dead."

Someone's gotta keep saying it. Someone's gotta have faith.

"If he's alive, where the hell did he go? He told me himself he didn't know how to survive anyplace but Bittersweet, or who he was when he wasn't here."

"Bet it wasn't just the money Johnny Tuller was looking for when he broke into the house," I say. "Bet it was these papers, too."

"Bet you're right about that."

The look on Denver's face about breaks my heart. It's the look of powerlessness, and I feel it, too.

A silent moment goes by. Then I ask: "You think I was stupid to ever believe he'd change?"

"Not stupid," Denver says. "Hopeful. That's the good thing about you, Sammy. You've got hope where most people would've lost it a long time ago. I'm almost sorry that Brayton guy turned out to be such a loser. It was nice to see you happy again, after Reed put you through the ringer."

"We put each other through the ringer."

"Even so. I know you think you're tough as shoe leather, and I'm not arguing otherwise. Your stubbornness won't let you give up. It's one of your best qualities."

He nudges me with his elbow till I smile. "That's why I never wanted you to know any of this stuff. Someone's gotta keep the light burning in the windows. Else we're all screwed, right?"

"Do you keep leaving 'cause you don't wanna be like him? Dad, I mean."

"I don't know that I could be like him. Remember how Dad says bravery is nine parts stupidity, one part not caring whether you live or die? Well, I'm not stupid, and I care a lot whether I live or die. Same goes for you, but you're sure as hell trying to prove the opposite, aren't you?"

I pick at the charm in my lap. Maybe it is just white country magic, but it makes me uneasy.

"Why do you say that?" I ask. "'Cause I won't give up on finding Dad? Or 'cause I took up with a rich boy knowing he'd break my heart in the end?"

"Did you know that?"

"I think I did, deep down."

"You went chasing that city boy because you really liked him. Anyone could see that."

I punch Denver in the arm. "Then why'd you and Gypsum set fire to it?"

Denver stands and offers me his hand. I let him haul me to my feet.

"I figure you've had enough of men lying to you about who they are so they can preserve your good opinion," he says. "Me, Dad, Reed… Brayton was one in a long line of sad sacks who kept you in the dark rather than make you hate them by telling you the full story, and I figured it was time that stopped."

"He ain't a rich city boy, not exactly," I say as we make our way back to the house. I tell him what Brayton said a while back about how he grew up: poor, not knowing his father, always at the mercy of someone else's generosity.

"So he's like us," Denver says.

"No he ain't. He got rich, didn't he? Even if it's someone else's money, he ain't wondering how he's gonna fill the pantry. He ain't about to lose his home."

I turn the broken remains of the charm over in my hands. "You gonna tell me to be nicer to Gypsum now? Apologize to her?"

"Hell no. You stay away from the Tullers."

We stop in front of Dad's old burn barrel. Denver asks, "You got fire?"

I pull a matchbook from my pocket. "Thought you didn't believe in hillbilly magic."

"I don't. But better safe than sorry."

He strikes a match. I hold the charm by a string over the burn barrel and Denver puts the flame to the dried leaves. Soon as it catches fire, I drop it in. Together we watch it curl and disintegrate, sending up a ribbon of gray smoke.

When the fire burns out, I fetch a hammer from the shed.

"So what do I do about Brayton?" I ask, yanking the three nails from the door.

Denver leans against the porch rail. "What do you want to do about him?"

"Like I know," I say. "He says he loves me."

"Could be he does," Denver says. "I don't know him well enough to guess. If he loves you, he'll figure out a way to get you back. Or he won't. Some folks just aren't stupid enough to be brave."

CHAPTER EIGHTEEN

The whiskey burns as it slides down my throat.

"What an asshole," Kenley says, stubbing her cigarette out in the dirt and wiggling her fingers for the bottle. She takes a swig. "I hate him."

"Me, too," I say.

We're sitting on the edge of Satan's Chin, watching night fall over the lake. Took me about ten hours of wallowing to work up the nerve to call Kenley and admit to what happened, but I can't keep it to myself, and talking to Denver about it ain't the same as talking to her.

"But do you?" Kenley asks.

"I don't know."

"How *dare* he cheat on you? Doesn't he know you're the hottest girl he's ever gonna get his hands on?" Kenley shakes her head. "Bet the girlfriend's a troll."

"She ain't," I say. "Not that it matters."

The whiskey warms me from the inside out and I feel calmer. Sadder, too.

"Last time a guy cheated on me, I nearly gouged his eyes out with a soup spoon," Kenley says. "I were you, I'd at least wanna egg his house."

"Guess I figure I should've known better. Guys like that don't stick with girls like me."

"Girls like you? What's that mean?"

"You know. Redneck townies. He's going to Yale, Ken. His family's got money, and his stepdad…"

I stop myself before I tell her. Sharing that information, even with my best friend, don't seem too smart.

"Anyway, he's different," I say. "You seen that boat, that house. I ain't never gonna be like him."

"Who'd wanna be? We got everything we need right here."

I grab the whiskey bottle. "Every goddamn thing we need."

We're packing up to leave when my phone rings. Half of me hopes it's Brayton, but I know he don't have my number. My heart leaps anyway.

"Sammy," Agent Pilson says. "We found your father."

Agent Pilson watches Denver and I from across the table in one of the interview rooms at the Bittersweet County Sheriff's Department. Sheriff Olina sits next to him, her usual sour look replaced by a somber one. It's freezing in here. I'm shivering in my tank top and shorts.

I pick at the fraying edge of my cutoffs and keep my eyes fixed on the floor. I feel like I'm in trouble, almost wanna confess something, one of the many petty crimes of my youth I never got caught for. Anything to avoid having to accept the reason I'm here.

"I have some photos of the crime scene in this folder," Agent Pilson says. "But I don't recommend you look at them."

"Don't you need someone to identify him?" Denver asks.

"We did that with fingerprints, since he's in the system. We wanted to spare y'all if we could."

"I wanna see the pictures," I say. I been trying to wrap my head around the reality of Dad's death. I know I'll never really believe it if I don't see the evidence.

"Sammy," Denver says. "It's been weeks."

"Been a hot summer, too," Pilson says. "The body has severely deteriorated, and there's evidence of animal activity on the remains. Not something you want to look at."

"Where'd you find him?" Denver asks.

"An abandoned farm out on Route 82," Olina says.

"The Collins place? Where?" I glance at Denver. "We searched it."

"Behind an old collapsed shed," Pilson says. "There was a lot of refuse in the area. The body was half-hidden."

The body. "I wanna see the photos."

"No." Denver's fingers close over my wrist. He used to grab me like that all the time when we were kids, to keep me from running out into traffic after a ball or a stray cat. I shake him off.

"It's really not a good idea," Pilson says. "Seeing a loved one like that, it can be traumatic, and after everything you've been through—"

"I understand. Show me anyway."

I tap my fingers on the tabletop. Pilson looks at Olina. She shrugs and slides the folder over to me. Pilson almost looks like he's gonna stop her, but he doesn't.

Everybody watches me like I'm about to defuse a bomb.

Maybe they're right. Maybe this ain't something anybody should see. But I can't back down now. I took the dare.

I ease the folder open with my thumbnail and lower my eyes.

One look at the photo on top, that's all it takes—I turn my head and throw up all over the floor.

Denver's chair screeches and then he's on his knees in front of me, cool hand on the back of my neck.

"It's okay," he says. "You're all right. Take deep breaths."

I pull away, wipe my mouth with the back of my hand. Sheriff Olina goes to the door and shouts for someone to bring paper towels and disinfectant.

"And some water," Denver says.

I sit up, woozy. "Sorry," I mumble.

Don't know why I thought seeing the pictures was gonna help. It didn't do anything to make losing Dad real to me—that mess of flesh and blood and *parts* lying in the red, red dirt don't even look like him.

Animal activity, Pilson said. Bits of him looked like they'd been gnawed on.

Some junior deputy cleans up my puke while I sit in the chair, shaking. Denver takes his seat and stares at me. My mouth tastes awful.

"You want to leave?" Agent Pilson asks. "Come back later, when you're feeling better?"

"No. I wanna know what else you found." Besides that *thing* in the pictures.

"Cigarette butts," he says. "Crimsons. Know anybody who smokes those?"

I think on it for a minute. Dad was a menthol man. Most people I know smoke Marlboro Lights, or American Spirits.

"I don't pay much attention to what people smoke," Denver says.

I spit into a paper towel and take a long drink of water.

"Johnny Tuller smokes Crimsons," I say. Sheriff Olina stiffens. "I seen him plenty of times. He even put out a cigarette in the street outside Decca's day care. Don't know how often they clean them, might still be there."

Pilson says they'll send a deputy to look for it, then continues his inventory: "Three spent bullet casings from a twenty-two, plus the slugs in the body, which'll most likely match. Marks on the casings don't match anything in any state or federal database, so it's either a newly purchased gun, or never been used in a crime before."

"The Tullers got lots of guns."

"What makes you so sure it's them?" Olina asks. "You got some information, you better share it."

"Those developers that are putting up Sweet Home on Gibson Bluff, word is they hired the Tullers to muscle people out of their land. Pretty sure my dad was one of the people they convinced to sell up."

I take the purchase agreement I found under the Oklahoma rock out of my pocket and slide it to Pilson.

"He never signed, but he did have that big wad of cash. This is probably what they were looking for when they broke into our house."

"We didn't find the money on the body," Pilson says. "Just a five and some change in his wallet."

"I don't know exactly what's going on, but I bet that cash had something to do with selling the land. Maybe it was a payoff? Whatever it is, the Tullers gotta be involved. Dad never rolled on Redbreast when he went to prison. They owed him. Maybe they made selling worth his while."

"There was a lien on the land," Denver says. "He could've used the ten thousand to pay it off."

"Doesn't look like it," Pilson says. "We ran his financials. He was in a fair amount of debt."

"That don't make sense. The lien is one thing, he hated paying taxes, but Dad's a cash-only guy. Didn't even have a credit card."

"Not now, but when he was married to Rainne Tremont, there were a lot of credit cards, and car loans, things of that nature. He's been paying them off slow, but there's still a mountain of it left. If he was selling his land, might be why."

"You know about that?" I ask Denver. He shakes his head. "No wonder there was never any money. So you gonna bring the Tullers in for questioning or what?"

"Which ones?" Sheriff Olina scoffs. "You want us to haul in everybody with that last name?"

"For a start," I snap.

"We'll try, but we called up at Rock Creek after the break-in at your house—they're not talking. And we don't have anything concrete tying anyone to the crime as of yet. We've got to do some more advanced ballistics testing, get the autopsy results back. We're still processing the scene," Pilson says.

"I thought you knew how he died."

"There's evidence of blunt force trauma to the head in addition to the bullet wounds, but given the state of the body we can't know for sure till we do a full exam. We'll see if we can track down that cigarette butt, test it for DNA if it's not degraded and compare it to the ones we found."

Pilson puts the folder aside. "You should go home, both of you, and get some rest."

"Like I'm gonna be able to sleep," I mutter.

"Sheriff, can you give me a minute with Denver and Sammy?"

Olina pushes back from the table.

"Do whatever you like, Agent," she says frostily.

When she's gone, Pilson says, "Let me show you something."

He starts lifting his wrinkled black polo shirt over his head. I put my hand out.

"No, thanks. I don't think I wanna see it."

Denver turns away with a snort.

"Calm yourself, I'm not trying to give you a show. I got another shirt on."

His wifebeater's a dingy gray color, like he put it in the wash with something dark. Pilson drops the polo in his lap and turns so we can see he's got some ink on his left shoulder, a number: 47.

"Know what that is?"

"Gonna guess you didn't get that in prison."

"It's an affiliate tattoo for the Devil's Guardians MC," Pilson says.

"You were in a motorcycle gang?" Denver asks.

"I wasn't in the club. My dad was. Granddad, too. Founded it with a couple buddies after 'Nam."

Pilson tugs his shirt back on. "Got that when I was about your age. Planned on joining the club soon as I turned twenty-one, but then my dad got stabbed by a rival club member outside a bar and died. They let him bleed out next to the garbage cans."

I lower my chin and stare at my hands on the table.

"Hey." He dips his head so he can meet my eyes. "I didn't tell you so you'd feel sorry. I told you so you'd know I understand."

"Understand what?" Denver asks sharply. "What it's like to have your dad killed?"

Pilson sits up straight. "I can see why you suspect the Tullers. And I respect how determined you are to get answers, but you're not exactly objective, and objectivity's what a good detective needs. There might be more than one possible explanation for what happened to your dad. I have to look at this thing from all angles, or else I'll be failing Bobby Ray."

"Did they ever catch them? The men who murdered your daddy?" I ask.

"Didn't get a chance to," Pilson tells us. "Couple Guardians got to them before the police could, dropped their bodies in the Arkansas River. Want to guess what happened to their killers?"

"The rival gang killed them, too?"

Pilson nods. "And on and on and on it goes. Till somebody puts a stop to it once and for all."

Denver and I go home, but I don't sleep, just toss and turn all night. I almost call Kenley three times, and Brayton seven, but in the end I delete his number from my phone and don't call nobody at all.

My phone rings 'round midnight. The screen flashes Rainne's name.

"Sammy, I just heard about Bobby Ray," she says when I answer. Her voice is hushed, like she's trying not to wake somebody, and my heart seizes at the thought of Decca sleeping, totally unaware that she ain't never gonna see her daddy again.

I can't shake the creeping feeling that she's in danger. That we all are.

"I'm so sorry," Rainne says. "So, so sorry, Sammy."

"Not too sorry, I bet." I ain't in no mood to comfort her today. "Now you can take Decca anyplace you damn well please."

"I ain't calling to fight with you. I just wanted to hear your voice. You and I, we're in a weird place right now, and God knows Bobby Ray and I had our troubles, but I never in a thousand years wanted any of this to happen. There was a time when I loved him, too."

"Uh-huh. And what about me?"

"What do you mean?"

"Did you ever love me, or was that an act? Play nice with your husband's kids to impress him?"

"Of course I loved you. I still do. I wish things were different. I hope they will be, someday."

"You keep my sister from me and I can guarantee you— things ain't never gonna be different."

She pauses. "What's all this drama about Waldo? When the police came by to tell me about Bobby Ray, they showed me some photo they took of Decca in MaryEllen's front yard. They wanted to know if the stuffed animal she was holding was Waldo. Why would they ask that?"

"Dad was supposed to be by your place the night he was missing, to drop Waldo off."

"But he never came. I told you that a million times."

"It's been a while since you gave me a reason to believe any word you say."

"Sammy, please. Don't make this harder than it's gotta be. Don't go using what happened to Bobby Ray to punish me.

Like I told the police, that stuffed animal was a rabbit Mary-Ellen bought Decca to replace Waldo."

Rainne sighs. "You were right, she can't sleep without him."

"Imagine how hard it'll be to get her to sleep once you tell her that her daddy's dead, and all this time you were working to keep her away from him."

"Ain't told her yet. How do you explain that kind of thing to a child?"

"Don't ask me." I hang up.

Denver knocks on my door 'round midnight, but I pretend not to hear. I feel betrayed—by Dad for dying, by Brayton for lying, by the whole damn world for trying its damnedest to break me in half.

And by Rainne, who told me when she married Dad that she would always protect me.

She was just a stupid kid back then, not much older than I am now, and maybe she even believed what she was saying at the time, but she didn't really mean it.

When people tell you they wanna protect you, they hardly ever mean it.

CHAPTER NINETEEN

I keep my phone in arm's reach all week, waiting for Agent Pilson to call with more information, but it's slow coming. The autopsy revealed Dad *was* hit in the back of the head. Pilson thinks it was a baseball bat, but it ain't what killed him. Probably just knocked him unconscious. They found some tracks near Dad's body, like he might've been dragged there.

They found the Crimson cigarette butt Johnny Tuller tossed outside Decca's day care—they knew it was his 'cause they already have his DNA on file, no surprise. But it didn't match the DNA they found on the butts near Dad's body. And the ballistics tests came up negative on all known twenty-twos in the Tullers' possession.

"Don't mean they didn't kill Dad," I insist.

"I know," Pilson says. He sounds weary—I get the sense he's tired of my desperate questions.

So am I, but I can't stop asking. My mind spins every minute of every day and I can't shut it off.

The one bright spot is I finally found a new job, at the Fuel 'N Fun. Even pays a little better than waitressing.

"And, bonus, free slushies," Kenley says when I tell her.

Business ain't exactly booming, which gives me plenty of time to stare at my phone, willing it to ring. When it does, I'm so surprised I drop it on the floor, and when I pick it back up I can't believe the name I'm seeing on the caller ID: Pourret Home. Reed's parents' house line.

I ain't gotten a call from anyone in Reed's family since we broke up, and Pete's the only Pourret I seen for about that long. I'm so freaked I almost don't answer, but at the last minute I do, like someone's operating me with a remote control.

"Sammy? Oh, Sammy, honey, it's Shirla Pourret." Pause. "Reed's mama."

"Christ, Shirla, I know who you are."

Soon as the words leave my mouth, I wanna kill myself out of shame. Her son just lost his leg and I'm snapping at her. But I'm rattled by the fact she's even calling.

I swallow and cough. "I mean, um…hi. How are you? How's Reed?"

"Oh, he's all right, honey. How are you? I heard that horrible news about poor Bobby Ray. I'm so damned sorry for you, and Denver, too. And little Decca, though I'm sure she's a lot bigger since I last saw her. They grow up *fast* at that age, you barely recognize them one day to the next."

Shirla talks too much when she's nervous.

"Thanks." I really don't know what to say. Everything going on with Reed, and she's so damned sorry *for me*. I barely got room to feel sorry for anyone but myself.

"Just wanted to let you know Reed's home now," Shirla says. "Not in the house yet, but he's back in the States. Down at the university medical center in Tehlicoh. Got his own private room and everything."

I let out a breath I didn't even know I was holding.

"That's great. I mean…I'm glad he's back. I hated thinking about him so sick and far away."

Sick, like he's got a cold. I squeeze my eyes shut and press the heel of my hand to my forehead.

"I told him he ain't never allowed out of Oklahoma again," Shirla says. "I told him, I said, 'Oklahoma is God's country, son. No harm'll ever come to you in a place that's blessed by our Lord.'"

My daddy was murdered in God's country, but you don't argue with Shirla about this—she'll wear you out before you can win.

"Reed's been asking for you, Sammy. He'd really like to see you, if you wouldn't mind popping down to the hospital for a visit sometime."

My first thought is: *I don't wanna go. I don't wanna see Reed.* I'm afraid I'll find I'm still in love with him, after all the work I did not to feel that way, and I'm also afraid I won't. I'm afraid I'll feel guilty about the pregnancy—if I'd kept it, the baby would've been born by now—and I'm also afraid I won't.

But mostly, I'm afraid of his injury. The Reed I remember is healthy and whole, but the Reed that exists now is neither of those things.

"Of course I'll come," I say. 'Cause what other choice do I got?

"Thank you, honey. That means more than you can imagine."

Shirla gives me the visiting hours and hints I should come soon as possible, so I tell her I'll be there tomorrow and hang up feeling sick with nerves—but also, in a weird way, sort of relieved.

I probably stand in the hallway outside Reed's hospital room for fifteen minutes before getting up the courage to knock on the door. I keep trying, and failing, to come up with a good opening line, something that'll make Reed laugh, but I can't remember how I used to make him laugh before. I got no idea if he even does anymore.

"Knock knock." I nudge the door open with the toe of my shoe.

"Come on in," Shirla calls.

Pretty typical hospital room Reed's got here, tiny and unnaturally bright, but Shirla's done her best to make it homey. Couple half-deflated Mylar "Welcome Home" balloons in the corner. Handful of cards propped open on the bedside table next to a battered old Bible. Cheerful yellow-and-green quilt on the foot of the bed.

Shirla sits in a chair next to the window with a book of crosswords in her lap and a pencil behind her left ear. She smiles when she sees me.

"Who's there?" Reed asks.

He's looking right at me. Stunning, how *the same* he looks. Kinda scruffy, probably 'cause it's a pain to shave, and his skin's pale, his eyes are bloodshot, but otherwise, same old Reed. I prepared for the worst, so I'm more surprised than I ought to be.

I force myself not to look at the sheet covering him from the waist down.

Does he really not recognize me? Ain't been *that* long. Maybe the same blast that took his leg took his memory. Shirla could've at least warned me. I wanna run straight out of the room.

"It's—it's Sammy," I say. "I brought you daffodils. I don't know why."

I hold out the bouquet of butter-yellow flowers. I picked them myself from Karen's garden and wrapped them in a cone of newspaper. Shirla takes them.

"These are so pretty," she says, patting my shoulder. "Gonna get some water for them. Be right back."

She grabs an empty vase and slips out of the room. I chew my lip and try to smile at Reed.

"Who's there?" he asks again. It's like there's an elephant sitting on my chest. I gotta force myself to breathe.

"Sammy." I press my hand to my heart. "I'm Sammy. You don't remember me?"

Reed laughs. My muscles uncoil and I sigh with relief.

"I know who you are, Sammy, ain't nothing wrong with my *brain*," Reed says. "You're supposed to say 'interrupting cow' or 'banana' or something."

"What?"

"You said 'knock, knock' and I said 'who's there?' I'm gone a year and you forget how to tell a simple joke?" He shakes his head. "Such a disappointment."

"You're a dick." I sink into the chair next to his bed. "Some things never change."

"*Some* things have," he says. My chest starts to feel tight again. "Are those new boobs?"

"Yeah, I won the lottery, and spent it on plastic surgery. Got a nose job, too."

He snaps his fingers. "I thought it looked bigger!"

I laugh. Shouldn't be this easy to sit here, talking to him, making jokes, like all that happened ain't happened. But things always were comfortable between Reed and me, till the end, and if I squint I can block out the hospital room and the stitches in his face and the space under the sheet where his leg ought to be and pretend it's a year ago.

We were still together a year ago. Still happy, I think.

I take Reed's hand. Ain't sure how he'll react but his fingers fold over mine. He shuts his eyes and leans his dark head back against the pillow.

"Nice of you to come," he says. "Wasn't sure you would."

"Wasn't sure you'd want me here."

I will never forgive you for this, Sammy. He said those words to me, and he meant them then. He looks like he might be remembering that conversation, too.

He lets go of my hand. "Yeah, I know. But I do want you. Here. Wish you'd been there in Germany, though I guess I might not've noticed if you were or not. I was on a lot of hard meds."

"The good stuff?"

"The *best* stuff."

"How you feeling now?"

"Okay," he says.

"That's convincing."

"Convalescence ain't no fun. I'm trying to get strong enough to leave the hospital and move back home so I can start PT and get back on my... Well. I don't do nothing all day and it's exhausting. Nice to have company. Someone to talk to besides Mom. Not that she ain't great, but there's only so many crosswords a man can take."

He rambles when he's nervous, too.

"Shirla's been gone a long time filling up that vase."

"She ain't filling up the vase." Reed points to the door in the corner of the room. "That there's a bathroom. Sink, running water, the works. She's giving us privacy."

Couple ticks of silence go by. Then Reed says: "Heard about Bobby Ray. I'm sorry. It's so awful, what happened. Part of me still has a hard time believing it."

"Me, too. I keep thinking I'll wake up one morning and he'll be in the kitchen making coffee and everything'll be normal again."

"You figure a way to unplug from the Matrix, let me know, won't you? I could use a reboot, too." Reed pats his thigh. "Sorry. We were talking about your dad."

"Don't be stupid. You lost a leg fighting for our country. Bring it up as much as you want."

More silence, and I know I done said the wrong thing. But he don't make a thing of it. Reed never was one for dramatics.

"Police got any leads on who killed him?"

I hesitate, not sure how much I'm allowed to discuss. But it ain't like I know a lot anyway.

"They found cigarette butts near...the body. Crimsons. Killer used a twenty-two. They're looking at the Tullers for suspects."

Reed whistles. "You think it was Redbreast?"

"Him, or on his orders. Probably the second one."

"Your dad was working for him again?"

I shake my head. "I think it's got something to do with our land."

I explain the situation with Sweet Home and the Tuller connection, how it all fits. Crazy, how easy it is to talk about this with Reed. Maybe easier than it's ever been, 'cause I ain't worrying if this is the thing that'll make him realize I ain't good enough for him. He figured that out a while back, so I got nothing to lose.

Since he knows my family, I give him the lowdown on Rainne's moving scheme, too.

"That bitch," Reed says. "She's got some nerve keeping Decca away from you."

He ain't the first person to say it, and God knows I been thinking it since this whole nightmare started, but I keep having dreams where Johnny Tuller reaches over the fence of Decca's day care and snatches her up, dreams of my sister finding Dad in the grass behind the Collins's crumbling shed.

What kind of monster would I be if I wanted that for her? What if the only way to really protect her is to let her go?

"Denver'll be going back to OU soon," I say, when Reed asks after him. "I don't know why, but I got this feeling in my gut he'll never come back once he's gone. Not this time."

"Even if he don't, it don't mean nothing," Reed says. "You guys were always thick as thieves, and with everything that's happened, he's gonna need you, whether he knows it or not. And if he don't step up, be a good big brother, you tell him to come see me—I'll set him straight."

"You're a real tough guy, huh?"

"Don't you forget it," he jokes, but then it's like a thought strikes him out of nowhere, 'cause the light in his eyes fades.

He looks away from me. "Heard you're with someone. He a tough guy, too?"

"Who'd you get that from?"

"Miscellaneous local loudmouths."

"Kenley?"

"No, Junior Miss Bittersweet ain't been by to see me yet."

"Ugh, that pageant! I wanted to compete so bad, but we didn't have the entry fee to spare."

Can't believe I thought Reed forgot me. He remembers goddamn everything.

"Is it true?" he asks shyly. "About the guy?"

"Maybe. Who told you?"

"Pete," Reed admits.

"Oh. Yeah. Reed, I—"

"Don't you go apologizing to me," Reed says. "It's okay. Not like I expected you to wait around crying this whole time. I'm glad you moved on. Better for both of us, I guess."

"Ain't that simple."

"Don't gotta be simple. I didn't ask my mom to get you over here so I could make a pass. Be sorta pathetic, don't you think? I knew you'd find someone else."

Reed rubs his eyes. "I'm tired."

"Okay, I'll just go then," I say, getting up.

"No. Stay. Get in here."

He lifts the edge of the sheet and I see his leg for the first time. It's normal till you get to the knee, then it disappears. The stump is wrapped up tight in gauze and clean white bandages. I try not to think of how it used to look.

Reed stares at me. "Does it freak you out?"

"Of course not," I lie. Ain't the look of it that disgusts me, but the fact he lost it in the first place. That it got stolen from him.

I climb into the bed, careful to avoid kicking him, and rest my head on his broad shoulder.

"How are you?" I ask. "Really."

"Depends. Helps having Mom here. And you. And Pete,

when he gets the chance, though he blubbers every time he sees me and I get pissed about that real quick."

He pauses. "I get pissed about a lot of things real quick. 'Course that was happening before…before this. Before I even joined the service, it was there, boiling, all that anger. I don't know where it comes from. I wish I could stop feeling that way."

He says this with shame, 'cause he was always such a calm guy, grace under pressure. He's got a right to his temper, after what he's been through, but I won't say a furious man don't make me nervous. I hope I never gotta see that side of him come out.

"I'm having a good day today. But there are so many bad days, Sammy. Sometimes I wish the blast'd just killed me like it killed my friends. I can live with the pain, I think. I been in pain before. It's everything else makes me wanna die. The way y'all look at me. How goddamn fucking scared I am."

I press my face into his shirt. It's a soft, well-worn Cherokee State tee I used to steal from him back when we were together. I'd take it with me when I left his house, sleep in it for days, till the smell of him was gone. Then I'd wash it, give it back, and the pattern would start all over again. I forgot he even had it. I thought I'd kept it, hidden it away in a drawer somewhere. It's good to see him in it.

"Ain't to say I ain't grateful to be alive," he goes on. "Grateful you're here, too. I want you to know I'm so, so sorry, for everything."

"Don't," I say, just about choking on the word.

"When I got hit, there wasn't much I could think about except the pain," Reed says. "I'll tell you, when you're dying, your life don't flash before your eyes—least not when you're dying like I was. It's all pain.

"But after, in Germany, when I was awake, which wasn't a lot, I kept thinking, 'I was so awful to Sammy. If I die and that was the last thing I ever said to her, I'm gonna be paying for it for eternity in the next life.'"

"We both said terrible things," I tell him. "It was a hard business."

He grabs my hands.

"I do forgive you. I do. I wish I hadn't said that nasty thing about you holding a gun to my head. Ain't your fault you got pregnant, or if it is, it's mine, too. I was already desperate to get out. I know you weren't trying to trap me. You just loved me. And I left you to deal with all of it alone."

"I did love you. I didn't know you felt trapped. But I get it now. I understand."

"That ain't on you. That's on me. I wasn't ready to be married, or have kids, same small-town Oklahoma life my parents had, no end in sight. Were you?"

"I was. But I don't think I am anymore. Least, not yet, not like that."

'Cause what if I could leave? What if I wanted to?

"You wanted to be free of me," I say. "I thought I was giving you that. But really I was giving me that, so I'm not sorry I did it. I'm only sorry it hurt you."

Reed nods. "I loved you, too, you know, even then. Still do."

"I still love you. Ain't the same…"

"No, it ain't." He stares at me, releases his grip on my hands, presses them against my chest. "But maybe there's a way it could be better. We both made mistakes, before."

"Ain't totally sure I'm done making them," I say.

Reed puts his arm 'round me. I know what he's trying to say, but I don't wanna talk about that right now. It's too soon after he's come back. He's still reeling. I'm still grieving. Ain't a worse time to talk about loving each other again.

Reed asks, "Who is he? Your new guy."

"Nobody," I say, wishing like hell it were true. "He ain't nobody at all."

CHAPTER TWENTY

Holler's old clunker of a car strains against the climb as I drive up into the hills. When I hit the turn that leads to Brayton's house, I consider taking it, in a moment of temporary insanity, but I force myself to pass it by.

The urge to see Brayton is stronger than I expected after spending the day with Reed. I feel lighter than before, like someone packed my body tight with stones and a few done fell out. I'm forgiven. But forgiving is different than forgetting, and if there's any future for Reed and I together, as friends or as something of our own making, forgetting is what needs doing.

Driving's good for thinking, always helps clear my mind. I was foolish for hoping Brayton and I had something that could last. But I did hope it, so secretly even I didn't know it till I lost him, till I saw I never really had him at all. If he don't get back together with that girl, he'll find another just like her and lose sight of me quick. Never been good at imagining my future, but Brayton's is easy to see. Life will scrub my red dirt leavings from his heart.

Night was falling when I left the hospital, and it's dark when I pull into the drive. The lights are off inside the trailer, which means Denver ain't home. Probably still working at the marina.

Last thing I want is to be in that house alone again after what happened, so I gather fast-food wrappers and old soda bottles from the floor and cup holders, check my phone for messages, anything to stall. But I can't stay in the car forever, inventing things to do.

I get out, juggling trash and my keys and my phone, trying to return a text from Kenley. A shadow shifts nearby and my heart stops dead for a beat, but it's just Dolly, slinking out of the darkness with a grin on. I pat her head and scratch behind her ears.

"You spooked me, girl," I tell her. She pushes her muzzle into my palm, nose wet and cold against my skin. "Come on. Let's go inside and get something to eat."

Dolly sniffs her way up the drive, and I feel tense, wondering what she's smelling that's got her so curious. Halfway to the trailer, she stops at a certain spot, circles it, nose to the ground.

"What are you, part bloodhound?" I ask her. She sneezes. I bend down next to her, rubbing her flank. "You find something?"

She sure as shit has. In the ankle-high brown grass, just past where the lawn meets the gravel, there's a single Crimson cigarette butt. I know it by its bright red filter.

For a second I think Johnny Tuller must've been back here, but then I remember the day Dad disappeared: that morning, Rainne stomping off the porch back to Duke's truck to wait for Decca. Duke flicking a cigarette out the window and into the dry grass.

I got no idea what brand of cigarettes Duke smokes, but I don't get the chance to think it through, 'cause just then I turn to see two people walking out of the woods.

The dark hides their faces, and at first glance I half believe they ain't human, but instead characters straight out of stories Granny Lester and Dad used to tell about giants and tree sprites that once lived in these parts.

The man's huge and bulky, a sackful of mashed potatoes on stilts, head that looks too small for his body. He's got on a leather cutoff vest and camo pants and great big combat boots, gun strapped to his hip: Luger Tuller. Next to him, looking a child in comparison, a girl with bushy red hair and a great beak of a nose—Gypsum.

I put my whole weight against Dolly, shoving her. "Run, Dolly, run!"

She takes off like a shot into the night. I drop what I'm holding and scramble to my feet, sprinting toward the car, thinking only that, of all the Tullers apart from Redbreast, Dad feared Luger most.

Nearly drowned his own brother in a stream up at Rock Creek, Dad told me once. *His head never was quite right.*

My heart is thumping so hard it might just burst right out of my chest.

My eyes are fixed on the ground, so I don't even see Johnny Tuller till I plow into him. He slams me against the car, pinning my wrists with one hand and my hips to the door with his own. I ought to be hollering my lungs out, but I can't get enough air in them, 'cause Johnny's got his right arm pressed down on my throat.

His cold eyes look direct into mine and he puts a finger to his lips: *Don't make a sound.* I look down and catch a glimpse of the vulture on his right bicep. Is he here to finish what he started?

"Got her, Johnnyboy?" Luger calls.

I glance frantically over at Karen and Wayne's house, hoping someone might've heard me scream, but it don't look like they're home. Car's not in the drive.

"I got her," Johnny says.

"Let me go," I gasp, squirming.

"Don't worry, Sammy, they ain't gonna hurt you," Gypsum says, sidling up next to me. "I told them they gotta be real gentle, 'cause we're friends. Ain't we?"

She looks so smug, taking real pleasure in my terror.

"Yeah," I say, fixing her with a glare. "Good friends. Best there is."

Gypsum motions to Johnny and Luger. "Let's go. Don't wanna keep Redbreast waiting."

They frog-march me into the woods, where there's a black SUV parked halfway down an old deer path, into the corps land—Sweet Home land now, though I guess ours just might be, too. Is that what this is about, or is it Dad? Or something different altogether?

I can only just barely see our trailer. They must've been hiding here awhile, like hunters in a blind. I concentrate on remembering every detail, on the off chance they ain't gonna kill me. I wanna know exactly what to tell Agent Pilson so he can arrest these sons of bitches if I manage to get away.

"What's Redbreast got to do with this?" I ask. If they really grabbed me on his orders, I'm in a whole mess of trouble.

Actually, in that case, I'm probably dead.

Gypsum shrugs. "He told us to fetch you, so that's what we're doing."

"I won't go."

Johnny ain't holding me anymore, but anytime I look like I'm even thinking about running, he steps close to remind me what'll happen if I do. Maybe I don't care. We've almost reached the SUV and I'm *not* getting into that thing if I can help it.

"Loog and Johnnyboy'll make you," Gypsum says.

"They touch me, I scream."

"Scream and they'll shut you up so fast nobody'll hear but the trees."

She opens the passenger door and hops in. When I don't follow, she stares at me from inside the darkness of the car, whites of her eyes shining like pearls in the moonlight.

"Get in," she says, "time's a-wasting."

I don't recognize Gypsum no more. I never really knew her, but she's been around more this summer than I ever remember from years past, and it's hard to make this version—calm and confident in her mission, bursting with Tuller swagger—add up with the desperate-to-please puppy dog I'm used to.

The night Ash Boford and his friends attacked me comes rushing back, the unchecked rage in Ash's eyes as he prepared to dole out my punishment for messing with the Tullers.

No sign of any such emotion in Johnny and Luger. They seem bored, like kidnapping is routine. Only Gypsum's getting joy out of watching me twist, and I figure that's mostly personal. I did say some awfully mean things to her.

Still, I'm scared out of my wits, and not just for me, but for Decca and Denver, Reed and Kenley and Brayton. What if I up and disappeared just like Dad? How would they ever understand it?

Luger shoves me and grunts at me to get going. I figure the best course is to pretend I ain't as terrified as I am—Lesters got swagger, too—so I climb in next to Gypsum and buckle my seat belt. Maybe if I can bluff my way through whatever's coming, I can survive it. If I try to fight my way out, I'm pretty sure I won't.

"Let me guess," I say. "It's a surprise party. My birthday ain't for a couple months, you know."

"Shut up," Gypsum snaps. Luger backs the SUV down the deer path till it meets the road, then takes off at top speed down the hill.

"So you know," Gypsum says, in a voice real low, "I don't want nothing to do with your brother. Uppity twats who done got above their raising ain't my type."

"How do you know what your type is? You even been with a guy before?"

Gypsum sniffs. "Not as many as you, I reckon."

She stares out the window. Johnny plays with the radio dial, like we're on any old car trip, trying to coax a decent tune out of the storm of static.

"Look here, Gypsum. I'm real sorry about everything I said. I was angry. My stupid heart was breaking and I took it out on you and I shouldn't've. So if that's what this is about—"

"I *told* you, Redbreast sent for you. Sit tight, Sammy. You'll know when we've reached it."

"Reached what? Rock Creek?"

God, I wish Dad were here to help me. That anybody were, but especially him.

"Shut the fuck up already. I ain't telling you nothing else."

That's the last time anybody talks till we reach Rock Creek. Least, that's where I assume we are. In the dark it's hard to see where we were going, and I lose the thread of country roads that lead us into the true Ozarks, up through the hills and hollers of the Boston Mountains, trees pressing in on both sides as we climb.

By the time Gypsum says, "We're here," I've given up trying to figure how to escape. I don't know this land—where would I even go?

Luger pulls off the road onto a dirt path. We drive for what seems like miles and all I can see is whatever the headlights show ahead. Finally—*finally*—we stop, in the middle of a large open meadow with one low-slung house spread out like a man taking a nap, looking like a kid built it, with a square center building made of stone, additions and lean-tos pasted on the sides when more room was needed. There are some lights on inside, but the place seems pretty well deserted.

Gypsum gives me a shove.

"Get out," she barks. "They're waiting for you 'round back."

My gut wrenches at the word *they*. Could be anybody. Tullers, of course, but maybe Ash Boford, too. The terrible feeling I'm going to my death grips me and I refuse to move out of pure instinct, fighting the inevitable. Luger grabs my arm and twists it hard till I gasp in pain, then drags me down a packed dirt path.

We round the side of the house and come upon a whole group gathered there, sitting in front of a fire pit, drinking whiskey out of Dixie cups.

I ain't seen Redbreast since I was younger than Decca, but I recognize him easy. He don't look like much, an old man with a big paunch hanging over his belt, face that tells the story of a life lived hard. He's got an unlit cigar between his fingers and a toddler on his lap, not barely three, sucking her thumb with a lock of curly red hair clenched in her fist. Her eyes are drooping. Gotta be past her bedtime.

"There you are." A woman standing behind Redbreast puts a hand on the back of his chair and frowns at Gypsum.

"Took longer than we thought," Gypsum says. She kisses Redbreast on the cheek. "Hey there, Grandpa. Want me to take that one off your hands?"

She reaches for the girl, who tips sleepily into her arms, and hoists her up on her hip.

If my eyes get any wider, they'll pop right out of my head. "You're his granddaughter?"

"Who'd you think I was?" Gypsum asks.

A third-rate Tuller, *at best*, not an heir to the hillbilly throne. Seems stupid now. Should've guessed she had more to do with Redbreast than a last name. Stuff's starting to clear up real fast.

Redbreast stares at me, raking his eyes up and down my body.

"You're late," he says.

I glance at all the faces gathered 'round me—no sympathy, no gentleness on any of them. No great curiosity, either. The Tullers look bored, or annoyed, like my arrival interrupted their fun.

And maybe it did. There's a table spread with burgers and hot dogs and salads. My empty stomach groans at the sight of it. There's a bonfire, too, kids sitting cross-legged in front of their mamas and daddies, watching us, Redbreast and me. Sometimes I forget the Tullers ain't just a gang, they're a family.

It'd be almost normal if it weren't for the spooky silence. Not a person is talking. They're all just staring at me.

"Didn't know I was expected," I say carefully, letting my gaze drift back to Redbreast. He's still staring. "Looks like y'all are having a party. My invitation must've gotten lost in the mail."

For a second, Redbreast don't react—then he laughs a laugh ain't got no joy in it at all.

"Gypsum told me you're a spark plug," he says, in a voice that ain't quite fond, but ain't quite insulting, either. "So'd Bobby Ray. Said you had spirit."

"That why I'm here? 'Cause of my dad?" I ask.

The baby girl starts to whine. Gypsum bounces her up and down to keep her quiet. Makes me miss Decca with the sudden fury of a twister, and hate Dad just as much. How could he get us into such a mess? How could he die and let his bad fall on me?

Redbreast puts his cigar in his mouth and lights it, puffs, blows smoke rings toward the fire. His eyes are like lumps of glittering black chert in the flickering light.

"Your daddy borrowed quite a bit of money from me," he says. "Gonna need it back."

I swallow hard. "Borrowed?"

"Advance against payment for something he ain't never delivered on."

"Well, you won't be getting it back from him. He's dead, in case you ain't heard."

"That is a predicament. In a civilized society, responsibility for an unforgivable debt falls to next of kin."

"But this ain't a civilized society. This is Lake Bittersweet," I say, hoping for another laugh. If he likes me—likes my *spirit*—maybe he'll cut me a break. Give me time to figure this out instead.

No laugh, but maybe the ghost of a smile. "You'd rather play by the rules of an *un*civilized society?"

"Not really. How much are we talking?"

"Ten thousand."

"I don't got that kind of money. Tight as things are right now, I couldn't pay you ten—ten thousand is out of the question."

"Then how's about we change the question," Redbreast says, easing his bulk against the back of his chair. "In exchange for the ten thousand up front and a couple days to break it to the family before he signed, Bobby Ray was supposed to sell up his land on Gibson Bluff. Since he never did turn over the agreement, and now he's dead, means the land belongs to you—you and that brother of yours."

"I guess it does," I say, though hell if I know. I never even thought to find out.

"Finish what your daddy started. Sell the land, get the price we promised Bobby Ray, I'll forgive the debt—pretty sure where that money went, anyway. We got a deal?"

"No."

He squints at me, frowns. "I trust you know who you're dealing with, girl. Just 'cause you got that damned pig Pilson sniffing around don't mean you're safe. I got ways of getting what I want."

"Ways like sending Johnny to break into my house and nearly kill me?"

"I don't know nothing about that," Redbreast says, in the same flat tone Gypsum used to deny it.

"I ain't selling. That's our land." And even if I could bring myself to sell it, I ain't handing it over to the man who murdered my daddy. But I know better than to say that to his face.

Redbreast throws a sharp look at Gypsum. "Thought you said she was reasonable."

"She don't trust us. Can't say I blame her. Maybe you ought to give Sammy her presents. That way she knows we don't mean her no harm."

"Clever girl. We'll put aside the land for now. I got a couple gifts for you, Sammy Lester."

"What kind of gifts?" Pretty sure ain't nothing the Tullers wanna give me that I'm keen to have.

"A name," Redbreast says. "And an opportunity. First, the name."

"Whose name?"

"I liked your daddy, you know that? There's people going 'round saying I must've had him killed for some reason. You wouldn't know nothing about that, would you?"

I shake my head.

"Good. 'Cause I'd hate to think Bobby Ray's own kin don't know him at all. He don't always make the best decisions high, but when he's clean he's smarter than all my other men put together. Too smart to do something that'd make me want him six feet under. Wasn't happy about the missing money, but ten thousand ain't nothing to me. I live simple, but I ain't been a poor man in a long, long time."

Ain't sure what to say to that, so I keep my mouth shut. What's the point of this ramble?

"So you see, when he done disappeared, I got curious. Didn't make no sense to me why a man who always talked about his kid, and making sure he got to be a proper daddy to her, would up and go with no explanation."

"Is that why he said he needed the money?" I ask. "For Decca?"

"Didn't give me no reason, and I don't see none to meddle in business that ain't mine, but I suspected it. Lawyers are expensive, even the cheap ones. Moving's expensive, too, especially when you gotta leave your job and the rest of your family behind to do it."

"Dad was gonna move? To Arkansas?"

"Like I said, I don't meddle."

"What's this name you said you'd give me?"

"I'm getting to that. Like I said, I was curious about Bobby Ray leaving, so I told Luger and Johnny to take their crew, see what they could find out. 'Course at first I didn't tell them *wh*y I wanted Bobby Ray, which means I owe you an apology for that graffiti on your door."

Not to mention the hole in my ceiling. "Where's my apology for Kibble?"

"What's that now?"

"Our dog. Your boys killed him back when Dad got arrested for Arthur Comstock."

"Did they?" He shrugs. "You wanna send a message, you gotta spill a little ink sometimes. Price of doing business."

I look away in disgust.

"My boys went a lot of places, talked to a lot of people, trying to sort out who knew what about Bobby Ray. Also had Gypsum watching over you, making sure you didn't come to no harm."

"She did a really great job," I say. "Ash Boford near about smashed my face in."

"We'll get to that. But first—you know a guy named Marco Goodman?"

"No. Should I?"

"He's just a junkie. Used to be one of mine, long time ago,

like Bobby Ray. Marco ain't got no love for your dad. Everybody knows that."

Everybody, meaning everybody who matters to the Tullers, which don't include me. Dad was part of a whole world I never saw. And it hits me: each new person I meet for the rest of my life, Dad won't know them. Every new place I go, if I ever go anywhere at all, he won't know I'm there.

"You're saying this Marco guy did something to Dad?"

Is it possible that, after all this wondering, Dad's killer could turn out to be a man I never even heard of?

"Not saying that at all."

"So why's his name mean anything to me?"

"You're gonna have to ask him about it yourself. But from what I'm hearing, let's just say even jacked up on meth as he is, Marco's got better sense than to kill somebody for money."

I feel like I been hit by a truck. "Somebody tried to hire him to kill my dad? Who would do that?"

"Like I said—that's a question you'll be having to ask Marco himself."

"Why didn't he go to the police? Why don't *you*?"

"Don't act stupid. We don't talk to police. Used to be Lesters didn't, neither, but y'all were raised wrong. Too straight for your own good. I blame your mama."

Redbreast puffs his cigar. "Marco might sing for the pigs, though, if you loosen the lid for them first. Man's gotta be *convinced*, you see, and ain't nobody better for the job than a pretty girl like yourself. Tell him I sent you. He'll talk if you ask real nice."

"Maybe I'll do that."

"Maybe you will."

The old man narrows his eyes at me. I hate those eyes. They're more alive than the rest of him.

"Was Bobby Ray right about you, Sammy?" he asks. "You a good girl like your mama?"

"Pretty sure *good* ain't how my mama would describe me."

Redbreast laughs, for real this time, and so does everybody else, cackling like a coop full of hens. How long am I gonna be stuck here with these rednecks? They ain't in any hurry to cart my ass home, that's plain, though now I'm thinking they might let me go.

Luger's cleaning his fingernails with a hunting knife, and Johnny seems mighty comfortable on the far side of the circle, lounging on an overturned log with a dark-haired teenage girl on his knee, hand up her skirt. Gypsum's the only one who ain't laughing at me. The kid in her arms stirs and Gypsum shushes her.

"You said you got two gifts for me," I say. "What's the other one?"

Redbreast's eyes brighten. "This is the fun part. Johnnyboy, look alive."

Johnny Tuller stops whatever he's doing with that girl and stands, dumping her out of his lap. She pouts.

"You want I should get him now?" Johnny asks.

Redbreast nods. "Our guest's waited long enough, I think."

"If it's all the same to you, I wanna go home now, please," I say.

"Now, ain't those impressive manners? Bobby Ray was right—your mama did raise you up good. Nice and polite. *Please* and *thank you*. Think I get any of those sweet words up here? Not out of this mangy bunch."

Everybody laughs again, but there's an edge to it all. I know

I'm being mocked. Gypsum frowns and hands the little girl over to a woman standing nearby.

"Take her inside," Gypsum says. But Redbreast puts a hand up and snaps, "No."

The woman freezes. The little girl blinks at him and sticks her thumb in her mouth.

"Everybody watches," Redbreast says coldly. Then he turns to me. "Don't worry, you're gonna like this."

He raises his eyebrows and angles his head to indicate there's something behind me.

"Now, what do you suppose you get for the girl who's got nothing?"

I nearly stumble backward when I see what it is Johnny's brought into the circle: Ash Boford. My pulse starts thumping, but then I see Johnny's got Ash's arms held together tight behind his back. Ash's head's hung low. Johnny shoves him to his knees in the dirt near my feet.

Ash scowls. "What the fuck is going on? What's she doing here?"

"Shut up, or I'll give Johnny permission to stop being gentle. Young buck like you'll recover from a dislocated shoulder, but not quick," Redbreast says.

I'm so busy staring at Ash, wondering what hell is about to be unleashed, I don't even realize Redbreast is out of his chair and standing right next to me. He smells like cigar smoke and cheap beer and body odor.

"Like it?" he whispers, soft like a lover. "My gift?"

"If you're giving me Ash Boford, I'm gonna need the receipt 'cause I ain't keeping him."

"Not forever, just as long as it takes you to give him what's due." Redbreast puts a hand on my shoulder and brings the cigar to his lips. "Unless you're not the vengeful kind."

Now I get it. "You heard what he did."

"Gypsum let me know our little *pro-tee-jay* gave you a licking not too long ago. When it comes to our ways, he's still a pup, but at least he ought to know better than *that*. We don't do harm to the families of our friends, do we, boy?"

"Bobby Ray Lester ain't my friend," Ash sneers. "Beat the tar out of my sister when they were married. He deserved what he got, whoever done it, and Sammy deserved what I gave her for making trouble."

"That ain't true, and you know it," I shout at him.

Redbreast grabs Ash by his floppy blond hair and yanks his head back. Ash is shaking.

"Ain't for you to decide who deserves what. That right belongs to our Lord and Savior, but he ain't been around much lately, so I suppose the responsibility done falls to me. You're gonna stay here, all calm and respectful-like, and let Sammy give you a whipping. When she's finished, she's gonna go on home, and you're gonna leave her alone till I tell you otherwise. You got that?"

Ash nods as much as he can with Redbreast holding a fistful of his hair. I ain't never seen him look so scared. Gives me an odd sort of satisfaction, that.

Redbreast lets go of Ash and walks away, knocking my shoulder as he passes by.

"Now'd be the time to show us all that grit you think you got, little girl," he tells me.

Everybody's looking at me. I feel the weight of their gazes like stones in my pockets. *Watch the uppity bitch from down at the lake take on the townie fool who thinks he's one of us.* I ain't innocent enough to believe Redbreast's doing this on my account. He's disciplining Ash for going rogue. Being humiliated by me is just part of the penalty.

"Here," Johnny Tuller says, slipping his belt from its loops and handing it to me.

Ash stares at the ground like he's willing it to open up and swallow me. He ain't a good guy, or a smart guy, or even an evil guy. He's just desperate to be accepted by these hard people, so he can tell himself he's hard, too. But he ain't yet, though this is one of the things that'll get him there.

If there's anything I've learned, it's that hard people come to bad ends. I got no interest in being a tool for Redbreast Tuller, and even less interest in being a stepping stone on Ash's path to a fate like Dad's—or worse.

"No thanks," I say, dropping Johnny's belt on the ground. "Far as I'm concerned, having to go through life as himself is punishment enough."

Ash lifts his eyes and finally meets mine. So much hate in those eyes, and to think he used to think he loved me. Or whatever passes for love when you're fourteen and an idiot.

Redbreast don't look happy. Maybe he was hoping to see a spark of Dad in me, something he could use on down the line. I shrug. I ain't Dad. Thank God.

"Should've known you wouldn't have the balls to hit me, you stupid, filthy slut," Ash says. He spits at my feet.

Redbreast's eyes widen with excitement. He knows what's gonna happen before I do. Without even deciding, I slam my fist hard as I can into the side of Ash's face.

Dad taught me how to throw a punch when I was twelve, but even so, a sharp, sickening pain shoots up my arm like a bolt of lightning and I got a tough time staying upright. My

knuckles cry out as I uncurl my hand but I ain't about to show
how bad it is in front of the Tullers.

Ash falls to the ground, clutching at his mouth, groaning
wetly and spitting red blood into red dirt. The sight makes
me woozy.

I turn to Redbreast. "I'd like to go *home* now."

Redbreast nods. "You think real hard about my offer. I'll be
after an answer from you soon."

"I'll drive her," Gypsum says, handing the girl to another
woman. Luger tosses her a set of keys and she grabs me by
my good arm, hauling me off like I'm on fire. "Let's get out of
here before—"

But there ain't no time. Redbreast nods at Johnny and Luger,
and they fall upon Ash, set about beating him to a pulp right
there in front of everyone. Ash don't make a sound except at
first, when Luger nails him hard in the stomach with a steel-
toed boot and he makes a wounded animal noise, somewhere
between a whimper and a grunt. I turn away, but I'm the only
one who does. *Everybody watches.* Gypsum tows me away.

Soon as we're out of sight of the Tullers, I sink into a crouch,
cradling my hand. "Holy *shit*."

"Bet you ain't never walloped nobody like that before," Gypsum says. "How'd it feel?"

"Good. Really good. Bad, too."

"'Cause of the pain?"

I shake my head. "I stooped to him."

"You got yourself some good old-fashioned country justice,"
Gypsum says.

"What's gonna happen to him?" I ask. I hate Ash more than
almost anybody, but what if they kill him? What if they kill
him and I'm right here and don't do nothing about it?

"Don't you trouble yourself—Luger and Johnny know how to give a beating without going too far. Most of the time. Up here, ain't nothing but a scolding. You don't even wanna know what happens to folks who really make Redbreast mad," says Gypsum. "Besides, Ash Boford had it coming for what he done. Think how far he would've gone if your boy hadn't put that semiautomatic to his head."

"You were there," I say. "You told Brayton where I was, that I needed help."

"Grandpa said to watch out for you. I was doing what I was told. Been doing it the whole time."

"You never said anything about being his granddaughter."

"Would you've been nicer to me if I did?" Gypsum grabs my good hand and helps me up.

"Probably."

"Well, you never asked."

"Did Redbreast tell you to watch *out* for me, or to *watch* me?"

"Bit of both. He figured you could use someone at your six, what with his suspicions about your daddy's disappearance."

"Which are…"

Gypsum smiles at me. "Nice try. Charms were my idea. What'd you do with them?"

"Took the nails out of the door," I tell her. She unlocks the SUV and we climb in. She looks like a rag doll behind the wheel of this monster. I ain't a hundred percent sure she can drive it. "Burned the charm."

Gypsum whistles low. "Boy howdy, Sammy Lester, are you in for it now."

CHAPTER TWENTY-ONE

"Looks like you got visitors," Gypsum says as we round the corner onto my street.

There's a handful of cars outside my house: Kenley, Holler, Agent Pilson, they're all here. Denver must've shit a brick when he came home to find me missing, my things scattered across the gravel drive, called everyone he could think of.

Gypsum slows the SUV.

"Better let you out here," she says, pulling over in front of one of the many empty houses just waiting for the Sweet Home developers to tear it down. "I don't want no trouble."

"I'm gonna have to tell them where I was."

"Make something up for the pig, or Redbreast won't be so nice next time he sees you. Which'll be soon enough. He ain't kidding about your land. He wants it, and you can't fight him forever."

"How long you think I got?"

Gypsum shrugs. "Couple of days, maybe. A week if he's feeling generous. You make up your mind before then, you call me. I'll set up a meeting."

"I don't have your number." I pat my pockets. "Don't got my phone."

"Gimme yours and I'll text later. You probably ought to go show your face so they know you're still alive. Bet your wimpy brother's gone out of his mind with worry."

"He ain't a wimp. Don't kidnap me next time and then nobody gotta worry."

Our trailer's so tiny, it feels mighty cramped even with just Denver and I living there, so when I walk through the door to find seven people and one very het-up Labrador retriever gathered in the front room, I wanna bolt.

The space is hot and stale-smelling. Everybody looks like they don't know whether to hug me or kill me dead.

Karen opts for choice number one.

"Sammy! Oh, thank God you're safe, honey. We were so worried," she says.

Wayne hugs me, too, then Kenley, then Holler. Even Dolly gives my hand a relieved lick, but Denver, Brayton and Agent Pilson keep their distance.

What the hell is Brayton even doing here? Goddamn me, it's so very nice to see his face again, mad as I still am at him.

I figure the best course of action is to play dumb.

"What's going on? Why's everybody here?"

"What's going *on*?" Denver snaps. "You disappeared right out of our fucking driveway with no sign of where you'd gone. I panicked. Where the hell've you been?"

"Went for a walk." I shrug. My right hand's a solid ball of pain and both of them are shaking.

"A walk? For four hours, after dark?"

"Needed to clear my head. Didn't mean to be gone so long.

Didn't mean for any of y'all to worry. Agent Pilson, what are you doing here?" I ask.

Of all the people gathered in this trailer, he's the one who looks most out of place. Even Brayton blends in better. My chest cramps whenever I look his way, heartsore from all the missing him I been doing.

"Denver called me," he says. "Really, Sammy, under the circumstances I would've thought you'd try not to cause your friends and family any unnecessary concern."

"I'm sorry," I say, cursing Redbreast Tuller to hell in my head. "I didn't mean to."

Since I'm clearly safe, Agent Pilson leaves, shooting me a disappointed look on the way out. Soon enough, Karen and Wayne and Holler are gone, too, leaving just Kenley, Denver and Brayton behind.

Much as I can't stand having Brayton here, reminding me, I'm not looking forward to being left alone with Denver, who's so angry he ain't even talking, just sitting in Grandpa Lester's armchair chewing on his tongue in agitation.

"Why're *you* here?" I ask Brayton.

He shoves his hands in his pockets, only half looking at me from under his eyelashes.

"I was worried," he says. "Can't I still care what happens to you?"

"No. I told you to forget me," I say. But I bet it's written all over my face, how glad I am he cares.

"Well, I can't. What's wrong with your hand?" Brayton asks. It's starting to bruise and swell, and I'm holding it funny to keep it from hurting too much.

"Slammed it in a door, not that it's any of your business. You better get out of here. Wouldn't want your girlfriend to get the wrong idea about us."

He frowns. "Sammy, I heard about—"

"Get out," I say, 'cause he's gonna bring up Dad and I can't talk about that right now.

He looks straight at me, like he's trying to send a message—*I won't leave you at a time like this*—but when I don't crack he gives up and heads for the door.

"I'll wait for you outside," Brayton mutters to Kenley as he leaves.

I turn on Kenley. "*You* brought him here?"

"Denver asked me to check with Brayton to see if you were with him, and when I told him why I was looking for you he freaked and insisted on coming along. What was I supposed to do?"

"How about not tell him why you were looking? Or, maybe, not look for me there—you know I'd never, after what he did."

Kenley narrows her eyes at me. "I'm starting to wonder if I know anything at all about what you would or wouldn't do. Where were you, really?"

"The truth, this time," Denver says.

"I told you. I was on a walk. Don't believe me, that's your problem."

Denver and Kenley exchange a look.

"I gotta drive Brayton back home," she says. "Glad you're okay, Sammy."

She hugs me on her way out, but I can tell she's pissed. I'm gonna have to fix that later. Right now I got bigger problems.

Like how, soon as the door closes behind Kenley, Denver explodes at me.

"What the *fuck* do you think you're playing at?" he shouts. "How dare you take off like that after what we just been through, and then have the *balls* to lie about it when you finally turn back up? Ain't we suffered enough, Sammy? Ain't we both fucking suffered *enough*?"

"Careful, Denny. Your country is showing," I say meanly.

"Fuck you!" he roars.

Denver's anguish is terrifying. I ain't never seen my brother act like this, never seen him so upset before. He was always the steadier one, the Lester who could control his emotions.

"Calm down, and maybe I'll tell you the truth," I say. "Why don't you sit?"

"Just say it. Your shit was scattered all over the lawn and Dolly was losing her goddamn mind. Something must've happened."

"Luger, Johnny and Gypsum dragged me up to Rock Creek to see Redbreast."

Denver's eyes get wide. "No bullshit?"

"No bullshit."

"Guess I ought to be thankful you turned back up at all, then."

"I ain't even got to the good part yet."

I tell Denver everything, from the second I saw the Tullers coming out of the woods to punching Ash Boford in the face.

He grins in spite of everything when he hears that part, goes into the kitchen himself to fetch me a bag of frozen peas to ice my swollen knuckles. A peace offering. Though I can't forget what he said. I sure as hell feel like *I've* suffered enough.

"Wish I could've seen you drop Ash like that," Denver says. "Jealous it wasn't me, too."

"Don't be. My hand hurts like a bitch."

"So this Marco Goodman guy, you ever heard of him?"

"No. You?"

"Nope. Redbreast made it sound like someone might've offered him money to kill Dad?"

"That's right."

"But he didn't say who, or why?"

"No. Looks like the only person we're gonna get that information from is Marco Goodman—if we're lucky. I bet he's like all those junkie types, don't trust nobody."

"Then we're just going to have to make him trust us."

"We?"

"Yeah. You're planning to talk to him, right? Sounds like the sort of crazy thing you'd do without telling anybody so as to put yourself into the most danger possible."

Denver gives me a small smile. "I get why you don't want to tell Pilson just yet, but I'm not letting you go alone."

"Who are you and what have you done with Denver Lester? You wanna come *with me*? Where's the lecture about taking matters into my own hands, about being good and obedient and not putting myself at risk?"

"I still believe all of that. I think you're crazy to keep sticking your neck out. But you'll just do it anyway, and you're my sister. Maybe we got other people on our side, but we're our own team, the two of us. And I'm sick of feeling like we're not."

"Me, too," I say.

Marco Goodman lives in a trailer park on the outskirts of Tehlicoh, the type of place I usually avoid, and now I'm here my nerves are going full throttle.

I told Denver he had to wait in the car. Redbreast made it sound like Marco would only talk to me, and even if that ain't true, seeing a big guy like Denver through the peephole ain't gonna motivate a drug addict to open the door.

Takes a couple knocks, but eventually I hear someone shuffling 'round inside. The door opens and a white woman with dark circles under her eyes peeks out. She's got track marks in the webbing between her fingers. I look past her, into the dim hallway. Junkies creep me out.

"Who're you?" the woman asks.

I tell her I've come to see Marco.

"He ain't here."

"I think he is," I say. If I know anything about addicts, I'm gonna bet Marco Goodman almost never leaves his house. "Redbreast Tuller sent me. You wanna check on that before you let me in, go right ahead, but don't take too long. It's urgent."

"Redbreast?" The woman stiffens. "I'll go get him."

She shuts the door and I hear the sound of muffled voices, but I can't make out what they're saying. Then the door swings open again and a man I assume is Marco stands there, dressed in faded jeans and a dingy wifebeater, looking like he just woke up. He squints at me.

"What d'you want?" he asks.

"I wanna talk to you about Bobby Ray Lester," I say. "And the person who hired you to kill him. Redbreast said if I asked real nice, you'd tell me straight. That true?"

Marco works his jaw back and forth, considering. "What's your name, girl?"

His voice is thick and drowsy. He looks me up and down and flashes me what I guess is supposed to be a flirty smile. Makes me wanna heave all over the dirty welcome mat.

"Sammy Lester."

"Bobby Ray's daughter, huh? Or maybe his new wife?" Marco cackles. "He liked 'em young."

"Daughter."

"Huh. Didn't know he had another one."

Gives me a chill, thinking about someone like Marco knowing anything about Decca.

Marco runs his fingers through his long, greasy dark hair.

Looks older than he probably is. I'd say he's somewhere in his early thirties, but if he'd told me he was Dad's age, I could believe that, too.

"Better come in, then," he says. "Ain't something we ought to be talking about all in the open, like."

I got no desire to step foot in that trailer, and I can just imagine how pissed Denver'll be if I do, but I know from experience with people like Marco that he ain't gonna tell me nothing unless he can be absolutely sure he won't be overheard. I follow him in and take the seat he offers on the least stained corner of the couch I can find.

There are ashtrays overflowing with cigarette butts—no Crimsons—and spent joints littered all over the tiny living room, bags of weed lying out in the open, a crack pipe sitting on a small chipped mirror on the kitchen table. I cover my disgust with a cough, but I ain't fooling Marco. Not that it really matters what I think. Junkies don't care much about the opinions of others, something you pick up right quick when you live with one.

His girlfriend, or whoever she is, peeks out from the bedroom, but Marco shouts at her to mind her own business and she scurries out of sight.

Marco flops down in a La-Z-Boy opposite me and lights a blunt with a plastic American flag lighter. He inhales deep, holds it, then spews smoke in my direction.

"You say Redbreast sent you? About Bobby Ray?"

"Yeah," I say. He offers me the blunt. I shake my head.

"Your...*daddy*."

He says *daddy* like Ash said *slut* last night.

"That's what I said."

"Look. I ain't saying this is what happened."

"I don't got time for games," I tell him. "You're gonna tell me what you know, and then you're gonna tell the police if I ask you, 'cause Redbreast promised you would and I think we both know Redbreast Tuller keeps his promises. Who hired you to kill my dad?"

"Whoa, whoa, whoa!" Marco jumps to his feet and holds his hands up. "I ain't killed *nobody*. And I ain't talking to no fucking cops."

"You will, or I'll tell Redbreast you didn't. I'm sure you don't want no trouble with him. He had a soft spot for my dad, you know."

"Oh, I know. Redbreast treated Bobby Ray better than his own sons, sometimes."

Marco spits on his own damn carpet. This place makes our trailer look like a palace and all of a sudden, I ache for it.

"I ain't killed nobody, girl. You wanna know what I know, let's get that straight, right now."

"I ain't no little girl. Let's get *that* straight."

He shoots me a grin, then drops it when he sees I ain't playing.

"I ain't killed nobody," he says again.

"Sure the cops'll be glad to hear it."

"Goddammit," Marco whines. "Duke'll tie my balls in a knot if he finds out I gave him up to the pigs."

I feel like I been body-slammed by a sumo wrestler. "What did you say?"

"What?"

"*Duke* was the one who hired you to kill my dad? Duke *Tremont*?"

"I don't kill people, not for money, not for nothing. I know the mandatories on that shit, they ain't worth it, and Oklahoma'll fry you up on murder for hire soon as look at you." Marco stares at his hands. "But yeah...he asked."

"Did he say why?"

Marco shakes his head.

"How much did he offer you?"

"Couple grand."

This is crazy. I mean, this is actually insane. Duke would never spend good money on hiring some junkie to kill Dad for his own reasons, so if he went 'round looking for a hired gun, it's gotta be 'cause Rainne asked him to.

But she wouldn't do that. Just 'cause she was having issues with Dad don't mean she'd actually want him *dead*…does it?

First thing that pops into my head is the memory of us searching the old Collins place, how Denver and I were about to look behind the shed, where the police ended up finding Dad's body, and only stopped 'cause *Rainne* distracted us, calling us over to the creek to look at that lump of rotted fabric that obviously wasn't anything.

And that picture of Decca cuddling the stuffed animal on MaryEllen's lawn. I could've sworn it was Waldo, not some random replacement rabbit MaryEllen got her. Maybe Dad *did* show up at her house that night like he planned. All we gotta prove he didn't is Rainne's word, but what if she's lying?

The cigarette butts they found by Dad's body, the Crimsons with the red filter—there's a Crimson butt on our lawn, too. Maybe it *is* Duke's.

Holy shit. Maybe it *is*.

A sick feeling like the one I got when I saw that photo of Dad's body rises up at the thought of Duke within ten miles of my baby sister. They're probably home right now, all together, the three of them. Little Decca, in arm's reach of Dad's killer.

How long before the same evil impulse that brought Duke to Marco Goodman's door makes him lash out at her, too? I'd like to think he'd never, that Rainne wouldn't let him hurt her. But how well can you really know the hearts of people like that?

"You know they found him dead," I tell Marco. "If you didn't kill my dad for Duke, who do you suppose did?"

"Could've been anybody. He asked others. Maybe one of them changed their minds later, said yes. Or maybe Duke did it himself. But I *didn't do it*. You got that? I ain't killed *nobody*."

"Yeah, I heard you the first hundred times. If you knew Bobby Ray showed up dead, how come you didn't go to the police?"

"I went to Redbreast," Marco says. "That's what *I* do when I got information. I told you, I don't mess around in other people's business, and I *don't* talk to *cops*."

I can't take being here any longer. My head's pounding, and I feel like I'm standing on a rocking boat with no sea legs to speak of.

Duke. Rainne. It's all too crazy to believe, but it makes total sense.

"Well, you're gonna. Better not run, Marco. They'll find you and they'll put you in prison for screwing with a police investigation." Don't know if that's true, but I figure Marco don't, either. "You wanna go back to prison?"

Bit of a wild guess, but Marco's got a tattoo on his left forearm, and it's got that same homemade look as a couple of Dad's. I'd bet money he served time in McAlester, maybe even when Dad was there. Maybe that's where the blood between them first went bad. Gotta say, ain't sure I care.

"You're a bitch, you know that?" Marco sneers. But he looks scared. "Get out of here."

I only just catch that last part, 'cause I'm already halfway out the door.

* * *

Denver and I drive straight from Marco Goodman's house to the sheriff's department, where Agent Pilson and his people are camping out while the investigation into Dad's murder continues.

Every time I walk into the interview room Pilson's using as an office, he looks less and less happy to see me, but this time, I don't care. This time, I'm coming with answers instead of questions.

Pilson listens patiently while I tell him what I learned at Marco's, and what I pieced together on my own. When I finish, Denver and I both stare at him expectantly. Don't know what it is we think he's gonna do—thank us for cracking his case for him, hug us, throw us a goddamn party?—but what I *don't* see coming is when he says, "I know."

"What do you mean, you know?"

"I've suspected Rainne and Duke Tremont might be involved in your father's disappearance for a while now."

"You have?"

"Remember when I told you a good detective considers all possibilities? The most likely one, in a case like this, is that it was perpetrated by a lover or spouse. Soon as you mentioned your father was having a custody dispute with his ex-wife, I was pretty sure where to start looking."

He reaches for a nearby stack of papers and pulls a file out.

"When we ran your dad's financials, we ran Rainne's, too. The debt is mutual so it showed up in both reports, but Bobby Ray was the only one making payments on it—till he disappeared. After that, Rainne started making payments. Different amounts on different loans and cards, but guess what it all just about adds up to?"

"Ten thousand dollars," Denver says.

Pilson nods. "Either Bobby Ray gave Rainne that money, or she took it from him."

"You don't happen to know what brand of cigarettes Duke smokes, do you?" I ask Pilson. "There's a Crimson butt on my lawn. My neighbor's dog sniffed it out last night. I think it might be Duke's."

"If you suspected Rainne since we first met you at that diner, what've you been doing about it all this time?" Denver asks. "They have our sister!"

"I've interviewed them both," Pilson says. "Separately. While we talked, I had a deputy put GPS trackers on their vehicles so we could monitor their movements. I thought they might revisit the scene, or go somewhere else that implicated them in your father's disappearance."

"Did they?"

"She didn't, and for a while, neither did he. After we found the body, I checked for any record of a gun belonging to Duke Tremont. He's got a few registered in his name, shotguns and a Glock thirty-three, but no twenty-two. None of his guns match the weapon that killed your father."

We must look disappointed, 'cause Pilson rushes to say, "But, we did notice something interesting when we were tracking Duke's movements. Once a week, Duke drives to Stillwater to visit his ex-father-in-law, his first wife's dad. Seems the two of them are still tight, even though Duke's marriage to the man's daughter went kaput. The father-in-law's suffering from the beginnings of dementia, but when I visited him last week, he told me one of his guns was missing."

"A twenty-two?" I ask.

Pilson nods. "Now we've just got to find it. In the meantime, we'll test that cigarette butt in your yard against the ones we found near Bobby Ray's body, and I'm going to talk to Marco Goodman."

"What can we do?" I ask.

The pressure inside me is so intense, I feel like I'm gonna shatter into a million pieces. I don't know whether to be devastated or ecstatic or enraged—it's all jumbled up inside of me, all those different feelings, and I need a way to channel it before it drives me out of my mind.

A way other than plotting an elaborate kidnapping attempt to get Decca out of Rainne and Duke's clutches.

"Be good, Sammy," Pilson says. "Just sit tight and don't get in the way. Can you do that?"

"I think so," I tell him, and it ain't a lie, 'cause when I say it I really want it to be true.

It takes three days to get the results of the DNA test on the cigarette from our yard back from the lab. In the meantime, Agent Pilson tries to interview Marco Goodman, but it ain't easy. Marco won't answer the door, or his phone.

Finally, desperate, I send a text to Gypsum. The next day, Marco walks into the sheriff's department and makes a statement. Ain't no mystery what compelled him to do that.

"What are you gonna do now?" I ask when Agent Pilson calls with the news.

"I want to see those test results before we talk to Duke again. If they confirm what we suspect, it might be the evidence we need to break his story."

My heart slams against my rib cage soon as I see Pilson's cell number pop up on the screen of my crappy prepaid phone the next day.

"Did the DNA match?" I ask.

"It did. The Crimsons at the crime scene and the cigarette

on your lawn were smoked by the same person, and that person *is not* Johnny Tuller. Whether or not it's Duke, well, we'll have to wait till we can test it against his DNA. I got a warrant for a sample this morning."

"Jesus. I can't believe this."

I glance at Denver and nod. He takes a deep breath and sits back in his chair, digesting it slowly, the way he always does with big news.

Neither of us ever once entertained the notion of Duke hurting Dad. I look at Denver sometimes and think, *Could he kill someone? Could I?* I wanna say the answer's no, but how can I be absolutely sure?

"We're bringing Duke in right now for questioning," Pilson tells me.

"What about Rainne?"

"We're going to talk to her, too, but right now all the evidence is pointing at Duke."

"No way Duke did this on his own," I insist. "Even if he's the one who—who killed Dad, she's the reason. She must've put him up to it. He's her *husband*."

"Gotta be able to prove it, and Duke's our best shot at doing that. If we make it worth his while, he might roll on her. From what I can tell, he's not much of a brave soul. He might be her husband, but I doubt he's going to want to go to the electric chair for her."

"Electric chair?" I taste copper in my mouth. I've bitten my lip so hard it's bleeding.

"Figure of speech. It's lethal injection now."

"Did Marco give you the other names? He said Duke approached a couple different people."

"No, but shouldn't be too hard to figure that out," Pilson

says. "It's a small town. I can narrow it down easy. You know what you have to do now."

"Be good," I mumble.

"Be good, and don't talk to anyone. Especially not Rainne. You've *got* to keep a low profile. Don't leave the house unless you have to, don't make stupid comments and don't do anything to tip her off we've got more information than she thinks. She makes contact, you fend her off. Okay?"

"Yeah," I say. "Okay."

Denver sits down next to me on the couch. It used to smell like Dad, but it don't anymore. There's a pile of folded laundry in the corner of the room, just sitting there like he might come back for it. I get up and fetch a garbage bag from the kitchen, start stuffing it full of his old T-shirts and jeans.

"What are you doing?" Denver asks.

"He don't need these," I say. "I'm gonna donate them. Someone can make use of this stuff. Can't stare at it anymore."

"Will you calm down for a second? Can you just chill?" Denver rips the bag from my hands. "We can go through his stuff later, together, when everything's less..."

"Awful? Ain't never gonna be less awful. Dad's dead. After all we went through—and Rainne—"

My throat closes up. We're silent for a long time, sneaking glances at each other but mostly staring at our hands, or the wall, or anything we can bring ourselves to focus on.

I breathe deep. "I don't know how to do this, Denver."

He rubs his hands together like he's cold. "Me neither."

"Who's gonna take care of Decca?"

"I don't know."

I want him to say he and I will take care of her, but I ain't stupid enough to think we could. Denver's in college, and he's gotta finish quick so he can move on to that good life we both know is waiting for him on the other side. We can't assume custody of a six-year-old, and no judge in the state is gonna give her to us.

"It's gonna be Rainne's mom, I know it," I say. "That bitch hates us. We'll never see her."

"Don't think about that now. Nothing you can do. I'm sure it won't happen, anyway. They'll have to let us see her."

"Why? No such thing as sibling rights."

"Maybe there are. And eventually she'll be older and she can choose for herself."

"By then she won't even remember us."

That don't seem to bother Denver as much as it does me. He's not as close to Decca. Why can't I get him to care like I do? What if someone told him he could never see *me* again?

Maybe he wouldn't care much about that, either.

"We already set a bunch of stuff in motion, Sammy. We can't take it back now."

He rubs his face like he's trying to keep himself awake.

"Best-case scenario, we make it so Decca grows up with no mother *and* no father, and the woman who helped raise us goes to prison. No happy outcomes here. You've got to square with that."

I never thought about it that way, that if justice is served, Decca will lose both parents 'cause of what happened to Dad. For a second, my heart stutters with something like guilt. What if she grows up hating me for helping put away the only parent she's got left?

"If Duke rolls on Rainne, they're both going to prison, and Decca's going to end up in foster care. Did you think about that when you told Pilson about Marco Goodman?" Denver asks. "Would you have kept that information to yourself if you had?"

"No." Don't even gotta think about that answer.

"It won't come without a price. Nothing ever does, especially the truth."

Denver sighs. "I've been feeling lousy about what happened with Brayton."

"Why? You did me a favor."

"Sure. But he made you happy at a time when you had a snowball's chance in hell of being happy, and I guess I'm sorry I ruined all that."

"Don't be. It wasn't real, him and I."

Can't deny Brayton made me happy. Denver would know I'm lying, but it ain't about saving face. It's about being honest with myself. I'm tired of pretending I'm strong all the time when that just ain't true.

"I'd've found out eventually, anyway," I assure Denver. "Brayton ain't exactly James Bond."

"He's a dumbass. But I could tell he cared about you."

That's about the last thing I wanna hear, 'cause Denver's usually right about stuff.

"You never seemed to like him," I say.

"Hard to trust a rich boy chasing after a poor girl in crisis."

"How come you didn't say nothing?"

"Felt cruel to put doubts in your head I wasn't even sure of myself."

We're both quiet for a second, then I tell him, "I saw Reed in the hospital the other day."

"Yeah? How is he?"

"About as good as you'd expect. But it made me think, you know, about family. How when you need someone, they're the people you're supposed to count on. I want us to count on each other, Den."

"You don't think you can count on me? What do you suppose I'm still *doing* here? I came back to the lake this summer because Dad asked, and I stayed because I know you need me."

"I don't want you to stick around just for me. This place is your home."

"But it's not, don't you see? Since I was ten, all I could think about was getting out."

"Yeah, and you abandoned us soon as you could."

"That's not fair. What'd you think was going to happen? We'd live here all cramped up in one tiny trailer for the rest of our lives? I've got plans for myself. Doesn't mean I don't care about my family. I wish you had plans for yourself, too."

I rub my eyes with the heels of my hands. "So do I."

"It's not too late."

But it is. 'Cause without Dad, with the rest of the family scattered through the county and beyond, and Denver down at college in Norman, I'm the lake's last living Lester besides Decca, and who knows what's gonna happen to her?

If I leave, how long will it take for this place to forget we were here? And if they do, will it even matter that we ever were?

CHAPTER TWENTY-TWO

Two days later, a group of Bittersweet County sheriff's deputies find the gun Duke Tremont used to kill my dad, a twenty-two that he took from his former father-in-law. Between the DNA on the cigarette butts, which ended up matching the sample the OSBI took from Duke, Marco's statement and the gun, things ain't looking great for Duke. When they drag the water under the bridge where Copper Creek flows into the Bittersweet reservoir, they know they got him but good.

"How'd you know where to look for the gun?" I ask Pilson. When they searched Duke and Rainne's house and didn't find the gun, I figured they threw it in the lake.

But Bittersweet is huge, and there are plenty of places to hide things where they can't never be found.

"We didn't," Pilson admits. "But we've had surveillance on the Tremonts for weeks. A few nights ago, Duke went out to Bittersweet Landing and stopped his car on the shoulder of the Copper Creek bridge. Just stood there, looking down into the water. Then he pulled off into the rec area and walked along the bank like he was searching for something. Gave us a pretty good idea where to start looking. We're lucky the current didn't take it."

"I bet it was Rainne who threw the gun in the water," I say. "And Duke was out there checking she hadn't screwed it up after you started asking about what kind of guns he owns."

"That's just speculation at this point," Pilson says. "We don't have any hard proof Rainne was even involved. All the evidence we do have ties Duke to the murder of your father, not his wife, and so far he's not implicating her. Even Marco says Duke never mentioned his wife when he was trying to hire him to kill Bobby Ray."

"*Why* would Duke kill Dad if not for Rainne? He's got no beef with Dad outside of her. She must've put him up to it. She must've *made* him do it."

"DA's got to be able to prove that," Pilson says. "That's how the law works."

"The law is garbage. What are you gonna do now?"

"Now I'm going to arrest Duke and test to see just how loyal a husband he really is."

I been spending more and more time at the hospital with Reed lately. It helps me, to focus on him, to think about someone else.

Today, I'm dragging Kenley along. I know Reed wants to see her—we all grew up together, she's one of his oldest friends—but she's nervous about visiting by herself.

Holler's old junk bucket ain't the most reliable car I ever drove, but it's wonderful having wheels again. We got the win-

dows rolled down 'cause the AC don't work, and my hair's getting all tangled by the wind.

I'm trying real hard not to worry too much about things I
can't help, to stay put and keep my mouth shut, but it's been
almost a week since I was up at Rock Creek and I still ain't
decided what to do about Redbreast's offer.

I'm nearly out of time, and Gypsum ain't shy about letting
me know it.

"What if I say something stupid about his leg?" Kenley asks,
gnawing at her cuticles.

"Just...don't do that," I say. "Only you can control your
own mouth."

"I ain't *planning* on it, but what if I say something accidentally?"

"You won't. You'll stop thinking about his leg soon as you
see him. He's the same guy, Ken. You'll be surprised by how
the same he is."

"He can't be the same," Kenley says. "Maybe he looks the
same, or close to it, maybe he acts the same, but he ain't the
same, Sammy."

"How do you know? You ain't even seen him yet."

"Are you the same?"

"As what?"

"As you were before all this horrible stuff happened with
your dad?"

"I don't know." I feel sort of the same, and sort of different,
too. I'm sad, and angry, but I always been those things. It's just
all on another level now.

"You ain't. I know you. You're different than you were before."

"How?"

"For one thing, the Sammy I know wouldn't still be mooning over Brayton Foster, not with Reed home and open to getting back together."

"I should've never told you that," I grumble. "And I ain't mooning over Brayton. I closed that door and painted over it. That's done."

"Okay, whatever you say. He sure as hell ain't over you, though, if that's what you wanted."

"He say something to you about me?"

"Thought you didn't care."

"I don't."

"Then why're you asking?"

"I ain't."

"You just did!"

"Forget it, then," I say.

"I ain't seen him since you took your mysterious four-hour 'walk,' but he was a mess that night. Totally frantic. He wanted to go searching for you like we went searching for Bobby Ray, and I think he would've, too, except for it was the middle of the night with no light to see by. When you showed up, he was just about to get in his car and drive 'round Tehlicoh shouting your name."

"Stop," I snap. "What are you trying to do?"

"Get you to admit you still like Brayton. You miss him."

"I don't."

"You *do*."

"What difference does it make?"

"We're about to go see Reed. I think when you're there you should maybe think of it as an opportunity. A second chance," she says.

I give her a sharp look.

"Y'all could make things up," she says. "Be happy again. You both deserve to be happy."

"No," I say.

"Why not? He's the one you ought to be with, not some big-city asshole who cheats on you."

"Maybe Brayton didn't cheat. We never agreed to be exclusive. It got serious without us even noticing, and when he realized that he tried to fix it. Maybe I overreacted."

I half believe these things, and I half don't. It's too complicated, and I mostly try to avoid thinking on it at all. Brayton's out of my life. I couldn't have him back if I wanted him. So what's the point in asking so many questions?

"Don't make apologies for him. Reed's always been your guy. Sooner you figure out how to make it work with him, the better."

"Why does this matter so much to you, Kenley?" She ain't never interfered so forcefully in my love life before. Never spoke to me like she don't trust me to make my own decisions.

"'Cause," she says, examining the blue tips of her dark hair. "Fall's gonna be here before you know it. Then I'll be up in Kansas City, and Denver's going back to Norman… I don't want you to be all alone up here. Not with everything still so uncertain about Bobby Ray."

"I'll figure something out. Please don't bring this up to Reed," I beg her. "Last thing he should be thinking about right now is having a girlfriend, especially if that girlfriend is me."

Kenley folds her arms across her chest. "Fine. But you know I'm right."

When we get to the hospital, Reed ain't in his bed. He's sitting in a wheelchair, staring out the window. His eyes light all the way up when he sees us.

"If it ain't the two hottest girls in Bittersweet County," he says.

I blush. His compliments embarrass me now. They never did before.

"Howdy, Ken," Reed says. "Nice to see your face."

"Nice to see yours, too, handsome." Kenley can't help flirting, even with my ex. She kisses him on the cheek. "We missed you 'round these parts."

Pain flickers across Reed's face, but he does his best to hide it.

"Same here, darlin'. It's good to be home, despite…" He trails off. "Well, it's nice of y'all to come see me. Hey there, Sammy."

"Hey," I say softly.

Is Kenley right? Do Reed and I belong together, even after all we put each other through? When I'm with him, I feel almost normal. It's like old times: the jokes, the friendship, the comfortable silences. If I don't look at his leg, I can forget things've changed, pretend it's two years ago, when we were so in love it felt like there wasn't nothing in the world could divide us.

But soon as I leave the hospital, I remember. The tears, the heartbreak—the pregnancy—not to mention Dad. And Brayton, who I can't stop thinking about even though I try.

Sometimes, when I'm with Reed, I wish he and Brayton could meet. I think they'd get along. And sometimes I wonder what the part of Reed who's still my friend would tell me to do about Brayton, but I can never, ever ask. The ex-boyfriend part of Reed is still too fresh a wound.

Kenley and I sit with Reed for a while, shooting the shit all casual like we're lounging on a boat with ice-cold Coors in our hands. Kenley's gotta work in the afternoon, so she catches a ride from a fellow waitress to the Deck around two, leaving Reed and I alone.

"Where's Shirla?" I ask when she's gone.

"Work," Reed says. "I'd like to get out of here, Sammy."

"How long till they let you go home?"

"Not sure. Couple weeks still, I think. But that ain't what I mean. I'd like to get out of this room. Right now." He unlocks the brakes on his wheelchair. "Wanna take me for a spin 'round the floor?"

"Is that allowed?"

He smiles. "Since when do you care?"

"I'm trying to be good."

"Sounds boring."

I laugh. "Okay, let's do it."

Don't take long for me to realize Reed's pretty popular with the nurses and hospital staff. People stop us every few feet to ask him how he's doing. He answers like the humble man he's always been.

"Grateful to be alive," he says. "Gotta keep going using the strength God gave me."

"How you really feeling?" I whisper as I wheel him down a long hallway.

"Like shit," he says. "Pain's constant. Sometimes I think it's always gonna be like this. They tell me I'll get better someday, but it's impossible to believe. Ain't never gonna get my leg back."

There's a piece of hair sticking up at the back of his head. He's had that cowlick since he was a boy. I smooth it down. He leans into my touch.

"It won't be like this forever," I say. "Nothing lasts, not even the bad stuff."

"I know. Sometimes the bad stuff gets worse."

He don't mention Dad, but I know Reed's thinking about him, and so am I.

'Cause standing at the end of the hallway, right near the entrance to Reed's room, is Rainne.

"What the hell?" I mutter.

Rainne looks up and notices us. "Sammy. Oh, thank God."

"What're you doing here?" My hand tightens on Reed's shoulder. He reaches up and wraps his fingers 'round mine.

"I need to talk to you," Rainne says.

I know Pilson told me not to let her near me, but a morbid part of me is curious about what she's got to say. What sort of harm can she do just by talking to me, in front of Reed, in a building full of security and personnel?

"About what?" I ask.

"I think they're gonna arrest Duke," Rainne tells me, clutching her purse to her stomach. "I'm so worried, Sammy. He didn't do nothing to Bobby Ray. This is all a huge mistake."

"Then you got nothing to worry about."

I'm proud of how calm I feel. How invincible I feel, how in control, especially 'cause all I wanna do is rake my nails down the side of her face.

"You gotta tell them," Rainne pleads. "You gotta tell them Duke wouldn't hurt Bobby Ray."

"I don't think they care much what I think."

Rainne's eyes are wet, but I don't buy it. Decca's good at those crocodile tears, too.

"Things were messy," Rainne says. "I know that. And maybe I was making it hard on everyone, including you, and I'm sorry. I just wanted to do right by Decca. You believe me about that at least, don't you? Think how much you love Decca. What wouldn't you do to make sure she's safe?"

"She was safe with us," I say. "You didn't have to try to take her away."

Reed squeezes my hand. I'm letting this go on too long.

"You know how your daddy was with me, rough and angry. How could I be sure he wasn't just that way with Decca?"

"Don't you dare," I say. "Don't you fucking dare even *imply* he ever would've harmed a hair on her head. Go home, Rainne. Where's Decca now, huh? You taking care of her now?"

"She's with my mama. That's where she'll end up if Duke and I go to prison for a crime we didn't commit. You'll never see her again, Sammy, if MaryEllen has her. You got no rights. Decca will grow up a stranger to you. She'll hate you forever for destroying her family. That what you want?"

"You threatening me?"

Rainne shakes her head. "Just giving you fair warning."

"You ought to get out of here now," Reed says. "Before I get security to make you leave."

I almost don't want her to go. I'm rattled by seeing Rainne, but thrilled a bit by it, too. If she's resorting to this, scaring me into believing I'll lose Decca altogether if she's put away, it means she's desperate. And desperate people screw up.

I only wish there isn't a part of me that half believes every word she's saying.

"Good to see you, Reed," Rainne calls over her shoulder as she makes her way to the elevators. "Sorry about your leg."

"I wanna kill her," I say.

"Honestly?" Reed says. "I wouldn't blame you if you did."

That night, Agent Pilson shows up at our house. Soon as I open the door, I know something big has happened. Otherwise he would've called.

I show him in. He takes Dad's chair while Denver and I perch expectantly on the couch.

"We arrested Duke Tremont earlier this evening," Pilson says. "Ballistics came back on the gun we brought up from the creek. It's a match for the bullets we found in your father's body, same serial number as the one Duke took from his ex-father-in-law. Whoever killed Bobby Ray killed him with that gun."

"You know who killed him," I say. I've had just about enough of this "allegedly" bullshit.

"We got a rule in this country—innocent till proven guilty. If he did it, a jury of his peers will convict him—not me, and not you."

"Be faster the other way 'round," I grumble.

"So you got the gun," Denver says, gesturing for me to hush up. "What else?"

"The Crimsons from the crime scene are slathered with his DNA—puts him right there, in a place he shouldn't've otherwise been. We can't confirm much about his movements that night, but given what we know from tracking his car after the murder, and the place we found the gun, we can make a good case he's the one who disposed of it."

"No." I shake my head. "It was her."

Don't know why I'm so sure of that, but I am.

"Can't prove it."

I start to say something, but he puts his hand up to stop me.

"Hold on. I'm not finished. This is what I think happened the night your father was killed—after he got off work, he went over to the Tremont house to deliver Decca's stuffed animal, just like he told you he was going to do. Something happened in that house after he arrived. Maybe there was an argument about the upcoming custody hearing, or about money. Bobby Ray was hit across the back of the head with a blunt object, likely a baseball bat. Might've knocked him unconscious, made it easier to transport him. All the blood 'round where the body was found makes it clear he was killed there. Duke hid the body, then dumped Bobby Ray's truck in the lake."

"How'd he get home?" I ask. "It's a long, dark walk from the bluffs back to town. Rainne must've picked him up."

Pilson shook his head. "We know who picked him up. Ash Boford, Rainne's younger brother."

"Fuck Ash and anything he ever says to you."

A flash of white-hot rage bolts through me. I wish Brayton *had* shot Ash Boford the night of his party. I wish I could stand over his body as he bleeds to death in a patch of red dirt, just like my daddy did. The shiner I gave him up at Rock Creek can't begin to make up for the ways he's damaged me and mine.

"Even if it's true, Rainne must've known," I insist. "She must've been there."

"Ash says she wasn't," Pilson says. "Claims Duke told him not to say anything to her."

"They're just trying to protect her! She's the one who put them up to it. How do you not see that?"

"It's not what I can see that matters, it's what the prosecution can prove in court," Pilson says. "We have to tell the jury a story they'll believe. So far, nobody's given us anything that implies Rainne was involved. Our best shot now is to get Duke to turn on his wife as part of some sort of plea."

"Like what?" Denver asks.

"Reduced sentence." Denver and I exchange a panicked look. "Fifty years, maybe. Or, hell, life—the DA could go after putting death on the table. Way things are going right now, if

Duke swears he was the only person involved, he's more than
eligible. He's all lawyered up, and you better believe the DA's
gonna hear from his attorney any day now looking for a way
to make sure he doesn't fry."

"So you think you can get him to implicate Rainne?"

"If he's smart—or his lawyer is—he's going to plead guilty
in exchange for mercy from the state," Pilson says. "But what
he may not realize yet is the mercy he's looking for probably
isn't going to come from the state—it's going to come from
you two."

"Us?" Denver looks confused. "Why?"

"Because you're Bobby Ray's family. I've seen this happen
before in similar cases—if an alleged killer wants to enter a
guilty plea on a murder one charge in exchange for life instead of death, the prosecutor often leaves the decision up to
the family."

Pilson stands. "I suggest neither of you think too hard about
that right now. Think about yourselves. Know that if all goes
well, Duke Tremont will be punished for the murder of your
father. If we do our jobs, he'll never be a free man again."

"Where is he now?"

"County lockup," Pilson says. "Arraignment's tomorrow, and
his bail will be set so high he won't be able to afford it. He's
not going anywhere. Ash Boford, too. Accessory to first-degree
murder carries a minimum of five years in prison."

"What about Rainne?" I ask. Maybe they don't got enough
to arrest her, but they got enough to question her some more,
at least.

"I think you know the answer to that," Pilson says. "She's
home. For now."

"She came to see me."

Pilson narrows his eyes. "When?"

"Today. I was at the hospital visiting a friend and she showed up. Wanted me to tell you she and Duke had nothing to do with Dad's murder. She said if I didn't help her, I'd never see Decca again."

"She *what?*" Denver snaps.

"You should've called me," Pilson says. "She's getting desperate. It's a good sign. If it makes her nervous we got Duke in custody, might be it's because she thinks he'll tell us something."

"That's what I figured."

"Don't talk to her anymore, Sammy. You see her coming, you turn around and walk the other way. She shows up here, you slam the door in her face."

"Shouldn't be too hard."

"I mean it this time," he says. "She's looking for information from you. You accidentally give it to her, I don't know what's gonna happen. If she was in any way involved with Bobby Ray's death, she's a flight risk and I've got no way to legally stop her from running. Goes for you, too, Denver."

"I've got nothing to say to that bitch anyway," he says.

"Good. I won't lie, this is going to get worse before it gets better. If Duke doesn't plea out, trials can be a long, frustrating, difficult experience. You may have to testify."

Pilson frowns. "I'm so sorry about your father. I truly am."

We thank him. What else is there to say?

That night, I dream about Dad. It's the first time that's happened since he disappeared, and in the dream he's sitting on the porch, looking into the distance, past Karen and Wayne's house, through the small empty patch in the trees, staring at the cool blue water of the lake.

I'm standing behind him. I say his name, and he starts turning his head, but before I can see his face I wake with my cheek pressed against a damp pillow and the first light of dawn streaming through the windows.

CHAPTER TWENTY-THREE

"He's not going to rat her out," Denver says.

We're sitting in the kitchen, drinking coffee that's gone cold. I'm smoking, and he ain't nagging about it, which goes to show how bad things are.

I ash into a plastic bowl that somehow made it through my childhood despite several bad run-ins with the microwave. It's half-melted, bleached white in places, but it still holds its shape.

"You don't think?"

"Duke's stupid. But he's not going to give her up. She's got him wrapped 'round her finger."

"Think he's willing to die for her?" I ask.

"We're not going to let them put him to death."

"Why not?"

"Because one murder's more than enough."

"It wouldn't *be* murder. It'd be justice."

"It wouldn't. You know that."

"Dad would want him to die," I say.

Bobby Ray Lester was a vengeful man. What happened with Arthur Comstock taught us that, and it don't matter how much he learned or grew or changed over the years since. Nothing could've trained that out of him.

Bobby Ray Lester was a vengeful man, and I'm his vengeful daughter.

"Well, Dad's not here, is he?" Denver says. "Pretend all you want, but at the end of the day, you'll never be able to go through with it."

"We might not get a choice. You heard Pilson—that's only likely to happen if he tries to get a plea bargain. Maybe he won't. Maybe he'll take his chances with the jury."

"Duke's stupid, but his lawyer's probably not. We should do what Pilson said, just forget till something happens."

"But it's been almost a week and *nothing* has happened."

That ain't totally true. Duke was arraigned the day after his arrest, but no matter how much the police question him, he won't give them anything on Rainne.

Meanwhile, I'm suddenly seeing her everywhere. I noticed her car outside the post office in Tehlicoh on Wednesday, and had to duck down the frozen foods aisle at Harps a few days later to avoid her seeing me. It was especially hard 'cause Decca was with her, clinging to the front of the cart like one of those wooden ladies on the prow of a ship.

I ditched my grocery basket in front of the ice cream sandwiches and left in a hurry with my heart in my throat.

"It's like she's just living her normal life," I say angrily. "Probably still planning on moving. If she takes Decca away from here, I don't know what I'm gonna do."

"Do nothing, Sammy. Don't fuck this up, not when we're so close."

Denver stands and announces he's going fishing with Holler. "You ought to come."

"No thanks."

"You need a distraction," he insists.

"Well, if you hadn't ruined things between me and Brayton, I'd have plenty to distract me," I say. "But you did. So."

Denver leaves with a half guilty, half grossed-out grimace on his face, a fishing pole in his hand.

Since Duke's arrest, I been too obsessed with Rainne to slide back into thoughts of Brayton, but now he's been brought up I can't stop. I take a beer and my pack of smokes out to the porch and sit in the shade, thinking of him. I imagine his hand on my thigh and his breath on my neck and his hair between my fingers and shiver in spite of the heat.

I think and think and think, and I smoke and smoke and smoke, and I drink and drink and drink till night falls.

Kenley's voice keeps floating through my head, what she said about me and Reed being it for each other. But the more I turn her words over, the less I buy them. Reed's important to me, and I love him, but not the way I did before.

It's hard to ask myself if I love Brayton, 'cause I think I know the answer and it's too late. But at night, alone in bed, I fantasize about him. I touch myself and think about him touching me and the release is sweet, but it ain't as sweet as when he was there with me.

It feels so much better when you do it.

Worst part is that the best night with him was the one right before everything fell apart, 'cause for the first time we matched, me and him. Our broken hearts beat in sync and our bodies craved the same thing and we trusted each other to give what was needed.

Should've known it'd all get taken away. I never get to keep the things I love.

At some point in the night I stop drinking and just sit, watching the sky darken with a blackness that spreads like spilled ink. Denver calls around ten saying he's crashing at Holler's.

"Lock the doors," he says.

But I got nobody to make me come inside and go to bed, so I don't. Around 2:00 a.m. I'm glad I deleted Brayton's number, 'cause I'd call if I had it.

I fall asleep in my chair and when I wake it's dawn. A dog barks and I crack open my eyes to see Karen leading Dolly down the road. She bounds up the porch steps to greet me, tail wagging like the world is perfect. I scratch behind her ears and bury my face in her fur.

"You got a nice life, Dolly," I say. "I wish I was a dog. Then nothing would ever be wrong."

"Hi, sugar," Karen says. "You're up early."

"Never went to bed."

"You been out here all night?" Karen looks worried. I nod. "Oh, Sammy."

"I'm fine," I tell her.

"I don't believe you. All this business with Duke Tremont… must be eating you up inside."

"I'm fine, I swear it."

Karen pets Dolly, who settles down at her feet with a disgruntled *woof*. I'm interrupting her morning walk.

"I know you don't wanna hear this," Karen says. "But it's

gonna get better. Right now the pain is all raw and mean, but eventually it'll scar. You're gonna survive this."

"How?" I ask.

"I don't know," she says. "But people do."

It's so easy to forget things like this—worse than this—have happened before. And they'll happen again. Humans are cruel, selfish creatures. They do awful things to each other.

When I was a kid, and Granny Lester was still alive, she used to tell me stories about giants. She claimed that before humans came along, the state was overrun with them. There's a town about an hour and a half south of the lake called Poteau, built in the shadows of a small mountain called Cavanal Hill.

Wanna know why it's called Poteau? Granny Lester would say. *'Cause a giant was walkin' through there one day and he stubbed his toe on Cavanal Hill, which was just a big ol' rock to him, not worth a lick of bother till it hurt him. He shouted, "Oh, my po' toe!" and that's how Poteau got its name.*

The giants of Granny Lester's stories were irritable, violent creatures. When the humans came along, they stole babies from their cribs and ate them, bones and all, crunching on them like hard candies. They raided human villages and pissed on their crops so the people would starve in the winter.

In the stories, humans were the heroes. They used their wits and weapons to bring the giants down, pushing them closer and closer together till the giants murdered each other. Till there were none left.

But the way I saw it, the humans were the villains, evicting the giants from their homelands, showering them with bullets, spilling so much giant blood the earth was stained bright red.

I never had the guts to tell Granny Lester what I thought of her stories. But now I know I was right all along. *We are* the bad guys, the murderers, the cheats. And we'll never, ever learn.

"I'm tired," I tell Karen.

She nods. "Go inside, get some sleep. You'll feel better every day that passes. Maybe not a lot, but a little, then tomorrow, a little more."

I give Dolly one last scratch behind the ear and go inside, flop down on my bed. I cry till I ain't got no more tears left, then roll onto my side and sleep fourteen hours straight.

When my eyes open later that night, I know just what to do. The solution came to me while I slept, in a dream so vivid I wake up shaking.

I take a shower and dry my hair pin straight, the way Brayton likes it. I remember him letting it run through his fingers like water, smiling at me in the dark.

I put a pink tank top and denim miniskirt on over a pair of black lacy underwear and matching bra, then line my eyes to make them pop and pinch my cheeks to give them some color. I throw my car keys, cigarettes and phone into a big black purse and sling it over my shoulder. Ain't carried a purse all summer, and it makes me feel like I'm hauling an anchor. I'm nervous to see him, but excited, too. I feel jittery, like I had too much coffee.

I don't even know if Brayton will be home, or, if he is, whether he'll be alone. Ain't no car in the driveway but his, that brand-new SUV with *Stella* hooked up to the back. I pat her flank as I pass her by on the way to the front door.

I ring the bell, then regret it. I shouldn't be doing this. But when the door swings open, all doubts evaporate. I look at Brayton, and he looks at me, and I know I love him, just fucking *love* him, can't deny it no more. I know it's the wrong thing to feel, and he's the wrong guy to want, but that don't change a thing.

"Jesus, Sammy. Come here."

He pulls me into a hug, crushing me so hard I can't breathe. Which is good, 'cause if I breathe, I'll cry. I press my face into his neck. He rubs my back.

"Thank God," he whispers. "Thank God you're here."

He lets me go and I shut my eyes, 'cause looking at him is too much. He kisses my left eyelid, then my right. He kisses my nose and the apples of my cheeks. He scrapes the hair away from my forehead and kisses my temples. Every time I think I can speak, he kisses some other part of me and my throat seals shut.

I put my arms 'round his waist and let my hands wander up his back, beneath his shirt, 'cause I wanna feel his skin under my fingertips. I count the notches of his spine to quiet my mind, which is roiling with questions and answers like the lake in a storm. He shivers. I quake.

"Come inside," he says softly, so I do.

He holds my hand as he leads me silently up the stairs and into his bedroom. There's a suitcase in the corner, all packed and zipped shut. He's leaving. He's almost gone.

But not tonight. Tonight he's here, and he's mine.

Brayton leans against the dresser and stares at me. He shakes his head. "I can't believe you came."

"When do you leave?"

"Tomorrow."

"For college?"

"For home. Then on to Yale. I waited… My mom kept telling me to come back to the city but I couldn't because I wanted… I needed to see if you'd come. And then you didn't, so I thought—tonight's the last night I can stay, though. And here you are."

I nod, hugging myself. I feel cold without him holding me. "Here I am."

"I wish you came sooner."

"I couldn't."

He lifts his eyes to meet mine. "I know."

I breathe deep. "I don't wanna talk about what happened."

"Okay."

"All that shit? I don't care."

I really don't. Maybe he ain't the wrong guy—maybe I'm the wrong girl. Or maybe I'm the *only* girl for someone like Brayton. Someone who gets what's hiding beneath all the swagger and charm, 'cause we share the same rock-hard mantle and lava-hot core.

Our lives ain't been that different till now. His just has more money to smooth out the wrinkles.

"I understand."

I know he does. I get why he did it, that it wasn't about me. He *chose* me, even though it would've been easier not to. He did it in a stupid way and I ain't pretending he didn't, but last night it all started to make sense to me. The guts it must've taken to leave his familiar world for my unpredictable one, and what it means that he wanted to. That he still wants to—I think.

"All I need to know is that you're here tonight," I say.

"I'm here tonight," he says. "But what about tomorrow? What happens to us then?"

"I don't know."

It's the most honest answer I can give him. After tonight,

everything's gonna change, and I can't make any promises. Not that I ever would.

"Okay," he says, nodding.

I open my arms and he crashes into me. One hand flies up my skirt, plucking at the lacy band of my underwear. The other cups my face as his lips find mine. His tongue's in my mouth and his hand's on my back and he presses me to him. I let my fingers wander along the waist of his jeans till I find his zipper.

We fall back on the bed and I roll over so I'm straddling him, and he watches me with eyes bright as the moon as I undo his fly. When he's naked, it's my turn, but in spite of the wildness in his eyes, Brayton's less frantic with me, peeling my top and skirt off slowly, taking care with the clasp of my bra, kneeling on the floor in front of the bed as he eases my underwear down my legs.

"I just want to say one thing," he tells me. I nod. "You were right about me needing people to like me, and doing whatever I have to do—good or bad or just plain stupid—to make that happen."

"Brayton—"

"Wait—can you just… I thought about what you said. I've been that way my whole life. And I was so obsessed with not giving anyone a reason to dislike me that I never asked myself if I liked *them* or not. But you—I like *you*."

He kisses my right knee, then my left one. I smile.

"And I think I'm okay with not everyone liking me, as long as *you* like me."

"I like you," I whisper, reaching for him. "Please, come here."

He crawls back into bed and settles between my thighs, tracing circles on the soft, sensitive skin of them with his thumbs. We stare at each other, taking the time to memorize each other's bodies. I wanna paint him behind my eyelids.

"You," I pant. He looks at me. "Don't know why, but you—" I put my hand over my heart.

He puts his hand over his heart. "You, too."

He spreads himself down on the bed next to me and shifts me onto my side, pulling me backward so I'm flush against his chest. For a minute, he just holds me, breathes the smell of me into his lungs. Then he lifts my hair and kisses the top of my spine. He presses his lips down the length of my back. I'm so loose and warm, I think I might just melt right there.

"Brayton," I whimper. He grabs a condom from his bedside drawer. Then he braces himself over me, watching my face.

"I love you," he tells me. "I love you so much and I'm so sorry."

I think about saying it back to him, both *I love you* and *I'm sorry*, but a great wave of sensation rolls through me and I'm overtaken by the moment, by him, by our last night together.

It takes a while, longer than it ever took before, 'cause we both know how little time we got left and we wanna make it last.

It can't take forever, though. I got somewhere to be.

When it's over, I glance nervously at the clock. If I know Brayton, he'll fall asleep soon enough. I just gotta wait till then, get my fill of him, try not to let the fact that I'm using him even as I'm loving him ruin these final minutes together.

Brayton rolls onto his side again. I nestle into the curve of his body. He kisses my neck and runs his fingers through the ends of my hair, hand drifting down past my shoulder, lingering at my elbow before settling on my hip. I grab his hand and place it flat against my chest, linking my fingers with his.

"I feel like I'm losing you right now," he murmurs. "I hate it."

"It's gonna be okay."

"I can't lose you, Sammy."

"You won't."

"I have to go to school." His breath tickles my skin.

"So go."

"And you'll be…?"

"Right here."

Later, when he finds out what I've done, what I was planning to do as he was cuddling me like some beloved thing, he'll let me go himself.

"Come with me."

"To Connecticut? I can't."

"Why not?"

I shake my head. "Not where I belong."

"You belong with me."

"So stay."

I only say it 'cause I know he won't.

He's silent for a while. "I would."

"But?"

"It's not where I belong."

"So we're at a crossroads, I guess."

"No."

Brayton turns me so I'm facing him. He's so beautiful, glazed with sweat and moonlight, I almost can't look at him.

"Just because you were born and raised here doesn't mean you can't leave," he says. "You can go places. Doesn't have to be Connecticut, but it should be somewhere. If you want."

"Thanks for the permission."

"It's not permission, it's encouragement."

"Only place my people tend to go when they leave here is prison," I say.

"Not Denver."

"No, not him. But I ain't Denver." I pause. "I gotta be here right now."

I kiss the center of his palm. I ain't never leaving the lake. It just ain't possible for a girl like me, from a family like mine. But the fact he believes I could means a lot.

"Someone's gotta be here. Else everything falls apart."

That's why it don't bother me that what I'm gonna do next will probably ruin my life. It was ruined anyway, the night Dad died and the lake swallowed me up forever.

"Everything's already fallen apart," Brayton says. "You want to stand guard over the rubble?"

"Hush now." I sweep my fingertips over his cheeks and kiss his mouth. His eyes flutter closed.

Within a half hour, Brayton's asleep. I untangle myself from him and put my clothes back on. Looking in the mirror, I smooth the wrinkled fabric best I can, what little of it there is. I dressed like this for Brayton. My next target won't appreciate it nearly as much.

I pick up my purse and walk through the second floor till I find the master bedroom, and the bedside table where Brayton's stepfather, Jack, keeps his gun.

CHAPTER TWENTY-FOUR

I don't turn on my headlights till I'm out of range of Brayton's house. The longer he sleeps, the longer it'll take him to realize I'm gone, and the better it'll be for him. When the police question him, he can honestly say he knows nothing.

My purse is on the passenger seat, heavier now with the gun in it. I keep glancing at my mirrors, sure that any moment a cop will pull me over.

I drive through the bluffs, up Route 82 into Tehlicoh. In the dark, it's hard to pinpoint exactly where the police found Dad's body, which I'm glad for, 'cause I don't know what seeing the place where he died would stoke up in me.

Rainne lives on the outskirts of town. There's a spot just a dozen feet from her house where the street dead-ends in a curve. I park there and sit with the gun in my lap. I pick it up, trying to get used to its shape and weight. Ain't no stranger to guns, but I never handled this one before, and they're all dif-

ferent. Much more comfortable with a shotgun in my hands
than a pistol.

I put the gun in my purse, step out of the car and make my
way up to Rainne's front door.

Before I knock, I check Decca's window. The room's dark,
bed's made up, but that's expected. Rainne's been keeping
Decca at MaryEllen's, which is the only reason I came tonight.
Makes this all so much easier, not having to worry about her
overhearing.

If she was smart, Rainne'd be hiding out at her mama's
place, too, but I know she ain't 'cause there are lights on in
the house and her car's in the drive. Dad bought her that car
when they first got married.

My blood, which has been on medium simmer since I woke
up, cranks to boiling. She took everything from Dad, even his
life. She don't deserve to keep a damn thing.

I knock sharply and clutch the purse to my hip. Without
even closing my eyes I remember Brayton's hands on that hip,
how comforting it was, how I'll probably never feel so secure
ever again.

The door opens. Rainne's eyes go wide when she sees me.

"What're you doing here?" she demands.

"I wanna see Decca." I try to push past her into the house,
but she blocks me.

"She ain't here," Rainne says. "She's at MaryEllen's."

"Good. Just checking." I pull the gun out of my purse. "You
and I need to talk."

"Put that away," Rainne says. She lifts her hands, palms out.
"Don't be ridiculous."

"Get inside." My voice is frosty as the ice that covers the
lakeshore in winter.

Rainne backs up and I ease myself into the foyer, closing the door behind me and locking it.

"Please," Rainne whispers. "Please don't."

"Living room."

I gesture with the gun. It feels like a part of me, a dangerous limb, not heavy at all anymore. I expected to feel more anxious and unsure when this moment came, but I'm calm. Squaring myself with the outcome has given me courage.

"Go."

"Okay." She nods, trembling. "Don't shoot me, please."

I grab her arm and tow her into the living room. Soon as I let go, she escapes to the other side of the room, putting the couch in between us. She wraps her arms 'round her waist and stares at the gun in my hand.

I wonder if Rainne thinks she's gonna die tonight. Wonder if she saw that same certainty in Dad before she told her husband to execute him, three shots to the back of the head.

"God, Rainne, you're such a fucking coward."

"I know you, Sammy. This ain't what you want."

"Sit," I say. She don't move. "*Sit*."

Rainne sinks onto the couch like she's being forced down by invisible hands.

"Tell me," I say.

"What?"

"Tell me what happened. I wanna know everything. I deserve to hear the truth, and I wanna hear it from you."

I'm proud of how my hands don't shake when I level the gun at her, 'cause inside I feel like I'm gonna pass out.

"You look so scared, Rainne. That how Dad looked just before you killed him?"

"I wasn't there!"

"I don't believe you."

"I didn't kill him," Rainne whimpers. "It was Duke. He admitted to it."

"Maybe it was Duke who shot him, but you're the one who asked him to. Decca's *your kid*. Why would Duke want Dad dead unless you made him want it? What'd you tell him? That it was the best thing for the family? What'd you promise him?"

"I don't know why he did it," Rainne says. She takes pause, long enough to gather herself. She squares her shoulders and sets her jaw. "He must've thought he was protecting me. Your daddy was a monster. He used some stupid excuse to come in here and rough me up about Decca. He hit me."

"Liar," I spit.

"He pushed me down and screamed in my face about how he wasn't gonna let me take his kid away," Rainne goes on.

She's so wrapped up in the lie now, it's possible she even believes it. If she thinks she's gonna convince me, though, she's got another thing coming. I ain't leaving till I get the truth. Till I get some motherfucking justice for my daddy, the kind I can't get any other way.

"He told me he sold his land so he could get the money to follow us to Arkansas. He told me I wasn't ever gonna escape him, and then he hit me," she says.

"No he didn't! Tell me *the truth*."

"Sammy, you've gotta calm down now. You're not gonna shoot me. You ain't that kind."

"You don't got any idea what kind I am! I was always gonna come after you for this."

"It wasn't me!"

"Yes it was! I know you. I know every disgusting, evil part of you, and I don't got nowhere to be."

I train the gun on her like she's a lame horse needing to be put down.

"All right." She holds her hands up again. "All right. Get rid of the gun and I'll tell you."

"I don't take orders from you. Start talking."

Rainne draws a deep, shaky breath. "Your daddy came over that night to give Waldo back to Decca. She was so happy to see him, I let him inside. I didn't wanna talk about the custody shit, but he kept bringing it up, right in front of her, telling me to stop trying to prevent him from seeing his daughter."

Her voice fades out for a moment. Then she says, "He was so cocksure, always, Bobby Ray. Always thought he had the upper hand 'cause he was bigger and stronger than me. Said it didn't matter what I did, he'd follow us anywhere we went. I told him not to press his luck, and he started shouting, telling me what a shitty mother I am, what a terrible wife I always was. Duke came home just then and got into it with Bobby Ray. I tried to stop them fighting, I *tried*, Sammy, but Bobby Ray wouldn't back down and Duke always had a short fuse, especially when he thinks someone's out to get me. He *snapped*."

She's crying now, but her tears don't work on me.

"What happened next?" I ask, though I'm starting to realize I don't wanna know. It's too terrible to imagine, but I can't stop playing it out in my head.

"Duke grabbed the baseball bat he keeps in the closet and hit Bobby Ray across the shoulders," Rainne sobs. "He fell and hit his head on the coffee table and he was just lying there, so still. I thought he was dead then and started to panic, but Duke checked and said he was breathing. I told Duke to get rid of him. I told… I told Duke to make it so he could never hurt me again, or take Decca from me. So he dragged Bobby

Ray to his truck and drove off. I swear it. I didn't think he'd kill him!"

"No," I say. "That's not what happened."

"It is!"

"You were planning to kill him," I say. "Duke tried to hire someone to do it, and when he wouldn't, Duke went and stole a gun so the bullets couldn't be traced back to him."

Rainne lifts her eyes to meet mine. "If Duke did any of that, I didn't know about it."

"Bullshit! Ash says he picked Duke up in the bluffs after he dumped Dad's truck in the lake. Don't tell me Ash helped him out of the goodness of his heart. Ash don't *have* a heart. He did it 'cause you asked him. God knows why your men are always protecting you—snakes don't need protecting."

"Takes one to know one, I reckon," Rainne snaps. "Whose gun is that? That the same one your little boyfriend put up to my brother's head?"

"While Duke was driving Dad's truck off Satan's Chin, you were tossing the gun into Copper Creek so nobody would ever find it."

"No."

I shove the gun in her face and flick the safety off. "Tell me the truth or I shoot you right now."

"Yes," she cries. "Okay, yes, I told him to kill Bobby Ray and then I got rid of the gun. Are you happy, Sammy? Are you happy knowing all of this?"

I press the gun into the fleshy bottom of her chin.

"You used to love me," Rainne says. "Do you remember? I used to play with your hair, take you shopping. We read all the Harry Potter books together one summer. You loved me, and I loved you. I still do. I didn't want this to happen, but he didn't give me no choice. I wasn't gonna let him take Decca."

I open my mouth to say something nasty, but I don't get the chance 'cause my phone rings, startling us both.

Rainne grabs me by the waist, throwing her full weight against me and dropping me to the floor. My head slams against the carpet and sparks explode in front of my eyes as the gun goes flying and my purse spills open. My phone skitters across the living room.

Rainne lunges for my phone and hurls it against the wall, where the crappy prepaid shatters into a dozen pieces and stops ringing.

Then Rainne goes for the gun. Even stunned, I got enough instinct for self-preservation to grab her ankle, taking her down. She screams, but the sound of another voice explodes through an open window, shouting my name: Brayton.

There's a loud thumping noise, and at first I think it's the sound of blood pounding in my ears, but then I realize it's Brayton throwing himself against the front door. He says my name over and over again, but the wind's knocked out of me and I can't call back.

Rainne grinds her foot down on my fingers as she hauls herself up from the floor. Pain blazes up my arm. I scramble to my knees but she kicks me hard in the stomach and I fall back long enough for her to grab the gun and plant her heel on my chest.

She's panting, gazing down at me with an expression of such hate I almost don't recognize her.

"You Lesters," she says, her lip curling in disgust. "You're all such fucking trash."

Then she pulls the trigger.

When nothing happens, Rainne stares at the gun in shock, giving me time to roll out from under her and get to my feet. I blow past her, aiming for the door, for Brayton, who's losing his mind on the other side.

Rainne reacts fast enough to grab me by my hair, but I pull away. Adrenaline dulls the pain of having a chunk ripped right out of my scalp.

I run to the door, fumbling with the lock, then yank it open and fall into Brayton's arms.

"*Run*. We gotta run," I gasp. He rushes me away, half dragging me to his car.

"Are you okay?" he asks as I crumple to my knees at the curb. "Are you hurt?"

"How did you even know I was here?" I ask, tears streaming down my face. I'm so relieved to see him, but I don't get how it's possible. Feels like a miracle.

"I woke up and you were gone, then I saw the open drawer in my parents' bedroom and I realized you'd taken the gun. Wasn't hard to figure out what you were planning to do with it."

He hesitates before he adds: "And why you were there in the first place."

"That's not—" I lean over and dry heave at his feet.

He crouches down and puts an arm 'round my waist, tugging me upward, but I can't move. I feel like I'm made of stone.

"We've got to go," he says. "You need to get away from Rainne. The cops are coming."

I glance over my shoulder at the house. The front door is still wide-open, but Rainne's nowhere. She's probably freaking out and getting ready to run.

"How do you know?"

"Because I called them. Let's go."

"You called the cops? Why would you do that?"

He releases me and steps back. "You took a gun into the house of the woman who had your dad *killed*. I thought she was going to hurt you! That gun isn't even loaded."

"I know," I say.

He sighs. "I know you know. I told you. The bullets were right there in the drawer."

"I wasn't ever gonna shoot her." I swallow hard. My mouth tastes like bile, and blood. "I just wanted to scare her into confessing to me. Even if she never told anybody else, even if she never got caught, I wanted to make her tell *me*."

"That was a really fucking stupid thing to do, Sammy."

"I *know*."

Brayton pulls me into his arms. I press my face into his shoulder and start to cry.

Sirens scream down the street and cop cars pull up in front of the house, tires shrieking, lights swirling. Officers pour onto the lawn and circle the house, preparing to enter with their guns drawn.

I look up and see Pete standing over us. He hunkers down and puts a hand on my back.

"You okay?" he asks. I nod.

"She brought a gun to my house!" Rainne shouts from the doorway. "She was gonna kill me!"

Pete stares at me. "That true?"

"No," I say. "I just wanted her to tell me the truth."

Brayton explains to Pete about the gun, how it wasn't loaded and I knew it. He looks torn over whether or not he believes.

"Sammy Lester."

Agent Pilson's here, and he's livid.

"What the *fuck* have you done?" he asks.

THE LAST GIANT

As Froygar approached the human camp, she worked on her plan for freeing Lubel.

Froygar knew enough about humans to realize that, even with her size, she was at a disadvantage. The humans had each other, and their guns, and their fire—which giants had a natural fear of—and Froygar only had herself. At least she knew where they were keeping Lubel, could see the shape of her body in the light from the human campfire, hands and feet bound with thick, strong rope. Froygar's heart sank just looking at her cub. How was she ever gonna fight off all those humans alone?

The one thing Froygar had going for her was the fact it was so late, and most of the humans were asleep. There were only a few of them up at this hour, guarding Lubel. Froygar was too big to sneak up on them quietly, and there was nothing to hide behind, anyway, but giants' eyes are better than human ones, and for a while the darkness of the night cloaked her.

The second the humans spotted her, Froygar knew it, by the sound of a bullet as it whizzed past her ear. Not knowing what else to do, she charged the camp, roaring fit to wake the dead, knocking humans clear off their feet as she ran past.

The first bullet hit her in the arm, and the second one scraped past her cheek, but she barely felt them, paid them no more mind than a human does when bit by a mosquito. The commotion woke Lubel, who cried out for Froygar, a sound like a siren wailing through the dark.

Soon there was just the fire between Froygar and Lubel. Lubel strained against the ropes 'round her wrists and ankles, but they were tied too tight and the humans hadn't fed her—giants gotta eat almost constantly or their bodies get weak. Froygar paused before the fire, afraid to cross it, but she dug deep down inside of her and found the courage that helped her protect the Little Waters for so long against the man-giants who wanted to take it from her.

She took a deep breath and leaped over the fire, scorching the bottoms of her feet but otherwise landing on the other side unharmed.

Lubel squirmed and sobbed and shouted to Froygar that the danger was great, that the humans had no mercy for their kind. This, Froygar already knew. She swept Lubel up in her arms and turned back to find that more humans were coming, crawling out of their tents with guns at the ready, aiming to take her down.

She rushed them, feeling invincible and unnaturally calm, gnawing at Lubel's ropes as she ran. Her burned feet screamed and ached. It wasn't long before she realized she couldn't run anymore, and she fell to her knees on the hard earth. Lubel tumbled out of Froygar's arms.

The pain was spreading up her legs, scraping its hot, sharp fingernails across her brain, and Froygar's vision started to fog. Lubel, freed from her bindings, tugged at Froygar's arm, trying to drag her away from the camp as the humans descended.

Bullets rained upon Froygar, each one of them adding a drop to the swirling ocean of hurt that was swallowing her up.

"Go!" she screamed at Lubel. "Leave me and *run*!"

Lubel hesitated. The humans were so close, and there was no way a tiny thing such as herself could carry Froygar all the way back to the woods. Froygar kept yelling at her to flee, but Lubel couldn't abandon her, the only mother she ever knew, the giant who gave her a name.

"Lubel, please," Froygar begged. "Get out of here! You gotta protect the Little Waters. You gotta save yourself."

It was the thought of the Little Waters that did it. Lubel loved that land almost as much as Froygar did. With one last look at Froygar, dying in the dirt, soaking it with her blood, Lubel ran. She ran and ran and ran till she made it to the tree line, crashing through the forest until she reached the Little Waters at last.

After Froygar was dead, the humans went back into the forest, looking for the giant cub that had escaped them. But they never did find her, though some looked all their lives. Might be Lubel's still out there, hiding among the trees, keeping watch over the land that was hers by right, the only thing her Froygar had to leave her.

Giants live a long, long time, after all, and one of them had to be the last.

CHAPTER TWENTY-FIVE

"I want to see her!"

I sit up in my cell and strain to hear the commotion outside in the sheriff's department bull pen. Denver's here.

"Hold your horses, tough guy," Pete says. "Your sister's in deep shit right now. You don't give the orders. You wanna talk to Sammy, you gotta go through Sheriff Olina and Agent Pilson."

"Then go get them," Denver demands.

Ten minutes later, we're all four of us sitting in an interview room with a long one-way mirror, me on one side of the table, Pilson on the other, with Denver pacing the room and Olina standing in a corner, looking right sick of every single one of us.

"Do I have to get her a lawyer?" Denver asks. "We can't afford a lawyer."

"In the event that you cannot afford a lawyer, one will be appointed to you," Olina says wearily. "Ain't you ever watched a crime show?"

"I wasn't gonna hurt her," I insist. Pilson rolls his eyes. "I wasn't! You saw the gun, you talked to Brayton, you *know* I didn't load it even though I could've. I ain't a murderer, Pilson."

"*Agent* Pilson," he growls.

I can see in his eyes just how betrayed by me he feels. It's awful. I never should've done what I did. I was so intent on getting answers, I didn't care what happened to me, but I should've thought of other people besides myself. Denver. Brayton. Decca.

Oh, God, what's gonna happen to Decca?

"You know what the law calls what you did?" Pilson asks. "Assault with a deadly weapon."

Otherwise known as aggravated assault. Dad did seven years for that in McAlester. I know the mandatory minimum.

But I did it anyway, 'cause I didn't think I had anything left to lose, and yet here I am, losing more and more by the minute. Pilson's respect. Money my brother don't have. Brayton's trust. Decca's childhood. I squandered it all.

"Lucky for you, Rainne Tremont doesn't want charges filed," Detective Pilson says. "Normally it wouldn't be up to her, but she's the only witness to what you did, and in light of that fact, the DA has elected not to pursue a criminal case against you, Sammy."

I sigh in relief. "Whatever you did, I really appreciate it."

"I won't deny my influence had something to do with it. Which is why I want you to tell me the whole damn truth about what happened in Rainne's house. Don't you dare leave anything out."

I tell him everything. When I'm finished, he says, "I see why she didn't want to press charges."

"Why?" Denver asks.

"Because if she did she'd have to testify against Sammy," Pilson explains. "And then Sammy could get up on the stand and swear under oath Rainne Tremont not only admitted to killing Bobby Ray, she also tried to kill Sammy. Sammy knew the gun wasn't loaded, but Rainne didn't, and she pulled the trigger anyway."

"So Sammy's free to go?"

"Well, that's up to the sheriff here."

"Legally, we can hold her for forty-eight hours," Olina says. She checks her watch. "It's been…fourteen so far. I figure Sammy needs some time alone to think about how she could've ruined everything for this investigation, so I'm keeping her in lockup till tomorrow afternoon."

"Jesus Christ, do you have to?"

"It's fine," I say, though I ain't looking forward to it. "I deserve it."

"Sure as shit do," Pilson snaps. "I don't have time for vigilante justice. You had the law on your side and still you acted like an animal. I'm disappointed in you. Thought you were better than that. Better than her."

"I'm so, so sorry," I say. But honestly, I ain't so sure I *am* better.

Detective Pilson sighs. "You have to get out of this town. It's all right for some, but it's not right for you. Get out before you don't recognize your own face in the mirror. Educate yourself. Do your life up right from now on."

"I will," I promise, though the task seems daunting at best, impossible at worst.

But someone's gotta care for Decca. With Dad dead, and Duke and Rainne in jail, where is she gonna end up?

"She will," Denver says. He puts his hand on my shoulder.

I give him a small smile, and he gives it right back, and in spite of all the bad that's happened, all the ways in which I've screwed this up for us, I got the stones to hope maybe things are gonna turn out okay.

They release me the next day. On our way out of the station, Pete hands me my personal effects, including the shattered bits of my cell phone.

In the car, Denver hands me a note from Brayton.

You,
I stayed as long as I could but they said they weren't letting you out till tomorrow and I have to go. Move-in is two days away. I know things are really messed up, and you may never forgive me for what I felt I had to do, but I promise I was only trying to help. If anything had happened to you, and I could've stopped it, I never would've forgiven myself. Please let me know you're all right ASAP. If you never want to talk to me again after that, I understand, but I need to know you're okay. Here's my number, in case you don't have it anymore.
Love, Me.

"Did he know I wasn't gonna be charged?" I ask. Denver pulls out of the parking lot and angles the car toward home.

"He wouldn't leave till he did," Denver says.

When we get home, I go out to the Oklahoma rock and sit for a while, looking out over the lake. From all the way up here, the boats on the water look like toys. I feel like one of the giants in Granny Lester's stories, towering over everything, watching in secret from the trees.

It's a beautiful place, my home. Unspoiled and calm. Lush and inviting. The lake whispers to you, telling you this is who you are, asking you why you'd ever wanna leave. Before this summer, I never, ever did.

But now all I can think about is how soon I can get gone. It ain't 'cause of what Agent Pilson said. I know he meant it kindly, but I can't be having folks telling me how to live my life.

It's 'cause I got this feeling in my gut that I gotta leave Lake Bittersweet or I'm gonna die. Not the way Dad did. Not even the way Granny Lester did, peaceful in her bed at eighty-eight.

If I don't go, I'll die the way a person does when the world crushes the hope right out of them, till they look in the mirror and don't recognize the face they see.

Someone kicks my bed and for a second I think it's Decca.

"Go back to sleep," I mutter, turning over and burying my face in the pillow.

"Get up," Denver says. "Agent Pilson's here."

I seen just about enough of Agent Pilson. He probably feels the same way about me. Still, he's sitting in my kitchen, playing with Dad's old Zippo lighter, which I left on the table next to an empty ashtray. He tosses it to me. I hop onto the counter as Denver takes the seat across from Pilson.

"I thought you'd want to know Rainne confessed to her part in your father's death," he says. "She's going to plead guilty to second-degree murder."

"Really?"

"What happened with you shook her up but good."

He says it sternly, so I won't think I did something right by confronting her, but I can tell there's a part way down deep inside of him that's glad I did.

"I was able to use what she said to you as leverage to get her to confess. I told her that if she cooperated I'd speak to the DA on her and Duke's behalf about a plea. Took a long time, but eventually she started talking."

"She admitted to being a part of it?" Denver asks.

"Still blamed the lion's share on Duke," Pilson says. "He's not saying otherwise, so she might not get quite as harsh a sentence as he will, but if the DA's feeling ornery she could slap them with conspiracy to commit in addition to murder. Any way you slice it, they're going away for a long time. Ash Boford's pleading guilty, too, as an accessory after the fact."

"What's gonna happen to Decca?" I ask.

"Might be lots of things could happen. Rainne's mother had the child when Rainne was arrested, but they've taken her out of that house and made her a temporary ward of the state. The Bofords can go after custody, but in my experience, family court doesn't like delivering a child into the hands of a murderer's kin. Is there anyone else?"

"Us," Denver says. Nobody's as shocked as me to hear him say it.

"You?" Pilson shakes his head. "I'm sorry, but a twenty-one-year-old and an eighteen-year-old? You don't even have real jobs."

"Sounds like half the families of the people I graduated high school with," Denver says, insulted. If there's any part of him that actually wants custody of Decca, it's there 'cause nobody thinks we can raise her well.

Hell, *I* don't think we can raise her well. A kid needs a stable home and ours is anything but.

"Well, good luck with that." Pilson stands to leave. He

pauses at the door and looks back. "But seriously, you two—good luck. With everything."

We thank him. Pilson nods at us, then walks out the screen door into the sun.

We don't get custody of Decca, but neither do the Bofords. Ain't no family on either side that's good or willing enough to take her, according to the court, so they put her in foster care, with a middle-aged couple over in Tulsa.

They've got their own kids, three of them, one near about Decca's age. Molly, Decca's social worker, assures us they're known to her and will take good care of our sister.

Turns out there is a thing as sibling rights, at least when it comes to visitation. Molly helped fix it so Denver and I can see Decca regularly, long as we're willing to make the hour-and-a-half drive from the lake, or the two-hour drive from Norman, where Denver's a senior at OU.

So I got a choice to make: move to Tulsa, where I don't know hardly anybody but can be close to Decca, or move to Norman with Denver.

In the end, I choose Norman. Denver gives up his scholarship-funded student housing and rents us an apartment near campus. We stay at the lake long enough to collect Dad's body and have it cremated. We borrow a boat and drive it into a quiet cove, where we scatter Dad's ashes over the water. Then I call up Gypsum and ask her to get me a meeting with Redbreast Tuller.

When the land is sold, we shove everything we can find into our car, and drive away for good. The minute the lake disappears in our rearview mirror, I feel something let go of me, and I know, whatever it was, I ain't gonna let it get close enough to grab hold of me again.

There's another reason I decide on Norman. Couple weeks after Pilson tells us Rainne confessed, I'm packing up my bedroom in the trailer when Denver raps his knuckles on the open door.

"Someone's here to see you," he says.

I put aside the clothes I'm folding, thinking it might be Reed. He transferred to a rehab facility in Tulsa to start learning how to accommodate his life to his injury, but he can come and go as he likes and he said he was gonna ask Shirla to bring him over sometime before I left, to say goodbye.

The love we had before is gone, but there's something still between us. Reed and I, we're gonna figure out how to be friends again.

But it ain't Reed at the door.

My heart jumps into my throat when I see Brayton standing on my porch. He's wearing those fancy black Wayfarers and the Technicolor board shorts he had on the first day we met. My eyes start to burn at the sight of him.

I gave Denver Brayton's phone number and asked him to text to let him know I was okay, but I never called him after I got out of lockup. Wasn't 'cause my feelings changed, and it wasn't 'cause I wanted to hurt him. I just wanted him to be free of me. College could be a fresh start for him, and I want him to have it. Would've been selfish of me to keep him tethered to this place, and the awful things that happened this summer.

Least that's what I told myself, so I wouldn't give in to the urge to call. I never even let myself dream he'd come back to me.

He's leaning against the porch rail, looking out over our land

and the lake beyond. When I open the screen door he turns and says, "Dammit, Sammy! You couldn't've at least *called* to tell me you were all right?"

I launch myself at him, wrapping my arms 'round his neck and pressing my face into his shoulder.

He pulls me in close. His lips brush my ear as he whispers, "I was worried about you."

"I'm sorry," I say. "I was afraid to call."

"It's okay," he says, softly kissing my cheek. He's holding something in his hand. At first I think it's a bunch of wild flowers, but then I get a better look.

"Where'd you get that?"

He turns the bundle of twigs and leaves over in his hands.

"Kicked up the welcome mat by accident and found it underneath. You want me to throw it out?"

"No, give it here."

I take the charm and put it in my back pocket. Goddamn Gypsum Tuller. The girl can't help herself, but I suppose I ought to be grateful. A little backwoods magic never hurt anyone.

"What are you doing here?" I ask Brayton. "Ain't you supposed to be at school?"

Brayton brushes the hair out of my eyes and smiles. "How about we take a walk?"

I slip on a pair of flip-flops and follow him down the porch steps, holding on tight to his hand. We stroll through my backyard, all the way up to the bluff's edge, where Dad installed a picnic table and a wooden swing years ago.

There's a bucket of golf balls and a few clubs lying nearby in the gravel. Brayton picks one up and starts chipping balls off the cliff. He peers over the edge, clutching the drunk rope so he won't fall.

"Think any of them made it into the water?" he asks.

"Probably not," I say, putting on my sunglasses. "It's harder than it looks. Dad was great at it, though."

"I'll bet." Brayton puts the club away and sits across from me at the table.

"You gonna tell me why you're here and not at Yale?"

"Yeah, so, the thing is, I went to Yale and realized it's not for me." I raise my eyebrows at him and he shrugs. "I pretty much knew it wouldn't be the second Jack told me he fixed it so I could go. I mean, do I look like the Ivy League type to you?"

"Not really."

"So I withdrew and decided to enroll someplace different."

He looks at me for a reaction, but I don't say nothing. I ain't sure yet what it is he wants to hear.

"I'm applying to OU for the spring semester. I think it's a better fit."

"You do?"

"Yeah. I do." He rubs his hands against his thighs. He's nervous. "I've been talking to Denver some. He says you're moving with him to Norman."

I laugh. "What, are y'all friends now or something?"

Brayton smiles. "We've got a common interest, that's all."

"Oh yeah? What's that?"

"You, dummy." He grins and reaches for me. "He says you might go to college yourself."

"Maybe. Let's not get ahead of ourselves."

All the time I been spending with Molly, trying to figure things out for Decca, has got me thinking I might wanna be a social worker. But I ain't sure. Molly's got a master's degree, and school never was my thing. I don't know if I could get through six years of it.

"I guess…" Brayton trails off. He clears his throat, then starts again. "I guess that means we could probably be together, you know, if you wanted."

"That's a real tempting offer," I say with a smile.

Brayton groans. "Give a guy a break, will you? I'm trying to say—"

"I know what you're trying to say."

I get up and walk around the table. He puts his hands on my waist, smiling like he ain't sure if I'm gonna make his day or break his heart. I push the hair back from his eyes.

"I love you, Brayton Foster," I tell him.

"You know, that's the first time you've said that to me," Brayton says, beaming.

"Not the first time I felt it, though," I tell him. I put my hand over my heart. "You."

He puts his hand over his heart. "You."

I bend to kiss him. He plays with the waist of my shorts and I grip him by the shoulders of his T-shirt, tugging him up. "I'm gonna show you something very special."

"Yeah?" he teases. "I think I've already seen it."

"First of all, that's not true. I got moves I never even showed you," I tell him. He grins. "Second of all, perv, that's not what I meant. Come on."

Brayton follows me into the woods. We walk a few yards before I stop and point.

"It's a rock," Brayton says, lifting his shades.

"It's a rock shaped like Oklahoma! Ain't that cool?"

Brayton comes up behind me and kisses the nape of my neck.

"It sure is," he says, though it seems there are other things he finds more interesting.

I close my eyes for a second, and when I open them, I see two animals standing not ten yards away: my doe, and her little fawn. She had him after all. It's a relief. I was worried something bad might've happened.

I put my palm against Brayton's cheek.

"Look," I whisper. He sets his chin on my shoulder and wraps his arms 'round my middle. "Ain't they beautiful?"

"They sure are," he says.

I'm washing dishes in the tiny kitchen of the apartment I share with Denver when a car pulls up in front of the complex. I toss the towel I'm holding onto the drying rack and run to the door, flinging it open to let the late-winter sunshine filter in.

I shade my eyes and call out, "Who's there?"

Decca tumbles out of the car. "It's me!" She jumps up, waving her arms. "Sammy, it's me!"

"Well, come on up here, beastie, and give me a hug already!"

She rushes for the stairs, but Denver catches up with her and swoops down to grab her. He hoists her over his shoulder and by the time he sets her down in front of the apartment door she's giggling so hard she can barely stand.

"Sammy, I'm here!" she shouts, even though she's about two feet away from me.

"I know!"

I crouch and hold out my arms. She throws herself into them and clings to my neck. I hug her hard as I can, doing my best not to tear up. Ain't the first time she's come visit, but every hour is precious. Denver tries to hide it, but he's looking pretty happy, too.

Decca puts her hand on either side of my face, squeezing my cheeks.

"Where's Brayton?" she demands. He's her new favorite. She asks about him all the time.

You two better not split up, Denver warned Brayton once. *Decca will be more heartbroken than Sammy.*

I rumple Decca's hair and sling her Dora the Explorer backpack over my shoulder.

"He's meeting us at the park for our picnic. It's gonna be the best! Day! Ever!"

I throw out my arms wide and she mimics me, giggling.

"Promise?" she asks, sticking out her pinky finger.

I link mine with hers. "Promise."

That night, I put Decca to bed on a cot in my room. It's been tough getting her to sleep. Only thing that seems to do the trick are my stories, the ones I make up. Don't matter what they're about, really. I think she just likes the sound of my voice. It's the silence she hates. Can't hardly blame her for that.

"Come on, beastie, you gotta be quiet now," I say, tucking her in. "I'm gonna tell you a story. You wanna hear a story, don't you, Decca? Well, I thought of a good one. And, best of all, it's true."

* * * * *

ACKNOWLEDGMENTS

It's hard to know where to start thanking everyone who helped me make this book, but it only seems right to begin at the beginning, with my longtime friend Cambria Rowland. If not for her, I think I can safely say I never would've found Oklahoma, nor would I be the person I am today. Thanks a million, buddy. You're the absolute best.

To Andy and Dianna Rowland, I owe a huge debt of gratitude. Thank you for inviting me to Oklahoma that first year, and every year since, for treating me like family, for asking about me and rooting for me from all the way across the country. Thanks especially go to Dianna, for sharing so many of her personal stories with me, for influencing the best parts of Sammy's character, and for telling me that joke about Poteau, which inspired all the stuff about the giants found in these pages.

To Karen and Wayne Brayton: I mean, where to begin? First, thanks for lending me your first names, your last name, your son's name, and your dog for use in this book. Hope it's okay I didn't ask first, but I did give you that fictional twenty-five-foot Cobalt, so…maybe we're even? Thank you for opening your hearts and your beautiful country home to this city gal year after year, for answering a million ridiculous questions, for introducing me to your wonderful friends and neighbors, for "weasel bitch" and Dolly Cove and Jägerbombs and chicken salad and a thousand other things that make Oklahoma like a home away from home.

I'd be remiss if I didn't also thank the literal dozens of amazing people I've met during my time spent on Lake Tenkiller. Leslie, I'm proud to be a charter member of your fan club. To one and all, thank you for your hospitality and your company. You might not see your names or faces in these pages, but—if I did my job right—your spirit, humor, and love for your home shines through all the spaces between the words.

Thanks also to Nikki Pavoggi and Mary Dubbs, who—aside from being two of my favorite people in the world—managed to make trips to Oklahoma even more fun than they already were.

Thank you to my Penguin family, and all the ways you encouraged me over the many years we worked together, especially those of you who read, loved, and commented on these other pages long before they went to print.

Thanks to the many incredible authors I've had the good fortune to work with, who make me a better writer through their own examples and cheer me on in my writing life as well as my professional one.

Thank you to Alex Bracken, whose friendship I so greatly value, and whose work I so deeply admire.

To Joanna Volpe, thank you for all you've done and all you

will do, for taking such good care of me and my books. And to everyone at New Leaf—you're incredible, and I'm proud to be part of the team.

To T.S. Ferguson, for loving and championing Sammy's story, and helping to make it the best it can be, and to everyone at Harlequin TEEN for your hard work on behalf of my little book.

And to my family, for being there and believing in me always.